EXTRAORDINARY ACCLA

deception

"Outstanding. . . . Mina's *Deception* is a deft psychological thriller."
— Adam Woog, *Seattle Post-Intelligencer*

"Wonderful. . . . Although the narrative engine that moves *Deception* along is strong and leads up to what they call a blockbuster finale, it's the twists and turns of Lachlan's mind as he struggles with deceiving us about Susie's deception that really make this a most satisfying reading experience."
— Dick Adler, *Chicago Tribune*

"When a book is called *Deception,* the reader is forewarned. And when that book's author is the dazzling, deception-loving Glasgow writer Denise Mina, readers might as well assume that the red herrings have red herrings. Or not. . . . Readers of Agatha Christie might feel certain this book is headed in one direction, but Mina is such a clever writer that within pages, one's suspicions turn to sympathy, then back again. . . . It's tempting to say that the prose rings perfectly true — except, of course, in *Deception,* it might not."
— Michele Ross, *Cleveland Plain Dealer*

"Fascinating. . . . *Deception* quickly emerges as an intense psychological study that careens along a collision course on which Mina has total control."
— Oline H. Cogdill, *Florida Sun-Sentinel*

"A masterly psychological web of people on the edge and the devils that lie beneath their apparent respectability. Engrossing."
— *Guardian*

"*Deception* leaves the reader as anxious as the betrayed husband to figure out how a seemingly happy wife, mother, and psychiatrist could go off the rails so completely." — Connie Fletcher, *Booklist*

"A shocker that's exhilarating in its energetic, witty sordidness."
— Ken Tucker, *Entertainment Weekly*

"The crime novel as intellectual puzzle is still with us. One good example is Denise Mina's bizarre, fascinating *Deception*. . . . A skillful piece of work. . . . Lachlan's diary is car-crash irresistible. . . . A smart example of the crime novel as postmodern puzzle, a work that coolly offers to match wits with the unwary reader and is not likely to lose the game." — Patrick Anderson, *Washington Post Book World*

"Those who have already encountered Denise Mina's gritty Glasgow-based Garnethill trilogy will find *Deception* a change of pace and a further example of Mina's not inconsiderable talent as a novelist." — Charles L. P. Silet, *Mystery Scene*

"There are plenty of shocks in *Deception,* which is only to be expected from an elegantly engineered novel of psychological suspense. . . . Mina executes a stunning shift in style and tone to come up with an entirely different perspective on her recurring theme — that domestic dysfunction breeds criminal violence. . . . Mina works an astonishing degree of tension — and a lethal amount of savage humor — into Lachlan's progressively unhinged behavior as he loses himself in his research, discovering secrets his wife never meant him to know."
— Marilyn Stasio, *New York Times Book Review*

"Something special. . . . A tour de force."
— *Times Literary Supplement*

"An entertaining and engrossing Rubik's cube of a novel."

— David Lazarus, *San Francisco Chronicle*

"*Deception* is as much an intriguing character study as it is an expertly plotted mystery. . . . Mina impressively balances a novel of unnerving suspense with the uncommon pleasure of being inside Lachlan's unreliable, charmingly vain, and appallingly funny head."

— Ellen Shapiro, *People*

"A dark, discomfiting tale of murder and obsession. . . . Lachlan is utterly, nakedly human and his compelling voice drives the narrative to a stunning, fitting conclusion. . . . *Deception* adds to Mina's considerable reputation."

— Lynn Harnett, *Portsmouth Herald*

"Denise Mina is one of Britain's hottest new crime novelists. . . . She is a master of Scottish noir. . . . *Deception* is superb, a full-rounded novel by a master of the heart's dark reaches."

— Tom D'Evelyn, *Providence Journal*

"Not only one of the best crime writers going, but one of the best writers of any stripe. Drawn in shades of gray with streaks of bright wit, *Deception* is true to its title, told from the point of view of the deceived husband, who is perhaps not a trustworthy narrator himself. . . . There are many small, fine moments in the book. . . . Mina's sharp observation and lovely prose shine a disturbingly bright light into dark corners of life. Don't miss this book."

— Jane Dickinson, *Rocky Mountain News*

"*Deception* could be a page-turner, but the reader will want to pause and think as the story unfolds."

— Judith Evans, *St. Louis Post-Dispatch*

Also by Denise Mina

Garnethill

Exile

Resolution

Field of Blood

deception

a novel

DENISE MINA

BACK BAY BOOKS
Little, Brown and Company
New York Boston

Back Bay Books / Little, Brown and Company
Time Warner Book Group
1271 Avenue of the Americas, New York, NY 10020
Visit our Web site at www.twbookmark.com

Originally published in the U.S. in hardcover by Little, Brown and Company, August 2004
First Back Bay paperback edition, May 2005

Originally published in Great Britain by Transworld Publishers

Margy Rochlin's interview with Denise Mina, which is reprinted in the reading group guide at the back of this book, first appeared in the issue of the *LA Weekly* dated September 17–23, 2004.

Library of Congress Cataloging-in-Publication Data
Mina, Denise.
Deception : a novel / Denise Mina.— 1st American ed.
p. cm.
ISBN 0-316-73592-2 (hc) / 0-316-05857-2 (pb)
1. Serial murderers—Crimes against—Fiction. 2. Women psychologists—Fiction.
3. Glasgow (Scotland)—Fiction. 4. Married people—Fiction. I. Title.
PR6063.I457D43 2004
823'.914—dc22 2003065861

10 9 8 7 6 5 4 3 2 1

Q-FF

Text design by Meryl Sussman Levavi

Printed in the United States of America

deception

prologue

Following the recent House of Lords judgment in *Harriot v. Welsh,* it is finally possible to publish, for the first time in the UK, the notorious Lachlan Harriot diaries.

These pages came to be in my possession through a series of happy accidents. In the winter of 1998 I was approached through mutual friends concerning some materials relating to Dr. Susie Harriot. A local doctor, Dr. Morris Welsh, had come to be in possession of a set of diaries written by Lachlan Harriot, the husband of Dr. Susie, and was deeply troubled by their contents. Dr. Welsh, a good man who is much maligned in this text, was keen to do the right thing but unsure how to go about it.

A week earlier, Dr. Welsh had taken Lachlan Harriot's old computer away as a favor. Knowing that Harriot's computing skills were minimal, Morris Welsh did a quick search of the recycle bin, checking for important files that might have been accidentally deleted. It was there that he stumbled across the diary files that were to make him famous and add yet another twist to the Dr. Susie murder case. Having alerted the police to the facts outlined in the files, Morris

Welsh sold them on to me, as a collector of true crime stories and the highest bidder.

A little over a month before this discovery, Dr. Susie had been convicted, in a worldwide blaze of publicity, of the gruesome murder of Andrew Gow. The public was still intrigued by the case: how could a mother and professional woman, previously of good character, suddenly turn into a vicious animal who would cut the tongue from a man lying restrained on a cottage floor and leave him to bleed to death? As his psychiatrist, did Dr. Susie know more about Gow than the rest of the world? Was it an act of revenge by a jilted lover? Had she indeed fallen in love with him? The answers to these and many other questions were afforded by these diaries.

This is the first time that the law has encountered a set of computer diaries being sold by accident on old hardware. Even before the final judgment was delivered, the case of *Harriot v. Welsh* represented a significant development in the intellectual property and copyright law of this country. It was in response to this that the ExLibris™ Author Assignation software was developed, a system now used worldwide and subject to a series of copyright challenges itself.

The right to publish the diaries was challenged but upheld on two grounds: Had Harriot reserved copyright he would have been able to claim authorship and stop publication. However, because the files were written on his wife's computer, Susie Harriot was deemed the user and by default the author, and the copyright defense was not available to him. Susie Harriot herself neglected to bring a copyright action. The second course of action was Lachlan Harriot's privacy case, brought under the Human Rights Act, but the House of Lords found that Dr. Harriot had vitiated his right to privacy, having courted publicity and given a series of interviews to the *Mirror* newspaper. He had, therefore, left himself with no defenses.

What follows is the transcript of those diaries, complete and unabridged. The sole alterations to the text are the additions of a start date to orient the reader and then numbered headings at the beginning of new entries, put there for the sake of clarity.

Denise Mina
Glasgow, 2002

chapter one

Tuesday, November 3, 1998

I'M SHOCKED. I WOKE UP AFTER FOUR HOURS' SLEEP THIS MORNING still trembling. It feels as if there's a bubble of bile at the back of my throat, ready to splatter out through my mouth if I try to speak. I was exuberantly sick in the taxi on the way home, all hot browns and greens, which is odd because I have no memory of eating for the last three days. I tipped the driver twenty and apologized over and over. He said, don't worry, pal, no bother at all, just get out for fucksake, quick, before it happens again.

How could they find her guilty? She's a doctor, for Chrissake, she's a mother. We're both professional people. Things like this don't happen to people like us. Now I understand why mothers stand over dead children and shout NO as if their soul were exploding. It's a primordial urge; fate has made a terrible mistake and needs to be informed; in a just world this could never happen.

The courtroom was packed for the verdict. Even the policemen from the other courts snuck in to stand at the back in the dark. The public galleries seemed to include the same faces each day, but they must have changed. The line was one hundred, two hundred yards long every morning. A ragged, untidy snake of people having one last cigarette, nodding and chatting to the people before and aft, sometimes hunched against a hard rain, sometimes upright as meerkats in the morning sun, ready to come and sit in the warm, watching our lives being ripped apart as they nibbled their candies and nudged one another. Almost all were quite old. I wondered if that's the optimum age for shamelessly indulging in ghoulish interests, but they're probably retired or unemployed and have more time for such activities than young people.

Surprisingly few of the audience were journalists. From the extent of the coverage, you'd think every hack in the country was there. The journalists stood out because they were there for a purpose, bored and bent over notepads, scribbling in shorthand, glancing up every so often when a new player appeared. A larger portion of the crowd watched in shiny-faced amazement. A bald man who smelled like mustard always managed to inveigle his way to the front row. He seemed to know everyone. A recurrent group of three septuagenarian women saved places for each other in line. They all had the same tight white perm. One afternoon one of the ladies brought fruit scones for them to eat with their cups of tea from the machine in the lobby. She had buttered them and wrapped them individually in cellophane. They tittered and giggled as they ate. I was sitting on the bench across the corridor from them, thinking to myself: they'll remember this trial because of the scones. My life's being fucked ragged and all they'd remember are the fruit scones and their chum's winsome wit in bringing them each a funny little snack.

I sat through the two weeks alone, the sole representative of Susie's family. She waved to me, made faces, and occasionally turned for a reaction. I pretended to be a journalist with exclusive access and wrote everything down in a poor man's impression of shorthand (jst shrt wds, rlly). The newsmen had worked out that I was her husband at the start of the case. They realized during the first day, because they saw me talking to Fitzgerald during the breaks.

Fitzgerald has become a bit of a celeb during the trial. He was lampooned in the press last Sunday: a cartoon showed his headmasterish scowl and his big gray eyebrows, dressed in lawyers' robes, driving an expensive sports car with APPEAL written on it and money flying out of the back. They're never, ever funny, those cartoons.

The journalists approached me at the start of the trial; some even slipped notes into my hand like lovesick schoolgirls. The answering machine is choked with messages every day. They want to buy my story or get some sort of comment about each new development. They offer money, fame, a chance to have my say. They approach and approach, ignoring my snubs, rebuffing my rudeness.

The public didn't realize who I was until we went back in for the verdict, when the journalists shouted questions at me outside the court. When we were sitting down, the man who smelled of mustard turned around and smiled, pointing at the back of Susie's head.

"Is that your missus?" he asked, surprised and pleased.

I was so nervous I didn't trust myself to speak, so I nodded.

"Oh," he said. "Very good. You look queasy."

I muttered something about the possibility of being sick and he gave me a mint to suck.

The court official with the ceremonial stick came in and we all stood up, sat down, genuflected at the Crown, whatever. The jury clattered back in along the little wooden benches and sat down. The room was so quiet it felt as if everyone had inhaled and frozen, sitting perfectly still for the seven minutes it took the clerk to declare the result.

Guilty of murder. A murderer. Murderess. My own precious Susie, my sweetheart, my funny valentine, my dear Christ Almighty. Every pore on my body swelled open, as if trying to absorb the news osmotically. A hair fell from my head. A man dropped a pen down the row from me, and I kept thinking: he's dropped it, he's dropped it.

Susie turned slowly in her chair, her black hair sliding off her shoulder like a lazy oil slick, the flannel of her pale gray suit jacket folding perfectly into tiny consecutive waves below her shoulder blade. She looked back at me, horrified and helpless. Instinctively, I reached out to touch her and smashed my knuckles loudly on the glass barrier. In the tense hush of the courtroom it sounded as if I were rapping jauntily on the glass to get her attention. Everyone—the journalists, the old women, even the old man—stared at me disapprovingly. It was the most private, despairing, appalling moment of our lives, and yet they sat there, watching us, disapproving of my reaching over to give a last free embrace to my darling wife. It was like watching a loved one die on the pitch at Wembley and then being criticized for your technique.

Finding me a disappointment, as ever, Susie seemed to shrink to half-size, to look more alone than before in her big wood-and-glass playpen. Sad and defeated, she dropped her eyes to her lap and turned away from me. My hand was throbbing. Everyone stood up. I felt as if I were sinking into a grave.

Sentencing has been deferred until psychiatric and social reports can be drawn up; exactly the same sort of reports that she used to draw up herself for a living. We have to go back for the sentencing hearing in a few weeks, but murder has a statutory penalty of life imprisonment, so that's what she'll get. Whose lives are they taking in payment? Susie's or mine? Or Margie's? The forces of justice are orphaning our daughter at nineteen months old.

Margie'll never know her mother. She'll never walk past a makeup counter, catch a smell, and remember a thousand days at her mother's knee. She'll never roll indignant teenage eyes and join the other girls bitching about their bloody mums during school lunchtime. Susie will never surprise her in her thirties with a story about little Margie saying something rude to a pompous visitor, about falls and friends forgotten, about the literal confusion of early childhood. I wanted to stand up and scream at them; they're taking the wrong life.

As I made my way out of the courtroom, I tried hard to blend into the milling public, but I'm too tall to be inconspicuous, especially in a crowd of the midgetized elderly. A cross-eyed woman ran up to me and asked for my autograph. The crowd turned on me, wanting papers of their own signed, poking at my hand with chewed pens. I kept my eyes on the door and plowed through them. What does my autograph mean? Do they want a bit of me? It can't be salable, surely.

The lobby was quieter than usual. Most of the journalists had been corralled into a side room, but some members of the public took flash photos of me and got told off by the policeman on the door. Fitzgerald took me aside to brief me, but I couldn't hear the words he was saying, just a vague rumbling mumble from a mile away about an appeal and statements for the press.

To my surprise I found I was nodding and then shook my head violently. What the fuck was I agreeing to? It felt like one of those no-trousers-at-assembly dreams I used to have. I managed to rub my ten-ton lips together. "I can't speak."

Fitzgerald nodded. "Aye, well, all right, then," he said matter-of-factly. "That's not a problem. We can proceed without your active, verbal participation. Leave it to me. Just stand next to me and keep quiet, no matter what they ask. They may try to provoke you."

A woman passed us and slipped, late, into the journalists' room. Through the swinging door I could see a gang of grown men, half of whom had never been in the public galleries, I'm sure. Pointing at the two seats set out for Fitzgerald and me were fifty beady eyes, fluffy microphones and cameras, boxy TV cameras on stands, and flashes on tripods. Their voices were high and excited. Sitting on chairs and swiveling around to talk, writhing, grinning at each other. The Dr. Susie Harriot Murder Trial was going to run and run for them. It was just an entertainment. I've seen it happen to other people and never considered the casual brutality of it. Distant participants in the story, who neither knew nor loved Susie, would sell their stories. They'd be paid little more than pocket money to attach their faces to a string of misquotes that would make Susie sound sexier than she is, more evil, more interesting.

"Can't go in there," I said to Fitzgerald, knowing this more surely than any other thing in the universe. "Just—I'm going to be sick."

Fitzgerald looked at my face, and judging from the way his head darted away from my mouth, he knew I was telling the truth. He put his hand on my forearm and patted it once. "Perhaps the best course of action in this instance would be for you to go home," he said. "Just go home."

"Can't I see her? Before she's gone?"

Fitzgerald shook his head and apologized. I fled.

A couple of photographers followed me and took pictures as I hailed a cab. I left the car there. I've driven drunk; I've driven at sixty through blinding rain; I've driven my dying mother-in-law to the hospital, but I couldn't have fitted the key into the ignition yesterday. The car's probably got a stack of tickets on it already.

The answering machine was full when I got in, men and women offering gazillions for my story. We pay more, I care, so sorry, remember me from the court? I was sitting behind you, over your left shoulder.

I'm in the papers this morning, hailing the taxi, looking shifty and portly and weird. I had no idea I looked like that. I've always thought having longer hair made me seem rakish and bohemian. Instead I look as if I'm inexplicably ashamed of the tops of my ears. I'm plump in parts as well, which is a surprise. A sagging roll of fat is perched on my belt, and my jaw's indistinct. I look tearful, and my back's rounded as if I'm waiting to be slapped across the back of the head. This may well be the only time in my life when I'm in the papers, and I look fat and ill-groomed and frightened.

I went out and bought all the other papers this morning to see if my strange appearance was the fault of a crooked lens, but it wasn't. It's bizarre being in the papers. I feel a thrill of something, a mixture of fear and pleasure. The pleasure is like the delight of seeing an unexpected photograph of myself at a party I don't remember being at;

it's confirmation that I exist and am up to stuff. The fear is more real. People will know me from those photographs; people I've never met before; odd people. They'll look at my photograph for too long; they'll laugh at me for having a fast, faithless wife and for not working; make jokes about my hair and fatness to each other on the train on their way home from work; use me as a nickname for a misguided sidekick whose wife is fucking a serial killer.

The arrant stupidity of the coverage is astonishing. They're selling it as a sexy story, making out Susie was a frustrated suburban type. One of the tabloids is telling people not to trust their doctors anymore.

I've brought all the papers up here to the study, to hide them from Margie. It's irrational, I know, but I don't want these stories near her. I don't want her perfect, tiny hands with their rosy fingernails to touch the paper they're printed on. It feels like an unforgivable act of brutality, to bring these terrible accusations into such a precious, innocent life. She'll see them one day. She'll be curious and look them up, and I can't protect her indefinitely from articles like this one from yesterday:

SEX DOCTOR VERDICT ON PSYCHO LOVER'S MURDER

A verdict is expected today in the trial of Dr. Susie Harriot, 30, former psychiatrist at Sunnyfields State Mental Hospital. Dr. Susie is accused of the brutal murder of Andrew Gow, 33. Gow, previously found guilty of the "Riverside Ripper" series of murders but recently released on appeal, was discovered in an abandoned cottage in the Highlands, having bled to death. The prosecution claims that Dr. Harriot was in love with Gow and, enraged at his marrying another woman, killed him.

The body of his new wife, Donna McGovern, still has not been found, although her blood was identified from a sample in the couple's white Golf Polo car. Strathclyde Police say that they would be willing to prosecute for Miss McGovern's death if Dr. Harriot is acquitted on the present charges. A spokesman stated yesterday:

"During the summer months the hills of Sutherland are busy

with walkers and we would ask people to keep alert and watch out for anything unusual."

We've got this to look forward to all next summer. And every following summer if they don't find Donna this time around. Every time they find the decomposed body of some poor depressed soul who has staggered off to the Highlands to die, Margie will have the whole story thrown back in her face. It's not an uncommon occurrence either. Last year, before I was interested in such things, I remember they found the remains of a young French guy who had walked off into the hills with no ID and the labels cut out of his clothing. It was a suicide. He'd left a note in a hostel. He just wanted to melt back into the land, he said. In the same month they also found a woman from London who'd died of starvation while camping next to a loch. Apparently she was vegan and was giving airianism a go.

The coverage in the broadsheets isn't much better. An intellectual phony has written three pages in a review section about the significance of Gow's dying in Cape Wrath. Just because it has the potential to be a metaphor doesn't give it meaning. He can't have listened to a word of the trial, because Susie didn't choose the venue; Gow went to Cape Wrath and she followed him. He talks about Gow's head injuries, saying maybe all psychiatrists want to bash their patients' brains in, smash the organ that offends.

I can't answer the phone. Mum called from Spain and left a message asking how we got on and saying she was worried. I heard Dad clearing his throat over and over in the background, like a phlegm-powered car revving at the lights. He coughs like that to signal distress. I can't stand it when he's upset; it makes me feel so mortal.

The English papers will have arrived there by now, so they'll know anyway. It might even be on the news.

I can't bring myself to speak to anyone. Instead I remind myself of the need to focus on the positive things. I must:

1. Keep Margie away from the television so she doesn't see pictures of me or her mother flashed up every two minutes. I don't want her to remember this. I want it to pass her by for as long as possible because it's going to be part of her life forever.

2. Remember to pay bills and keep going.

3. Get back into a routine. Routine is comfort and as close to normal as we can hope for over the next short while.

4. Have a purpose. Before, when we discussed the possibility of a guilty verdict (Me: "Oh, my Jingo, that'll never happen," followed by hearty laugh. Susie grinning heavenward: "No, darling, of course not. Nothing bad ever happens to young professionals like us," followed by brittle, tinkling laugh and a little sip of sherry), Fitzgerald asked me to look through all of Susie's papers and see if I can find anything that might give us grounds for an appeal. We can't appeal against the sentence because life's mandatory for murder. We can only appeal against the conviction. We have to show that the evidence was flawed and claim a miscarriage of justice. It's the only grounds for appeal.

I've already spent forty minutes this evening in Susie's study sorting through piles of newspaper cuttings and tapes and professional files. I'm going to come up here night after night, and go through every note and paper with microscopic care.

chapter two

I FORGOT. I WOKE UP THIS MORNING WITH TIRED EYES AND LINgered in my bed. I pulled the crackling duvet up to my chin, warming my neck against the crisp November air seeping through the window. I heard Yeni and Margie downstairs, la-la-singing the Happy Happy Hippo song together and the high tink of cutlery against crockery as Yeni emptied the dishwasher. I smelled bittersweet coffee brewing on the stove.

The house yawned and stretched as the heating warmed the wooden floors; beyond the garden wall neighbors backed their cars out of garages, wheels rolling over damp leaves. Then I became conscious of the cold, dead space next to me in the bed.

For a fleeting, cozy moment I wondered why Susie was up already. I saw her in the kitchen, sipping a mug of coffee and eating an orange. I thought, she's been up long enough for the sheets to cool down, and then I remembered.

I couldn't face breakfast or a shave. I got a mug of coffee, hugged Margie for a bit, and then came straight up here.

* * *

I've found a box file with Gow's prison files in it, the ones the hospital sacked Susie for stealing from the office. Sinky Sinclair's suspicions were right all along. I bet he still wonders about that. Despite being a senior member of staff, she still wasn't authorized to take them off the grounds. She was adamant that she hadn't taken them. She lied to me. She was so insistent that she said "fuck" in front of Margie. Now I've found them here, five paper files and a computer disk sitting in a box file, on the right of the computer where she could reach them easily.

There are a number of matters I want to raise when I go to visit Susie:

1. Why has she never denied having an affair with Gow to me?
2. Where are the insurance papers for the house?
3. What in the name of the almighty fucking bollocks was she doing stealing these files and then lying to me about it? Does she think I'm an idiot or something? Does she think I'm going to take an infinite amount of shit from her and still stand by and save face for her? Has she no regard for my dignity? Am I some sort of pointless prick she thinks she can push around?

I think those three months of us both knocking around the house after Susie had been sacked, before the phone call and her taking off to Cape Wrath, I think they were the happiest of my life. I knew she wasn't happy; she was forgetful and ratty. She'd lost her wedding ring and was sure she'd left it at Sunnyfields. I bought her another one, a smaller one, which she never wore, and fooled myself into believing that she was adjusting to a new pace of life. I thought she'd get into it, slow the rhythm down. I thought, it's okay, we're fine for money, we can spend more time together, just the three of us. I even dared to wonder whether we might have another kid.

It was during that time that the mist came into the front room. It was July and I'd left the front-room window open when I went to bed. When I came down in the morning, the garden mist was all through the room, a swirling fog at chest level. I walked slowly through it, and the damp cloud closed in around me. As my bare feet came down on the red kilim carpet, they smashed the settled dust of water droplets and left perfect photographic prints. I told Susie when she came down for breakfast, but the mist was gone by then, and she listened but didn't understand. It felt like a dream sequence, and now I think maybe it was. No one around me was living in the same reality. What sort of self-centered buffoon would mistake a cataclysmic event in his wife's life for a splendid opportunity to spend quality time together? I'm a fool, a selfish fool. I hadn't a clue what was going on. Rome was burning and I played Dixie on the spoons.

This study's a mess. Susie's left bits of paper everywhere, all over the floor, on the desk, Blu-Tacked to the wall; there are even some on the window. I haven't been in for a while because she'd taken to locking the door and I didn't want to pry (another clue I *completely* missed/rewrote/dressed up as a lady rabbit). There's a photograph stuck to the glass on the skylight, a picture of Gow and Donna's wedding, with Blu-Tack smeared angrily over Donna's face. The light shines through it so it's a translucent picture of Andrew Gow standing with a headless woman. It's creepy. I'll take it down.

These prison files trouble me intensely. I want to talk to Harvey Tucker, Susie's colleague from Sunnyfields, to ask him if what he said in court was right, if Susie had been seeing more of Gow than could be justified professionally. I got the feeling he didn't mean to insinuate that. During his evidence I looked up at him and he seemed uncomfortable, as if he'd been railroaded into saying things. I've got this in my notes:

PROSECUTION: How would Mr. Gow come to be spending time in Dr. Harriot's office?

HARVEY TUCKER: I'm sorry, I don't understand.

P: How would any prisoner come to be in the office of a psychiatrist? Can they just walk in and demand to be seen?

HT: No, of course not. They'd first of all have to approach an officer and ask to see someone. Then the officer would refer them on to the psychiatrist.

P: *[looking incredulously at the jury]* Is that the ONLY way? *[He raised a hand in a rainbow gesture as he said it. He really was the most awful ham.]*

HT: No, well, we could ask to see them as well.

P: A psychiatrist can call a prisoner to their office?

HT: Yes *[faltering]* within reasonable hours . . . some prisoners—

P: *[cutting him off]* We have submitted into evidence Dr. Harriot's appointment book for the two months immediately prior to her dismissal. Is four hours in the space of three days a usual amount of time to spend with a prisoner?

HT: That's hard to say *[looking very shifty]*.

P: In this sort of case, where the initial paperwork is done, the risk assessment is done, no one has asked for a new report: would it be usual in such circumstances?

HT: I don't think it's poss—

P: JUST a yes or no will suffice, Dr. Tucker.

HT: No.

P: Not a usual amount of time?

HT: *[quietly]* Not usual, no.

Tucker was very uncomfortable when the prosecution dismissed him, as if he had something else to say.

Anyway, I phoned him just now but got no answer. I left a message asking him to call back, said it was important. I hope he doesn't think I blame him or anything. I know Sinky Sinclair was responsible for Susie's getting sacked, not him, but I don't care about that either at the moment, I really don't. I can see how the lawyer got Tucker to say what he did. I'm not in a blaming frame of mind, I just want to ask him about it.

It's obvious in hindsight that Susie was going through some huge crisis before she took off for Cape Wrath. Looking back, it's so clear.

At the time I thought she was just being huffy and withdrawn. She was so insistent that she hadn't taken Gow's file, even after they sacked her. That was a massive, throbbing, neon-ringed clue. Sunnyfields only has one applicant per post. It's so hard for them to recruit for forensic psychiatry, they wouldn't have fired her unless they had absolutely no other option.

Margie's gone down for her nap, so I've come back up here to do a bit more tidying. This is a nice room. I never thought that before. It's more of a converted closet than a room. It's warm because it's at the top of the house, and there's a wee stereo. The skylight Susie had put in last summer frames the top of next door's oak tree and stops the room from being suffocating. The plain white walls and the low bookcase keep it airy and fresh. And of course there's this computer, which I've never been allowed to use because I'm a Luddite and might break it. All I need is the word processing to write up the papers as I sift through them for the appeal. I know how to put the machine on and off and I can save the things I've written. That's all I need to do, really.

Once you're sitting at the desk, the narrowness of the room and the high sloping ceiling make it feel cozy. It's only when you're standing in the doorway, balancing on the shallow top step and looking in at someone else sitting here, asking them when they're going to come down and spend time with you, that it seems claustrophobic.

chapter three

EVERYONE'S IN BED, AND I CAN'T CONCENTRATE ENOUGH TO watch TV. It's been two full days since the verdict now, and Susie still hasn't called. I thought she'd want to talk to Margie at least. She may be finding it hard to get through here because our phone hasn't stopped ringing. There are constant messages from journalists offering money and sympathy. One of them said I should see ratting my wife out as "a kind of justice." A *Mirror* journalist called four times today. His name is Alistair Garvie and he's from London. He keeps saying "London" over and over and over, as if it's a magical place a hick like me would never have heard of.

Susie has my mobile number, though, so she could phone if she wanted to. I expect she's on the induction course for convicted prisoners. They send them on a course in the first few days of their sentence, to tell them the rules and so on. Susie says it's really to keep them busy, so they don't get the chance to think about killing themselves, because the reality of a long sentence starts to sink in during the first few days.

We saw an induction group walking across the grass once. The whole valley was swathed in sheets of biting cold rain, and I was in the visiting room with Susie during her brief spell on remand. The pretrial women averted their eyes from the window, as if any contact with the freshly convicted might jinx their chances. I watched them, though, only curious then, not thinking it relevant to me or us. All the women were dressed in blue jogging pants and sweatshirts and walked in a gaggle, topped and tailed by four female officers, as they made their way across to Bravo block for a talk about something. They all looked hard-faced and sad, even the officers. I remember the heavy way they walked, as if they were cosmically disappointed, let down by everything they'd ever seen or done or watched or eaten. They were a poor-looking bunch, not that the remanded women were much better, but at least they had a spark of hope and were allowed to wear their own clothes.

It's easier on the eye if prisoners wear their own clothes. Then you can categorize and distinguish and dismiss them from your mind quickly. Tracksuit and no bra: drug-addled loser. Stonewashed jeans and high heels: tart and/or shoplifter. Elegant gray cashmere crew neck, jeans, and soft baby-blue running shoes: wife, keeper of my tender heart, absent verb in my life sentence.

The induction group wore a blue uniform, which is supposed to strip them of their individuality, but for me, watching through the barred windows, the uniform made them all matter, made them all potential friends and neighbors. Convicted prisoners didn't seem real to us then. Susie was innocent and she was getting out on bail anyway. Her biggest problem at that time was getting to the bail hearing on the Big Blue Bus.

The blue security-reinforced minibus starts its morning journey at six-thirty a.m. with a pickup of the accused women, including for a short while my dear wife, from the Vale of Leven, Her Majesty's Prison. After traveling all over the central beltway picking up single and multiple miscreants hither and thither from any secure holding place, the BBB doubles back on itself and two and a half hours later sheds its load at the Glasgow High and Sheriff Courts. The wheels on the justice bus go round and round and round. As Susie said herself, a three-hour bus drive at six-thirty in the morning would be nightmare enough, without the added burden of ten traveling companions, many hungover or coming off drugs, who are about to meet their families and (not always the worse of the two) their doom.

A fat woman from Falkirk tried to talk to her. Susie said she swung her big red face over to her and said all men were bad news, kept calling her "my friend." Her new chum complained that the police had put her into a cell with a sleeping man. Evidently, they were confused as to her gender. Susie did a great impression of her accent. "I says to the polis-man, 'Fit's this oen ma chest, well? Them's tits!'"

Susie was so glad to get bail and be allowed to go home. She went for occasional meetings with Fitzgerald, but other than that we just stayed in. Mostly we sat around and watched TV, and she came down from this study to eat with us. She wouldn't let me touch her, though, and she didn't want to talk about any of it. Every time I asked about Gow or Donna or her going off to Durness, her eyes would fill up and she'd say, *please, Lachie, please, just till after, be my friend.* I am your friend, Susie, but I want to know, I need to know. I'd plead with her, stroking her hand, afraid I was begging. *Please, Lachie, please, just leave it.* And then she'd punish me by hiding up here for hours at a time.

I wish she were downstairs, sleeping, breathing deep and slow, feeding on the air inside our safe, dark house. And in the morning I could take her up a big milky coffee and toast and apricot jam and open the window and let the smell of the garden in.

Shit shitshitshit shit shitishitshit shit shit.

I can't think of Susie today without seeing her in the Vale, walking endlessly back and forth across grass in the shitting rain, being forced to sit through disappointing talks, told to expect nothing ever again, and trained in the disappointed walk. Maybe she can't get to a phone. Maybe they don't let them phone out when they're in the induction course.

* * *

I've got to find something for this appeal. I've emptied out two boxes of receipts into a bag and I'll use them to keep potential appeal papers together.

Box 1. Formal papers: Gow's prison file, plus all the formal papers from Susie's trial.

Box 2. Less formal stuff from plastic bag under this desk: Susie's collection of newspaper and magazines articles re Donna, the wedding, and Gow, plus video and cassette tapes.

I'm afraid Gow will be on the video and it'll creep me out, knowing he's dead and how he died. I've hidden the tape under the papers in the box. I will watch it, but not just now.

Box 1 Document 1 ***Indictment***

It is hereby charged that you, Susan Louise Emma Harriot, née Wilkens, of 7 Orchard Lane, Dowanhill, on September 26, 1998, did assault Andrew Alfred Gow, then residing at The Firs, Lenzie Road, Kirkintilloch. It is charged that you did stab him in the chest and throat, remove his tongue with knives and pliers or similar instruments at The Bothy, Inshore Loch, Cape Wrath, or elsewhere in Scotland, to his severe injury, and you did murder him.

It is further charged that you did assault Mrs. Donna Helen Gow, née McGovern, there or elsewhere in Scotland and you did murder her.

This whole second para was crossed out.

Mum phoned this morning and left a shrill message. She heard about the trial on the news and said she'll come over if I don't call her at once. I heard Dad coughing furiously in the background. I need a visit from my parents like a twisted testicle.

They've never liked Susie, they don't understand children, and they complain about not being warm all the time they're away from Spain. But they do worry about me. They'll read the papers and the speculation about the sentence, which was all exaggerated, of course.

I hope none of their friends out there saw the photos of me. I often feel that I've gone from being their son to a thing they boast about to their friends, a form of social leverage. A doctor? No, qualified as a doctor but got out before all his friends. Saw it was a career trap—*leave out the reason: that I couldn't stand the incessant contact with random people. Leave out the fact of my disenchantment with working, my house-husbanding career, and skip straight to*—wife's a doctor, of course, dear Susan, a psychiatrist, so clever. Mum often asks me to send a BIG card to Dad or phone friends of hers I've met once or twice to inquire after their grandchild/trip home. It's all about appearances. It would matter so much to them if I'm in the papers and recognizable. I'd hate to shame them, especially Dad. They're dejected at my progress as it is. I haven't the confidence to tell them about my writing in case nothing ever comes of it.

I went back into town to pick up the car this afternoon. It's been there for two days. Miraculously, it didn't have a ticket on it, but someone had scratched a long line into the paintwork on the driver's side. It was bizarre being back there. It seemed very quiet. Bits of paper fluttering through the narrow streets. Pink vomit on the pavement. People walking past me without a second glance. I felt invisible enough to walk up the steps of the court. This is how it'll be now. My days of being a minor, provincial celebrity are over and no one'll remember except those sick fucks who take an interest in such things. I'd like that very much. I stood at the top of the stairs and looked out over the green. The view's completely different when you're standing upright.

When I got back home, a few camera crews were sitting in folding metal chairs outside the wall, watching the wooden door to the garden. They weren't here during the trial and don't seem to have noticed the back door to the alley. Maybe they do know about it but can't get their trucks down there. They saw the garage door open before they noticed my car and scrabbled around, shouting at each other, pulling the cameras off the tripod and running over to the car. The automatic door seemed to take forever to open. Just as they were halfway across the road I took my foot off the brake and let the car roll in, pressing the remote button so that the door began to shut. I almost clipped the back of the Saab. One of the crews was Japanese. Why on earth would the Japanese be interested in this? They're probably still out there, filming the garden wall.

I'm beginning to realize how ill-equipped I am for this. I've been waiting for Susie to ring and tell me she's arrived and settled in safely, as if she'd gone to a professional conference or a hen weekend in Dublin. I can't get my head around her being away. I went to the shop on the way home and bought Jesti-jesters. I've got a cupboard full of Susie's favorite biscuits, and she won't be home for ten years. I'm still sleeping on one side of the bed, putting the lights out as soon as I lie down in case I wake her.

We've got to win this appeal. I've been sorting out the big plastic bag of papers and newspaper clippings and tapes under her desk. There's the copy of *GLT* magazine with the interview they printed with Susie (bastards), a Dictaphone tape, clippings about Gow's case that look quite old, as if she'd been gathering them for some time, and masses of notes about Donna. She must have every single interview Donna ever gave to the papers.

Susie's written notes about Gow and Donna on some of the newspaper articles, single words mostly, like "grandiose," "vicarious fame," and "stupid"—that word recurs *a lot* on Donna's clippings. Sometimes, especially from around the time of Gow and Donna's wedding, she has articles from different newspapers on the same day. Where was she getting all these papers? I don't remember the News of the Screws being delivered here, and she certainly didn't get them at her work. She must have bought them in secret, on the way to work or at the shops, and cut the stories out so that she could keep them. They date back for almost a year. This has been going on for fucking ages without my knowing a thing about it.

* * *

I phoned Susie's colleague Harvey Tucker again and a man answered. He hesitated, then said Harvey wasn't in. I've never spoken to Harvey on the phone before, but it definitely sounded like him.

"Will you tell him I'll phone back?" I asked.

"I will, of course, yes. Certainly," he replied.

We both sounded very stiff and suspicious. I hung up. It might not have been him. Maybe the guy had seen my name in the papers and felt awkward because of it. Or he'd heard Harvey talk about the trial; that's more likely. I think it was Harvey, though.

I miss her. I even miss the irascibility, the slights. I miss her coming up here to work alone rather than sit with me in front of the telly after Margie's gone to bed. I miss knowing she's up here, doing whatever. It should be easy to comfort myself. She was absent a lot of the time anyway, but it seems especially hard just now. Perhaps it's because she's been sitting at home for the past two and a half months. It's just sinking in, I think.

Last night I sat in front of the television and tried to pretend Susie was upstairs, ignoring me. Yeni wanted to watch *Friends* on a satellite channel and sat down on the other settee. I could hardly say piss off, I'm assuaging my grief by pretending to be ignored by my absent wife. I watched Yeni out of the corner of my eye. She's very young, and I don't think she understands what the characters are saying, but she smiles along with the jokes and nods sometimes. I suppose for most men this would be a creamer: left alone in a big house with a lonely Spanish teenage au pair. But Yeni is fat and has a prominent mustache, and her breath smells perpetually of yogurt. I think she's self-medicating for thrush. Susie chose her.

chapter four

I GOT A LETTER FROM SUSIE THIS MORNING. IT DIDN'T SAY ANY OF the things I want to hear, like I love you and didn't kill those people. It said she was there and safe, and feeling a "little under the weather" . . . blah blah, missing you and Margie blah blah, much hope for the appeal blah blah. She tells me what the weather's been like the past few days. She's in a facility forty miles away, for Chrissake, we're in the same weather system. She could have been writing to anyone from anywhere, except that just before the end there's an unguarded moment when, apropos of nothing, she writes "It's awful here."

I caved in and phoned the prison to check if she was safe. I recognized the voice of the squat-faced receptionist who was there when I visited Susie before she got bail. She's a sullen little gremlin with a flat nose covered in blackheads. Her uniform was too tight and her white bra strained against the blue blouse, her name badge tottering on a peak like an erect nipple. There was a proud, well-spoken old woman in front of me in line last time, there to visit her drug-addict daughter, she told me later, and the squat-faced guard rudely asked her to repeat her name four times, making her say it louder and louder so that everyone could hear it. The old woman was so upset by the time she sat down that I had to give her a hankie and the promise of a lift to the bus stop to stop her weeping. It's important not to cry when you go in to visit prisoners. They've got enough on their plate.

Anyway, I recognized the receptionist's voice. She wouldn't put me through to anyone but left me on hold for ten minutes while she asked around. Susie's fine. I asked when she might get the chance to phone me and the guard sounded surprised that she hadn't already. I said I thought maybe she wouldn't have a phonecard and could she put me through to her? The receptionist said it wasn't a hotel, *sir*, and she couldn't page her. I thanked her and hung up.

I wonder if the induction is going okay and what sort of things they do with them. Maybe they show them uplifting films about life, and how nice it is to still have one. I hope it's working, I hope she isn't thinking about suicide. I couldn't stand the world without her in it. I wrote back in longhand because I can't get the printer to work up here. I asked her lots of sanitized questions, told her I was thinking of her constantly, and described the garden. I enclosed a nice photo of Margie breaking a cup.

Box 2 Document 1 *Dictaphone Tape*

I was messing with the machine and turned it on, not realizing that the volume was up full. Her voice, calm and untroubled, filled the room like a sudden warm wave, washing through me, an embrace of noise reverberating off the walls. I felt faint suddenly. I wasn't listening to the words on the tape; I was just sitting there, flooded by her, wishing her home. I had to turn the tape off and rewind. It's Susie's voice from the beginning. She must have put the Dictaphone down pointing at herself because the interviewer's voice is distant and unintelligible. Susie sounds perfectly in control, as if she knows what she's doing.

> "Well, ask and we'll see. [Mumbled questions.] I'll tell you if I'm not prepared to answer. [Long mumbling.] Okay, yeah, that'd be nice. Yeah. 'Kay. It's got it on it, yeah? [Mumbling.] I'm not completely naive about the press. I'd like to keep my own record of what we say here. It's not a problem, is it?"

She thinks she's being really clever. I wonder if the journalist knows how utterly out of her depth she is. Even telling him she's not naive sounds like she's accusing him of being a bastard, like she's challenging him to fuck her over. But that's Susie employing her junior doctor's credo: protest competence regardless of the evidence. She hadn't the first idea. This is the interview the prosecution used to damn her, the one where she said she hated Donna.

An obsequious voice, a mumbling waiter, I suppose, asks a question and Susie lets the man opposite her order.

"Yeah," she sas flirtatiously, "I'll have one of those too."

> "I hated Donna from the first moment I saw her. She looks ridiculous—you must have seen her picture? She gave an exclusive to almost every national paper and charged them a fortune. All that cleavage and lipstick. She looks like a female impersonator."

Susie either coughs or laughs. All I can hear is her voice, as if she's talking into my ear, with the uncracked timbre she had before her confidence was shattered and her creamy voice curdled. I hear her sip a drink and sit back. She's sitting on leather, good leather judging by the sound, and it shrieks and sighs as she shifts her weight.

She shouldn't have given an interview, not to anyone, but she'd been sacked and was bitter and probably a bit panicky. She didn't tell me until the magazine came out in September. She went off early in the morning, saying she was going to get the papers or stamps, I forget which. She didn't come back for three hours, and when she did she had red eyes and was shaking.

I asked what was up. She put the magazine on the kitchen table and looked out the window. "It's a disaster," she said, quietly. "I'll never get work again."

I thought she was being overdramatic until I read the interview. It definitely contributed to the end. If she'd felt she had anything to lose, I don't think she would have gone to Cape Wrath. Which means, of course, that her career mattered more in the final instance than me or Margie or the house or our way of life or her freedom.

I never understood why the interviewer hated her so much. It seemed to me that she was doing him a great favor. And he was a pal of Morris Welsh's, which should have been a warning, I suppose. Of all the magazines to give an interview to, *GLT* was probably the most unprofessional. They sandwiched the article between an interview with a retired gangster and a chart of the biggest tits in porn. When she gave the interview, she didn't know it was for *GLT,* just that Morris's pal was starting out and could sorely do with the scoop. The photograph was unkindly lit and made her look old and wizened. Wizened; my beautiful Susie.

I think she agreed to be interviewed because she was hoping for a completely new career as a media psychiatrist. She's always watching telly and criticizing the psychiatric pundits on it. Forensic psychiatry's a small world. She wasn't in any hurry to suffer job interviews or explain her departure from Sunnyfields. She kept speculating about who'd heard about her sacking. Now I realize that this speaks volumes about her state of mind; she never wondered if nice people had heard and felt bad for her, only whether all the shitty bastards in the profession had heard and were pleased. And there are nice people in the profession, a couple of really nice women, like Tabitha Morley and that Finnish woman with the nose. If I'd been fired it wouldn't have mattered, but Susie's career is a huge part of her identity. It was a sort of death to her, I think; all her hard work being denied.

She had bought a suit for the *GLT* interview, a pale blue woolen one with a shorter skirt than she'd normally go for. She hid it from me, hung it at the back of her closet and pretended it wasn't new. She looked lovely in it. She couldn't wear it to court because it pinched her at the waist and looked sexy. She had to wear somber blacks and blues, straight-sided jackets that hid her shape and made her look sexless. She didn't have anything like that in her wardrobe. She sent me out to buy them before the trial. I got her a navy blue blazer that had ridiculous gold buttons with anchors stamped on them. It was graceless and horrible and she wore it almost every day. When we still thought she'd get off, we were having tea in the kitchen and she said she liked the blazer because it reminded her of who she wasn't.

I loved her in that pale blue woolen suit, loved the way she moved in it, the modest way she tugged at the hem when she sat down. If we can't find any grounds for an appeal, she might never get to wear it again. She'll be too old when she gets out.

I rewound the tape and pressed play. As I listened I imagined Susie looking great, sitting on a modernist leather sofa, legs crossed at the knee, gently swinging her free foot, holding an elegant espresso cup.

"All that cleavage and lipstick. She looks like a female impersonator."

Susie's right: Donna did look extraordinary. There are a lot of pictures of Donna in the plastic bag and on the walls around the office. For a blushing bride concentrating on her husband's appeal, she managed an astonishing number of interviews.

She was five feet two and wore clumpy high heels that made her walk as if she were falling forward the whole time. She dressed in frilly über-feminine dresses with plunging necklines and many gold chains. She looked a bit country-and-western with her big hair and sticking-out bum. The newspapers portray her as thoughtful but grasping (they nearly all mention how hard she negotiated the price of the interview), and the magazines have her as an ecstatic newly married nut case. In one women's magazine there is a particularly tasteless photo of her throwing a wedding bouquet backward at the wire fence around Sunnyfields State Mental Hospital. And some of the stuff she's quoted as saying, honestly, the League for People with Shit for Brains could sue her for bringing their name into disrepute.

I turn up the volume:

> "Yeah, it's a recognized phenomenon, prison romances. They're sad, sad women mostly. Often the men are in the course of serving their sentence when the women start writing to them. They meet them on a visit and start an affair. [The interviewer asks something that I can't make out.] No, Donna hadn't met him before. She saw him in the paper and fell in love with his picture."

Susie starts to laugh, and Morris's pal laughs politely along with her. He doesn't find it as funny as Susie. She gives such big, barking laughs that it ends up sounding forced, as though she doesn't find it funny either.

I have a picture of Gow from the bag under the desk. Susie has marked it "Donna's 1st view of G." This must be the picture Donna saw of him, the one that she fell in love with. In the picture Gow is looking over his shoulder at the photographer. His hands are cuffed together and he's wearing a green prison jumpsuit. His head is shaved, but he has the elaborate facial-hair arrangement of a man who's in no hurry to get out to work in the mornings: a pencil line along the jaw, a mufflike hair cap on his chin, a thin mustache. His eyes are small and beady. He's about as attractive as an anal prolapse.

chapter five

I WAS EATING A SANDWICH IN THE KITCHEN JUST NOW AND I GOT SO freaked out that I had to come up here. This is not a joke. They're really going to keep my Susie in a prison for years and years and years. It's grotesque. My heart will starve.

All the papers are in tidy piles now, some on the floor, some on the desk, waiting for me to work through them. Yeni is downstairs giving Margie a bath. Margie's in a terrible temper this evening. She's crying at everything. I keep turning around to talk to Susie about it and finding she isn't there anymore.

What happened to us? We shouldn't be worrying about murder convictions and appeals. We should be buying bigger houses, moving up the career ladder, fighting about next summer's holiday destination. The worst of it is that it wasn't just a random bolt from the blue. Susie had been gathering clippings about Gow for nearly a year, she got the sack over him, she followed him up to Cape Wrath. Let those who have eyes see.

I rewound the Dictaphone tape and sat looking at the picture of Gow, and I suddenly understood what Susie was laughing about. I started laughing myself. I felt so much affection for her and her bizarre take on everything that I ended up crying and laughing at the same time. I couldn't stop. I couldn't catch my breath or keep the noise down in case Yeni heard me. I was sobbing and laughing and coughing for about ten minutes.

I managed to clean my face up before I went downstairs. Yeni had put Margie to bed, thank God, and she didn't see the mess I was in. Margie hasn't asked for her mummy once since the conviction. I don't think Yeni has told her that Susie isn't coming back, she just seems to know.

Before we left for court on the morning of the verdict, Susie sat in the hall for ten minutes and just held Margie, smelling her hair and watching her move, as if she were trying to absorb her, memorize the sensation of her. Margie didn't want to be on her lap. She squirmed and tried to get off, but Susie just held on, rubbing as much of her face as she could into her soft skin and hair, stroking her tiny ears with her lips. Sometimes, when she's holding Margie, she gets this beatific look on her face as if nothing can hurt her because she has her baby. She never looks like that because I'm there.

I finally phoned Mum. Her voice was high and panicked, and she said she was on the verge of calling the police to come over to the house and check on me. I asked her why on earth she would do that. She fluffed her reply but basically seems to think I might try to kill myself and Margie. I told her not to be stupid: if I kill myself, who'll organize the papers for the appeal? Then I realized how depressed and subordinate this made me sound. She wants to come over and visit. I said she could if she liked but it's unnecessary. I have a lot of support, and Susie will be home just as soon as this gets sorted out. Mum didn't sound convinced but promised not to book a flight just yet. She said she didn't mind that other people would read about us in the papers; what was important was my health and Margie and Susie. As long as we all had our health, it didn't matter what other people heard about our family troubles. Everyone had problems, and our family need be no different. I think Mum and Dad've talked about this a lot and this is the line they've come up with.

Dad came on and struggled to clear his throat for five minutes. Eventually he said he was sorry about what had happened. I accepted his condolences. He said they didn't care about other people hearing about my problems (suddenly they're *my* problems); what mattered was that we were all healthy. The devil-may-care posture was wearing thin.

He said, "They can't take your health away from you, can they?"

I said, "Well, they can if they shoot you in the face," which, far from sounding chipper and cavalier, only confused and frightened him. I hope he doesn't repeat the comment to Mum; it would scare her as well. It's imperative that they don't come here.

Dad kept saying never mind, never mind, things will buck up. I suspect he always thought Susie was a bit racy because of the money and is glad to see the back of her. He actually said, "Chin up." What happens to expats in Spain? He was a GP in Ayr for fifty years, and suddenly he starts talking like a regimental sergeant major, all Colman's mustard and fucking Bovril. They ended a discussion about my wife's murder conviction by asking me to send them water biscuits. I felt like shitting in a box and sending it registered.

I keep thinking about Cape Wrath. There have been a lot of different versions printed in the papers. The articles reproduce a map of the cape with the red Ministry of Defense training area warnings saying DANGER AREA all over them. It's very dramatic.

My version of Cape Wrath is different from the others because it doesn't start with a long drive or a beautiful, dark-haired psychiatrist walking into a small hotel. Mine starts with Margie eating breakfast and an early-morning phone call: it was a Friday morning in late September. Susie answered the phone in the hall, said, "Oh, it's you," and turned away so I couldn't hear what she was saying. In the police's version it was Gow on the phone, telling Susie where he was, perhaps inviting her there. In the Susie version it was Donna asking for help. In the Lachie version Susie hung up, came into the kitchen, and told me she was popping over to the supermarket, back soon. Bye, Susie. Bye, Lachie darling, and the door shut behind her. She drove for eight hours to the very north coast of Scotland and the pretty little hotel on the beautiful banks of the Kyle of Durness. She walked straight into the lobby and told the owner's wife, a Mrs. Zoe Pascal, who she was and who she was looking for—not exactly the behavior of a woman who was sneaking about or intent on committing two murders. The woman handed her a sealed letter. Again Susie said it was from Donna; again the police said it was from Gow, but there's no dispute about what it said. It must have mentioned Loch Inshore and the hut because, without even stopping for a cup of tea, Susie took the ferryboat across the kyle. (It is literally a ferry boat. It isn't a ship or a steamer. It's a wee man with a boat who rows foot passengers across.) Susie was alone, not agitated but quite serious. She got off on the far bank, pulled her green leather coat closed, and walked off into the dusk. Three hours later she was back in the hotel bar. She was standing at the bar, drinking whiskey and looking disheveled when the police came to arrest her. His blood was all over her shoes. She was holding the glass with two hands, said Mrs. Pascal, because she was shaking too much to drink with one.

I can't sleep again. I've been lying in bed for two and half hours, and I keep getting rushes of adrenaline that make me want to sit up and start punching. I sat in a hot bath, breathing deeply, and drank a hot toddy, but when I lay down again, I wished I could go for a mad, high-kneed run around the garden. Tasks and their possible permutations keep coming into my mind when I lie down. I feel as if I'm trying to remembering things, things that will slip out of my mind if I don't wake up and write them down immediately. There are bits of paper all over the house with pointless things like "shop—get veg," "Phone Fitzg. re times," "clothing—ENOUGH?" Sometimes I can't remember what these important notes mean the next day. More often I can remember and they don't matter. I think I'm hoping that

I will stumble across the single shred of relevant information that will make sense of the whole episode. Maybe that's what I'm doing up here in the middle of the night.

I press the button and Susie's voice fills the room.

> "No, Donna hadn't met him before. She saw him in the paper and fell in love with his picture. [Mad laugh.]
>
> "Gow is an interesting character. Like many serial killers, he was very taken with his press coverage. He remembered the names of journalists who had written about him, imputed an admiring relationship between them. He actually referred to them as 'my fans.' . . . No, he didn't like all the coverage, sometimes he'd get very angry. He was terribly angry with his ex-wife, Lara Orr, but that all stopped when Donna came along."

The interviewer interrupts her. He tells her a quick story, which I can't hear, about a friend called Harold, I think, and then asks her a question.

> "Yeah, lots of people do visit. Gow comes over quite well. It's the set-up that gives him the edge. You see, he's very confident, self-assured in the way that only people with no self-doubt or insight can be, and meeting that sort of certainty can feel quite intoxicating. A lot of sensible people came under his spell."

He asks another question, and Susie's answer is adamant:

> "He is, yeah. He's insistent that he's innocent, even though he confessed in the first place and then pled guilty at the trial. . . . He claims innocence to make himself more likeable. Think about it: if he admitted he was guilty, he wouldn't get the sort of coverage he does, would he? Ian Brady doesn't get that sort of coverage. Sutcliffe doesn't get it. Just Gow. And the fact that he can claim innocence in the face of all that evidence may mean that he's more psychopathic than either of them.
>
> "That's what psychopaths do: they tell you what they think you

want to hear. If you want them innocent, they'll be innocent; if you want them guilty, they'll tell you that. Their purpose is to get under the skin of whoever they're near, to control them. The main variant with psychopaths is how bright they are, how capable they are of making the lies consistent. It's as close as they get to emotional contact with other human beings.

"If you look at the past three years' articles about Gow, you can see that. In one year alone he has declared himself a born-again Christian, a Seventh Day Adventist, and last year he became a Muslim by changing his surname to Ali and refusing to eat bacon."

The interviewer guffaws. Susie doesn't. She doesn't think it's at all funny and tries to continue talking over him.

"You see, he was being visited by a number of people with different religious convictions, and he joined anyone who came to see him. It may seem funny to you, but it actually reflects a very dangerous trait. He isn't trying to please these people. He's getting a hold over them. The Seventh Day Adventist was an extremely vulnerable man. His son had killed himself, and he wasn't converted. To the man, that meant his son was going to hell, and Gow used that belief to torture him. He was prepared to make that sort of investment in controlling people for his own amusement."

The interviewer has stopped laughing. He sounds disappointed and offended, as if she has insulted his favorite comedian or something. He asks a question, and I realize that he's goading her. This interview took place two months before Cape Wrath. It's his first-ever interview, and he's already guessed what eluded me for a year: that Susie has strong feelings about Andrew Gow. Now she's talking quickly and defensively.

"Not *my* skin. No, he didn't. . . . That's my job, giving nothing away. The purpose of what I do is objective assessment. . . . Well, it's important for Donna's safety. I've told her, but she won't listen to me. He'll hurt her, of course he will, that's what he does. I don't know if any appeals court could possibly refuse him now, after that poor student's murder. That's exactly why I'm giving this interview: I want people to know Donna isn't safe. I want people to watch out for her when he gets out."

Even I know that this last bit is a piss-poor excuse for committing professional suicide. Donna wouldn't read *GLT,* and I don't suppose her friends would either. They didn't print that comment. I expect the mag's lawyers combed it out. It must have been sub judice at the time.

"If Donna was a friend of yours, you'd be afraid for her, wouldn't you? It's not surprising she was attracted to him. Psychopaths are often compelling, as are celebrities, and Gow was both. . . . No, I'm not saying all celebrities are psychopaths. There are parallels, but I'm not saying it's the same thing. Celebrities give us an instant connection because we have prior information about them, while psychopaths can anticipate things familiar to you and mimic them back so that they *seem* familiar. . . . They have little conception of other people as fully sentient beings, have a limited capacity to empathize. They think of other people as objects to be used and moved about."

Susie takes a drink while the interviewer asks something. I can hear him saying "Gow."

"No, look, I can't talk about the murders or Gow's history. You can get that information yourself, anyway. I have to be careful what I say, especially now that the appeal is coming up.

"You shouldn't make him out to be a hero, you know. Serial killers're not heroes to the police or the families of their victims. They're inadequates worshiped by inadequates. D'you know what he did to those women? I read once that the people who buy the records by American gangster rappers are generally middle-class white teenagers. Same thing. That luxury of distance."

The interviewer's talking, coaxing Susie, and her voice gets closer. I think she's looking at the Dictaphone. "No. No, I'm not afraid of Gow. He won't come for me." They made a lot of this phrase in the court case: whether Susie meant *he* won't come for *me,* in other words, I'll come for him, or whether she just meant he wouldn't come. I'm glad they only had the printed interview to go on. From the intonation on the tape it definitely sounds like she's hinting that *she'll* get *him.*

There are books on her shelves up here, professional and sociology books and a couple specifically about women falling in love with prisoners and killers. The spines are broken and the top corners of the pages are dirty where Susie's been doing that disgusting thing she does when she reads: cleaning gunk out of her nails on the top corner of the page.

She's sought these books out and taken her time reading them. She hasn't opened them on the table and run her finger down the margins, paring out the relevant information for a work-related article or argument. She has luxuriated over the contents, which means that she probably read them in here, in this room. I've seen her reading in here, she sits sideways at her desk and opens the bottom desk drawer to rest her feet on, her mouth sitting slightly open, inner lips moist, drawing her nails slowly, one by one, over the corner of the page. I asked her once, huffily and pointlessly, because the answer's obvious, why couldn't she read downstairs? She said the light up here was perfect, and she's right. The window is just overhead and the branches of the overhanging tree diffuse the directional light, even now that most of the leaves are gone.

She read a lot up here, and yet we never talked about books. I never asked her what she was reading, but she didn't bring it up either. I have a vague memory of asking her about a book by someone we both knew at university. She said it was good, not a comprehensive look at treatments, but it had a thorough literature search at the beginning. It's no wonder I didn't ask again.

It makes me speculate, though: what else did she think about a lot and never mention? I wish her here. Suddenly I want ten clear, clean minutes to talk without the baggage of the past few months, few years actually, from before Margie was born. I want to ask her what she thinks about all sorts of things, as if we were first going out together and I was still listening to her.

I spent so much time with Susie ignoring her. What must she have seen when she looked at me? A fat guy with a weird haircut who doesn't want to do anything but read obscure novels and pester the garden.

We should have done things together instead of pissing the time away. We should have talked more, done stuff, sat with the television and the radio off and taken the time to look at each other. After we moved in together, so much of our time was spent simply stumbling along, thinking forward or sideways or about cars and clothes and furniture and pensions and Margie. We haven't even been on a proper holiday together, and I can't blame anyone but myself. We kept going to my parents' in Marbella and having a fraught time, whispering in hot rooms about annoying incidents and having quiet sex, never really being off duty.

Susie resented using her holidays to visit them. How would I like it, she used to ask, if she made me spend all my time off at her parents'? My excuse was we needed to see them as a family, but I could have gone there on my own. The truth is I wanted her there as a buffer. She said often, right from the very beginning, that she wouldn't be one of those wives, that she refused to be the point of emotional contact between me and my parents. "It's not my job," she said. "Do it yourself."

She was right of course, but I still found myself putting her on the phone, asking her to speak to them about specifics or comfort Mum about flat-roof leakage. I shouldn't have used our holidays like that. I should have taken her to Mexico and the Maldives, like she wanted.

She should be here with me. My yearning for her is so strong that it feels as if all the panels of our fractured picture will inevitably slide back to true and we'll be as we were before.

In my head I run through the last ten minutes of a cheesy film about a couple chasing each other on the beach, barbecuing fish, horseback riding, etc., and then I remember it's Susie. I snort, thinking about it; imagine her, slathered in sunscreen, turning to me and saying, "This beach is chemically unsafe."

chapter six

IT'S COLDER TODAY. I MIGHT NEED TO BRING A HEATER UP HERE. My feet are quite warm, but the top of my head gets cold. I think all the heat rises from the house and gets sucked sideways, out through the attic space next door. I'd like to insulate this room for Susie coming home, paint it maybe, and buy her a new computer and not say anything so she comes up here and gets a nice surprise. I could convert the whole loft area and give her a really big office. We don't keep that much stuff in there, just Margie's baby clothes and the LPs and some suitcases that were here when we moved in. I'd like a building project, something big, as a sign of good faith that she will come home. I think it would cheer me up. But, then, she probably doesn't want a big office. The claustrophobic feel of this little room, squashed in next to the chimney stack, has an intense privacy about it. If anyone else were in here, they'd be standing indecently close to me. It's like a physical incarnation of personal space. The nights are coming earlier and earlier, and as the skylight deadens, the slow black oak waves softly in silhouette, reminding me that there is an outside to this small, tall room. In case I forget.

I find myself craving this study when I'm downstairs coping and feeling tired and worn and put upon. It's not just the room, though, it's because of the Dictaphone tape as well. I've been looking forward to getting back to it all day. It's as if Susie's up here waiting for me to come to see her. It makes me feel as if I only need to die of love and sorrow until eight o'clock in the evening. Then I can leave Yeni to deal with Margie's final, stalling requests for water and come up here to the virtual woman in the attic.

I find I'm rewinding the tape to the start each time on the pretext that I need to check if I'm getting it down correctly. But as it plays, I'm not reading what I've written, I'm just glazing over and losing myself in the texture of her voice. I wonder if Susie wished herself up here when she was downstairs with me. And if she did, who was in here waiting for her?

I got another letter from her this morning. It's longer than the first but just as cagey. She tells me she's been seen by the psychiatrist and he's drawing up the report about her. The sooner we get to sentencing, the sooner we can start the appeal. It must be weird being assessed by a colleague. She'll almost certainly know them, at least vaguely. She's sounding less shocked, although it still doesn't sound like her. The letter is stiff and formal, as though she's trying to pass on a coded message. But then we've never written to each other, so maybe that's just her writing style. I asked her to phone me. She still hasn't and doesn't even mention it in the letter.

I rewind the tape for a moment and press play: ". . . are generally middle-class white teenagers. Same thing. That luxury of distance."

The interviewer asks a long question.

> "We screen all potential visitors to make sure that the prisoner hasn't misrepresented himself. Also, we need to know that the new visitor won't try to kill the men they're visiting. Yes, it is. It's a very real worry actually.
>
> "I had been in charge of screening his letters. The law's changing and we won't be able to read their mail for much longer. It's an

important security function at the moment. Strangers get in touch with them, and they don't always wish them well, I'm sure you can imagine.

"Donna'd written four letters to Gow, and they were fine, nothing untoward. Declarations of love from the first letter . . . not smutty. Some of the unsolicited letters are very smutty. Donna's sounded like a child writing to someone she had a crush on. Her letters are published on his website, so I'm not breaking a confidence. Stevie Ray, Gow's manager, he scanned them in."

Susie had told me about the letters to Gow. Apparently a lot of women sent in pornographic photographs of themselves, and some of their letters were filthy. But Donna wrote about love and loving him and how she'd known he was the only man for her for years. You can see the picture she sent him of herself. It was published in one of the magazine articles. She seems sad and is wearing a crucifix, but she's also managing to show quite a lot of tit.

Mumbled question.

"So, yeah, she seemed reasonable enough. How sensible is anyone who writes unprompted love letters to a self-confessed serial killer? Actually, when I interviewed her, I was surprised by how bright she was. She's intelligent, has a quick mind, and she's quite well read, too. Strange accent—have you heard her speak? Donna saw his picture in the paper at a time when she was vulnerable herself. You know about her father? He died two months before. . . . No, two months before she wrote to Gow." [She sounds exasperated.] "Honest to God, have you done any background work on this? Well, you won't get very far doing that."

I suddenly understand why the journalist wished her ill. She sounds so contemptuous. She used to talk to me about my writing using just that voice. It sounded like she was being a cheeky cow, but she is just a very practical person, very goal-oriented. She doesn't understand anyone pursuing a career with an uncertain outcome, or doing anything just because you enjoy the process.

> "The background is that Donna's mother died in childhood and she was raised by her father. He was very authoritarian, a strict Catholic, and was routinely violent to her. He broke her collarbone when she was seven. She married young. Then, when her father had a stroke, Donna and her husband moved back in with him. Both men were violent to her."

Susie moves in her chair, bends forward or something. The waistband on her skirt gently squeezes a breath from her as it contracts on her smooth, down-dusted belly. She lets out a sigh so small, so intimate, it makes me want to cry. It's as if she's brushing her lips past my ear, a small breath easing from her throat, past the palate, brushing between her lips, and out. She takes in a tiny rasping breath to compensate before she carries on, and when she does, her voice has changed. She's giving a lecture, a tutorial report, regurgitating information. She is hesitant, not because she is unsure, never that, but because she is summarizing, compressing, simplifying.

> "She threw her husband out, got a restraining order against him, and her father died shortly afterward. A few months later she wrote her first letter to Gow. It may have prompted her to write to him, actually. A cross between a relief and a grief reaction."

The interviewer says something.

> "I don't know about Donna. I wouldn't like to guess. What I can say is that there may be a number of different motives at play in prison-romance situations. They might just be romantic, or the women could be religious and approach the prisoner because they're looking for someone to save. Or they might be looking to get

something off the prisoner, like money or attention or vicarious celebrity.

"Of course some of them are just sickos who fancy killers. We try and weed those out at as early a stage as possible. It's a very negative sort of contact for the men to have. It reinforces their justifications for their crimes, especially if the crime has a sexual element. It buoys up the delusion that the victims are complicit. . . . No, 'sicko' isn't a technical term, but everyone understands it, don't they? I can give you the clinical term if you like: hubristophilia. Doesn't clear it up more than 'sicko,' does it? Hubristophilia is an attraction to someone who has committed outrages on other people. Some women view it as very masculine to have done something like that. Perhaps the ultimate expression of masculinity."

He asks, "Do you?" His voice is as clear as mine. He's sitting next to her now, facing the same way as her, and his larynx sounds compressed, as though he's sitting back and is relaxed. They seem to be getting on quite well now. Susie's flirting with him, and I can picture her leaning forward, sipping at her drink.

"No. [She sounds very sure.] That's an insulting construction of masculinity. It's a fearful construction. It's focusing on the most appalling aspects of gender-stereotyped behavior and making it the core. Like passive-aggressiveness in women, or compulsive cleaning."

I wonder why the interviewer didn't mention this part of the conversation in his evidence to the court. Susie specifically says she didn't find Gow attractive. Or she says she didn't find the violence attractive. It could have a bearing on the appeal. I think it might be worth my bringing this to Fitzgerald's attention.

"I need the loo," Susie says on the tape. She seems to lean forward, letting out another tiny sigh, and the tape stops.

It starts again abruptly, and her voice sounds lighter because she's had a break.

"These jail romances are very much an active search by the women for a partner within that community. If they're approaching a famous prisoner, they'll send an introductory letter, and if they get a response, they're off and running with an imaginary love affair. The hubristophiliacs show themselves pretty quickly. They always ask for details of the crimes. The more benignly inspired correspondents can get all the way to a visit, but visits are fraught, especially first ones. If they turn up, they might not go in to the visit.

"If they do go in, they're always surprised at the guy's ordinariness. Once they discover that the man has a spark of humanity, say he likes dogs or his granny or collects stamps, well then, the visitors ascribe all sorts of lovely qualities to him. A woman goes in expecting Attila the Hun, minus the charm, and he is *so much better* than she expected. Mind-blowingly better. She's awash with relief in his presence and she mistakes it for love. The impression that he is supernice isn't contradicted by reality because they never live together and they rarely meet. It's perfect for a fantasist: it's a reality-proof romance.

"Of course, a lot of it is that they're celebrities and that gives everything prisoners do a rosy glow, even brutal murders. Attaching themselves is a way for the women to achieve a higher social status. It may even be a way of committing vicarious murder. If they're very angry and have contemplated murder themselves but haven't done anything, it helps them understand the urge, helps them normalize and excuse it."

Susie really knows what she's talking about, but the interviewer doesn't seem to be listening. "Are the letters any good?" he asks, "Or are they full of pervy stuff?" He sounds very smug and nasty and stupid and unthinking. I remember suddenly that he's pals with Morris and may share his creepy attitude toward women.

"They're private," says Susie, squeaking across the leather settee. Away from him, I hope, and I want to kiss her for it. The journalist asks why Donna would have written to him in the first place. Susie can't say for sure. I stop the tape and rewind. She makes this strange *whung* noise, and then her voice sounds higher. I wonder whether his hand is on her knee or something. I rewind again. She sounds odd but carries on talking. I'm sure she'd have said fuck off if he'd done something she disapproved of. It must just be the mention of Donna. When she says her name in the next sentence, her voice cracks, showing the strain.

> "I think Donna identifies with Gow as a vilified figure, as an underdog, and feels that she, uniquely, can understand his pain. More pressingly, he fits the pattern of violent men she's familiar with and attracted to. It's smart really, if you think about it. She's attracted to violent men, can't resolve it, and so she reaches a compromise by choosing someone violent who happens to be imprisoned forever and can't get to her."

It doesn't sound as if she hates Donna when they talk about her properly, but the journalist didn't mention this bit of the conversation. I should ask Fitzgerald if he wants this tape. That journalist's evidence was definitely prejudicial.

I turn off the tape, tip the chair back, and look up out of the skylight. Why would Susie think about prison marriages so much? It doesn't happen that often. In all the time she has worked at Sunnyfields, only one other prisoner requested permission to marry, and the wedding fell through because the bride got drunk and took a weekend trip to Oban instead. But the books on the shelf have long indecipherable notes in the margins, whole paragraphs underlined, and she's thought enough about Gow's relationship with Donna to distill all that information and explain it in small sentences to a journalist.

The waiter comes back and puts some china down on the table. He states a price and thanks the man. The interviewer asks: "How can these women, like, get romantic with guys when they've done such, like, mad things to other women? What would you say to those people who'd say it's all really pervy?"

He keeps saying that word, as if he thinks all sex is wrong. It makes me think he's never had sex, or has no penis, or is sexually compromised in some giant way. But maybe it's just that he's sitting next to my wife in her sexy suit and I'm not and I dearly wish he had no penis, or at least wasn't pals with Morris, who's a bit of a cripple-dick himself.

"Overtly, none of the women believe their boyfriends are guilty. If the evidence is undeniable, they think up mitigating factors. But deep down, most of them know the man did commit the crime and that blood lust is enormously erotic to them. Even the religiously motivated ones are attracted to the violence. Think about it: that entire connection is contingent on the sinful behavior of the prisoner. They never target Social Security frauds, do they?

"In some way all the women who get involved with these men are religious really, all hoping to be that one special lady who changes him. They think if they make enough effort, are feminine enough, groom themselves, keep a clean house, they can make it work. What they don't realize is the pattern is already set."

Susie realizes that she's rambling. She sits back and coughs, asks the interviewer if she should go on. There is a silence; perhaps he's writing.

"Yeah . . . uh-huh . . . go on."

"Well, you see, the solution to violent men isn't to alter the stimulus; it's to effect change in the actor."

"You mean the women are being stupid?"

"No, no, no, it's not stupidity. It's much deeper than that. It's a quasi-religious belief: be good and God will favor you. It's redemption through another's eyes."

Even I'm cringing now. She's obviously rehearsed that spontaneous observation and it comes out sounding hollow and stagy. I know she's smirking as she says this last bit. I can hear her swallow another mouthful of drink, and I realize suddenly that she's been drinking wine and is a bit tipsy.

> "The men are blank canvases for them to imagine onto. It's love blindness in extremis. But that's true for all of us, isn't it? Isn't that what love is? Fantasy projection? Ignoring the facts until you're too committed to get out."

chapter seven

I CAN'T BRING MYSELF TO REPLY TO SUSIE'S LETTER. I COULDN'T say all the bland things she wants me to say: things are fine, I am well, much love, well done, get well soon.

What the fuck was she doing in Cape Wrath? I wonder about the details that don't fit. If she did go up there to save Donna, why didn't she phone the police when she saw Gow's body? Instead of phoning the police, she went into the hotel and ordered a large whiskey. She was there for thirty-five minutes and didn't alert anyone.

She was slightly nervous when Gow was released, I remember that, but she'd been sacked only two months or so previously, and I thought his appeal was a reminder.

She went straight into the kitchen the night she was sacked; she didn't come into the front room with me and Margie. She didn't even reply when I called her. I found her at the table, drinking our second-best brandy and smoking a cigarette *indoors.* I knew something big had happened.

I was pleased when Susie told me she'd been sacked. Finally, I thought, we'll get to spend days and days together. I can show her what I do all day, introduce her to my small enjoyments; she'll slow down. We'd be all right for money; we could live on the interest and I could work again if we ran short. Let's travel together, I said. Let's get another nanny and go and see Africa or China together before we're too old.

"There are things"—Susie squeezed my fingers together, pressing the knuckles so tight it hurt—"things you don't know about, Lachie." Her eyes overflowed and she climbed onto my knee, pressing her face into my neck to hide the tears. I held her, felt her rib cage deflate, stroked her bony little back as she struggled to breathe in. I held her until she caught her breath again and she called me her Lachie. I remember that strong, possessive feeling, that she was my girl, that no one could give her this sort of comfort but me. At the time, I thought to myself, I'm not a completely useless bastard after all.

She had told me that, despite all the public pressure, Gow would never get out because her risk assessment of him was so bad. She was shaken when they sacked her, because she knew they'd get her replacement to do another RA. Gow's lawyer could easily argue that her report was biased because she'd been accused of stealing his files. But she wasn't *scared* when Gow did get out. She didn't introduce any new security measures to the house and said, "Nah," when I asked whether we should get rid of the decoy box and buy an actual alarm. Did she think he'd hurt Donna? Was she afraid he'd hurt other women? I must ask her when I visit.

I think she was more afraid when Donna and Gow went missing than when he got out. They had disappeared for over a week before the call. All our phone records show is a forty-second call from the hotel in Durness, and then Susie took off.

I mustn't give in to this insistent self-pity. Yesterday evening was the zenith. After tea I went into an apoplexy of miserable self-loathing: I ate a whole box of Celebrations in front of the television and almost choked on the irony. Yeni had put Margie to bed by the time I finished the chocolates, and I suddenly felt that I was missing her growing up. I went upstairs and stood by her bedroom door, looking in at her sleeping. I stood there, wishing I was less ineffectual, until I realized that nothing could be more ineffectual than standing about in dim halls, wishing I was otherwise. If I were a friend of mine, I'd give me a slap.

At the start of all this, when Susie was first arrested, I promised myself that I'd be a good man. I promised I'd put my own feelings aside and attend to those of my family, but time and time again I find it's beyond me. The whole thing has been so emasculating: having the mother of my child taken from me, then sitting in the court like a spare prick, listening to the prosecution suggest that she was in love with Gow. It makes me so angry. I have an urge to go about smashing people in the face just to prove I'm still here, still making my stamp on the world, still a man.

I phoned Susie's colleague Harvey Tucker again, but he wasn't in. I need to talk to him. Tucker didn't pick up this time, but he must have the message by now. He obviously doesn't want to talk to me. I left a message saying I wasn't angry or anything. Just wanted to ask him a couple of things to set my mind at rest. He still hasn't called back. Maybe I could use Gow's prison files as an inducement to Tucker to get in touch; I could promise him a swap.

The disk that's with the prison files has a list of people who had contacted Gow in the past two years, like Stevie Ray and Donna. The entries have notes next to them like "letter, sexual content," "letter, request to visit," and then the final disposition like "no action," "visit," "Gow refusal," or "Scottish Prison Department refusal." Some of the correspondents wrote three or four times. One of them wrote twenty-three times, every one of them an "admiring letter, violent content" with a request to visit. Interestingly, it was Gow who kept refusing the visit. Even rapist serial killers must find some people distasteful, I suppose.

I've got to hang on to Susie, my own Susie. The images from her arrest and the court are so overpowering that I have to strain to remember her from before, when we were just two private people, before we became a byword for privileged suburban professionals lusting after a bit of rough.

I've been looking at photos all day, thinking about when we met. I was the only guy in our crowd in med school who married another doctor. All my pals, Rosso and Bangor and Morris, they all said it was a bad move, marrying someone like Susie. They didn't mention Susie, of course; they just said someone who wasn't a nurse.

Susie Wilkens was in the year above us, and her grades were legendary. She was determined to do psychiatry from the beginning. Not surgery, not the high-prestige technical stuff. She was so good she wasn't even competing with the rest of us. I thought she was marvelous.

I've brought up some photos from our student days to stick on the walls here, to remind me of my Susie. I should put them into an album and leave it around the house so that Margie can see her mummy in normal situations.

Three of the pictures seem especially significant to me:

Photo One

Susie in our crowd from the student union. She is small, five feet four in heels. Her dark, thick hair is long and pulled over one shoulder.

It was one night among many in the beer bar, special only because I'd bought a disposable camera to take pictures of my room in the medical residence to send Mum and Dad so they could see where I was living and agree to the high rent. The rent wasn't high at all, but they'd been in Spain for a year and were used to nothing costing more than a tenner. I used the end of the film on the beer bar pictures.

There is a lot of movement in the picture. Everyone is mugging furiously, shoving each other around and drinking pints of lager, the amber and froth sloshing up the sides of the glasses. Susie is in the middle of it all. She's making a silly face, sticking out her tongue slightly and crossing her eyes, as if making ugly faces is something she finds terribly hard. She is holding a bag of crisps: cheesy puff balls.

Photo Two

Susie and I in the sunshine, outside a church. It was a student wedding; one of the guys from the union got married suddenly because his girlfriend was pregnant. The marriage was over before we graduated.

Neither Susie nor I could afford good clothes at the time of this picture. She is dressed with studied abandon in a shocking-pink pencil skirt and black dinner jacket. She thought it was studenty to dress like that. I loved it, loved it when she got things so wrong. She was so rarely wrong.

I have my cheap gray suit on, shiny around the pockets and crumpled at the elbows. I didn't have the money to dry-clean it. I wore that suit for about four years without having it cleaned or pressed. I remember the semicircular creases on the back of the jacket, like tidal sand. I wore it to christenings, weddings, interviews. In the end it was unwearably smelly and I had to throw it away. This photograph is probably the last time my hair was nice this length, quite Paul Weller, and that was six years ago.

Susie is much more attractive than I am. Her dark hair was long then, rich and shiny because she was young, worn over her shoulders, falling halfway down her upper arms. Her velvet blue eyes flash. She leans into the camera, saying something and pouting as she finishes a word. I notice my arm around her waist is holding her up: she can bend over at an acute angle because I am holding her weight.

Photo Three

Susie is sitting on my knee. We are on vacation with friends, eating dinner in a Corfu restaurant with white plastic chairs and a blue oilcloth on the table. It is nighttime, in an open-air taverna. Twelve shiny, sunburned faces grin around the table. It was our last year of med school, and we all went on a cheap package tour together. They were my friends. Susie came everywhere with my friends. This strikes me as significant somehow. She didn't seem to have a crowd of her own, or if she did, we don't have photographs of them.

I'm very involved with her in the photograph. I'm smelling her hair and my hand is on her slim, brown thigh, my index finger disappearing up the outside leg of her high-cut shorts. I remember how completely wrapped up in each other we were. We kissed in public and touched each other, behavior I find appalling when I witness it now. But then, in the very early days, nothing seemed real or important but that we were together.

It wasn't all blindness. Susie's wrong about that. I did know she had flaws, and I didn't fall in love just because I projected things onto her, either. She had qualities that I had never even thought of before I met her.

She had a sharp analytical mind, could tease the essence from a phrase or picture, see grades of meaning in statements. I'm just not that bright or interested in dissection. She'd think of a joke and laugh uncontrollably before she told it. She wouldn't ever give an inch over the house cleaning and always made me do my share before we found Mrs. Anthrobus. I loved the fact that she had principles and was so self-contained. Those weren't qualities I went out looking for. They blew me away. It wasn't blindness at all.

Margie's sleeping through the night and seems to be adjusting finally. I wish I'd paid more attention to her before the verdict, but I was sure Susie would be coming back with me that night. We should have introduced the possibility that Mummy might not come home. I think she knows how bad it is. When she says "Mummy," she immediately looks at me and Yeni, waiting for whatever reaction we've unknowingly been giving. She's more clingy than she used to be.

Still, she asks for Anna, her little friend from nursery, more often than she asks for Susie.

I know I should take Margie back to nursery as soon as possible, but I'm dreading it. They'll have read the verdict in the papers. I told Mrs. McLaughlin that I wouldn't see her for a while because Susie would be dropping Margie off for the next few weeks. I'll look like an idiot.

If the other parents snub me, I'll feel terrible, and if they're nice, I'll feel even worse. I'd like to move Margie into a different nursery and never see any of them again, but she likes it there and has made friends.

I wish I could sleep.

chapter eight

FOUND A CONTACTS DATABASE ON THE COMPUTER, AND WHEN I typed in "T," I found this: *Harvey Tucker, 191 Orca Road, Cambuslang.*

Susie's comment on the tape, about how love is a mistake, wasn't directed at me. She could just have been pissed and showing off to the journalist, flirting with him, letting him think she was available. She's entitled to a bit of private head space, allowed to talk to people without me there. That's all she was doing. In some ways it speaks well of our relationship. I want her to feel autonomous. I wouldn't want it any other way.

She managed to call me this morning, a full seven days after the verdict. The phone rang while I was standing in the hall eating hot garlic bread (all that's left in the freezer). If I'd been in the living room, I could have used the cordless and gone off somewhere private, but Susie said that she couldn't talk for long anyway. She's been given a job in the laundry, Monday is their heaviest day, and it doesn't pay well.

"I'll need to phone Fitzgerald a lot in the next few weeks, and I should keep as much of the phonecard as I can."

Why would she need to talk to Fitzgerald a lot? I thought the sentencing hearing was straightforward. Perhaps they've thought of something for the appeal, but I didn't think to ask that until after she'd rung off.

"Susie, it's great to hear your voice." I kept saying her name to remind myself that she wasn't dead, that she'd just gone away for a while. It was difficult to hear what she was saying. A woman was shouting in a singsong voice in the background. Another woman told her to shut up or move away from the phone area, and the singer let rip a string of expletives.

"But, Susie, Fitzgerald can phone you, can't he?"

"No." Her voice sounded distant, as if she were looking away from the phone, back at the shouting woman. "Well, I don't know all the rules yet. Maybe that's right." Then, in a quietly muttered aside: *"Shut her up, will you?"*

"You can reverse the charges to here, as well, you know."

"I think we've spent quite enough money already, don't you?" she said flatly. "Anyway, we've got to buy our phonecards out of the wages they give us."

"Can't I send you some?"

"No."

"Why?"

"Because otherwise the rich prisoners would get a lot more talk time than the poor ones, and that wouldn't be fair." She sounded scornful. I couldn't tell if she was being sardonic about the system, the rules, or my stupidity in not instinctively knowing the rules about convicted prisoners' phone calls.

"I've booked you visits on next Friday at three and the following Wednesday at eleven," she said. "Bring cigarettes and a transistor radio and a big PP9 battery for it."

"Okay." I jotted the items down on the phone pad. "Did you get my letter?"

"No." She sounded suspicious. "Why? What does it say?"

"Nothing special, just, you know, hello. You didn't get it?"

"I got one. Did you send two?"

"No. How often can I visit you?"

"Four hours a month. Four visits really."

"Oh," I said, hiding my disappointment. "At least that's one a week." It didn't seem very much at all.

"Yeah. We could have one or two big ones instead, but I'd rather the one-hour ones. Gives me more to look forward to."

I was briefly resentful at the forty-minute drive each way but pleased that I would be the high point of her week.

"How are you, Susie?" I said. "I miss you." I had the phone pressed to my ear, my chin to my chest, and was talking quietly, privately, when suddenly a shriek on the other end made my eyes water. I dropped the receiver. It was swinging by the leg of the phone table, but I could still hear the noise of a scuffle and Susie demanding that I answer her.

"It's frightening in here," she said quickly. "There's a lot of disruptive people."

"Don't worry," I said, shifting the phone to the other, non-bleeding ear. "We'll get you out of there, just hang on, Susie." I felt quite manly saying that.

"Is Margie there?"

"Well, no. She's just gone to the park with Yeni. I'm sorry."

She sighed heavily, sounding like a blustery wind in the earpiece. "I wanted to talk to her," she said, near to tears.

"I'm sorry. I didn't know you'd phone today, I'm sorry."

Neither of us talked for a moment. We just listened to one another breathe.

"Is she okay?" she asked.

"She's fine," I said. "Really fine. She's been talking more."

"Has she?" I heard a hopeful lift in her voice. "What's she saying?"

"Yesterday she said 'Teddy' and 'sleepy' and 'Yeni.'"

I should have known. I should have thought it through before and known how upsetting that would be, but I hadn't planned the conversation that way at all. Susie howled. She howled from the depths of her ruined soul.

"Don't bring her," she bubbled when she could finally speak. "Don't bring her to see me."

And she hung up.

I tried phoning back, but you can't call in to the number because it's a pay phone. I desperately wanted to comfort her, offer to let Yeni go, anything. I've been carrying the phone around with me in the hope that she'd call me back, but she hasn't. I've had an emotional hangover all day.

Other telephone news: Mum and Dad phoned from Marbella this evening while I was tidying up. Mum said not to worry, the papers seem to have dropped the story. So that's all right then. They invited me out for an extended visit, and by all means, feel free to bring Margie. She's not even two yet. I can't leave her alone in the bath. The card they sent for her first birthday had a Monet print on it and a tenner inside. They might as well have sent her duty-free cigarettes.

I drove into town to see Fitzgerald this morning. I always expect his office to be near other lawyers, or next to the courts, or somewhere more atmospheric than an office block with a charity clothes shop next to the entrance. I took in my notes of points to query for Susie's appeal. He didn't seem all that interested in getting my input. He frowned as I spoke, drawing his gray eyebrows down over his eyes like duvets. I felt like a deluded idiot who'd been wasting my own time and was now intent on wasting his. I was reluctant to leave the Dictaphone tape with him in case it got lost, because he didn't seem very concerned at all. I explained what it said anyway.

He sat me down and told me that the reports were being done on Susie. They were due to have the sentencing hearing in a few weeks, but of course I must understand that murder always meant life. He was a lot less friendly than he has been, for reasons that I can't fathom. I'm touchy, I know I am, but it makes me feel suspicious, and I wondered briefly whether he threw the case. It's stupid. He did very well, even the papers said he did well. I must come up with better things for him to base an appeal on. I need to work harder.

When I came home, I wrote a long letter to Susie, an encouraging letter, telling her that I'd had a good meeting with Fitzgerald. I finished it and got halfway through dialing Harvey Tucker's number, but I hung up. He's not going to phone me back. Even if he did, I don't know whether I could stand to ask him about Susie. What if he tells me all the things I don't want to hear? There's just the faintest possibility, but it niggles me. If I'm going to find any grounds for appeal, I have to approach this with an open mind. It doesn't really matter what I feel about Susie spending time with Gow. If she did, well then she did, but I need to know so we can answer those points in an appeal. I have to put my own feelings aside. I'm determined to make a contribution to her appeal; I want to help.

Box 1 Document 2 ***Notes from Susie's Trial***

Police Constable McCallum, who gave this evidence, was very young and seemed scared of the court. He gave a lot of details that I thought irrelevant. He was then quizzed about the details by both sides. This is word for word as I took it down:

> PC: Mr. Gow's body was found in the abandoned bothy above Inshore Loch.

Prosecution asked for a definition of "bothy." PC said it was a "single-room dwelling on hills, used by walkers for shelter." Judge snickery because the lawyer didn't know what a bothy was.

> PC: Approach to bothy over a mile from road. Well-worn path, familiar to hikers. Out of season, no one there. Police alerted by anonymous caller. Never discovered identity, but call came from a public phone booth that would only be known to a local. Bothy facing

north on loch side. Windows broken, no door. Roof collapsed in on west side. Bothy itself: very dark on entry. [PC shaking.] Victim lying on side, facing back wall. Could see hands tied tightly behind back with plastic tag.

Prosecution asked why "tightly"?

PC: Hands very, very swollen.

How swollen?

PC: Hands about double size and purple. Thought they were gloves at first. Plastic digging deep into skin; wrists bloody. Victim missing one shoe, never found. Stepping to left, PC noticed Gow's injuries. A lot of blood on the floor and under his head. Mouth obscured by blood. No, sir. . . .

I think he was questioned by someone here. My writing goes all wonky, as if I'm not sure I should bother taking it down.

PC: I couldn't see. It was very dark. . . . Yes, sir, I use a flashlight. Even then, it was still v. dark. Couldn't see a weapon at this stage [I think this is what I'm writing here.] And the tongue . . .

Oh, God, the tongue. The dreaded tongue.

PC: had been . . .

He gulped here, I remember. Everyone leaned forward to catch what he was going to say. Even the impassive stenographer tipped one degree toward him. The blood drained from the PC's face as he said it.

PC: removed.

Everyone in the public galleries recoiled and gasped. The mustardy old man who was sitting in front of me clapped his hands to his face, as though they were coming after his tongue next, and a couple of old women in front of me held on to each other. Who were these ridiculous people? It really must be the height of cant to wait for a place in the public gallery at a murder trial and then act surprised when violence is mentioned. Why go to so much trouble to hear the details and then get indignant the very moment their prurience is satisfied?

Susie did herself no favors by turning around and tutting at them. The papers said she was callous, but she's a medic: she was having bits thrown at her when she was in her teens.

The only genuine response came from Stevie Ray, who sobbed loudly. Everyone knew he was Gow's manager; he'd been on any TV show that offered pocket change. He's effectively unemployed now that his only client is dead, but there was no sympathy for him in the gallery. Everyone just looked away and left him crying like a bullied boy in a playground.

PC: Clean removal from the root, not gouged.

How would he know?

PC: Tongue later found in corner of room. Sitting on newspaper. Lot of blood from mouth on floor. Face clean on upper cheek, suggesting not moved since tongue cut. Deep wound on underside of head, probably initial wound. Checked for pulse.

F'sake! Half his head f'ing missing!

PC: Found victim was dead.

No!

PC: For ten minutes searched front and back of bothy for other persons. No one there. Called for backup.

From the crime-scene photos and the aerial photograph in the paper, it was clear that the bothy was a single room with one doorway, sitting on a continuous slope. There was nowhere to hide. The PC could have searched the whole area by stepping outside and turning his head left and right, but neither lawyer asked about the missing ten minutes. I think they assumed he was out the back being sick. Maybe we could make something of this? He could have been contaminating the evidence in some way.

Susie didn't do it. I've known this from the moment they raised the evidence about the tongue and the hands. Gow may have been left in the fetal position so that he bled to death, but anyone with a rudimentary knowledge of first aid could have done this. She wouldn't have cut his tongue out or stabbed him on the side of his head either. Because she's a doctor, she would have killed him more cleanly and she'd never have tied his hands up like that. I knew she was innocent before this evidence, and I've never doubted her. I still don't doubt her.

Box 2 Document 2 ***Interview with Donna,* Woman's World, *4/24/98***

The photographs of Donna make her look pretty. She had an electrifying figure and a nice smile, that's undeniable. There's a picture of her standing underneath the maximum-security prison sign in full wedding gown. The sentence structures in this article are horribly clunky. Imagine the corrosive effect this sort of magazine has on the language of people who read it week after week.

A woman's wedding day is supposed to the happiest of her life, yet Donna McGovern was searched on her way into the service and spent her wedding night alone. Alone she may be, but Donna, 23, has no doubt that she made the right decision.

"Andrew is the man for me," says Donna. "I know he is innocent and I will stand by him until he is released."

But Donna may be waiting for the rest of her life, for her new husband is one of Britain's most notorious serial killers. He has been called the Water Rat, the Riverside Ripper, and "just plain evil" by the daughter of one of his victims.

"People don't know the real Andrew. He's the most caring man I've ever met—very loving and sweet and gentle. He's the most popular person in the prison. The other prisoners love him."

After four years behind bars, Andrew Gow, 33, finally feels he has found true love. Speaking through his manager, Stevie Ray, Gow announced on the day of his wedding, "I have finally found love forever. Donna is a true lady."

Gow was a minicab driver before he was convicted of murdering five Glasgow prostitutes in 1993. He was arrested after being stopped for cruising in the red-light district of the city and confessed to police that he had committed the terrifying series of murders. At the trial Gow pled guilty but now claims he is innocent.

While in prison Gow studied art and has become a poet. He writes to his new wife every day and sends her poems and drawings he has done of her.

They've reproduced one of his handwritten poems. McGonagall would blush. The script is neat and boxy, and he's drawn flowers and knives all over the paper. Badly.

When I saw her I knew she was the one for me.
A very special lady.
Eyes of love like lovely diamonds.
A smile of joy.
Maybe it's the light.
Maybe I'm dreaming.
Maybe there right.
Maybe I'm insane.

Although married, Donna and Andrew have met only four times.

The first time was after just three letters had passed between them. For the visit, Donna wore a red dress, which Andrew had chosen for her from ten photographs she had sent in of herself in different outfits. Donna says their first meeting was a special day.

"It was as if we'd known each other all our lives. We cuddled and laughed together. We weren't awkward. It was a relief because I had finally found my Andrew. I always knew there was a special man out there for me, and when I saw the picture of Andrew in the paper, it was as if I recognized him. It was love at first sight."

Donna was born and grew up in Leicester. Currently living in Kirkintilloch, near to the prison, she aims to train as a travel agent and wants to do exams so she can support her new husband when he is released. Sadly, Donna's dad died recently, leaving her without a family of her own.

"Andrew and I are incredibly close," says Donna. "Probably because I have no one else."

But Andrew has been married before. Shortly after his conviction, his first wife, Lara Orr, was quoted as saying she hoped she never saw him again. "He is a violent man who made me dress up for kinky sex games," said Lara at the time. "I hope I never see him again. He has ruined my life."

Although they were separated immediately after the touching service, Donna insists that she does feel married. "We weren't able to consummate the marriage, but we were allowed an hour together, under guard of course, and that was great. We just held each other and kissed and laughed. Andrew doesn't want to see me sad. He said if he ever sees my tears, he'll hang himself."

What a nice man. The article continues and gets more and more anodyne and hard to read. It finishes: "As soon as Andrew gets out, we will go up to the north of Scotland and start a new life together."

God help the Highlands. They are cluttered up with incomers from all over the country, running from whatever. Mr. and Mrs. Petty-Fury from Shropshire who can't maintain a harmonious relationship with any neighbor anywhere. John Q. Bankruptcy, living on a yacht with a suitcase full of cash. Ms. Adulteress and her suspiciously young friend. It's almost impossible to stay in the Highlands for any length of time without seeing all the subtexts float to the surface, bloated and obscene, like rotting day-old corpses. And Donna and Gow were going to add to that.

The article finishes with a picture Gow has drawn of Donna with her hands behind her head. I don't think he meant it to be a sexy drawing, I think it's just because he can't draw hands. It's not a bad drawing, actually, although she looks as if she's squinting and the tip of her nose is dirty.

I understand what Susie means in the Dictaphone interview now: when she's talking about projection, she means love like this. All this stuff about Gow's being gentle and kind and everything, it's so obviously not true. They found the blood of the women in his car and his spunk on them. They proved he was in the area during the crimes. Reading these interviews, it's as if Donna were trying to turn a really fervent hope into a fact by being adamant about it.

chapter nine

I WAS A BALL-HAIR AWAY FROM WRIGGLING OUT OF TAKING Margie to nursery, but I gave myself a talking-to. I felt a bit cocky anyway because I had a dream last night, about myself and Susie. We were swimming through the living room in Otago Street. The water was amniotic and comfortable. We slid past each other in the warm currents, touching fingertips, smiling in the blue light. It felt prophetic somehow, as if everything were going to be okay. I woke up feeling sure again, thinking that she'll be back, certain I can cope. This lasted until I got to the doors of the nursery.

I need to get Margie back to some sort of normality. She needs routine, I need to sort these papers out, and Yeni needs to go to English classes. She's been fantastic and has done the bulk of the child care while I mope about and come up here. She's not required to do so much, and would have been within her rights to leave us when Susie was first arrested. She's a kind girl. I think back on myself at eighteen and I know I'd have run away at the first sign of trouble, but she's mature for her age, emotionally. She told me she has four younger brothers, so maybe that explains it. I thought of buying some thrush suppositories and leaving them in her bathroom, but that's probably a bit presumptuous.

I'm avoiding writing about the nursery. As I walked through the park, I could see up the hill. Beyond the park gate parents, mums mostly, were parking their big cars and pulling the little kids out of the backseats, lingering in the street before they took them in, chatting to each other. The trendy brigade, what Susie calls the MILTers (Mums in Leather Trousers), were gathered around the doors of one of the urban jeeps, looking in at something on the floor. I began to wish I'd sent Yeni, but I want to be with Margie during any potential unpleasantness. If anything happens, I want her to remember me being there, not simply handing her over to Yeni all the time.

Margie was messing about, picking up leaves and showing me them. I picked her up, put my head down, and walked up the final hill to the park gate. My heart was thumping like a gallows drum. Margie realized where we were going and got excited, squealing and stiffening her body to be put down. I held on to her tightly. Luckily, a small boy had caught his coat on the cast-iron railing at the head of the stairs, and some parents were engaged in trying to untangle him. I slipped down the stairs to the basement without catching anyone's eye.

Usually I just let Margie run in, but Mrs. McLaughlin waved me over and asked how I was: syrupy concern, head tilting and hand rubbing. They keep the playroom incredibly hot, so by now I was sweating heavily and could feel my blood pressure going through the roof.

"Fine, fine, fine," I said, over and over, panting, trying to cool down and calm down at the same time. I looked far more distressed than I felt. All around the room parents tried hard not to look at me.

Margie ran off and tugged at a fire engine a small boy was holding. The boy's hand slipped and he let go. Completely unnecessarily, Margie smacked him over the head with it before crouching down to run the wheels on the floor. A horrible quiet descended in the room as the little boy tipped his head back and let out a rolling air-raid-siren wail. We all thought the same thing at exactly the same time. But Susie's innocent, so how could it be genetic?

The boy stopped crying and crouched down, watching Margie play and putting his hand on top of the engine so that he was doing it too. Everyone looked ashamed because of what they had been thinking. A very young assistant ran forward and stroked Margie's hair with ostentatious affection, smiling back at me and at Mrs. McLaughlin. God, it was awful. I muttered something ridiculous about loving my daughter very much and McLaughlin nodded wildly and I left. I don't want to go back this afternoon.

I forgot about the press and came in the back way. There was only one camera crew this time. They scrabbled out of the van, but I sped up and managed to get through the gate before they got their stuff out. I could hear them over the wall, swearing in French. It's frightening. Even when I'm sitting in the house, I sometimes break into a sweat, imagining I'm being watched.

I've just found a book about the psychology of love hidden under this desk. Susie hid the book but not the files she stole from Sunnyfields. What does this mean? What does all the stuff in this room mean? I feel like an Egyptian grave robber in here sometimes, as if I'm crashing around in a room full of signifiers and symbols, unknowingly smashing through a hundred subtle strata of meaning.

Otago Street: the cramped, new-built flat. We were the first people to live there and it was our first home together. They had knocked down the tenement block that had stood there previously. The whole area was subsiding, sliding slowly down the hill to the river. During our first week there, the lintel above the bathroom door began to skew. The windowsill in the living room shifted, and the front door got jammed open. The workmen said it was normal settlement for a new-build. We were just grateful that we were renting.

It was tiny. The bedroom was so small that the double bed touched three walls. We had to climb over it to open the window. We used to lie in the dark and listen to the river and talk about our day. Sometimes Susie would get up and make a plate of buttery toast and two mugs of tea and we'd sit up and watch late-night clubbers walk home across the Gibson Street bridge far below. I was her world then. She adored me. She did things, like the toast, gave gifts, thought of me all the time. She phoned me during the day to say she missed me. Sometimes we'd be watching television and I'd turn and find her just staring at me, doting. She wrote notes and stuck them around the house for me to find, saying she loved me, sending kisses.

She loved me more than I loved her then. It was a bit scary, how much she loved me. When I daydreamed about ending it—just for a distraction, not because I was going to—when I thought about it, I worried that she'd stalk me. She had never been in love before. I'd been in love twice before I met her and knew how to hold back and defend myself. I made a decision to be kind to Susie when I could have been otherwise; I deigned not to hurt her. I was only ever tempted once, when I saw Sandra again and we went back to her house. It felt wrong and cheap and stupid, and I was angry with her before she even made a move. I couldn't touch her. I went back to Susie's room in the med residence and had to resist the urge to make a huge fuss of her, because that's a dead giveaway that you've been thinking about doing something wrong.

How did it happen, then, that her benevolent tin god ends up getting the tail end of her phonecard? How come I'm hanging about at the back of the court, acting calm as I hear that she loved a serial killer over me? When did the dynamic change to the point where she doesn't even feel the need to explain to me that it isn't the case?

I was still in charge before the wedding. I knew it and so did she. She even said it sometimes, that I didn't love her as much as she loved me. We laughed about it and I reassured her. I said that I would never leave her; that I was set with her for life. I'd stroke her hair and roll the flesh on the top of her ears gently between my lips: tiny hairs, skin that had never rubbed against anything, never been sunburned.

Corfu was the first time she had ever been abroad, and she had that perfectly translucent skin little Scottish girls have. It was the softest skin I'd ever felt until Margie was born.

Before we were married. I remember that time so well: it's the most vivid memory I have. Two days before the wedding, we sat in the car outside here, in Orchard Lane, looking at the SOLD sign looming over the high garden wall. I didn't know this house existed until we came to view it. It's hidden away, and the lane looks like a delivery slip because it cuts down the side of two large houses. Beyond the wall, in this overdeveloped, trendy square mile of a busy city, sits our fat little white house with our apple tree and fruit bushes and our three small hills of private green heaven. I love it here.

Susie pulled the car around and parked. We couldn't see past the wall, but we sat together and imagined our way through the gate, across the garden, opening the French windows and walking into the kitchen. We imagined eating with the doors open in summer and gathering in the front room for Christmases with family. Not our own families, who are quite tricky and grim, but cheerful families who are nice to each other and enjoy a good time. I said I'd cook with our own fruit and plant carrots and cabbage. This house cost a fortune because of where it is. Susie's father gave us a big chunk of the deposit. Said he'd been saving up. It should have made us suspicious but it didn't.

As we sat in the car, Susie said that the storeroom next to the attic could be a small study for her, if I didn't mind. I didn't even remember it from the viewing. I'd been looking for a comfy television room, enough bedrooms so we didn't ever have to move, and a nice bit of garden. I wasn't looking for a study when we first saw it. We both knew she was the one with ambition. I said of course she should have it, and she started to cry because she was so happy. I held her hand across the gear stick, kissed her fingers, and called her sweet names while I thought of Sandra and all the other women; well, all six of them. It didn't seem like that many. I mean, statistically, it isn't that many. Compared with most people. I still had the upper hand at that point, I'm sure of it.

After the wedding, after our honeymoon, when we came back and began the task of doing the house up, we were probably still equal.

It's strange to know a house as well as I know this one, to know its guts and drainage system, to have seen inside each and every wall and under every floor. Everything needed doing: rewiring, replastering, replumbing, central heating, painting, and furnishing. I got the estimates, chose the workmen, and timetabled everything. She liked it that I did that: took control. She chose the colors and furnishings, but she was working hard at the time, so I did everything else.

Maybe the change happened after her mother died. It must change you, becoming an orphan with no parent to chastise or please, no one at the back of your mind to keep you in check.

I was downstairs just now, listening to the *Mirror* journalist offering the answering machine untold wealth (Alistair Garvie, from godalmighty *London,* where barter economies are a thing of the past and they have *schools*). I went off and made a cup of tea, and it occurred to me that Susie grieved differently for her mother than for her father. She was bewildered by her father's death, stunned and saddened, but her mum dying made her angry, as if the old woman had committed the ultimate submissive act when she pegged it.

Maybe the change came when Susie inherited all that money. That would make you feel powerful. She must have felt that she didn't need to be subservient to anyone. Even I felt powerful when she got it and paid off our mortgage. Just knowing that all that cash was sloshing around in the bank with my name attached to it in some tangential way made me feel strong. She got pregnant a month after her mother died, just when the money came through. Three years of trying and she gets pregnant then. She never worried about money until she inherited. We never even talked about money before, but afterward we did. We talked about little else for the duration of her pregnancy.

I still don't know exactly when our relationship shifted in her favor, but it did, and I didn't even notice until we were in court and I was drying my damp palms on the knees of my trousers, staring at the back of Susie's head, wishing with all my might that she'd turn around and smile at me.

The clues were all there: her hassles at Sunnyfields as she struggled to win back lost ground after her maternity leave. I thought she was just going back to herself after giving birth, but actually she was hardening way beyond what she had been before.

She was my sweet, soft-hearted Susie, and then, quite suddenly, she was someone else.

chapter ten

When I went back to collect Margie at nursery yesterday, the tanned young assistant was embarrassingly overfriendly. She kept patting my arm and back and grinning unhappily. They had obviously had a staff chat about me and decided I was a pathetic, unknowing mug.

It's rare for people to pity me. I did well at school, had pals, wasn't crap at sports, and got straight into medical school. I had good-looking girlfriends, met Susie, and we both graduated. Even though I didn't go into practice, everyone knows that was because I chose not to. I don't think they even pity me for giving up work and staying at home. The women love it because they think I'm caring. Most men my age have realized that seeing patients day after day after day isn't the unmitigated joy they had supposed. They try to pretend that I'm missing out, but they know, most of them, that their careers will climax in a whimper of boredom. At least being at home there is a possibility that I will write something one day, something important and useful. I'm just not ready yet. I have to let the ideas form first.

Anyway, the women at nursery pitied me, and I have to say, I rather liked it. I don't know if it's because they're female, so I don't feel threatened, or if I'm too bigoted to think women could possibly challenge my position in the social hierarchy. The pity felt like a comfort, like empathy, as if they understood. Some other mums came in while I was there, and they felt sorry for me too. They all came up to talk to me and rubbed Margie's hair, cupping my elbow and issuing distant invites to bring Margie over to play. I found myself standing bravely, nodding sadly and sighing quite a lot. My tragic tableau was spoiled when Margie bit another child on the head and we had to leave. I used to get Yeni to drop Margie off on Thursdays, but I might just go myself tomorrow.

I keep thinking about Harvey Tucker. What an utter, utter bastard. Is there any need for him to snub me now, at this moment when I couldn't be more down? Mum phoned from Marbella this morning. I told her she didn't need to phone every day and reminded her that it would be costing a fortune. It didn't work. It was just the usual: more nagging and coughing and needing to be reassured.

It is just possible that Harvey Tucker has the wrong number and is leaving kind, considerate messages on someone else's machine. I don't ever recall his phoning here for Susie. One digit out and he could be doing that. Psychiatrists' writing is awful, so it wouldn't be hard to get a scribbled phone number wrong if Susie had written it down for him. But that's crap, because I've left him our number every time I've phoned. So that's crap. Tucker, Tucker, you motherfucker.

Yeni has gone out for the afternoon with her friends from the English class, a pimply boy who may or may not be her boyfriend and a fifty-year-old hermaphrodite woman with a jolly-hockey-sticks attitude. Margie's having a nap now, but before she went down I got our wedding pictures out and we looked at them together. I told her the story of our wedding. About the big cake and dancing with Mummy, and the big car. She said "Vroom" and spluttered orange juice on the couch. Margie's teeth have come in quite sharp with gaps between them. Her head is big as well, or maybe her hair is just so thin and dark that it makes her head seem unusually big and square. I hope she won't grow up ugly.

Looking at the wedding photos, I can see nothing untoward in them. Susie's not brandishing steak knives or anything. We are a normal happy couple, standing stiffly on church steps, in a garden, by a tree, wearing stale smiles. The photos took hours.

The whole wedding felt like it had nothing to do with us. Susie's parents, her father really, took over. He ordered the biggest, fanciest everything, with knobs on the knobs and extra bells. Both sets of parents were beside themselves with joy; two only children, each marrying a soon-to-graduate doctor. Her parents told me several times they were pleased—even though I was a Catholic. Susie and I laughed about it behind their backs: the joke was on them because I'm a *lapsed* Catholic. She didn't want to tell them about that. She said it made me seem even more dangerous.

Mr. Wilkens ordered the biggest dress, the biggest dinner (five courses in a plush Glasgow hotel by the river, free wine, and liqueurs at the end), the biggest kilt outfit for himself and me. In the pictures I've got the kilt and shoes and the socks, skean-dhu, sash, jacket, and I'm holding a silly bonnet-type thing. I'm so over-Scottish I look like a visiting American. Mr. Wilkens (call me Alan) measured everything by the size of the bill. Susie ended up lying to him and saying that the return to Corfu cost thousands, just so we didn't need to go to Barbados. He was pushing for us to get a prenuptial agreement—he pushed quite hard behind the scenes—but I insisted that I wanted Susie to have anything I owned. It didn't make any sense until he died.

Her mother worried about money. She was alarmed by the cost of everything, even the price of the inscription inside the rings. Once, when we were ordering the cake and the favors out of a catalog, she inadvertently let off a little worried squeal. Mrs. Wilkens didn't know that her husband was loaded. She didn't find out until he died two years later. Mr. and Mrs. Wilkens and little Susie Wilkens went to Portpatrick for their fortnight's rainy holiday every year and used his old undershirts for dusters. The old bastard had almost three-quarters of a million sitting in different accounts and the same again in a low-risk shares portfolio. The money came from way back, and he'd always kept it quiet. Double lives seem to be something of a theme in her family.

Susie was furious with her mother for never questioning him, never finding out. Her mother said that the money was her husband's business; it wasn't her concern. No matter what happened in the family, Susie got furious with her mother. The family cat died, blame Mrs. Wilkens; Aunt Trisha broke her foot, blame Mrs. Wilkens; father lied to his family consistently during his thirty-seven-year marriage, blame Mrs. Wilkens. She had a lot more respect for my mum, who I think is a bit of a bully.

Surprise killed Mrs. Wilkens. She was fine when her husband died, but finding out about the money upset her desperately. She had always assumed they were on the verge of poverty and had fetished watery baked beans and walking everywhere into a kind of fiscal piety. She found herself facing a massive windfall when she was just too old to change her values. Her psyche sort of short-circuited, and six months after her husband's will was settled, she had a series of heart attacks. We were with her in the hospital at the end. She looked so surprised. I'm sure she saw his bank statement during her final seizure.

Looking at our wedding pictures has made me feel quite happy, as if I were back in that time when everything made sense. There were good times, I'm sure of that, before we forgot one another and got caught up in endlessly meeting work and domestic obligations. Susie didn't always keep secrets from me. Sometimes we got Saskia, the old nanny, to baby-sit and went out alone together. Over dinner we'd reassure each other that the relationship was still alive, tell each other how great it was to have someone to depend on, like beautiful background music. Maybe she was lying, I don't know, but I meant it.

Once we went to the Pecorino for dinner; it must have been a birthday or anniversary, I forget which. We were both dressed up and enjoying the food and I looked up at her and fell in love all over again. She had that white sweater on, the fluffy one with the wide neck, and a diamanté starburst on a chain. It was her hair that made me catch my breath, as thick as a pillow. She had recently given birth to Margie and still had that formless softness. I knew that her body was flooded with relaxin and even her joints were soft. She was sheepish, vulnerable, and unsure. It was so unlike her and completely precious. They were really good times.

Looking at the wedding photographs has made me miss her. My breastbone aches, but not, I realize, for her *now.* I miss her then. The verdict and the difficult phone call have left me exhausted at the thought of seeing her. I'm supposed to be going out to visit her in two days' time, and I don't want to. I'm angry at Susan-now for ruining my relationship with the Susie I thought she was. I won't be able to face her if I go into the visiting hall with this attitude. I need to remember her as she was before.

Memories to Consider Previsit

1. Honeymoon: the hot nights and days. Sleeping on the balcony. Having drunk sex in the grassy hills behind the beach on the way home from a nightclub.

Neither of us really wanted to go to a nightclub; we only went to feel young, and then we got fed up because there was nowhere to sit down. It was just a boring disco, lots of bam-bam-bam music we didn't recognize, and then, within the space of fifteen minutes, everyone there became incredibly drunk. People were shagging on the banquettes: girls with miniskirts up around their waists, tits out, guys half-coming, one guy finishing himself off in the cubicle in the toilet.

Susie was drunk and thought it was funny; she found it exciting, and we had a shag on the way home. It was just a quick one and we got up quickly afterward and kind of ran home, but we never forgot it. It was the highlight of the honeymoon. She wondered if she was pregnant afterward. I didn't like that. I didn't want us to conceive after having dirty sex, which is stupid and prudish. I felt it should have been more missionary somehow. Prim. We never touched on that sort of thing again, never went there together again. Susie didn't like to talk about it. In truth, if she had, I think I wouldn't have liked it.

2. The first summer in this house, the day the kitchen arrived. We got the suppliers to fit it, and they did it all in one day. It cost extra and they were rude and sulky, but they were quick. Afterward, sitting with the French windows open, looking out into the garden, sipping wine (cheap wine—not nice, as I remember, but it added to the pastoral picture). Looking out past our perfect kitchen units and beechwood worktop, thinking how lucky we were, to have each other and everything else anyone could possibly want.

3. The day Margie arrived. No, that's a bit of a scary blur actually.

4. Just before Margie arrived. Lying in bed next to Susie, who was gigantic and propped up on a pillow, talking about the sound of the river in Otago Street and how she wished she had taped it and could play it now to calm herself. She was scared and couldn't get comfortable.

When she told Dr. Mackay at the Queen Mother's Maternity that she was frightened, he said it was too late to back out now, ho ho ho. Susie gave him a rocket. What a stupid thing to say to patients; did he think it helped? What was he thinking, saying things like that to women? I think he gave her an elective caesarean because of it. She was jumpy until she got out of the hospital. There was never any question: she wouldn't do it again. Even though we both know how hard it is to be an only child, she wasn't going through that again. She couldn't wait to get back to work.

5. The best night we ever had: there are so many nights it's hard to say what the best night was.

Best for being madly into each other: the first time in Corfu. One night in the first weeks when we went for dinner with everyone else and then went to a disco. We might as well have been alone. I don't remember who else was there or what anyone else said or anything. Just Susie, slinky and slim, sitting on my knee, slipping her fingers through my hair, tilting my head back when she caught a tangle, pulling quite hard as if she were annoyed, and her face breaking into a smile as she kissed me. I knew then that I didn't ever want anyone else. The knowledge that I had found her bloomed warmly in my gut. I never told her that, and to be honest, I'm glad now.

Her best night for telling other people about: the night I proposed. New Year's Eve and I was working as a resident in the emergency room at the Western. She missed a party and came to meet me for the bells. We sat on a bench in front of Glasgow Uni, high on Gilmorehill, watching the fireworks go off in the city below, and I took her hand and asked her to marry me. She laughed and said we'd already decided to get married, but I wanted to ask her properly. She liked it. She's very conventional, deep down. When she tells the story to other people, when her dad told the story during his speech at the wedding, they didn't mention her laughing at me.

6. Best sex: the night in Corfu on the beach. Definitely.

I'll remember the beach at Corfu before I go in to visit her. I don't want her sensing rejection from me or feeling that I'm tentative about her in any way, because I'm not. She's my wife.

chapter eleven

IT'S THREE-THIRTY IN THE MORNING AND FREEZING UP HERE. MY finger joints are aching, and I've got two sweaters on over my pajamas. Mentally and physically, I'm completely exhausted.

I was thinking about Harvey Tucker while I fed Margie her tea. I've been leaving messages for a week now. All he needs to do is pick up the phone. I started rehearsing what I'd say to him if he did, what I'd tell him if I was clearing my mind, which is always a mistake. I used to do that in the Western and invariably ended up having fights with people when it would have been much better just to shut up.

I was thinking about how unnecessary it was to be unkind and not return the call, how it was kicking a man when he was down, etc. I got really angry and lost my temper with Margie for knocking over a plant pot and treading soil into the crack in the kitchen lino. I should have known then that I was losing control. I kept coming back to Tucker, thinking about him and getting hot.

It was only four-thirty, and it occurred to me that I could phone Sunnyfields and ask for him. I felt nervous thinking about it; they often didn't put me through to Susie if she was in a meeting, and he could have successfully dodged me again. I realized that I would be better off just turning up at his door.

I hurried Margie through her tea, abandoning her yogurt so soon after the first refusal that she got confused and ate two-thirds of it before starting the "no" game again. Yeni settled down with her in front of the television, and I said I was going out to the supermarket. Won't be long. They wouldn't even notice I was gone.

Harvey Tucker's street isn't far off the motorway. It's narrow and dark, with big old houses set back in wide gardens. At the foot of the street, hemmed in behind a low wall of bollards, a stream of slow-moving rush-hour traffic passed like a lazy herd of migrating buffalo, kicking up dust. The lights were on in the houses neighboring Tucker's, and cruising slowly past in my dark car, I could see kids turning on televisions in front rooms, families settling in for the evening.

Harvey wasn't in when I got there. The lights were off: no Mrs. Tucker, then, no grizzly little Tuckers to deal with. Just Harvey living alone, and, I thought, so much the better.

His house is much grander than ours. It's one of those solid, tall Victorian villas with a crunchy red-gravel drive and big, clean bay windows with swaths and swags of expensive material thrown about all over them. I've only ever met Harvey once, at a Christmas party, but I could have guessed he lived somewhere like this. He's an angular, splindly man with thin legs that match his thin hair and thin smile. He's about fifty and has a faintly jaundiced pallor. He looks as though he would have been a sickly, whining child.

It was six o'clock, and I know they finish at Sunnyfields at five. It took Susie about fifty minutes to drive home, and we're diagonally across the city, so I knew he'd be home soon. I waited outside in the car, rehearsing all the hell I was going to give him and watching until I saw a silver BMW pull slowly into the driveway. Tucker turned the engine off and stopped for a moment before he undid his belt. He climbed slowly out of the big, sleek car, opened the back passenger door, took out his briefcase, and shut the door again, pressing the beeper to lock it.

I suddenly realized how near the house he was and thought he might dodge indoors before I caught him, so I opened my car door and, slamming it shut, ran across the noisy gravel to him. He flinched at first, looking terrified, and raised his briefcase as if he were thinking of lashing out with it, but when he saw it was me, he let the bag fall to his side and watched me back off, lock my car, turn again, and come back toward him. It was eerie: he didn't say hello or anything. It was as if he knew my coming to him was inevitable. When I drew close, he just turned around and opened the front door, switched off the burglar alarm, and shut the front door behind me. Our commonality of purpose felt like one of those creepy gay pick-ups in films about the fifties. But I'd left about twelve messages asking him to tell me something quite specific, so perhaps it wasn't all that prescient.

When he turned on the light in the hall, I suddenly felt quite unsafe. The house was very dark, the hall papered in navy blue with gold stripes. The light had a small, stained-glass cone for a shade, but all it did was mute the light on the ceiling. From below, it was an elaborately decorated bare bulb, casting sharp shadows about the hall and Harvey's already Gothic face. A tall, dark wood bookcase housed the phone, a series of never opened green-bound books, and several scrawny stuffed birds, one about to take off, one staring at its feet, another (a little owl) staring startled at the opposite wall.

Harvey was standing close to me, a little too close, as if he were afraid of the hall as well. Behind him gaped two large black doorways, one leading to a front room, one to a back. I tried smiling to diffuse the atmosphere.

"So, Harvey Tucker, I've been trying to get you," I blurted. Of course I meant "get you on the phone," not "get you and attack you physically," but his face convulsed in consternation, and he stumbled away from me, across the hall to the mouth of the dark front room. "No," I said. "I mean *on the phone.* Get you on the phone."

He didn't look convinced. "You've been phoning me a lot. Too much." He took a long-limbed step back into the front room, until he was swallowed by the dark. "It's threatening."

I followed him in. "Look, Harvey, I don't mean to be threatening, but you can understand how upset I am—"

He was standing in the dark, holding a long, gnarled and knobbled walking stick over his head. He looked terrified as I came through the door and sort of brandished it in a tiny circle, as a warning. The man had just left his work at Sunnyfields, a containment facility for Scotland's most dangerous criminals, and he was knee-tremblingly afraid to be alone with me. A car passed by outside, twin white headlights fanned across the dark wall opposite, and I noticed, for no good reason at all, that his fly was open.

"Come on, Harvey. I'm not the fighting kind," I said, cheerily. "I need to talk to you. It doesn't seem much to ask. I've had a terrible time."

Still he hesitated, afraid to give up the stick, until I leaned back and flicked the light on. "I just want to ask you some questions about Susie."

The room was cluttered, again decorated with a lot of money, some obviously inherited furniture, and very little taste. It was done in dark, depressing colors, blue and red paper, two green chenille armchairs and matching couch, a coffee table with bow legs, a massive gray marble fireplace with a black belly, and a posy of crunchy dried flowers in the grate. On the mantelpiece sat posed professional photographs of a ten-years-younger Harvey and a pinched-faced woman. They were dressed in eighties shoulders and sharp angles, and they were sitting next to each other in front of a "stormy sky" backdrop. Next to it, in a matching thin gold frame, was another picture of Harvey sitting with the same woman and two young girls of about ten, again in front of a stormy sky. Their knees were all pointing in different directions, father left, mother right, children front and side. It gave the picture a splintered quality, as though they would all try to run away from each other the moment the shutter closed, which, judging from the quietness of the house, they had.

Harvey let the walking stick drop to the ground, the end of it hitting the nasty nylon carpet with a loud thunk that reverberated through the house, reminding us that we were alone.

My talking seemed to have calmed him a little, so I rambled on. "I'm sure you can imagine how many questions I must have about what happened to my wife. I'm pretty much in the dark about everything that went on. I thought she was going to the supermarket and then suddenly she's arrested in Durness for a gruesome murder. I don't even know anything about her job or what happened there with Gow and Donna. All I know"—I was being sneaky, I knew I was—"is that you were responsible for getting her sacked."

It had exactly the effect I wanted it to: he shouted at me.

"*I did not get her sacked.* No one got her sacked. She stole Gow's files from the hospital. She was caught on videotape putting the files into her bag. That's why she got the sack." He leaned back against a mock-Georgian liquor cabinet and panted for breath.

I couldn't breathe. My mind raced over all the cozy nights we had spent together since her dismissal speculating about Sinclair's motives: whether he was jealous of her professionally, whether he was a misogynist. I was flattered that Susie'd included me in a discussion about another man's misogyny. It blinded me to her bald-faced lies. She had known it would. It was so unfair. I'd tried hard to be a good husband and she'd just stood there and lied to me.

I nodded at the liquor cabinet. "Please, can I have a drink, please, Harvey, please?"

Harvey led me by the arm to a chair and sat me down, handing me a tissue. Then he gave me a glass of a nice malt whiskey to sip. I was glad it was only Harvey I cried in front of. I said I was sorry, it wasn't his fault, not his problem at all, but I needed to know some things. He got himself a big drink and sat down opposite me, on the other side of the marble fireplace.

"I'm sorry for all that's happened," he said. "I like Susan very much. Before all this started she was irreproachably professional. She was a good friend to me as well." He looked up at the photos on the mantelpiece. "My wife and I separated last year, and Susan talked me through it. I don't think I could have survived it without her. That's why I felt so bad in the court. I didn't want to give evidence against her, but they forced me to."

I said I thought he had seemed a bit ambivalent, and he nodded. "I couldn't look at her in that dock without thinking about all the help she'd been to me. I felt awful about it all." His voice cracked, and I looked up. He was staring absently at his glass, looking vacant and old. A dark opening gaped in his trousers. He still hadn't noticed. "They made me give evidence against her. I liked Susan." He was talking about her as if she were dead.

"What about Gow? Did you like him?"

He snorted joylessly. "He was a psychopath."

"Did Susie spend a lot of time with him?"

He put his glass down and looked straight at me, saddened by what he had to say. "An inordinate amount of time," he said softly. "Inordinate. Hours at a time. We questioned her about it. Sinclair knew there was something wrong. He brought it up at a case conference, and she got very defensive. Said she was concerned about the wedding and wanted to make sure nothing was going to happen. Sinclair said that if she thought there was a security risk, she should report it immediately. It wasn't that at all, we all knew that. We all knew and none of us did anything about it. If we had done something, none of this would have happened. Sinclair wanted to ask Donna McGovern what was going on, but I and a social worker convinced him it would be unprofessional to go behind Susan's back. None of the people who were at that case conference can look at each other now." His chin sank to his chest; a string of hair fell over his forehead, and he caught it between his thumb and forefinger, placing it back. "It's a terrible thing to have happened," he whispered. "Just terrible."

"How would Donna know?"

"Eh?"

"What would the point be in Sinky speaking to Donna about it? How would she know what was going on?"

"Well, Susan spent a lot of time with Donna as well, didn't you know?"

I shook my head. There was very little I did know.

"Yes, Susan spent a lot of time with Donna, more time than Gow did, technically. Trying to convince Donna not to marry him, I suppose. Have you found the files?"

I shrugged. I could hardly admit to myself that Susie was a liar, much less to a stranger.

"The files Susie took from the office?" continued Tucker. "They should be returned. They're Prison Department property. You haven't come across them?" He took a drink, watching me over the rim of his glass.

"Tell me what it is you're looking for, and I'll keep my eyes open."

"A disk with a table of Gow's correspondents over the past two years. Susan deleted all the copies, but I was rather hoping she kept one on a disk. We were writing an article together. Because of the Human Rights Act, we're not supposed to read prisoners' mail anymore. We won't be able to collate that sort of information ever again. It could be a unique bit of research."

It would have been Susie's idea, we both knew that. She'd have read ahead and anticipated the change in the law, thought about it, and drawn up the research outline, and Harvey was hoping to get all the credit now that Susie was in prison.

"I'll look out for it," I said, swirling the last of my drink and swallowing it.

"Please phone me if you find it. It's Prison Department property."

I don't think he had anything to do with that research at all.

Tucker watched me drive away. I think he wanted to make sure I actually left. He stood on the step of his dark, empty home and saw me off like a visiting relative, waving for too long, making sure I was out of sight before he went back in.

I stopped the car around the corner and dropped my head to the steering wheel, concentrating on breathing in and out. My head was bursting. My chest ached. I opened the car door and threw up into the street.

They've been right about her all along. They were right and I was wrong.

chapter twelve

A TERRIBLE, TERRIBLE DAY. I'M SITTING HERE IN FRONT OF THE computer with this document from Gow's files, and I can't even be bothered to read it:

Box 1 Document 3 ***Note of Circumstances 1994***

1. This note of circumstances represents the Secretary of State's understanding of the circumstances surrounding the offense for which Mr. Gow is serving a life sentence. The information in it has been obtained from a number of sources. If Mr. Gow disagrees with any of the details in the note, he should record the disagreement on the form provided for written representations.

CONVICTION AND SENTENCE

2. At the High Court, Glasgow, on March 4, 1994, Mr. Andrew Alfred Gow was convicted of murder by a unanimous verdict and given five consecutive life sentences. There was no appeal against conviction.

INDICTMENT

3. The indictment bore that Mr. Andrew Gow did:

3.1 On March 23, 1993, while acting along with people or person unknown, assault Mrs. Elizabeth MacCorronah, then residing at Flat 3/1, 6 Ochil Place, Milton, Glasgow, push her bodily, repeatedly punch her on the head and body, knock her to the ground, forcibly detain her in motor vehicle registered number B513 DSF, and abduct her from Mitchell Road, Anderston, Glasgow, and there, or elsewhere in Scotland, repeatedly strike her on the head and body with a hammer or similar instrument, repeatedly strike or slash her in the chest with a knife or similar instrument, all to her severe injury, and in Ferry Road, Yorkhill Quay, Glasgow, did remove said Elizabeth MacCorronah from that motor vehicle and abandon her there, whereby she died of her injuries there, and did murder her.

3.2 On May 19, 1993, did assault Karen Dempsey, then residing at 46 Glen Tanar Street, Lambhill, Glasgow, repeatedly punch her on the head and body, repeatedly strike her on the head and body with a hammer or similar instrument, abduct her from Waterloo Street, Anderston, Glasgow, abandon her at the Netherton canal bank, Temple, all to her severe injury, whereby she died of her injuries there, and did murder her.

3.3 On June 12, 1993, while acting along with people or person unknown, did assault Martine Pashtan, then residing at Flat 1/1, 236 Saltmarket, Glasgow, repeatedly punch her on the head and body, knock her to the ground, forcibly detain her in motor vehicle registered number B513 DSF, and abduct her from the bus station at Anderston, Glasgow, and there, or elsewhere in Scotland, repeatedly strike her on the head and body with a hammer or similar instrument, repeatedly strike or slash her in the chest and face with a knife or similar instrument, all to her severe injury, and in Water Row, Govan, Glasgow, did remove said Martine Pashtan from that motor vehicle and abandon her there, whereby she died of her injuries there, and did murder her.

3.4 On July 28, 1993, did assault Alice Thomson, then residing at Flat 16/3, 5 Calder Street, Polmadie, Glasgow, repeatedly punch her on the head and body, and there repeatedly strike her on the head and body with a hammer or similar instrument, forcibly detain her in motor vehicle registered number B513 DSF, and abduct her from Dundas Street, Glasgow, all to her severe injury, and in Millerfield Road, Dalmarnock, Glasgow, did remove said Alice Thomson from that motor vehicle and abandon her there, whereby she died of her injuries there, and did murder her.

3.5 On October 1, 1993, did assault Mary-Ann Roberts, then residing at Flat 1/2, 38 Langa Street, High Carntyne, Glasgow, repeatedly punch her on the head and body, and there repeatedly strike her on the head and body with a hammer or similar instrument, forcibly detain her in motor vehicle registered number B513 DSF, and abduct her from the Broomielaw Road, Glasgow, and repeatedly strike or slash her in the chest and face with a knife or similar instrument, all to her severe injury, and at the Garden Festival site, Govan, Glasgow, did remove said Mary-Ann Roberts from that motor vehicle and abandon her there, whereby she died of her injuries there, and did murder her.

PREVIOUS CONVICTIONS

4. Mr. Gow had six previous convictions, including theft (x 4), taking and driving away (x 1), breach of the peace (x 1), and drunk and disorderly (x 1). The convictions were disposed of by three short periods of detention and two fines. The last sentence was completed in 1990.

SITUATION AT TIME OF OFFENSE

5. Mr. Gow was aged 28 at the time of the indictment.

The police found samples of blood in his car from all but the second woman. Gow started off with someone else helping him sometimes, and then he killed alone. The killings got closer and closer together and more frantic. He cut their tongues out, initially, it was thought, as a symbolic gesture so that they couldn't talk if they survived. The tongue became part of his fetish, though, and they found evidence that he watched them bleed to death. His DNA was found on several bodies, although I heard that the bleach he threw on them degraded the semen samples. I remember them showing a cheap bottle on a TV crime show and asking for information. Dowsing a cut on someone's skin with bleach—the intrusion of that small, imaginable domestic detail, somehow makes him seem unimaginably callous. The bleaching seems much worse than what was done to Gow himself, much worse.

It was all over the papers around the time of our wedding. They called him the Water Rat because the bodies were always abandoned near the River Clyde. The name was alarming; it sounded as if the killer was climbing out of the water, hunting people, and then slipping back into the dark river. A historian on television at the time said that when the River Clyde stopped supporting Glasgow, when the ships went to be built elsewhere, then the brokenhearted city turned its back on the water. I realized that he was right: everything in Glasgow faces away from the river, all the buildings have their backs to it, and the fast roads skirting it keep pedestrians away. The Water Rat felt like the river's revenge on the faithless city. The name stuck until the national press got hold of the story and changed his nickname to the Riverside Ripper. I think Water Rat was better.

The city changed during that time: women wouldn't go out; men were afraid to slow their cars down in dark streets in case they attracted suspicion. Everyone who had been in the city on the nights around the killings claimed that they saw something, a shape, a car, felt someone watching, smelled fusty river water a mile from the bank. The city glowered, every dark corner and deep shadow became a moist and needy mouth waiting to swallow the careless. Our wedding reception was in a riverside hotel. Later on, when the band had finished, I remember groups gathering around the glass walls, looking out at the dread water sneaking past the window, exchanging gossip about the case in an undertone.

It stinks in this study this evening. I've regressed so completely to teenage sulkiness that I'm smoking a cigarette up here in the dark. I resisted starting again for a whole year after Susie did. She used to smoke up here. She started again one year to the day after Margie was born, as if she were celebrating having her body back. I read somewhere that it's a sure sign a woman is having an affair: weight loss and starting smoking again, going back to old habits. I didn't think she could possibly be seeing someone at the time because all she did was work, and I knew what her colleagues looked like.

The last year and a half have been coming to me in flashbacks all day today. Every minute we spent together since she went back to work after Margie. Every word she said to me has another aspect now, an extra side that I knew nothing about at the time.

The day she got fired I found her in the kitchen drinking brandy and smoking a cigarette. It was late June, and the door to the garden was open. The delicious smell of freshly cut grass wafted around the room. I recall the kitchen as dirty for some reason; maybe Mrs. Anthrobus was on vacation.

"How can they fire you? Don't they have to give you warnings before they fire you?"

She didn't answer me. She shut her eyes, pursed her mouth, and sucked on her cig, holding the smoke in her lungs, exhaling reluctantly. She had been warned, however many times they have to warn you—it's usually three, I think. A trinity of warnings, and she never told me. When I think back, she didn't tell me very much about anything. She'd say, "Oh, yeah, by the way, the car needs oil," or "I met so-and-so at Sainsburys on the way home." I suppose I thought I was getting the big picture because she told me the details.

"Fucking Sinky has been putting in reports about me behind my back. It's like an orchestrated scheme to oust me from the department." She slapped the table, a gesture that now seems overemphatic. "D'you know, I wouldn't be surprised if he stole those files himself."

"Why would Sinky do that?"

"Because"—big inhalation, eyes closed—"he can't fucking *stand* to have a woman on staff in a position of power. He's the most misogynistic man I've ever met. He honestly loathes women. That's one of the reasons he works at fucking Sunnyfields, he's looking for an exclusively male environment."

I wonder if it was just luck or she knew the impact this assertion had on my ego. She has known me long enough. She knew how it would blind me.

"It's just a dreadful shame"—big sigh, sad nod—"that all men don't appreciate the wonder of women the way I do."

I probably didn't say that, but I feel as though I did. I feel as though she played to my weakness so completely that I might as well have smiled and shrugged and told her to fabricate anything she liked about what had happened, however implausible, because really, Susie, I'm such a self-involved prick, I'm not even really listening.

Sinky had, according to Susie, been building up to making his big move for quite a while. Having noticed that she was off when Margie was running a fever and hadn't filled out her time sheet accordingly, he filed complaints about her timekeeping (strike one). He then complained about the record-keeping in the addiction group she ran on Thursdays. No one had ever kept proper records, and although it had been established at a previous departmental meeting that the group was supposed to be closely minuted, no one had ever done it or worried about it until now (strike two). Strike three was pretty close to not being a lie. Strike three was some records missing from the back office, and Sinky accused her of taking them, although she hadn't. Strike three was not that she stole the files and was caught on film slipping them into her bag and tiptoeing out of the room, creating a huge potential security risk for the prison because they couldn't be sure what she had taken out or who she had taken it out for. That was not the representation of strike three that she presented to me.

The next morning, the first day of our new lives together, she got up early and came up here to work on some unspecified thing. When she came down for lunch, her eyes were very red and her hair stank of smoke. I don't think we've had an honest conversation since.

* * *

I remember when they were going to release Gow, I commented that the news programs were using nicer photos of him now, and she sat up and asked me if I thought he was attractive.

It's the betrayal of trust that smarts the most, makes me feel stupid and gormless. I trusted Susie so much. I was naked before her, and she was wearing an invisible trench coat. I wonder if she told Gow about me, how I called to her every night as she came through the door, asking how her day was, honey. That irritated her, I know it did, but I kept doing it because it made me laugh. I wonder if she was seeing him when I gave her that antique watch for her birthday. She didn't like it very much and only wore it to please me. I can imagine them together: "He gave it to me. I feel so bad. I don't know whether to wear it or not."

I wonder if she told him about the time I couldn't get it up; whether they had a laugh about it. But that wouldn't be her style at all. "I feel so bad even discussing this with someone else," she'd say. "He'd be so hurt. I feel awful." She'd be a better person twice: once for tolerating my private failings and again for being kind about it.

My world has shifted sideways suddenly and I find that I'm not even a central character. I've never felt less in my life. The evolutionary biologists must be wrong: if we're not designed for monogamy, why is infidelity so excruciatingly painful? Shouldn't I just shrug and move on?

It's so long since I smoked that the man in the shop said they didn't make Piccadilly anymore, much less packs of ten. I fucking need a smoke. Over and above Tucker's revelations last night and my getting two and a half hours' sleep:

1. Margie and I were rushed on the way to nursery this morning.
2. We have a most unwelcome guest.

Unannounced and uninvited, Susie's Aunt Trisha has come to stay with us. I need a bit of time to take in what Tucker said, instead of which I can hardly find a quiet corner of the house to be alone in. She actually knocked on the door while I was having a long leisurely shit this evening. We have three fucking bathrooms in this house and she was standing outside the one I was in, clutching a vanity case. She couldn't find those other bathrooms, she said. It was not without a frisson of compensatory pleasure that I stood on the landing, holding my limp newspaper, and watched her lock herself in with the rank stench of my lower intestines.

This morning Margie and I were walking slowly through the park. I was busy mulling over what Tucker had said last night, trying to think of alternative explanations for Susie and Gow's long chats but drawing a blank. It had been raining and the leaves and grass glistened bright and white, trembling in the searing breeze. Margie was hitting the ground with a twig she had found and making talky noises, intonation without vocabulary, which I love because I can hear what her little voice will be like when she does start talking properly. We walked on past the trash bins, following the path we always take, when a man with a big camera leaped out at us from behind a shed door and took our picture. I grabbed Margie and shouted at him, stupid things like how dare he, stop it at once, and what a rotten thing to do. I forgot to swear or act hard at all. The photographer didn't even reply to me, just walked away looking at his camera. It was as if I wasn't talking to him at all, as if I wasn't a person. My shouting upset Margie more than he had.

She was crying when we got to nursery, but the mums at the door couldn't have been nicer.

A little blonde who has a son called Harry kept smiling at me. "How awful," she said, through a big grin. "That's awful." She kept standing on her tiptoes. I think she was quite excited by it.

I called Fitzgerald the moment I got back. His office has been phoning the papers all day, issuing lawyerly threats. He assures me that none of the national papers will use Margie's picture. It brought it home to me for the first time how much of a burden this is going to be to Margie. She'll always be The-Girl-Whose-Mum. It'll never leave her. I mentioned the notes I'd made to Fitzgerald—about the search of the bothy—but he didn't seem very excited. He didn't leap to his feet, pull his coat on, shout "I'll be right over," and slam the phone down. He sort of sighed, burring his lips. Maybe I could make a list of all these points and drop it at the office, he said. He'd have a look at it. It's pretty annoying. He was the one who asked me to have a look through the papers. I'm spending hours doing this for him.

Afterward I made a cup of tea and was sitting in the garden, thinking about raking and bonfires, when the front doorbell rang. I peered around the curtain in the front room and almost passed out with dismay. It was Trisha. Bad enough in itself, but she had a big suitcase with her.

The mums were lovely back at nursery. I think they'd phoned each other during the day because they all knew about the photographer. A tiny fat mother, with a hat jammed so low on her head that she had to tip her head back to talk to anyone above five feet tall, said she'd had a lot of trouble with the press during her husband's bankruptcy but it all blows over. They'll forget you soon enough, she said cheerfully.

As she left with her eight-month-old baby, I noticed a drip of vitrified baby puke on the back of her black coat. I asked McLaughlin about her. Her husband was a corrupt councillor who had an affair with a lady pilot. She, the hatted-vomit-woman, walked away with everything plus a new boyfriend in the lawyer who had represented her. It was all in the paper, apparently. I don't remember any of it.

Harry's little blond mum was there again this afternoon. She seemed to have been waiting about until I came in, and made sure she caught my attention by sticking her chest out as she put her coat on. Harry is a sad-eyed child, the eldest of three, who knows his time in the maternal spotlight is over but has not the words to say it. Even smiling, he looks as if he wants to cry. When he waves good-bye, he twists his little hand from the wrist, slowly, as if he's being taken off to be killed and wants us to remember him.

* * *

Margie doesn't know Trisha or she wouldn't have been so friendly to her. She sat on the old shit's knee and tried to pull her cheeks off. Trisha gave her a bath and put her to bed without a story.

"I am the child's great-aunt and Susan Louise has no one else," she explained later when I asked her why she was here. "As the only surviving member of her family, I should be here."

"If you're so keen to lend her support, why didn't you turn up at court during the trial?" I said, knowing full well she couldn't have stood the humiliation. Susie would have recognized her and waved, and Trisha couldn't cope with being publicly associated with an accused person. "Maybe she could have done with a bit more support then, did you think about that?"

"I had commitments"—Trisha was scratching the back of her hand slowly, raising welts on the thin dry skin—"that I simply couldn't walk away from. I came as soon as I could."

"Does Susie know you're here?"

She looked straight at me. "She asked me to come and visit Margery."

She then deflected attention from herself by demanding a cup of tea, a bath, the use of the guest bedroom (too small), and by quizzing Yeni as to where she's from. Yeni didn't really understand, but she was uncomfortable at the accusatory tone, I could see that.

When Yeni went upstairs to her room, I told Trisha that Yeni had been a rock during the whole bloody episode. She stayed with us throughout the trial, I said pointedly. Trisha pursed her lips. She said that was fine then, as if Yeni were an unsuitable friend who would lead me into smoking and the use of slack grammar and tube tops and other modern evils.

I gather that Susie didn't really send Trisha here. They've been writing to each other, and Susie agreed that it would be nice for Margery to see other members of the family. It was Trisha who decided she was needed; whether she was wanted here or not is of no concern to her. She knows I hate her and doesn't seem to care. I wonder how she now feels about taking Susie aside before our wedding and telling her she thought I was a drinker. I was a student then and it was a friend's graduation. I wasn't even that drunk, I'd only had about four pints. How unforgiving can you get?

She drives me insane with her endless pronouncements. She seems never to have mastered the art of interaction, and her conversation, which cannot be discouraged or stopped (not even dammed to a trickle by food), consists entirely of her imparting information. Social acceptance is still important, apparently. Having a daughter is a great responsibility, especially for a man alone. Nutrition is the starting point for intelligent growth. I asked, intelligent growth, Trisha, what is that? Is it growing intelligently, i.e. upward, and not diagonally like all these malnourished young ones with their fancy ideas today? Or is it growing in intelligence during the course of normal physical development? She doesn't have a sense of humor and knew I was conversing obliquely but couldn't quite put her finger on the meaning. But she didn't give up. The government will have to improve the education system or lose the next election. These and many other sparkling gems were cast before Yeni and me, swine that we are, over the macaroni on toast. Yeni smiled and nodded, trying to be friends with everyone, as usual. I sighed and tutted just enough to make Yeni finish eating quickly and stare uncomfortably at the table until pudding came.

Mum phoned later and was horrified to hear that Trisha had arrived. She demanded to know what she was doing, had I asked her to come? I said of course not. Mum gave the phone to Dad, he asked all the same questions over again, and then she snatched the receiver back from him and asked them again herself. There's a serious danger of their coming over, even though I told them that there are no spare beds now.

I want to teach Margie to say "Great-aunt Trisha is a bastard," but she'd be taken off me by the social workers.

So I'm up here after everyone has gone to their respective beds, smoking in a sulk, making this nice room smell horrible. I've opened the skylight, and the November air's fresh outside. It floats down the chimney-shaped room and nibbles at my fingers and forehead and bare ankles, keeping me awake.

In the past twenty-four hours I've been emasculated, violated, snubbed, and invaded. To cap it all off, I've got to go and visit Susie tomorrow. I don't want to go. I want to be back at the nursery surrounded by sympathetic, pitying mums. I want to press my face into their big warm tits and stay there forever.

chapter thirteen

WORSE. AN EVEN WORSE FUCKING DAY THAN YESTER-FUCKING-DAY was. I'm up here, hiding in my own home, so I don't have to talk to Trisha or tell her about Susie and the visit.

Today started out okay. I got a letter from Susie that didn't say much but did make me think it would be quite nice to see her. I went to the shops to buy the batteries she asked for and found my picture in one of the papers. Margie has been cut out of the photo, which is good, though you can just see her little hand. I actually look quite attractive. It was windy (you can see the wind-ruffled trees behind me), and my hair was brushed back off my ears. Also I had an overcoat on, which covered my belly. Instead of fat and afraid, I seem angry, defiant—even, at a stretch, a little handsome.

(I'm wondering if we could make anything of the press coverage for the appeal. It feels as though we've never been out of the papers. Surely one of them must have broken the rules?)

I put three copies of the paper in my cart, right side down, and walked around the shop in a flush of excitement. I thought the cashier would recognize me, but she didn't. I'd drawn myself up, ready to explain that I was gathering material for a case I would be presenting to the Press Complaints Commission, but she didn't even notice my buying three copies because they scan them in upside down. I was a bit disappointed.

The story itself is horrible, all about me struggling on with my pathetic devil-spawn child. There's no mention of me as an independent person, just Susie's unemployed husband this and that. They'd never say that about a woman. She'd be a housewife, an attractive housewife maybe, or a stay-at-home mum, but not unemployed.

I half wanted to cut the picture out and take it to Susie, to show her I'm not a complete loser dog, but the story would upset her, and I thought she might have other things on her mind. When I came home from the shops, I took the picture up to the bathroom and used Susie's hair spray to flatten the hair at the sides of my head. I look cool, whatever Susie says. I know I do.

I keep going back to the picture and looking at it. I may feel like a neurotic fool, but when I look at that picture, I'm a tragic hero. I can see the story from the far distance for the first time, and I come off rather well. I'm tall, not at all bald (a major boon at twenty-nine), and I've stuck loyally by her. If I were slightly thinner, I think I'd cut quite a dashing figure.

Trisha's being here was good for one reason only: she agreed to take Margie out for the day. I'd rather do that than leave her with Yeni. That wouldn't be fair to either of them.

I turned the car radio on to keep myself from thinking and drove onto the motorway. It's a long time since I've been out of the city. It was windy, and all the high-sided vehicles were leaving the road or stopping on the shoulder. I could feel the car being blown sideways on exposed stretches. When I got all the way out into the flat Leven Valley, the traffic was backed up to a complete standstill, and I was afraid I'd miss visiting time. I was cursing whatever feckless bastard was causing the obstruction when I saw an ambulance weaving against the traffic. It passed, and the cars began to move again. Two hundred yards farther on a large truck lay on its side in a field like a big dead beetle, down a sharp slope from the motorway. It was at such a crazy angle from the road it must have tumbled over several times before coming to rest. The ambulance had been attending here, and I realized that the driver might actually be dead.

I was making good time, so I stopped in the local village and bought a big bag of toffees. I sat eating them in the car, one after another, chomping and slurping the toffee juice, unwrapping another before I'd even finished the last. I tried to remember all the lovely times we've had together. My Susie. My Susie-suse. But all I could see was the back of her head in court and the death-trap truck on its side, and all I could hear was my jaw grinding the hard toffees, my saliva sloshing glucose onto those hard-to-reach surfaces of my teeth.

I could have claimed that the conditions were too bad for me to drive out. It was the perfect excuse. There were bad accidents everywhere; it would be confirmed on the news. But I couldn't do it to her. Whatever she had done, I couldn't leave Susie Wilkens sitting in a women's prison waiting for a visitor who wouldn't come. I thought about the real reason I didn't want to go. If she admitted she was having an affair with Gow, I'd sob. In front of everyone.

I sat looking out the window and chewed through three more toffees before I made up my mind. I decided (cowardly, I know) not to ask her about Gow today. I put the rest of the toffees behind my seat in disgust, so that I couldn't reach for the bag while I was driving the final mile to the prison. I promised myself that when I got there I could take three toffees in with me, one for the reception area, one for the waiting room, and one for the way out.

The Vale of Leven doesn't look like a prison from outside; there are no high brick walls or spotlights or watchtowers. The bars on the windows are 1960s-style curvy iron, painted beige. The prison complex consists of a series of two-story buildings, like an army training camp, set deep inside a wide perimeter fence made from what looks like chicken wire. I guess the fence is stronger than it looks.

The high wind whistled through it like a "blasted heath" sound-effects record.

The Vale has a suicide problem. They have seasonal rashes of women, usually drug addicts on remand, who kill themselves. At its absolute worst, they had four deaths in three months. It was a national scandal. I heard once, during the last suicide craze in the Vale, that a woman had hanged herself from a radiator. A radiator? How much determination must it take to hang yourself from something three feet off the ground? Until the very last second of her conscious life there must have been not a shadow of doubt in that woman's mind that she'd be better off dead. The conviction must have been so complete that even the instinctive urge to put her foot on the floor and lift the weight off her neck was overridden by the certainty that she didn't want to live. She had four daughters, ranging from twelve years old to six.

Trisha just came in there. She burst through the door and whispered that she'd heard me creeping about up here. This room's too small for two people. It's a closet really, and with the chair behind the door, there's barely room for two sets of feet. She stood in the room, realized that her belly was inches away from my face, and stepped back out onto the shallow landing. Then she found that she was too far away to whisper properly. She moved forward, standing on the raised threshold, keeping her balance by holding on to the wall as I, lowering my voice so as not to waken Margie, asked her to get out, this was a private study, and anyway, what was she doing up at quarter to two in the morning? She said she might well ask me the same question. What was I doing and what was that on the computer screen? I kept my finger on the enter button so the text disappeared up and away. I said it was just some work, and listen, you, this is my house. I can do what I flipping well like. (Why can't I remember to swear at people when I'm trying to be angry?)

Trisha asked what all the pictures on the walls were. What were the photos stuck to the skylight for? You'll make the room dark, you'll strain your eyes. I lied and said I only came up here at night anyway, and what was she doing up? Go and have a cup of tea if you can't sleep. Fuck off downstairs, in other words.

She got embarrassed and looked at the floor, tottering on the step, staying far enough away from me to remain decent. "I do worry about you, Lachie," she said, and for an awful moment I thought she was going to come on to me, rub her ghastly old body on me, touch me. "I've never liked you, I've made that plain in the past, but I can see that you are a very good father and I greatly appreciate you standing by Susan Louise."

"Her name's Susan," I said, finding, to my surprise, that I was speaking quite loud. "Susan. Or Susie. That's her name." It was alarm, I think, at the mental image of Auntie Trisha pole-dancing in a thong and brogues.

"Well, she'll always be Susan Louise to me," she said, stepping away and nodding, pleased that she had said what she came to say. "I'll leave you alone." She shut the door and threw it open again immediately. "Unless you'd like a cup of tea?"

"No."

Now I'm bristling with guilt and shame. I feel as if Trisha's just peered into my brain. What I'm writing is private but it's not shockingly private. I'm not looking at porno on the Internet or anything, though I might if I knew how. Had I been jerking off when she came in, I'd probably have felt less embarrassed. The bit of the page I was most worried she might see was the bit about Susie maybe having an affair with Gow. Is that what I'm most worried about? Being superfluous?

I feel odd writing now. I need more privacy if I'm to write in here. Susie had a padlock on the outside of the door, but I unscrewed the attachment from the wall because I didn't have a key. I'll put a Yale on the door, one that'll lock automatically when I come in and go out. In the meantime I feel this room is very compromised. I don't want

Trisha coming in here, but I can't watch her all the time. I'll leave a bit of paper behind the door so I'll know if someone's been in during the day.

There was a line when I got to the prison door. I and the people off the Glasgow bus had to wait outside in the freezing gale, all shivering with sideways hair, stamping to keep warm while they processed the group already in the reception area. In front of me was a gang of three, obviously related, female troglodytes. They were wearing identical purple anoraks with the hoods up and smoking wee rollies, held between gnawed and nailless fingers, sucking the smoke through atavistic, stubby teeth.

Their chiefess looked up at me. "Ye right?"

I nodded and looked away.

"Yur gonnae freeze out there; mon intae the doorway."

I would have looked like the world's snootiest asshole if I'd turned down her offer of shelter. I had to squeeze in between the three of them and smile cheerfully while they made a series of almost incomprehensible, largely dirty jokes about me not telling their man about this or us being engaged now. At full height, not one of them reached my nipples.

Eventually our group was called into the reception area, and we had to tell them our names and who we were there to see. I was stumped for an answer when they asked me why I was there. The guard had to prompt me. "To see your wife . . . ?" she suggested.

I had to hand over my mobile phone and sign for it (everyone was very impressed that I had one) and let them check any gifts I had brought in (took ages). Then I had to go and sit in a waiting room behind a glass wall. The heavy door shut behind the last person and locked with a definite "click." There were gray plastic chairs clamped to the wall and ladies' and gents' toilets at one end of the room. The three women sat near me, as if we were there together. Around the room sat sad, damp visitors in ones and twos, some with small children, some barely adult themselves. Antidrug posters adorned the walls, along with bus timetables for Glasgow and Edinburgh and notices advertising support groups for the families of prisoners. A teenage boy with the most tenuous mustache I've ever seen kept getting up and going to the toilet. Every time he came out he was smiling sneakily. He was either wanking in there or drawing on the walls.

I allowed myself a bribe toffee. Eventually, twenty minutes before the visit was due to begin, an unsmiling guard came through and stood outside the glass wall. The locked door buzzed open, we were ushered into the corridor, and then a second door, leading into the prison proper, buzzed open. We all walked through, the guard made sure the door was shut behind us, and we followed her to the second waiting room. I had another toffee. I don't know why they had to keep us there for so long, but it was another gray room with the same haranguing posters. The troglodyte family started laughing at something, hee-hawing through smoker's phlegm, rocking back and forth in their chairs, elbowing each other. A guard came through the door and flicked a finger at me, motioning me to follow him. He took me into a side room off the main corridor. There was a narrow table, a white curtain, and a burly male guard standing next to a sharps bin, pulling on latex gloves. I stalled at the door.

"Mr. Harriot," said the first man, "under the Prisoners and Young Offenders' Institutions Scotland Rules 1994, we are authorized to search you prior to your visit with your wife."

I looked back at the open door. They were going to search me, strip me and stick a finger up my arse in a room with an open door. I managed a strangled "No," but it was so small I don't think they heard it.

"We are authorized to ask you to take your jacket off."

"My jacket?"

"Yes, sir, your jacket. Please, take it off. Do you have any sharp instruments on you? Any syringes or knives that we should know about?"

The guard took my jacket, stroking it carefully, while the other man patted me everywhere, my underarms, between my legs, the soles of my shoes. His fingers brushed the underside of my balls and made me wince. I know he noticed. He paused momentarily, cringing, I hope, and then looked in my mouth and got me to waggle my tongue around. They looked through the stuff Susie'd asked me to bring. The waiting room was chock full of suspicious and desperate characters. Why search me?

"Because, sir, you are a doctor and we have reason to believe that your wife is suicidal."

So that was how I found out Susie was on suicide watch. I don't know if they felt sorry for me or what, but they decided to leave it at that and let me go back to the waiting room.

I've just been downstairs to make a cup of tea and found Trisha watching television and drinking cocoa. She'd changed her tune and said, rather accusingly, that she'd have brought up a cup of tea if I'd said I wanted one. I will not be chased around my own house. I said I didn't want one then, but I do now. I almost resent her insomnia more than I resent her presence. Night is my time to be alone in the house, my time when I don't need to be self-conscious. I don't like her creeping about.

We lined up by the prison door and traipsed single file across the ten-foot stretch of windy grass, guarded on either side by prison officers. The door behind us locked before the door in front opened. Inside the door the troglodytes dispersed: they were there to see two different people. The convicted visiting room is disgusting, furnished with knee-high brown tables and spongy yellow chairs with no arms and melted fag burns all over them. Everyone was smoking; it looked like a Philip Morris laboratory. A vending machine selling Coke and crisps in the corner had a thick metal belt around it, strapping it to the wall, presumably to prevent anyone from ripping it off its foundations and throwing it.

I tried to remember who Susie and I were in Otago Street, a lucky pair of scamps, not a man who could be patted on the balls with impunity and his murderess wife. Then I saw Susie across the room. She looked like shit. Her black hair was frizzy at the top and her eyes were swollen from crying. She had lost weight in the week and a half since I last saw her. She was dressed in a shapeless blue sweatshirt and jogging pants that were too short for her. The elastic cuff clung to her calf above the ankle, showing off her white socks and the black slip-ons I'd bought her for court.

She scowled at me and waved grimly. Eager visitors swept past me, and I stood there, not wanting to go to her. I wanted to turn around and run away and keep my Susie safe, but I clutched the final toffee in my pocket, walked over, and bent to kiss her.

She gave me her cheek, which annoyed me. She sniffed the side of my head and asked me why I smelled strange.

"Oh, I, um, flattened my hair," I said, self-consciously.

"With toffee hair spray?" She looked annoyed. "You didn't bring Margie, then?"

When I said she told me not to, she got tearful and stared at the table. I said I'd brought the radio and the battery and the other things she asked for, but she didn't speak then either. I put my arm around her shoulder and told her that we'd get her out of there, that we were doing everything we could for the appeal, that things would be fine, she'd see, things would be okay and not to worry. She started to cry. She just shook and shook. All around us groups of people talked quietly while the women in blue uniforms hugged the kids on their laps. I stroked Susie's hand and said Fitzgerald wouldn't let a single thing go. I felt awful for finding her vulnerability so frightening. I used to love it, but then, I suppose she was only ever a little bit vulnerable. Even when she was in labor she just seemed very, very angry, not broken like this.

"Susie, they said you're suicidal."

She rubbed her red eyes hard. "Well, I'm not. They use suicide watch proactively sometimes. I'm a high-profile case, and if I killed myself it would cause an uproar. They're being cautious."

"What does 'suicide watch' mean?"

"You're put in a special cell and they look in on you every fifteen minutes. The cell has all the corners taken out so you can't hide."

She tried to chat. The sentencing reports were coming on well, she said, and should be ready in a couple of weeks' time, but then she ran out of things to say and sat, miserably still.

I took out a pack of cigarettes, and she fell on them. We smoked together. We haven't smoked together since we lived in Otago Street. She caught her breath, managed a shaky smile, and thanked me. She told me to leave the pack for her. I said it had been my full intention to pursue that course of action from the outset, and that made her smile. I asked her what she was reading, whether she wanted me to send in some books. She drew on her cigarette, inhaling heavily, and said she couldn't read, couldn't concentrate. The atmosphere was nicer between us then. She took my hand, gave it a little squeeze, and we smoked in silence for a while. I thought suddenly of her with Gow, and I felt myself dying inside, atrophying through moral compromise, like a Nazi general's fat wife. I wanted to whip my hand away and tell her I knew what she'd been doing with Gow in her office, dirty bitch, that Harvey Tucker had told me. I had to breathe in deeply, over and over again.

After a while I started talking quietly, and just to have something to say, I told her not to worry. I was going through all the papers at home and would find any tiny detail we could use for an appeal.

She sat up stiffly and looked at me. "What papers? What are you talking about?"

"The stuff in the study," I said. "Around the computer and on the disks."

"But that's my stuff. Those papers aren't about this, they've got nothing to do with this." She was speaking very quietly, angrily, spitting words at me, and then she stopped and looked suspicious. "How did you get into my study? I put a lock on the door."

I reached over for her hand but she whipped it away from me.

"Come on, Susie, it was just a teenie wee padlock. I wanted to use the computer."

"You ripped the padlock off my fucking office door?"

"It was only a small one," I said, chasing her hand around her lap.

"You took the lock off . . . ?" She stopped still again. "How . . . You've been using my computer? How can you use my computer? How can you know the password?"

I said, come on, Margie H wasn't exactly hard to guess, the joint account code is Margie's birthday, our movie channel request code is margiel, every secret code we have is Margie.

But Susie wouldn't allow me to make light of it. She had turned a strange lemony shade. "Just leave it alone," she said. "There are confidential files in there. They're nothing to do with any of this."

I thought she was talking about the Gow files from Sunnyfields, and I dropped my voice and said, "Look, don't worry about Gow's prison files, I've already found them. I'll burn them when I'm finished."

Susie slapped my hand away and shut her eyes, taking deep breaths, trying not to lose it. If we had been at home, she'd have left the room to cool down, but we were in an open-plan visiting room surrounded by nosy bastards with nothing better to do than listen in. "Forget the study," she said through gritted teeth. "Just stay out of there."

"Susie," I said softly, "come on . . ."

She stood up, pocketed the pack of cigarettes, turned on her heels, and left. A guard opened the back door to let her through and glanced at me, curious and faintly accusing. I'd driven forty reluctant fucking miles to be blown off for trying to help.

I pulled over onto the hard shoulder on the way home, pretending to the passing drivers that I was afraid to go on in the high winds. I put my elbow up to the window and hid my face with my hand. It was the search, and fighting with Susie, and the strain of not asking her about Gow. She was in love with him, I know that now. I don't think she hates me, but I can see in her eyes that I'm irrelevant. I knew it when we sat and smoked together. She was thinking about him, wishing I were him.

I was glad Margie hadn't been with me. I don't want her left alone with a prison guard while someone pokes her dad in the balls. I went for a walk around Kelvingrove Park so that I didn't have to go home early. I sat on a bench and watched people walking their dogs. It was cold, I could see my breath, and I remembered the Christmastime when we were expecting Margie, how hopeful everything seemed and how pretty the frosted grass was in the garden, like a moat of jagged glass all around the house.

The journalists were gone from the back lane when I got back. I still feel that they're watching me. Trisha was watching television with Margie in the front room. She asked me how the visit went. I shrugged. She didn't tell me off or make any statements about what had happened, which I was grateful for. Yeni was hiding in the kitchen, looking uncomfortable. I think Trisha has been hounding her all day. It's obvious that Yeni doesn't like Trisha at all, and I feel I can trust her because of it.

I was suddenly struck by the terrifying thought that Yeni might leave and I'd have to find another au pair and explain the situation to her and the agency and her parents. No one in their right mind would let their teenage daughter come to the house of a lone man whose wife's a murderer. I realized that I must be much nicer to Yeni, so I asked her if she'd like pizza for dinner and ordered it in for us all to share. I got a big one with artichoke and olives because that's what she likes. I know she appreciated it because she went out to the deli later and bought me a bar of marzipan ("Fur jyou, Lachie") and left it in the fridge.

I wonder about Susie. I wonder how I could live with her and know her so little. I keep looking at the picture of us in Corfu and realizing that we've hardly seen each other since Margie was born. I thought that was normal when couples have a baby. I thought you had to take each other for granted and concentrate on the child. I was looking forward to it, actually. It's a normal part of the rhythm of life. It doesn't mean one of you can go off and fall in love with a psychopathic convict.

chapter fourteen

THEY PHONED AT SIX-FORTY THIS MORNING TO ANNOUNCE THAT they were coming and arrived just after five p.m., dressed for an Arctic winter. We left their suitcases in the hall and sat around the kitchen table. The place looked nice because Mrs. Anthrobus had been and everything was clean and polished. Mum had brought a basket of pretty red and yellow jellied fruits from Marbella, and we had them with a high tea in the old manner, bread and jam and cakes and Marmite and several strong pots of Ceylon. The garden had never looked so inviting, and I wished I were out there, alone, working up a sweat pruning the apple tree and raking the leaves, kicking up the damp smell of the earth and settling the beds for winter.

Dad's getting old. He never speaks when Mum's there, and Mum is always there. He's smaller than ever before, and his eyelids are coming away from his eyes. He looks awfully tired, not long-trip tired but life tired. I tried to hug him, but he sort of brushed his forehead against my chin and pushed me away.

As with Trisha, Mum and Dad were not invited to my home, nor did I in any way encourage them to come here. However, my wishes and well-being are of little concern to this elderly triumvirate. I'm little more than a sideshow, a useful prop for them to prove to each other how caring and family-oriented they are. Afraid Trisha was usurping her by coming here first, Mum's been fussing around the house, spraying her scent in corners and doorways. She knows Trisha warned Susie about me before the wedding and is very suspicious of her.

They've begun a vicious exchange of tit-for-tat pleasantries that can only end in bloodshed. Trisha says how well I've done, and Mum trumps that by saying she knew I would do well, having known me since childhood. Trisha wants to give up the guest room in favor of Mum and Dad, but Mum and Dad want to sleep in the coal cellar so that Trisha won't be disturbed by dad's snoring, because you do snore, don't you, Ian? Eventually I gave M&D my room and said I'd sleep downstairs, that it didn't matter because I wasn't really sleeping much anyway.

Mum stroked my hair and looked accusingly at Trisha. Trisha smiled and muttered, "So kind." The irony of this sort of comfort is completely lost on both of them. They have nary a care that their support has resulted in my being put out of my bed.

Margie is loving it, though. They held her, one at a time, and fed her, cooing and gasping at her every move. It is lovely to see her through fresh eyes, because I forget how enchanting she is. The proportions of her facial features are perfect really, and she's very clever. She plays little jokes, hiding things and so on, and her singing and talking is very advanced. She chats away all the time, to toys and walls and floors and shoes and the telly. She tries to boss everyone around, getting us to sit in chosen seats, hold a particular doll, eat things, and she claps her hands with pleasure whenever we do her bidding.

I was hoping with everyone here that Yeni might get a few days to herself, but Mum and Dad insisted that she join us for afternoon tea and quizzed her in pidgin Spanish. Having gone to the trouble of bastardizing her language, they were quite indignant to find the discourtesy unreciprocated. Yeni apologized in Spanish and reacted to their stonewalling by blushing and wobbling her head from side to side. Then she sloped off to hide in her room. She really must not leave.

I said I was going to the loo and went up to her room to see if she was okay. She was sitting on the end of her single bed, looking at the pictures in a book about the Romans. She had wound up the noisy little circus clock that Susie had as a child, the one with the seal balancing the ball on his nose. The anxious, tinny tick-tock bounced from wall to wall, making her seem like a child waiting out her time in detention. I gave her a quizzical thumbs-up. She raised a limp thumb back and stretched her lips across her teeth. I made a wait gesture and brought the portable television through from my room. I sat it on the chest of drawers at the end of her bed and plugged it in. I pointed at my watch. *"Friends,"* I said, and her big fat face lit up.

"Friends?"

"Yes," I said and turned it on, fiddling with the aerial until I found good reception. Mum called me, and as I went to open the door and go back downstairs, Yeni darted from the bed and caught my arm, turning me around. She gave me the toothiest, cheesy grin and a big, affirmative thumbs-up. We both giggled behind our hands as Mum called again, and I dragged my heavy feet back downstairs to the unwelcome support and comfort of my family.

I got a locksmith to come this morning before Mum and Dad arrived and install a Yale on this door. It makes the room feel so much more private. When I came back up after tea and heard the firm lock slide shut, I found myself smiling and looking around, rubbing my hands, secure in the knowledge that I was up in my high attic room, alone.

Susie'll be pleased when she does get out. I'll give her both keys and let her get on with it.

* * *

Harvey Tucker had the cheek to phone and leave a message reminding me to look out for that file for him. I found it on the disk with the Gow files from Sunnyfields. It's a table of the people who contacted Gow, dates of when they did, and notes of whether they came to visit or not. I can see from the top left-hand corner of the document that the table has been made up by both Tucker and Susie, so he's not lying. He did do some of the work. I'm reluctant to hand it over, though. I can't bring myself to admit Susie really did take the files, and I don't want to contribute to anything else being published about Gow. Susie must have had a reason for erasing all the other copies: she obviously didn't want Tucker to get ahold of it.

Donna McGovern's name is in there. It says she contacted him ("2/2/98 letter, romantic content, photograph encl."). Then the first visit ("Scottish Prison Department approval for visit. Gow approval for visit") and a flood of letters, one a day, until the file entries stop abruptly around the time Susie got the bump. A rush of letters from strangers accompanied Gow's wedding, presumably people wishing him well or ill or just freaks who had seen him in the paper. The most worrying correspondent is the one who wrote fifty-three times in two years (all "sexual content") and was knocked back for a visit every time, often by Gow himself. But that was a man, a Mr. Thomas Wexler whose address is given as 221 Grape Street, Bristol. I like knowing that. I may go to Bristol one day, and I wouldn't want to run into Mr. Wexler without knowing that about him.

I've started reading that "Lovers in Prison" book that I found up here. It's a collection of case histories of women who fell in love with murderers in America. Initially I thought I was reading about Donna, but after meeting Harvey Tucker, the book takes on a whole new complexion. It's interesting in a human-interest-story kind of way, but there aren't a lot of surprises in it. Apparently, if you want to fall in love with a convicted murderer, it helps if you're a fool and find it easy to lie to yourself.

The chapter I finished last night, before I fell asleep on the couch (at four-ten a.m.), said that generally the women are dissatisfied and disillusioned with their lives and see it as their last chance to attach themselves to "someone powerful." Which means that Susie *didn't* see herself as being attached to someone powerful and was trying to bridge the gap. Can every fucking thing in this unholy mess be down to my failings? I was interested to note that being Catholic, whether practicing or not, is also a predictive factor. I wonder why? Could it be the emphasis on redemption or just the ability to believe a lot of improbable shite? It's interesting, because Donna was Catholic but Susie isn't.

Box 2 Document 3 ***"Serial Beast Kills Prostitute," 10/3/93***

This is the newspaper article Gow's tongue was found sitting on in the corner of the bothy. Susie downloaded a copy of it from Stevie Ray's "Gow—Hard As Nails" website. The download is dated *months* before he was released, which just goes to prove that she didn't have a copy to start with and so can't possibly be the killer.

I've heard the website mentioned on TV, when Stevie Ray was doing his tour of the chat shows. Susie's printed a lot of articles from it, but they're all poor-quality. In some of them the printed text is illegibly tiny. Some have titles or paragraphs chopped in half. Nearly all of them favor the photographs over the text, even though they all use the same famous picture. Gow is standing with his shoulders hunched, fists together, elbows out to the side, pumping himself up like an end-of-pier muscle man. He has shaved the word "Growl" into his chest, although it seems to read "Groul" because his body hair is quite straight. He's wearing a pair of children's white plastic sunglasses. It disturbs me that they're children's glasses; the shaded eyepieces are much too small for his big face, and the little white legs splay out at the side of his head. But perhaps it's only me who thinks that's creepy: I saw a middle-aged man riding a child's red bicycle down Dumbarton Road the other day and found it sickening, watching his old knees smash up against his chest as he tried to beat a red light.

The prosecution read this article out in court, so I've heard it before. I don't think there's anything special in it, but it was an original cutting and was five years old when the police found it, so it must have meant something to whoever left it there with Gow's tongue on top. They'd hung on to it for long enough.

Two pictures: police tape strung around weak-looking trees on an industrial skyline and a photo of Robbie Coltrane looking moody.

Police are hunting for a serial killer after a fifth body was found yesterday, strangled and dumped on waste ground in Govan. Police say that the murder fits the profile of the Riverside Ripper. The murdered woman is believed to have been a prostitute working in the Anderston area of Glasgow. All the victims have been prostitutes so far; all have been strangled and mutilated with a knife.

Actually, they weren't strangled. Everyone now knows that they were stabbed and had their tongues cut out, so that they bled to death. This strangling stuff must have been fed to the papers at the time to put off crank confessors.

A police spokesman called for calm and asked the public to come forward with any information they might have about a man behaving suspiciously in the Broomielaw area between the hours of twelve midnight and four on Friday morning. Women are being cautioned not to walk home after dark.

Top Criminal Psychologist Dr. Joe Fennie, who was the basis for TV's *Cracker,* starring Robbie Coltrane, talked exclusively to our reporter. "This man will kill and kill until he is caught," stated Fennie. "He will give in to his sick compulsion until we stop him."

Previous victims include Alice Thomson, 33, Martine Pashtan, 24, Karen Dempsey, 21, and teenager Lizzie MacCorronah, 19. Lizzie, whose body was the first to be found, left behind three children now being raised by her mother.

Women's groups are calling for greater action, claiming that police protection is inadequate.

Joe Fennie was in the news a lot at the time. He was being quoted by every paper on every case that came up in Scotland. He'd been at Sunnyfields for a few years in the eighties, so he knew all that crowd. I heard he went to work in a special facility for sex offenders down in Surrey before coming home in disgrace for some minor infraction. Susie doesn't know him, but his appearance in the press always elicited a big eye-roll and muttering. We met him at a wedding in Carlisle four years ago. He has very bad skin and a squint. Susie says that's why they always use a picture of Robbie Coltrane.

I can't see what is special about this article or why the person who murdered Gow would choose it above all the rest of the coverage. It might not be special, it could just be a random article about his case, or it might be that the woman whose body was found in the article was important.

I'm sure the police have already done all this stuff and done it better than I can. I should concentrate on the stuff only I know. I keep going back to the morning of the phone call from Cape Wrath, pulling it apart, pressing my eye so close to the details that they distort and I can't remember if I'm remembering them or filling spaces between the events. I've worked out the following so far.

It was a Friday morning in September. Susie was in the house and not having a lie-in. I was busy feeding Margie in the kitchen. The phone rang twice, she picked up, listened. "Oh, it's you," she said. She turned away from me, facing down the hall so I couldn't hear what she was saying. When she picked up she must have heard someone speak, and they must have said "Hello" or "Listen" or "Help," because if they had introduced themselves (said "Hi, it's Donna McGovern" or "Hi, it's Andrew Gow"), she wouldn't then have said "Oh, it's you." It makes no sense to say "Oh, it's you" to an introduction. So, given that there was no introduction, she must have recognized the voice. She'd have to know it quite well to recognize a voice from such a short greeting.

After the call she came into the kitchen and beamed at me. It was, I realized later, the first time I had seen her smile in months.

"Can I take the car, Lachie? I just want to nip out to the shops."

I said, yeah, sure, honey, I don't need it. She kissed my forehead and called me her darling. Good-bye, my darling. Something like that. See you soon. She knew that she was going all the way to Durness. She was setting off for an eight-hour drive, yet she took just her purse, threw her green leather coat casually across her arm, and told me she was nipping out to the shops.

I've been going through the boxes again.

Box 2 Document 4 ***News in Brief, a broadsheet, 12/19/93***

A man was charged with the murders of five Glasgow prostitutes this morning. Police report that after being stopped for cruising, Andrew Gow, 28, spontaneously confessed to the murders of Elizabeth MacCorronah, 19, Karen Dempsey, 21, Martine Pashtan, 24, Alice Thomson, 33, and Mary-Ann Roberts, 41. Strathclyde Police Service issued a statement stating that the investigation was still ongoing.

That means Mary-Ann Roberts was the one found in the tongue article.

Box 1 Document 4 *Social Background Report 1994*

Strathclyde Social Work Department
India House, G1

Name	Andrew Gow	DOB 6/23/65
Religion	N/K	
Address	3582 Cumbernauld Avenue, Cumbernauld	
Occupation	Minicab driver	
Marital status	Married	

Is to appear on Monday, March 2, 1994, at Glasgow High Court in connection with the offense of murder.

This report was compiled from one interview with Gow.

HOME CIRCUMSTANCES

Before he was arrested Mr. Gow was living with his wife, Lara Orr, at 3582 Cumbernauld Avenue, Cumbernauld. They have no children. Ms. Orr is a shop assistant. Their house is in one of the nicer areas of Cumbernauld, and records show that it is furnished and maintained to a high degree.

PERSONAL HISTORY

Gow was born and educated in Bridgeton, Glasgow. His mother and father separated when he was eight, and his father is now deceased. Mr. Gow no longer has contact with his mother. The second of four children, he has three sisters and reports that he has no contact with them either, having split from his family over his marriage to Ms. Orr. His family does not like her.

Gow enjoyed school until the fifth year. He states that he had many friends there and was extremely popular. His arrests for theft followed his falling in with a bad crowd. He claims he was shoplifting to show off to them. The police stopped him and he confessed to the crimes. The car theft occurred near his home. Again he confessed and was given and served a one-month custodial sentence.

The breach of the peace offense was committed while drunk. Gow reports that he had too much to drink on the way home from his work on Christmas Eve and started shouting at a bus driver who tried to eject him. The drunk and disorderly offense related to the same incident. He had not been charged with any offense for three years before his arrest.

Gow informs me that he has always enjoyed good health, never having suffered from any serious mental or physical illness.

He was employed as a minicab driver at the time of the offenses charged.

CONCLUSION

During his period in custody, he has been visited regularly by Ms. Orr. Neither his mother nor his sisters have visited him, although his youngest sister, Alison, has written to him three times. Mr. Gow states that he does not wish contact with his sister and will not be replying to her.

At school he was thought clever enough to sit five GCSEs but failed them all. He claims his sisters would not leave him alone to study and his mother made him take care of his sisters at this time and that is why he failed.

Gow tells me that Ms. Orr intends to continue with their relationship no matter the outcome of the trial.

Thomas H. Granger
Social Worker
THG 3/21/94 (AndrewGow)

Box 1 Document 5 ***Letter re Donna***

Scottish Prison Department
From S. Jackson
Supervisor
H-Hall
Sunnyfields State Mental Hospital
Lanarkshire
March 21, 1998

To: Dr. Susan Harriot
SPD Psychiatric Services
Sunnyfields

ANDREW GOW (30757): REQUEST TO MARRY
Mr. Gow has lodged a formal request to marry Miss Donna McGovern. I have spoken to Mr. Gow, who informs me that he does intend to marry Ms. McGovern. He informs me that the intended date would be sometime in April. Please conduct an interview with Ms. McGovern to determine her intentions.

Yours sincerely
S. Jackson
Supervisor

What is Susie so wound up about? There's nothing in these papers that's especially confidential. I've been checking through the files on the computer all morning, and they're all like these, all straightforward notes about different cases, a couple of book reviews, and some sketched-out ideas for professional articles like the table of correspondents.

I still haven't watched that video and can't now that the house is full of people. I don't mind getting upset in this study, where I can be alone. I wish they'd go. I don't know if I can hold it together for much longer, and I don't want to frighten my mum. I hope they aren't planning to stay until after the sentencing, which could be weeks away.

I can't understand why Susie wants me out of here. Why would she object to my finding material for her appeal? It's as if she'd be happier stuck in there with her privacy intact than out here with me, facing up to whatever problems we have. I know we do have problems; I'm not brushing over them. I'm just saying they don't need to be as big as she makes them.

Supposing, just for argument's sake, that Susie was in love with Gow and was jealous of Donna, supposing all of that, I still don't think she'd kill them. She's sensible, a problem-solver, and killing both of them wouldn't advance her cause in any way. Surely a guilty woman wouldn't hang around in the bar at a nearby hotel after committing a double murder? And who phoned the police? The "helpful local" theory the prosecution came up with didn't sound at all plausible to me.

But then what the hell do I know? Maybe Susie wasn't acting rationally. Maybe she'd tried everything else she could possibly think of and was at the end of her tether. She made a lot of bad decisions around that time. She gave that interview, which was contrary to all of her interests. Still, it's a leap from bad decisions to committing two murders.

If she was truly in love with Gow, I think it might break me.

chapter fifteen

I've been out on my own for a couple of hours, and the break has done me good. I think having everyone here has been more of a strain than I'd like to admit. It's hard falling asleep on the sofa. Almost as soon as I managed it, Trisha got up and clattered around the kitchen, banging plates together, trying to make herself useful. Mum heard it somehow and rushed downstairs, determined not to be last up, and before I knew what had happened, I was sitting at the breakfast table arbitrating their conversation.

After returning from mass this morning, Mum looked through the cupboards and found that the gravy powder was two years out of date. Evidently this was the start of the rot, the lack of Sunday gravy. I think she was more disgusted by this than my refusing to go to mass. She sent me out to get the makings of a Sunday roast. Yeni still wasn't back from chapel, and for a terrifying moment I thought she might have run away.

The supermarket was quiet, and I nipped around in record time. As I was loading the bags into the car, I looked across the road to McFee's and, through the condensation dripping down the window, thought I saw the back of Yeni's yellow anorak at the table by the door. She could only have been hiding; the coffee's terrible there.

She was sitting on her own, frowning hard and trying to read a Sunday tabloid, when I sat down opposite her. She glanced at my arm, politely sitting back to afford me a share of the tabletop before she realized it was me.

She pressed a hand to her chest. "Lachlan," she said, as she always says, as if her tongue were negotiating its way around a mouthful of oily marbles. "Jyou give me, mm, big scare."

I smiled and said I was sorry. I nodded at the menu and asked if I could buy her an ice cream. She doesn't have a lot of money and seemed quite pleased. Still, she tried to pay for the egg rolls she'd already had. I think she's trying to make it clear that she is not available for good times. I didn't know how to say "dream on, fat bird" in Spanish, so I smiled and let her pay and then ordered two Knickerbocker Glories and a pot of tea for two.

"My wife and I can't thank you enough for staying during all of this," I said.

She shook her head, but I could see she liked my mentioning Susie.

"My wife asked me specifically to tell you that she says thanks. You have been so good to Margie just when she needs extra care. Any other au pair would have left us. You are very kind."

Yeni shook her head again and nodded and waved her head about some more. When she realized I'd finished, she smiled a beamer. "I like Margie very fine. She is good for to me."

Her English is shocking. I suppose it's my fault; I should talk to her more. We nodded and smiled at each other some more, and shrugged and were reduced to giving each other thumbs-up by the time the ice creams came. They looked great. The sun shone in through the window and lit up the strawberry sauce neon-clear. They looked gloriously indulgent.

Afterward we sat, drowsy with carbohydrates, sipping tea and ripping up paper napkins by wiping our sticky fingers on them. I read the papers while Yeni flicked through the pictures in the supplements. It was nice being with someone and not having to interact, just having the comfort of a bit of company. I noticed that she'd stopped smelling of yogurt, so she's either sorted out her thrush problem or given up eating it. We didn't talk about Trisha or my parents, but it was obvious why we were both hiding there. Afterward, when we could delay it no longer, I gave her a lift back to the house. It would be nice to have a pal.

Box 1 Document 3 ***Note of Circumstances (cont.)***

SITUATION AT TIME OF OFFENSE

5. Mr. Gow was aged twenty-eight at the time of the indictment. He was married and living with his wife, Lara Orr, at 3582 Cumbernauld Avenue, Cumbernauld. They had no children.

6. The victims were all working as prostitutes in the Glasgow area.

6.1 Victim Mrs. Elizabeth MacCorronah, resident of Flat 3/1, 6 Ochil Place, Milton, Glasgow, had three children, all of whom were in local authority care at the time of the offense. She was a registered heroin addict and had attempted methadone-assisted withdrawal four times. She was married at the age of sixteen. Her husband, Davie MacCorronah, was killed in a house fire in 1991. He was also a registered addict. Mrs. MacCorronah was nineteen at the time of her murder.

6.2 Victim Karen Dempsey, resident of 46 Glen Tanar Street, Lambhill, Glasgow, was single and had a dependent mother. Although not a registered addict, she had a high level of both alcohol and codeine in her blood at postmortem. She was twenty-one years of age.

6.3 Victim Martine Pashtan, resident of Flat 1/1, 236 Saltmarket, Glasgow, was married and had a child aged four months. She lived with her husband of three years, Mr. Alvin Pashtan. She was twenty-four at the time of her death.

6.4 Alice Thomson, of Flat 16/3, 5 Calder Street, Polmadie, Glasgow, was thirty-three at the time of her murder. She had two children, aged thirteen and twelve, both living with their father, John Livingston, in East Kilbride.

6.5 Mary-Ann Roberts, of Flat 1/2, 38 Langa Street, High Carntyne, Glasgow, was single and childless. She was forty-one at the time of her murder. Ms. Roberts had convictions for prostitution stretching back to 1971, when she was nineteen.

7. Although Mr. Gow confessed to the murders, he was unwilling to talk about the commission of the offenses. DNA matches were made between Mr. Gow and the semen samples on the bodies.

PRISONER'S ACCOUNT OF OFFENSES

8. Gow volunteered a confession to the murders upon being stopped by two police officers for cruising in the Anderston area. He admitted to murdering the women, told police where he had left the bodies, and revealed details about the arrangement of the corpses. Forensic examination found traces of the women's blood in his car. A preliminary DNA match was established between Mr. Gow and the semen samples left at the scene of the crimes. He has entered a guilty plea.

Subsequently, he refuses to discuss the offenses despite his guilty plea. On all other matters he is happy to talk. He is a pleasant, articulate man and presents himself well.

It's now teatime and I've spent the best part of today up here hiding from the crossfire. Firstly there's Trisha and all the nasty questions I've been avoiding: How did Susie look when I visited? What did she say? Is she well, not being mistreated, I hope? Does she have her own room? Is she having to empty her own slop bucket? How the hell am I supposed to know all this stuff? Trisha wants to know if she can come to visit Susie, but I said no, probably not. I've promised to ask Susie about her living conditions the next time I go, but I won't. I'm not driving the forty minutes there and back with Trisha in the car and having her watch me being searched. Susie only gets four visits a month, anyway, and it may be wrong, but I want them for myself. Then Mum pipes up, standing up for me, telling Trisha to write to Susie if she wants to know these things, leave the boy alone, let my people go.

It takes eight hours to drive up to Cape Wrath from Glasgow. Susie could surely have changed her mind and thought of me, or at least of Margie, once during the eight-hour drive. They showed security film from a service station during the trial, and we all watched as Susie stopped to gas the car up and bought a family-size bag of wine gums and a can of Diet Coke. On the film she is laughing and chatting with the girl behind the counter, pointing back to the car because she didn't know the number of the pump. As the prosecution said, not exactly the behavior of a woman beside herself with worry about Donna. I'd like to think she was buying the wine gums to bribe herself onward, like I was with the toffees, but I don't think she minded going up there. I don't think Susie'd go anywhere reluctantly. I wonder if she'd come and visit me in prison if the situations were reversed, and I can honestly say, I don't think she would.

My chest has been hurting from all the smoking, and I've got no one to blame that on but myself. I've been up here since lunch, transcribing and playing computer solitaire. It's a dull but hypnotic game. I've cut a picture of a Greek seaside town out of the Sunday papers and stuck it up on the wall. There are whitewashed buildings in the foreground and a steep cliff over an electric-blue sea. It relaxes me. Just looking at it, I can almost feel the sun on my neck. I want to go back there.

This time two weeks ago I was still hopeful that the verdict would go our way. This will be the worst of it if she never gets out, these interminable Sundays stretching off into the future until Margie goes to university. By that time I won't remember what it is to be happy, the loneliness will be all through me like a cancer.

I wish Susie was home. I wish she was up here working and I was downstairs shouting up at her to come down and talk to me. Even if she was up here fantasizing about Gow, I wouldn't mind. I wouldn't care even if she was up here thinking about touching him.

That prison-lovers book says that the women hear whatever story about the murder they want to hear; if they want him to have been protecting a helpless friend, then they'll hear that in the story he tells; if they want to excuse him on the grounds that he was forced to kill an abusive wife, then they'll hear that. And if they can't mitigate the cruelty, then they'll factor in drugs or drink to explain it. But Susie couldn't have misheard Gow. She had his records. She was his psychiatrist.

I'm so tired of thinking about it all the time. I'm tired of second-guessing every moment we've spent together. I can't sleep for thinking. Even when I manage to fall asleep, I wake up with my mind careering back and forth over a big map of what-ifs and did-shes. Some did-shes bring me close to despair. Last night on the sofa I played with a did-she that made me feel elated and warm and centered. Suppose she didn't care for Gow at all and it's all just a mix-up. She was talking to him in the office, nothing more. She's my wife, still my wife, and she lies in her little prison bed, hands behind her darling head, and sees me on her ceiling, longs for my presence as I long for hers.

Maybe Susie wasn't working all the time she was up here. Maybe she was hiding the way I am now, bristling with resentment at the people downstairs. Maybe she was sitting here in this tiny closet thinking fuck them, smoking angrily, avoiding coming down.

What is it she doesn't want me to see in here?

Box 2 Document 5 *Donna's First Letter to Gow*

48 Evington Road
Evington
Leicester
2/2/98

Dear Andrew Gow,

Forgive my writing to you out of the blue but I have been in love with you for three years now so its about time we spoke!! I saw a picture of you in the paper and knew by your eyes your a kind man. You say your not guilty of those crimes and I know it's true. In my heart I know you will not be trapped in prison forever.

Well who is your mystery admirer!?! I am twenty three and have already been divorced. My first husband was not a kind man. He drank and did not understand that I need room to breath and grow. I am not a complete dummy. I have a GCSE in typing as you can see and an HND in catering. I have a job in a health center where I work behind the reception desk. I like dancing and going out and having a good time on the town.

Sadly my dad died two months ago and it has made me see that I should grab life while I can. That is why I am writing to you. My friends tell me I am mad but I can see an angel from heaven when I look at your picture. I LOVE YOU! I dream about you at night and think about you all day!!

Maybe you will write back. If not just remember there's a girl out here who thinks your the greatest guy in the world!!

Take care of yourself in there.

Yours sincerely,
Donna McGovern

Fucking hell, Donna!! Learn to punctuate?! I shouldn't take the piss out of the dead, she might come back from the grave and beat me to death with an exclamation mark. Hope not!?! I should feel an affinity with her, I suppose; she was betrayed by Susie and Gow too. Why would Gow get married if he was involved with Susie?

I found this psychology report about Gow and keep thinking that one exactly like it is being drawn up about Susie.

Box 1 Document 6 ***Clinical Psychological Report 1994***

CLINICAL PSYCHOLOGICAL REPORT ON ANDREW GOW (DOB 6/23/65): HMP BARLINNIE

1. In response to a request from the governor of the above-named prison and from Mr. Telford of the Scottish Office, I now submit this report on the above-named prisoner. The report is based on an interview of just over one hour, together with analysis of the data from a diagnostic personality test, the Minnesota Multiphasic Personality Inventory (MMPI), which the prisoner agreed to complete. The writer has not canvased the views of any of the prison officers, since she understands that their impressions will be recorded elsewhere.

2. The prisoner, charged with murder, was admitted to Barlinnie prison on December 23, 1993. He is a large man who nevertheless moves easily and talks comfortably in interview. He told the psychologist that he considers himself to be a survivor and the sort of person who adapts easily to new situations. He foresees no problems in coming to terms with a lengthy sentence. He claims he is "easy-going," can "get on with anybody," and is "very popular," although he prefers his own company. Later in the interview he became very angry when asked about his ex-boss at the minicab firm who had sacked him after his arrest. He said he would like to "teach him a permanent lesson."

3. His early family life seems to have been quite troubled. He was born and educated in Bridgeton, Glasgow, a less than salubrious area. Mr. Gow's parents fought, principally over his father's excessive drinking. He enjoyed school and did well up until fifth year, when he failed his GCSEs and left. His parents separated

when Mr. Gow was eight. He states that his relationship with his mother was "shite." When asked to elaborate on this statement, he declared that his mother was "a cow" who never cared for him. He became quite agitated in discussing his mother. He said she made him take responsibility for his siblings and "spoiled his chances in life." Asked whether his relationship with his mother related to the crimes he was charged with he smiled and refused to speak on the matter. He is high on anxiety and may well have more trouble forming social bonds and restraining impulsive behavior than he declares.

4. His father is now deceased. Mr. Gow no longer has contact with either his mother or three sisters. He is married and states that his wife will remain with him whatever the outcome of his trial.

5. Mr. Gow's early criminal career centered on shoplifting minor items such as cigarettes, a newspaper, and a pair of lady's tights. As regards to car theft: Mr. Gow took a neighbor's car and drove into the country until he ran out of gas. He was picked up walking along the M8, making his way back to Bridgeton from Lanark.

6. With regard to the theft charges, he states he was "angry with himself" but wavered when questioned as to whether he regretted getting caught or stealing in the first place. He claims that he did not get caught but confessed to the police of his own volition, showing them the items and the shops he stole them from. He had intended to give the stolen items to girls to "try to get them to like him," a statement which belies his claim to universal popularity. The charges of drunk and disorderly and breach of the peace were brought in relation to a single series of events. Having gone for a drink after work Mr. Gow became drunk and tried to catch the bus home. He argued with the driver and resisted being ejected by holding on to a seat-back. He was not violent during this or any other incident prior to the present charges.

7. With regard to the present charges, he will not talk. When questioned, he smiles and will not be pressed further. He claims he does not "fancy" talking about the incidents.

8. Throughout the whole interview, Gow was systematic and

clear in his report. The veracity of what he told has of course to be taken on trust by the writer, who has only known him very briefly. What Gow has told me has to be taken as the image of himself he wishes to portray to a relative stranger at the moment. He showed no disturbance of thought or emotion at interview, although he tends to be guarded and given to inconsistent posturing, as in his claims to be easygoing/uncrossable, very popular/a loner. No intelligence test was administered on this occasion but he is probably of at least good average intelligence.

9. Gow was slightly wary of subjecting himself to the MMPI. The latter is a well-researched inventory-type test used on both sides of the Atlantic in clinical and forensic populations. Its purpose is to scan for significant personality malfunctions or psychopathy and to measure certain factors which may have predictive value for the person concerned. It also has reliability indices which measure attitudes to test-taking, e.g., tendencies to lie, to alter responses to fit in with anticipated expectations, to exaggerate, or to deny adverse features, all of which are helpful in determining how much weight to give the overall test.

10. These indices were well above normal limits, suggesting that Mr. Gow has either a tendency to lie all the time or a desire to disguise his true profile in this test. However, the attempts to lie were done in a surprisingly intelligent and consistent manner, suggesting a degree of ability when it comes to duplicity. None of the scale scores were outside normal limits apart from the psychopathic personality scale which had a significant T score of 76. Clinically this is of note, being a relatively high score. The general pattern of his test scores and attitude to the psychologist suggest that attempts at rehabilitation may be problematic. Of particular concern is his attitude to the charged offenses. He is either refusing to talk about them because he cannot excuse them, or he simply has no memory of them. The former seems more likely. In light of his high score on the psychopathic personality scale, it is suggested that future treatment of this man should probably involve: (a) limiting his work and activities; (b) perhaps group work to attempt to prompt him to talk about his offenses; (c) always approaching his self-report with care and skepticism.

11. I will be pleased to clarify or expand on anything in this report if necessary.

I hope that it will serve some useful purpose.

Yours faithfully
Valerie Elliott

chapter sixteen

I'VE GOT A HANGOVER.

Morris and Bangor came over last night and took me out for a pint. When I saw them coming through the gate, I threw the kitchen door open and ran across the lawn to them. I found myself getting a bit carried away. Luckily Morris punched me on the arm and I could pretend that it brought tears to my eyes. It's essential never to show fear or pain in front of Mum or she'll sit you down and try to make you talk about it. It's inconceivable to her that anyone would rather not talk, or would like to talk to anyone but her. Of course, I wouldn't be saying this if there weren't a lock on this door.

Mum was delighted to see Bangor. She's always liked him and is pleased that I've stayed friends with what she refers to as "degreed folk" (like the little folk but with better prospects). I think it comes from not having been to university herself. She thinks you have to be clever to get in. When Bangor flirts with her and calls her Mrs. H., she clasps her hands in front of her and looks contented.

We went for a pint and talked about football. Neither of them mentioned Susie or the papers or the trial, apart from asking me if I was all right. It was great. We sat in the snug, next to the fruit machine, and sipped Guinness and ate smoky bacon crisps.

The business of the evening: Morris is still having an affair with the receptionist in his practice, and Bangor says he thinks his new girlfriend, Nurse Julie, has heard about it from the district nurse.

"Well, she either knows or she doesn't," says Morris.

"Well, she does," says Bangor.

"How do you know for sure?" asks Morris.

"Because she told me."

"What did she tell you?"

"She told me she knows that you and the tart with the fat arse from Kingspark are at it."

"Is she going to tell Mrs. Morris?"

"Nurse Julie thinks Evelyn already knows."

"What if she doesn't?"

"Julie's going to tell her."

"She can't. The bitch just can't trample all over people's fucking lives like that. Has she no feelings? No sense of propriety?"

During this exchange I think of Gow and Susie, and I know they weren't shagging. They couldn't possibly have been shagging. We're sitting there getting more and more pissed, and I feel great. I'm not the one with the problems, and there's nothing strange here. We've all known each other forever, and Morris is up to mischief again and Bangor is trying to trick him into doing the right thing. I sip and nod along and laugh because I'm not the focus and all we have to talk about is frivolous shit. It feels roomy and comfortable.

But when I went to the bar to get a round in, the guy serving kept looking at me and frowning. Finally, as he was giving me my change, he asked where he knew me from.

I was feeling cocky because of the drink, so I said, "Dunno, mate. In here?" But we both knew it wasn't.

I got back here at ten-thirty. I was standing in the dark kitchen, making a big buttery sandwich with the leftover roast lamb, when Mum came down and switched on the light. She put the kettle on and made us both a cup of tea. We sat at the table together. Full of drink and goodwill, I said thanks for coming. We had quite a nice chat. She said what nice friends I have, how good of them to come over and cheer me up. I didn't tell her that I phoned and told them to come. The Guinness made me mellow, and I leaned across and kissed her cheek and said it's been nice having her here, talking about it in the *past tense,* hoping she'll get the message. She patted my hand and washed her cup before she went to bed.

I put the lights out again and opened the French doors to the garden. I sat on the step as if it were summer, as if there were nothing wrong. The dead leaves evaporated, the sky lightened, and the cup of tea in my hand turned into a can of beer. I looked out at the paper plates thrown in hedges and the bits of burger bun strewn across the lawn and decided to leave it all until the morning, what the hell, give the foxes a treat.

Behind me Susie was chatting about something Bangor had said to Saskia and laughing. She came over and sat next to me on the step, lifted my arm over her shoulder, and took the beer can from my hand. I squeezed her waist.

"What a pretty garden, Lachie. Aren't we lucky to live here?" she said. "One day we'll have kids of our own and they'll enjoy it, too."

"We'll have hundreds of kids," I said, burying my face in her neck.

"Well"—she smiled and patted my knee fondly—"tens of kids, maybe."

I heard a noise behind me in the November kitchen. Yeni had crept in and was standing uncertainly by the door. I stood up and waved to her. Without making any noise, she waved back, glancing up at the ceiling nervously. I motioned for her to come over, I don't know why; I didn't have anything to say to her. She got the marzipan bar out of the fridge, brought it over and halved it, and we sat on the step in the dark in the cold, cold kitchen watching the moonlight slither about the grass. It was great marzipan. It had a spongy chocolate bit in it with pistachio stuff on top. We munched through it silently, nodding and smiling at each other like top pals.

Today I can actually feel my liver throbbing, although I may be imagining it. The alcohol is making something bad happen to my innards. It never used to be like this. I used to get pissed and bounce back the next day and go for a fry-up. I never want to eat a roast dinner again, but even through the bitter haze of a terrible hangover, I still remember how nice the marzipan was. I must find out where Yeni bought it.

chapter seventeen

I GOT A LETTER FROM SUSIE THIS MORNING ASKING ME NICELY NOT to come up to this study anymore. I wrote back and didn't mention it. She can piss right off. I've got to go and visit her tomorrow and I don't want to. I don't want to talk about this being her room. I want it to be my room.

I've been looking at this report for days without realizing it was written by Jon Compton, Susie's old supervisor. She did all the typing for him, and I remember she said she sat in on this interview as part of her training. It was probably the first time she ever met Gow. She said he was creepy and stared at her tits.

Box 1 Document 7 *Gow's Psychiatric Report 1994*

State Hospital

Sunnyfields
Lanarkshire

PSYCHIATRIC REPORT ON ANDREW GOW
DATE OF BIRTH: JUNE 23, 1965

I hereby certify on soul and conscience that at the request of the Procurator Fiscal, Glasgow, I examined Mr. Andrew Gow in Barlinnie prison 2/13/1994 and that the following is a true report.

I am recognized in terms of Section 20 of the Mental Health (Scotland) Act 1984.

The report that follows is based upon statements that Gow made to me during my meeting with him and my only other source of information is certain background details provided for me by the Procurator Fiscal at Glasgow. The fact that I record Mr. Gow's statements here does not mean that I accept them as being true and accurate.

THE CHARGE

I understand that Mr. Gow faces several concurrent charges of murder. He will not discuss the charges. Although he refuses to talk about it when questioned, he claims that he does understand the nature of the charges, that they are for murder, and that he fully remembers the events of the nights in question. Questioned about the charges, he smiles inappropriately but is aware of the meaning of murder and can recite the names of the women he is charged with killing. He says he never met any of them and had not heard of them before he was charged with their murders. Asked what the women had in common he says they were all prostitutes. Asked about his attitudes to prostitution he shrugs and says he wouldn't want his sisters doing it. He claims to have a full memory for all events and was in a normal state of health throughout the period charged.

FAMILY AND SOCIAL BACKGROUND

Mr. Gow grew up in Bridgeton. His father had a drink problem and separated from his family when Mr. Gow was eight. His mother does not drink. He has three sisters, one older and two younger. He states that his childhood was unhappy. He blames his mother's reliance on his looking after the other children for his failure to do well at school. He has worked as a minicab driver since school. His father died of cancer two years ago. He has fallen out with his mother and sisters because of a dispute between them and his wife. He seems quite bitter about his family's unwillingness to accept his wife. Mr. Gow and his wife have no children.

Past Medical History

There is no history of psychiatric treatment or contact of any kind. He attempted suicide when he was twelve by taking an overdose of acetaminophen. His mother took him to Casualty and claimed he had taken them by accident. He does not recall why he took the overdose. There is no past history of physical illness.

Alcohol and Drug History

Regarding alcohol, he told me he used to drink, sometimes heavily, but "got a fright" after his arrest for drunk and disorderly conduct and stopped drinking. He has never taken drugs. He has been offered them in prison but does not want them.

Behavior Pattern

He told me that he does not want to discuss the charges with me but is fully able to discuss them with his lawyer and understands what is about to happen in the trial. He is fully oriented and aware of his surroundings during interview. He is a healthy-looking man who, when not discussing the charges, smiles readily and appropriately and presents well.

He performed well in the reading skill and memory functioning. His handwriting is neat.

There was no evidence of abnormality either of the form or content of his thinking and no evidence that he has ever experienced perceptual disorders.

There was no evidence of primary abnormality in his mood in either direction.

OPINION
Gow is sane and fit to plead.

There was no evidence of mental illness or mental handicap.
There are no psychiatric grounds for diminished responsibility.
An EEG examination is not indicated.

J. Compton, MD MRC Psych, DCh.
Physician Superintendent

Reports like this one are being drawn up about Susie right now. I wonder what they'll say about our home life.

1. Husband is unemployed/unemployable.
2. A dispute about her husband has led to tensions with her sole surviving relative, her Aunt Trisha.
3. Her husband is sticking by her even though she was having an affair with a half-man/half-monkey-type creature.

There must be something in among all the dross in here; something Susie doesn't want me to know about. I've been through all the computer files in the "My Documents" file and they're all cases, notes, timetables, research ideas, stuff like that. If there is a faint possibility that we could base an appeal on something in here, it's got to be worth my looking through it, whatever she says. She can't be objecting on the grounds that this stuff is confidential. She can hardly take a hard line on patient confidentiality, given that she was dressing up like a tart and giving interviews about Gow to lads' mags.

It occurred to me while I was bathing Margie: Susie had a lock on the door *and* a computer password, which suggests that there might be something in the room, not just in the computer, that she doesn't want me to see. I'll start at one end and work my way around the walls.

I've spent the day with Mum and Dad and Trisha, being chirpy to reassure them all that I'm all right, that they can actually go home. We took Margie to the Haughhead center and let her run amok in the playroom. Mum and Dad like it out there because it's warm and everything's indoors. They wanted to leave Trisha behind and spend a bit of time just the four of us but it seemed so unkind to leave her out. We were talking about it in the kitchen and she came in to make a cup of tea, clearly feeling excluded, staying away from the table and looking out of the window with her arms crossed. I invited her to come out with us, and she pretended that she might have something else to do before agreeing enthusiastically. I wish she got on better with Mum so that they could go clothes shopping and I could get a chat with Dad. Trisha isn't warm, but she is nice to Margie. When we got to the mall, she watched Margie climbing about in the playroom for nearly forty minutes while Dad and I walked around the supermarket and Mum went looking for an electric blanket to take back to Spain.

It's scary spending long tracts of time with Dad; it reminds me how nervous and elderly he is. He's lost half a foot in the past three years, and we're not allowed to mention it because of the implication that his bones might snap in a high wind. But I know it's not brittle bones or bad hips that make him old, it's the fear. He treads carefully, is nervous around rough children, tries not to lift heavy stuff. In the supermarket he came to a complete stop at a spill of milk. I saw it happen to Mrs. Wilkens. Once the fear gets hold of them, they start to think that every fast-running child or hot bath or mild bout of diarrhea is the start of an inexorable descent into indignity. The fear is all-pervasive until they're sitting in all afternoon watching the matinees on TV, afraid to leave the house in case they die.

I'm visiting Susie tomorrow, and I don't want to fall asleep because then the morning will come sooner. Mum and Dad have insisted on accompanying me, saying that they'll look after Margie while we're in the car. Coincidentally, a big antiques fair is taking place nearby on the same day and they might just pop along to look while we're in visiting. Trisha has told Margie that she will see her mummy, so there's no backing out. Each time I think of simple questions to ask about the food and conditions, another, bolder, question leapfrogs to the tip of my tongue. What did I ever do to you? How could you come home and look at me in the evenings? Why were you fucking Gow? But Margie'll be there, and Susie will pay scant attention to me. It occurred to me as I lay awake and burning-eyed on the settee that she only stayed with me for the sake of Margie. She was counting on my bringing up her child for her while she got on with her life, having affairs and progressing in her career. I'm like Yeni but paid better.

I actually found myself praying. Please, God, let me know the truth. Let all the wondering stop. Let my thoughts rest. But I don't believe in God. I don't even believe in the cognitive value of prayer.

chapter eighteen

IT'S FOUR-THIRTY IN THE MORNING, AND I'D GIVE ANYTHING TO BE able to sleep. I wish these old bastards would piss off home and leave me be. I want to go for three hours without talking. I want to get back into my own bed. I worked it out: In the past forty-eight hours I've had four and three-quarter hours' sleep. In the past seventy-two hours I've had nine and a half hours' sleep, as opposed to the generally recognized requisite twenty-four. That is a deficit ratio of 1:2.5. I should be sleeping two and half times more than I am.

All the numbers in the world are sloshing about in my head, forming themselves into answers to questions that I don't fully understand. I'm lying down, knowing that it is imperative that I fall asleep right now because Trisha will be up at seven, smashing about the kitchen, emptying the dishwasher, and all the time I'm trying to sleep, I'm thinking about Susie and the Vale and Margie and Gow, and when I switch off, I think of numbers and hard sums. So I gave in to the noise in my head, made a cup of tea, and came up here. My head is bursting.

While at university, hanging out on the eighth floor of the library trying to get the attention of some girls, I was flicking coolly through a journal and read a study about the effects of sleep deprivation. The US Army found that it can induce temporary psychosis, hallucinations, both auditory and visual, and mood swings. I know this. I haven't been awake for sixty hours, being chased around a square mile of tarmac by a sadistic CIA experimenter, so the effects are more subtle, but they're there, especially the mood swings.

For the first few miles of the drive out to the prison, I was sad and anxious. When we stopped at a Little Chef for Mum to go to the toilet, I became angry. Then Dad got back into the car and started feeding Margie sweets made of sugar and ADD-inducing additives. I asked him to stop it and he pooh-poohed my objections. I became more and more furious as Margie became more and more hyper. She began to wriggle, shrieking intermittently when she didn't get the paper/keys/attention/chance to run the sugar off. She was going berserk by the time we got to the prison. I swore in front of her, a thing I hate to do. I told them to fucking stay in the car; the antiques fair turned out to be four miles away, and I wasn't prepared to wander around for hours and hours after the visit looking for them. Now that I'm so tired and the fight has gone out of me, I can see perfectly clearly that I was nervous and looking for someone to blame. It wasn't their fault at all. So now I feel angry *and* guilty.

The guard at reception saw me holding a screaming, wriggling Margie around the waist like a paper parcel and didn't comment, but I could sense her disapproval. A couple of scary women with bad dye jobs sat up as I came into the glass waiting room. Margie was turning red and close to vomiting. The gnarled women came over, gathered around her in a solid wall, and cooed over her beetroot face, stroking her and making clucking noises. Somehow, they managed to mollify her so that she sat up on my knees, breathing heavily and holding tightly on to my arm as she looked around. I thanked them as they dispersed, and they said things in indignant Edinburgh accents. I didn't understand the words but guessed that they were meeting my thanks with dismissal and statements of solidarity. I had dressed Margie in the faded red corduroy pinafore dress, which doesn't look too expensive. I didn't want to make Susie stand out, and I was glad of it now: I don't know if they would have helped me if she had been head to foot in Burberry check, but maybe that's just me being a middle-class prick. I'm stalling because I don't want to go through the details of the visit again.

They didn't search me this time. They just let me through with everyone else, and I saw Susie sitting at a different table at the back of the room. I expected Margie to run across the room to her darling mama, but the first thing she did when we got in there was to start coughing. It was incredibly smoky. Susie stood up when she saw her girl. She kept her eyes on Margie as we walked over; she didn't look at me once, didn't even offer me her cheek to kiss this time. Her hair has been cut straight across just below her shoulder blades and she looks even thinner than she did last week. Her lips are dry and have turned slightly purple. Her skin is luminescent and waxy, and her blue eyes are sad and hollow and more expressive of every nuance of thought than I have ever seen them.

She took Margie from my arms and sat down, hugging her tight and straightening her little red skirt as if she were dressing a dolly.

"I picked the red dress so she didn't look too middle-class," I said and gave a kind of wet snort as if to say "we're better than every-one else here, *fnar fnar.*"

She frowned briefly at my feet. Margie seemed completely un-affected by her mother's presence, and for a fleeting moment I wondered whether we could just never come back here. Maybe we could run away, Margie and I, take all of Mr. Wilkens's money and go and live somewhere warm, like Greece; perhaps take Yeni for the first year or so. I was thinking that Yeni wouldn't come because she's supposed to be over here to learn English, when I heard Susie whispering into Margie's hair. She was repeating "I love you," telling every strand, letting the words spill across her lips and soak her hair.

I sat across from her (resisting a cigarette for Margie's good), feeling sick and angry and exhausted. Ten words from her would let me sleep and bring me peace of mind. A mere ten words would keep me on her side for the next thousand years.

I'm so sorry.

I've been faithful.

I love you still.

Instead she looked over the top of Margie's head and said, "You look knackered, Lachlan." Using the formal name, pulling back from me.

And instead of ten words that would soothe her soul, I said, "I am, Susan. I am."

We sat across from each other, unhappily watching Margie so we wouldn't need to look at each other. I told her Trisha had come to stay. She didn't make a joke about it or say any of the usual things. She sighed as though I'd reproached her unfairly and apologized. I said my parents had come to stay as well and they were all competitively caring for me. She didn't smile. Well, she said, that must be nice. It seems as if all we learned to do during our marriage is not talk. We stared at Margie some more. She'd wriggled off Susie's lap and was holding on to the low table, trying to grab the far edge.

"Did you get my letter?" she asked.

I said I did, yeah, and asked when the next visit was.

She smirked miserably. "We're hardly ten minutes into this one yet."

I stopped to breathe and gather my courage. "Look, Trisha wants to come and see you, and, well, you're obviously not bothered about seeing me, so I'll send her next time."

She melted. It's the only way to describe her face: her jaw dropped, her eyes drooped, and she keened quietly, "Oh, Lachie, no, please."

I know that prisoners will do anything, promise anything to keep their families coming to visit them—we'd talked about it when she was still working—and I knew that she was begging as a friend, asking me not to abandon her.

"I'm not leaving you," I said. "But I can't do this. . . . I can't come here and be treated like this . . . like I don't matter."

She covered her face and wept. Margie turned and tugged at her hands, muttering "Mummmumm" noises, poking the tears off her face and yanking her hair to distract her.

Susie sniffed hard. "Please, Lachie, please." Electric blue eyes half closed in dire warning of the consequences, she shook her head at me; a perfect strand of midnight black hair fell over one eye, ending in a kiss curl on her dusky cheekbone. She pushed the hair behind her ear and pulled Margie onto her lap, enveloping her. "Please?"

I didn't speak. I couldn't give the hollow reassurances that she wanted, say that I'd come and see her for the next ten years, make a go of our empty marriage, talk about the garden and the apple tree and oh, goodness, Mr. Tottery at number thirty-seven had a foreseeable accident, what a pity. I was so tired and raw already and, dreading the slip of meaning from lip to ear, didn't dare tell her how I felt.

Margie spotted another child across the room, a five-year-old boy, and ran over to play with him. I don't know why small children are magnetically drawn to older kids who never want to play with them, but I couldn't help seeing parallels in our situation.

There weren't as many people visiting today as there were the last time. A cancer-thin man of about fifty, wearing denims and an anorak that were too big for him, was visiting an emaciated woman with yellowed-white hair. They sat silently together and smoked matchstick rollies, her arms wrapped across her stomach as though it ached. The women who had calmed Margie down were sitting at different tables on different visits. The relationships between the visitors were usually obvious: mother, daughter, big sister, wee sister, pal. Some of them chatted; most looked a bit bored. One prisoner got up to go to the toilet. She had her eyebrow pierced and homemade cross tattoos on her hands. She tipped her chin at Susie, checking me out as she walked by. Susie pressed her lips together and nodded back.

"Who's that?" I asked.

Susie shrugged. "Someone."

"Someone who?"

"Just someone. She cut my hair."

I hadn't thought of Susie having a social life in prison. I had imagined that she would be static in aspic while the world outside revolved. I asked her if she was being bullied or anything.

"Women's prisons're not like that. It's more like being at school. Games, popularity contests. Margie, come here, baby."

She spent the rest of the visit coaxing Margie back across the room. She only came back after the older boy had pushed her and she ran over, crying, wobbling on her chubby wee legs. Susie picked her up again and hugged her tight, stroking that part of her cheek that makes her sit still. It's below her right eye, a patch of skin so sensitive that it hypnotizes her with pleasure when it's touched in a particular way. I can never find it.

The thin woman with the rollie was looking over at us. When she caught Susie's eye, the woman smiled down at Margie, and Susie raised her head and smiled slowly, taking the compliment on the chin. It was a codicil to a long conversation had elsewhere.

A bell rang and everyone in the room stood up. Susie let Margie down to the floor and cupped her hands over my forearm like a begging dog.

"Come back, Lachie, please?" she said, looking up at me.

I frowned. "Give me something," I said, but we both knew that I meant anything.

She paused, thinking hard, looking for a place in her heart where I provoked a positive response. I waited for a year.

"I miss you," she said eventually, but she was looking at Margie.

Still, I felt the electric neediness flood through my feet into the ground. I nodded. "Okay," I said. "I'll come back."

"Thursday next week? One o'clock?"

"I'll come."

We were standing close together. She floated slowly up to meet my face and let her plump purple lips brush mine. A flash of hope shocked me. For that golden moment, things were fine. It was okay between us and I had a future.

She walked away toward the short line at the back door. A male guard pointed the women into a straighter line, asserting his power over them. They shuffled into place as the visitors gathered up their things and made for the other door. Susie twisted from the waist and looked back at me. I was standing exactly still, tipped forward at an improbable angle into the space where her lips had been.

"Stay out of the study," she said and turned her attention to Margie. She splayed her fingers open-shut in a starburst and Margie raised her little hand and did it back. Nothing more for me. I'd had all I was getting.

"I'll go where I like," I said, loud enough for her to hear.

She took a step out of line and jabbed an angry finger at me. "Stay. Out."

"Back in line," called the guard.

Susie's right, I shouldn't be up here. I was lying on the couch in the dark, watching the green minutes count by on the video recorder, when I suddenly remembered the night we went to the opera. We were students and still open to new things, hadn't yet rejected whole swaths of cultural experience, so we ended up going to see *Duke Bluebeard's Castle* by Bartók. We paid a fiver each for our seats. We were so high up that we were looking down on the singers' heads, and their bodies were dramatically foreshortened. The set was good, but the music did nothing much for me. I found it a bit dreary. Susie loved it, though, and I bought her the CD for her birthday.

I got up off the couch, put the lights on, and found the CD. I wanted to play it, but it was the middle of the night. I sat reading the libretto and was struck by this line of Judith's: "I came here because I love you. Let me enter every doorway."

I'm firmly on Bluebeard's side. I said so afterward; he specifically asked her not to go into the seventh room, he gave her the run of the castle and everything she wanted, but Susie disagreed.

"Could you?" she said in the pub on the way home. "Could you know that some amazing piece of information was behind the door, have the key, and resist the urge?"

I said yes, I definitely could, but Susie didn't believe me. She teased me, alluding to a raunchy lesbian experience she'd had in the sixth form. She said it was with Tina, a buxom girl we'd bumped into at a party once. She wore tight trousers and a fluffy bra; I couldn't stop staring at her tits. This irritated Susie, but Tina looked like a prostitute. Did I remember her? I grinned; yeah, I remembered Tina. We sat silently smiling at each other, and she ended up laughing. I didn't find it hard not to ask about Tina because I knew it wasn't true.

The point is that in abstract I agree with a no-entry policy for seventh rooms, but in this raw reality I'd rip the plaster off these walls to find out what was going on. I'd face the fact that Susie was in love with him, admit she killed him and cut his tongue out, deal with every sordid detail because I suspect—and I might well be wrong—but I suspect that I wouldn't feel just as bad if I knew the truth.

What am I looking for in here anyway? The truth? A fact? Her motive? At the moment, on a day-to-day, hour-to-hour basis, I think, speculate, wonder about Susie's motives more than any other single thing. Yet motive is the most slippery of truths. After an utterly honest, undefensive, unpropagandizing three months of incessant talk, a brilliant, insightful psychiatrist couldn't hope to uncover my true motives for taking an unsatisfactory dump this morning. They could call it tension, stress, a mother complex, and I could call it a desire for world peace. All of them could be equally true. It could be a fleeting vitamin deficiency or a dream I don't remember having. I know this and still I'm wasting time trying to determine what someone else's motives were for a series of out-of-character actions months ago. I'm up here for hours at a time searching for a completely unknowable quality.

In conclusion, my being here is both wrong and pointless. And still I'm here, scrabbling through the rubble.

A good, true husband would want his wife to be autonomous, could comfortably allow her to leave questions unanswered, and I used to. I loved being so sure of her. I loved having a wife who could go off to a conference and come in and grunt, "Hello" without elaborating. I was proud that she was free to make her own choices, and so was I. Now pain and insecurity make me want to control her, like the arsehole men who kill their wives and girlfriends in the prison-lovers book. I could never have anticipated this hurting and preoccupying me so much. I don't want Susie to be free to do things that make me feel like this. I don't want her to have free will at all. If I could, I would rip the free will from her, rip it out and keep it from her.

No one who knew what this feels like could assent to it. In a way it's proof that God doesn't exist. If there were a God, and he did love the world, he wouldn't have given us free will. He would have anticipated this feeling, deemed free will a flaw, and taken it out. Maybe there is a God but he simply doesn't care what we feel or how much it hurts, in which case any and all pleas for succor or help from him are just about as useful as a nun's cunt.

God forgive me. That's the worst curse I've ever read or said or heard of.

chapter nineteen

MUM AND DAD CAME DOWN TO THE KITCHEN AS I WAS FINISHING my porridge this morning. They tumbled bleary-eyed into the room as though afraid to have left me alone during the hours of darkness. By my watch it was six-forty-five. It's an insult to insomniacs, voluntarily getting up at that time. I went upstairs and found Margie standing in her cot, good as gold, chewing Lizzie Limber Legs and watching her mobile. When I got back down, Trisha had appeared. They were all sitting around the table together, chatting politely. They look a bit scary in the mornings because nighttime dehydration and pillow-creasage exaggerate their wrinkled smiles into horribly sarcastic sneers.

I gave Margie a piece of toast and let her run off into the living room, and then I took a deep breath and turned to the assembled crowd. I told them that I had something to say to all of them: I greatly appreciated their coming to support me, but I wanted them to go home now and let me get Margie back into a routine. Susie will be home soon, I said, and everything will be back to normal. They stared at me, dumbfounded at my gall. Mum was annoyed that I was speaking to her in front of Trisha; I know she wants me to choose her to be on my team first, but I'm too tired to play those games. Dad, sensing what was going through her head, twitched nervously and glanced at her. Mum asked me if I was quite finished, and when I said I was, she stood up, pressing her fingers on the table as if she were addressing a public meeting.

"I think Trisha should go," she said. "She has been here for a whole week—"

Determined to be evenhanded, I interrupted her. "No, I want you *all* to go. I didn't invite you. This is the worst imaginable time for me to have visitors."

"Lachlan," she said patronizingly, "you're not well enough for us to go home."

"Mum," I said, closing my eyes. "I am perfectly well."

She huffed disbelievingly, and her voice rose to a familiar brain-gouging pitch. "*LACH-LAN,*" she said angrily, "your eyes are bright red. It is clear that you are under a lot of strain. To be quite honest, and I don't mean this in a bad way, I'm actually afraid to leave you alone with the child. There, I've said it. You're not sleeping, you're being very moody—"

"I CANNOT SLEEP BECAUSE YOU'RE IN MY BED," I shouted, dropping a plate to the floor. It broke and spiky shards shot across the kitchen floor. "When I *can* get to sleep, you wake me at six a.m. Having you here is driving me crazy. Just get out, will you? Will you all just get out and leave me alone?"

Trisha deliberately misunderstood and said, "Cheer up," weakly. Speechless with impotent rage, I picked up her cup and threw it at the wall. The toffee-brown tea splattered across the white emulsion, flecking at the outer edges. They all looked suddenly very old and brittle. In the living room Margie put the television on. An interviewer was questioning someone about a bombing in the Middle East.

"Young man," said Mum, "it's about flipping well time blah blah blah." I can't remember her exact words, but I was supposed to shape up, ship out, and something something. I wasn't listening, I was sitting at the table, sagging and bent, wishing I were asleep or at least winning the fight. The more emphatic I was, the more they thought they should stay with me and deprive me of a bed. "And furthermore—"

Trisha stood up suddenly. It's easy to forget how tall she is. She stands about five eight, which isn't eugenically freakish or anything, but in Scotland, where all the women are tiny (smallest in Europe), and especially among older women, she seems supernaturally long. I was only half listening, so this is a paraphrase. "I think Lachlan has done incredibly well. I think he deserves a little peace and quiet now. The very least we can do is go and stay at a hotel."

I don't even think it was just to piss Mum off, either. I think she believed it.

"I don't need you to tell me what to do, you sneaky prig," Mum shouted, and I covered my face. Name-calling. Always death to rational argument. "I think I know what's best for my own son."

"I'm not telling you what to do," said long tall Trisha. "I'm telling you my opinion as to what we should do. I think we should leave him in peace and be supportive from a distance."

"From a distance?" Mum was really fired up now. Dad and I have both seen this scenario a hundred times. When Mum gets past a certain degree of annoyed, she starts crying and blaming and lashing out with accusations of all sorts until only physical exhaustion can calm her down again. I see the same pattern in myself sometimes. Knowing that an emotional tsunami was imminent, Dad stared anxiously at the table. Mum turned on me, wagging her finger. "If you don't get some sleep and sort out your marriage PDQ, young man, there'll be hell to pay, you mark my words." She was shouting and trembling and just about to blow when Trisha interrupted her.

"Any idiot can give advice," said Trisha calmly. "It's taking it that's hard."

It was such a sensible observation that we were all stunned into silence. Then Trisha picked up the newspaper and sauntered off.

Mum's head was twitching, side to side. She blinked hard, and her anger just sort of subsided as she sank down into her chair again. Dad, as surprised as I was, caught my eye and pressed his lips together. Margie came running in and climbed onto Mum's lap. I went next door and turned off the television, came back into the kitchen, and we all continued our breakfast as if I hadn't smashed two bits of crockery and shouted at a crowd of benignly inspired pensioners.

Ten minutes later we heard Trisha lugging a suitcase downstairs. I ran up to help her with it, whispering, "Thank you," under my breath. I was so pleased I felt like asking her back to visit again.

She patted me on the shoulder and looked over at Mum and said something like, "You'll sleep now that I'm unselfish enough to leave." Margie ran over and kissed her knees as she pulled her coat on. Mum and Dad stood in the living room like guilty children waiting to be told off, half watching her.

Trisha turned to address them, "Good-bye, Margery. I hope you have a safe journey home," she said, not only taking the high ground but building a small, sustainable, eco-friendly resort there. "Good-bye, Ian."

It would have been a splendidly dramatic exit if the taxi hadn't taken forty minutes to arrive. We had to call three times to find out where they were.

When she had gone, Mum said that since there was a spare room now, there was no need for them to leave, but Dad cleared his throat sharply, and she spontaneously changed her mind. He's so rarely insistent that it's compelling when he is. They phoned the airline and changed their return flights to the next day. At Dad's insistence, they booked into a bed-and-breakfast for the night. Mum went upstairs to pack and left me and Dad alone. I offered to come and get them the next day and take them to the airport, but he said no, they could manage perfectly well on their own and I should have a quiet evening and try to sleep. We were standing in the living room, facing each other, and he reached out to me, almost showing affection, but chickened out at the last minute and slap-patted my shoulder, muttering, "Well done." I appreciated it, I really did.

He offered to get me a prescription for some sleeping pills, but I said I'd rather do it naturally. He chuckled indulgently as if I were opting for primal-scream therapy instead of taking an aspirin. I'm always amazed at how prescription-happy that generation was. I suppose if they now admitted it's wrong, they'd have to own up to turning half their patients into drooling addicts.

I insisted that they allow me to drive them over to the bed-and-breakfast. I had to drop Margie off at nursery at the same time, so after an infinity of packing, dressing, and general organizing, we all bundled into the car. Margie started singing the noises-in-our-car song—*parp parp peep peep*—and I felt my heart swell in elation. I was going to be alone, actually alone, very, very soon. I joined in, singing the choruses, perhaps a little too joyfully. When I caught Mum's eye in the rearview mirror, she looked terribly hurt. I apologized.

She sniffed and looked out of the window. "In front of *her* . . ." she said, or something upsetting like that. I pretended not to hear.

My attention was elsewhere: Mum and Dad were leaving. I was going home to be alone for the first time in over a week, and I had arranged for Yeni to pick Margie up at lunchtime so that I could sleep. I was days ahead of myself. Margie ran in to nursery, kicking her little legs up behind herself, working her fisted hands at her sides, all her gestures expressive of her absolute determination to enjoy the day. She stopped inside the door, scanning the horizon for the jolliest children as I pulled her coat off, and then lolloped off across the room toward a ginger-haired boy. The mums were sweet to me. Gathering around, they said they'd seen me in the paper but not to worry. I know I looked nice in the paper because they were all either smiling at me or trying not to smile. One woman got flustered and pointedly ignored me. Harry's little blond mum was on the other side of the room, and then suddenly she was standing at my shoulder, slightly behind me, behaving like a politician's supplicant wife on the campaign trial.

I don't understand why she is selling herself so hard. She has perpetually untidy thin hair, which looks as if she has just got out of bed. Her eyes are small and green, the smallness being a positive benefit in one's midthirties, in the sense that small eyes age better than big eyes. The divorcée's tinge of bitterness and regret that infuses her conversation doesn't show on her face. Her lips are swollen and red, as if she's been eating all the red candies in the box and needs admonishing. Even the way she stands is profoundly sexy, with her butt sticking out, emphasizing her chest. She flirts with me, with glances and looks and the way she turns away and then back toward me. It flatters me so much I get quite flustered. Until today I comforted myself with the thought that she was probably a vacuous idiot, but now I know she isn't. I'm quite taken with her.

I only realized Harry's mum was there because the mum who was talking to me glanced behind my shoulder a couple of times, as though addressing my partner. She was standing so far back that I had to turn a full 180 degrees (away from everyone else) to see her. She was wearing a low-cut green sweater with a silver stick on a chain that sort of pointed down into her cleavage. Our eyes locked, and I nodded hello just as a hush descended over the room behind me. Even the babies were momentarily quiet. Everyone in the room stared at the kitchen door and sort of gasped under their collective breath.

I turned to see the young woman assistant standing in the middle of the room. She was so brown she could have been working on a sugar plantation in the Caribbean for a month. Her eyes were an eerie blue, her dark skin, her white-bleached hair making her look like a photographic negative. Aside from dramatically increasing her risk of developing a melanoma, she'll ruin her skin using a sunlamp that much, and she's only young. Aware of the effect she was having, she drew herself up. She actually seemed quite pleased with herself.

"Good God," I muttered. "She shouldn't do that."

"She can't help herself," whispered Harry's mum. "She's tanorexic."

It was so unexpected, I laughed out loud, even though it was obvious who we'd been talking about. I couldn't stop myself. It would have been even more rude to stare straight at the girl and laugh, so I turned my shoulders to Harry's mum. She laughed back and fingered her necklace.

I pointed at her. "Funny lady," I said, and blushed. I sounded like a horrible old creep, but she didn't seem offended. She smiled coyly and ran the tip of her index finger up and down the silver drop pendant on her necklace in a way that made me think fondly of my knob.

Back in the car, the atmosphere was thunderous. It had turned into a wet, gray day. Dad had booked a B&B somewhere in Paisley because it was quite near the airport but outside the two-mile rip-off radius. Unfortunately neither of us was familiar with that area. We couldn't find the right street and ended up stuck in a grubby one-way system of streets near the city center. The rain washed across the windshield, and we couldn't read the street signs. Big red sandstone terraces sat back from the pavement just far enough to make the house numbers unreadable. The streets were short and litter-lined. Mum barked from the backseat that no way on God's green earth was she staying the night here.

Every time I felt my blood pressure climb, I thought of Harry's mum's joke and smiled. I wish I'd said something debonair and charming back. I couldn't think of anything, so I imagined myself laughing comfortably and brushing my fingers down the back of her arm and sliding away across the room, leaving a trail of aftershave.

We finally found the place. I parked illegally and carried their suitcases upstairs as Dad signed in. It was a nice spacious room with a big window and tea-making facilities. As I was leaving, I weakened and invited them back over for dinner this evening. Mum breathed in to speak but Dad coughed and she said no. We left it on an uncomfortable note. Mum kissed me grudgingly, sighed tremulously (twice, in case I hadn't heard the first one). Dad gestured to me to get out of the room before she started a scene, so I did. She never used to be this self-indulgent. Dad feeds it in a way. I think he quite enjoys the drama of it since he's retired.

I shed all sense of worrying about them as I left Paisley and hit the motorway for Glasgow. I came straight home and took a long, hot bath in my house, leaving the bathroom door open. I got out and walked, gloriously, balls-swingingly naked to the bedroom, where I pulled on a pair of underpants and slid into a big cream-puff bed.

I slept like a barbiturate-sodden housewife, waking up at four o'clock this afternoon. The sun was already setting outside the window. Margie was standing at the end of my bed, drinking from a cup and staring at me. She grinned when she saw my eyes open. Blood red Kool-Aid spilled from the sides of her mouth (I've asked Yeni not to give her that stuff). As if she knew that peace had come to our house, Margie climbed up on the bed and lay down, spooning me. I wrapped my arms around her, crossing my hands on her chest, tucking my fingers into her damp little armpits, feeling her heartbeat on my thumbs.

In moments of perfect clarity, when I'm not tired or upset or worried, I know that Margie eclipses her mum and me, that her life and health matter more than the respect of my peers, the history of literature, my financial security. Everything I loved was there at once, every precious thing. She wriggled her tiny bum backward into my chest, bending forward and sticking her legs out. My darling, all-encompassing comma.

chapter twenty

THIS IS THE FIRST OF A SERIES OF ARTICLES ON GOW'S CASE BY Fergus Donagh. Later on the articles were published as a book, and he read them out himself on the radio; I remember it being on. His voice was very ponderous and slow, but it was an interesting series because he spoke to people who were central to the story but peripheral to the court case and tended to be ignored. He interviewed most of the victims' families, and Lara Orr as well. Susie has most of the articles. I don't think there's any point in my transcribing them all. They're pretty samey, more or less descriptions of the interviewees' poverty-ridden circumstances interspersed with heavy hints about how melancholy Donagh feels about the murders and how grim the world looks to his sensitive yet manly and unafraid Irish soul. His writing is a bit florid for my tastes.

Box 2 Document 6 *Article by Fergus Donagh, Guardian, 3/16/94*

Karen Dempsey is one of the least important people in the Andrew Gow story. Karen was raped and mutilated, her tongue was cut out, she was dowsed in bleach and left to die by a stinking river. It is a telling indictment that in a word search of the last four weeks, the five leading British newspapers have mentioned her name 17 times. Andrew Gow's name has been printed 203 times. Lara Orr Gow, Gow's wife, has been named 97 times.

Karen was twenty-one years old. Last week a box of evidence relating to her death was returned to the police, unopened by the courts. There will be no trial. Gow has pleaded guilty to the charges and has been convicted. He will be sentenced next week. The box held the clothes Karen was found dead in: the thin shirt, short skirt, and flimsy silver bomber jacket, ripped at the pocket. An officer on the case told me that the sole of her high heels was worn down on one side, the result of her lopsided walk. She had a hip operation when she was a baby, and the other girls nicknamed her Hop-along. She had done a lot of walking in those shoes.

Karen worked as a prostitute in Anderston. It is a derelict area by the waterfront with many dark doorways for illicit trysts. She was last seen approaching a man in a baseball cap at the corner. The streetlights are all overhead, and the CCTV did not capture his face. She should have been home that night. She had promised to baby-sit for a friend, but a sick child occasioned a cancellation. If the baby had been well, she would have stayed in. If she had stayed in, she would still be alive today.

Unusual for the area, Karen had no children herself. Friends have told reporters that Karen began prostituting herself to support her ailing mother, but it seems more likely that she did it to get money for drink and drugs. She was well known on the club scene but had stopped going out recently after a fight with a young woman. The police were called to the fight, but Karen and the other girl had left by the time they arrived. Had they arrested her, she might still be alive today.

Fate created a plethora of chances for Karen to escape Andrew Gow, but she didn't take them.

Approaching Karen's home on this cold winter morning, I found the next-door tenement block burned out, sheets of gray fiberboard nailed over the windows, and the open stairwell scarred with gang graffiti. It is an unsafe area in a bleak corner of the world.

Karen grew up and lived her short life in Lambhill. This, one of the roughest council estates in Britain, has a per capita rate of burglary and muggings three times the national average. Council houses bought in the eighties are now selling for a fraction of their original valuation. It's an all-too-familiar story, a tale of disempowered, marginalized families surviving in an economy determined to ignore them.

Veronica Dempsey, Karen's mother, opens the front door to her dark flat. She ushers me in, anxious that the neighbors don't see me. Shame enough, says Dempsey, to have had a daughter killed while on the game, but to be seen talking to journalists about her would be much worse.

Hers is a poor house, neither clean nor proud. The hall has no carpet, just bare hardboard streaked black with trips from room to room. In the spare kitchen, a whitish mist I mistake for net curtains turns out to be dirt on the windows.

Dempsey is a stocky woman, looking much older than her thirty-six years. Despite a heart condition, she chain-smokes Kensas Club. The fingers on her right hand are tobacco-stained. Karen was conceived when Veronica was only fourteen, but she is at pains to point out that she didn't give birth until she was fifteen. Her parents put her out of the house and the child's father moved away, but Veronica refused to give up her untimely daughter. She kept her child and did her best to bring the baby up decently. Veronica has never worked herself and knows few who have.

I'm the only one Dempsey has spoken to, she wants me to know that. She promises that she won't speak to the other papers. It is only at the end of our conversation that I realize Dempsey expects to get paid. She doesn't know that it is customary to negotiate payment in advance of giving an interview. I tell her I'm from a broadsheet and we don't tend to pay people for stories. She doesn't know what a broadsheet is, she says. All she knows is that Karen was all she had and now Karen is dead.

Veronica Dempsey is typical of the Riverside Ripper families.

Hopeless people at the bottom of the social scale striving to make sense of a brutality that is beyond them. Their families are poor and helpless, neither able to organize nor well-resourced enough to take on the powers that be.

Now that the trial is over and Gow has been convicted, an army of questions remains unanswered. How could Gow cruise the same small group of women in an area the size of Regent's Park, kill five, and only be caught because he confessed? Why was a multiphasic task force not set up until after the third death? Why did no one in the NCSOD claim jurisdiction over the series of crimes? Where is the companion who helped him with the first and third murders?

The DNA evidence was not foolproof: the semen samples from the bodies were badly compromised by the bleaching. Other than that, all the evidence the police had against Gow was the blood in his car and his lack of an alibi. Why didn't his defense argue that Gow, while admittedly a rapist and possibly the driver, was not the killer? It hardly feels like justice at all.

Alice Thompson's name has not even reached seventeen hits in the coverage. She has been mentioned only twelve times because her family refused to release a photograph to the press. Her two sons are thirteen and fourteen now. They came to the court with their father and sat next to him. Their father was drunk and shouted abuse at Lara Orr in the lobby of the court. He hadn't lived with Alice Thomson for six years. The boys hadn't seen her for three.

Elizabeth MacCorronah was a registered heroin addict. Her husband, also an addict, had been killed in a house fire two years before. Her three children were in care at the time of her murder. No one from her family came to the trial. Martine Pashtan's husband moved back to Birmingham, taking with him their son, now a year old. Mary-Ann Roberts was forty-one years old and the most experienced of the women. She left no one.

This series of articles is depressing, but I think they're meant to be. Excused as a cry for justice and a forum for pointing out the inadequacies in the police handling of the case, they're really designed to give the middle classes a frisson of terror at the missing social safety net. I heard Donagh argue on a radio-show debate that he wasn't cashing in by writing these articles. He was moved to pursue the case because none of the victims' families were able to demand answers or to comment on the quality of the police investigation. He got a big round of applause, and I think he was right. These victims won't be celebrated; they won't be remembered as anything other than a footnote in a true-crime book. Not for them the self-named foundations doing good or ardent family campaigns advocating a cosmetic reform to some small point of law. Grief-stricken campaigning families used to mystify me, but they make perfect sense now. If I could think of anything to campaign about, I'd love to set one up for Susie. I could pour my energies into it, meet new friends through it, work really hard at wrestling order from a chaotic universe.

Donagh makes you feel sorry for Veronica Dempsey, but still, there does come a point where you have to admit it: you need to be pretty thick not to know what a broadsheet is at thirty-six.

The description of Lara Orr in his last article is genuinely touching. The poor woman isn't very bright and doesn't know how to present herself. She seems not likable, exactly, but certainly very innocent.

Box 2 Document 7 ***Article by Fergus Donagh, Guardian, 3/23/95***

Lara Orr sips her cup of tea and looks out the steamed-up café window. The shadows under her eyes show the recent strain, and her roots need doing. It took twelve phone calls to arrange this meeting. Her friend Stevie Ray fields all phone calls and controls access to her husband. Stevie, she says, has been looking after both of them. He has given up his job at the minicab firm where he met Gow and is dedicating himself full-time to managing Gow's career as a serial killer and celebrity. Of the £1,000 he is charging me to interview Lara Orr, she will get £750 and Stevie Ray will get £250, twenty-five percent of the final deal. Lara isn't worldly enough to know that Stevie's cut is far too high and Stevie isn't smart enough to make it a proviso that I don't mention the money in this article. It's a case of the blind managing the blind.

Lara was born on the south side, the middle daughter in a family of five girls. Her mother was a telephone operator and her father a park keeper. They were not happy times. As she grew up, her ambition was to move out of the family home. She got her wish at sixteen. She was sent to live with an aunt in Liverpool while she studied hairdressing. It was in Liverpool that she met Andrew Gow. It was an August night in the Taboo nightclub; Lara was with some girls from her hairdressing school; Gow was alone. They got to chatting because they were both Glaswegian and one month later Lara and Andrew were engaged. After Laura had a fallout with her aunt, Andrew brought her home and they stayed with his family, sleeping on the floor of his young sister's house until the council allocated them a flat of their own. They were married in the spring of 1991, two years before the first riverside murder.

"I didn't know he was a monster," says Lara, looking out the window. "He was always gentle with me. He was kind to me."

I ask her about the story she sold to the *Mirror*, about Gow dressing her up as a prostitute for rough sex games. Lara looks sick, curls a tress of bleached hair around her finger, and says she was afraid of him. This means that Gow was simultaneously gentle and kind and frightening. It's hard to know which is true. Both sentiments seem quite genuine.

She's divorcing him, she says, at some point in the future, perhaps when the financial value of being his wife is mitigated by the passage of time. She is alone now. Having fallen out with her family and her husband, she's sorry to say that Gow will be keeping Stevie Ray as his manager, so she will have to cope with being his ex-wife alone. I suggest that she might get a better agent.

"There is no one better," she says. "Stevie knows how to do it all."

Donagh never got to interview Stevie Ray and went on about it later in the radio series. Ray kept charging him money and then not turning up. Donagh titled the series after him, something about Stevie Ray—"Good-bye, Stevie Ray" or "Tell Stevie Ray Hello" or something like that.

It occurs to me that Stevie Ray might be interesting to talk to. He was in contact with Gow and Donna right up until the end. Susie has a photo up on the wall here, taken on the steps of the court on the day of Gow's appeal. It was on the front page of the tabloids. Stevie is holding Gow's hand up in the air like a triumphant boxer, and they are both grinning maniacally. Gow has those white children's sunglasses on. He seemed to wear them all the time. Donna was camera shy suddenly and is lurking in the background. Stevie Ray might even know something about the phone call from Durness.

I didn't get to know Stevie during Susie's trial, but I don't think I'm being presumptuous in saying that he understood what I was going through; after all, he'd watched someone he was close to go on trial for horrible crimes. We spoke only once: we were waiting to get back into the court after lunch and he was crying. As I remember the incident now, it doesn't seem at all strange or alarming to me that he was crying, so it must have been around the time that the prosecution brought evidence about the extent of Gow's injuries. Stevie Ray was standing next to me, crying silently. I remember little silver trails of snot on the backs of his hands catching the light in the dark corridor. I said, "Sorry, pal," and handed him a disposable tissue out of a packet.

He took it between two fingers, nodded sadly, and, without looking up, said, "Sure, sure," and moved away. I'm sure he'd talk to me.

I don't know why I keep coming up here to write this rubbish down. I find myself tramping up here night after night, my eyes smarting and wanting to sleep, and still I pass the door to the bedroom and come up here. I've always wanted to write, but not all this rubbish about feelings; I want to write clever things about the death of empire, about big theories and themes that will win me the respect of Martin Amis and get me into Soho House. Writing this stuff down has become a sick compulsion, and the only reason I can find for it is that, like a petulant child, I want to have my say. I'm presenting a defense to an absent audience and I haven't even done anything wrong.

It's the diarist's dilemma: if no one's ever going to see it, there's no real reason to bother writing it, spell-checking it, or taking time over the grammar and phrasing. Why not just think thoughts? If there is a secret desire to be read, does that make what I'm writing any less honest? Who are these literary pyrotechnics meant for? If I knew for sure that no one would ever see these pages, I think I would write differently. I'm going to try to be completely honest, bare.

Still, without knowing what my motive is, the function all of this writing serves is clear: while I'm writing down every small thing, I don't need to participate fully in my life, which, at the moment, is pretty shitty.

I've just found this. I was opening the lowest drawer on the desk and it got stuck. I tugged and tugged and heard the rustle of something falling from the underside of the drawer into the well underneath. I had to take all of the drawers out to get my hand in there. It had been stuck to the bottom with a big lump of Blu-Tack.

It's handwritten, but it's definitely by Donna; the grammar's all wrong and there are no commas.

Box? (not sure which to file this under yet) **Document 1**

DURNESS HOTEL

Keoldale

PROP: MR. W. PASCALE

Susie—
he is taking me to the broken little cottage above
Loch Inshore. Im scared of him.
Come please please come please
Donna

My first thought was that I should go to Fitzgerald's house with it and wait for him to get up in the morning. Finally, this is something we can use for an appeal. But then I stopped: Susie had this letter all along and never gave it to Fitzgerald herself. Why? I can understand that she might have been confident she'd get off—I was confident she'd get off—but she could have told him about it since. She could have told *me* about it since. If she was worried that she'd get into trouble for withholding it, she could have told me and I'd have claimed I'd hidden it or something. I'd do six months in prison for contempt if it meant she'd get out. I would. I'd do that for her.

This letter might be what she and Fitzgerald spent all the phonecard money during the first week talking about.

I know I should take some sort of urgent action, but I don't know what to do for the best. What if she's been telling the truth all along?

chapter twenty-one

Stevie Ray, 14 Hamilton Drive, Priesthill 876 2454: 10:30 a.m. Greggs the Baker's.

INTRIGUED BY MY FIND, I GOT INTO THE CAR LAST NIGHT AND drove out to Kirkintilloch. I wanted to take a look at the house Donna lived in while she stayed in Glasgow. It has been pictured in the papers often enough, but I wanted to look for myself. I can't stop thinking about Susie since I found the note.

Donna's old house is off a fairly busy road, but you'd have to be looking to find it. She rented it when she first moved up here from Leicester and Gow lived here with her for a week when he was released, before they took off up north.

The night sky was cold and clear when I went out there; the moon lit the countryside as brightly as a forty-watt bulb. The house is on a patch of flat land outside the town, and a mile away, straight across fields and grass, the massive Campsie Fells rise suddenly like a mammoth back wall to the valley. The one thing you really notice is how remote the house is from anywhere. I wouldn't have expected a twenty-three-year-old to want that sort of isolated place.

It's squat, like our house, but only one story high, with two attic rooms. It's whitewashed and peeling, with small, deep, inset windows. It seemed empty. Overgrown bushes in the front garden make the house look ramshackle, and big bushy weeds have sprung up on the drive. A few dead bunches of flowers were perched against the front door, presumably left there by locals to commemorate Donna, or perhaps even Gow. I peered into the dark windows and saw dull, brown furniture, an armchair, a small sideboard, a table and chairs, but no personal effects. The windows felt cold, so there was no heating on a timer coming on to cozy the house for the residents' return. There were no signs of life at all.

I stood, trying to imagine Donna pulling up alone in her little Golf Polo, taking the keys from the real estate agent, excitedly unpacking her luggage from the trunk. I imagined her living there, shopping, coming back dreamy-eyed from visits to Sunnyfields, returning alone to a cold house after her prison wedding. Next to the house, across a small pathway to the garden at the back, sat a crumbling garage with wooden doors. I had been sure the house was uninhabited, but as I walked down the lane at the side, I heard an intermittent high-pitched whirr. I froze. It was coming from inside the garage. I listened for a while, approaching the doors, before I realized it was a deep freezer coming on and off. Someone probably was living there. Guilty and ashamed, I tiptoed back to the main road and my own car.

As I drove home, I tried to imagine the Cape Wrath scene again with the letter in it. Susie gets a phone call early in the day, Donna asks for help, and she sets off up north (leave out the lie to me about nipping to the shops because that just distracts my attention). Susie drives for about eight hours, morning to early evening, stopping to fill up the tank, seeming happy when she does. She drives through rain and sunshine, through high winds and deep valleys, and gets to the Kyle of Durness and the hotel, where Mrs. Pascal gives her the letter. Donna asks her to come to the bothy. She sounds helpless in the letter (I know it by heart now)—*he is taking me*—and desperate—*please please come.* Without phoning anyone for help (which I don't understand), Susie goes to Donna, not covering her tracks, not hiding; she goes alone in the ferry across the kyle at dusk, unafraid. Three hours later she is back across the kyle (the tide was out and she walked across the sands; her driving shoes were covered in sand). She is standing in the hotel bar, again not hiding, drinking to stem the shakes, unaware that Officer McCallum has already received the call and found Gow with his hands bound, his tongue pulled out and cut off at the root, left to drown in his own blood. He must have known he was going to die from the moment they tied him up. He must have lain on his side and felt the blood pulse from his mouth, warm and wet under his cheek. He must have looked at someone's shoes and known he was dying. When I imagine his fate in detail, it doesn't seem to matter that he did such awful things to other people. Officer McCallum had time for a good hurl out the back before calling his pals and telling them to go and pick Susie up from the hotel bar.

Only a local knew where the phone box was, they said, and Fitzgerald didn't challenge it. I've been looking at it on the map, and the phone box is on the B-road into Durness; you'd know it was there, unless you'd been helicoptered in.

Finding the hotel letter has spurred me on: I'm determined to be more focused about this whole thing. I'm going to sort this out, even if Susie hasn't the brains or will to survive. I'm going to search this room methodically. I'm working counterclockwise around the walls, starting from the door.

My first find is a paper bag tucked under the leg of the bookcase, behind an envelope of credit-card bills. The open end of the bag had been folded over so that the things inside were held snugly. It's a small white bag, like the bag a birthday card might be put in when you get it from the shop. I'll put it into Box 2, which is getting quite full.

Box 2 Document 8 ***Contents of Paper Bag***

There is a carefully cut out "news in brief" paragraph about Donna and Gow's wedding and three photographs, all the same size, all of the wedding. I know that Susie took them herself. The prints have the matt finish and white borders that she always asks for at Snipper Snaps, and I can tell that she was using our camera because she never zooms in properly.

She didn't tell me she was at Donna and Gow's wedding, a fact that haunts me now.

According to the press cutting, the wedding took place on a Tuesday in April this year. I've been trying to work out what we would have been doing, what happened on Tuesday nights at that time. Nothing. I looked up the television listings for that time in an old Sunday supplement Susie had up here. Nothing special at all. None of the dramas during the week seemed familiar, none of the soap story lines rang a bell, and then I realized why: Margie was teething and wasn't sleeping for longer than five hours at a time. Susie was working, so I'd taken over nights. I was spaced out, just coping from one screaming fit to the next. It was after Saskia left and before Yeni arrived.

Susie would come home from work, drop her bag by the chair in the hall, take off her coat, and hang it up in the closet. She'd kick off her shoes and come into the sitting room. I'd ask her how her day was. Fine, yeah, okay. No, nothing much really. If Margie was awake, Susie'd put the telly on for the news. It wasn't really for the news, I knew that, it was for an excuse not to talk to anyone for an hour or so, but that was okay, I understood.

Margie and I lived in the sitting room in those days. I kept all of her toys in the big storage box on the parquet floor under the window. It was a mild winter, just a week or so of really cold, head-down weather. I remember buds on the branches outside the sitting room in the first week of January. I remember birds' nests in the bare trees, like tangles in fine hair, gradually being covered by foliage. It was

Margie's first-ever spring. The view from those windows was my world in those days. I used to do the ironing with the telly on and feed Margie in the kitchen by the door, where the laminate flooring is. I was proud of how efficient I was with her. I've never felt closer to anyone. We'd sit next to each other on the settee when the lunchtime news came on and I'd say, "What do you think about that, Margie-Pargie?" And she'd look up at me and smile. It was just because I was talking to her, I know that, but her smile made my heart swell and synapses zing. She was mine. I loved her and each unrecapturable moment. She was mine alone. The minute she went to nursery it all changed. She has her own social life now, and our relationship has never been quite the same, it can't be. Yeni arrived soon after.

PHOTO ONE

The first photograph is informal and cut in far too close. Donna is getting ready for the wedding, checking her makeup in the reflection on a brass plaque commemorating Princess Anne doing something at the prison in 1976. It's a good photo actually, technically very competent. Donna's putting lipstick on, using the brass as a mirror, looking down at her lips as she does it. Her eyelashes are long and hide her eyes. Her hair is pulled up at the back, and the willowy hairs at the nape of her neck are visible. Her neck is incredibly white; a small black mole nestles off-center between the two ligaments. The skin on her neck is soft, powder-soft, and fringed by the smallest hairs, like Margie's baby hair. When I think of Margie's newborn head, I can almost feel my fingertips running over it, the duckling softness of it. It was so soft I never knew for sure that I was touching anything at all until I looked at my hand.

I sat looking at the photo for a while, and then I realized that it's a very telling picture. The reflection is so clear you can see red dots on the soft skin under her eyebrows where she's overplucked them. You can see where her makeup stops on her neck and how thick her mascara is. She worked hard at it, Donna. I can't imagine what Susie would have made of her, this brassy doll, permed and over-made-up. She never talked about her to me.

Donna doesn't seem aware that she is being photographed, but she would be able to see Susie's reflection on the brass plaque. It's as if she knows Susie's watching, aware of eyes on her, but acting casual. It seems so knowing, this movie-star calm: she's saying you can look at me but I won't acknowledge you, I won't react. Mind you, with a cleavage like that and the low-cut tops she wore, she must have been aware of eyes moving over her all the time. She'd have to be oblivious to dress like that.

The photo's so close in on her that if you didn't know about Susie's trouble with the zoom, it might seem creepily intimate. It's hard not to interpret the picture as Susie sneaking up on Donna to batter her to death.

PHOTO TWO

The second picture is Donna and Gow together. He is wearing a crumpled gray suit with big shoulder pads, curling lapel-tips, a white shirt, and dirty sneakers. I recognize it from the old pictures of him being bundled into the prison vans: it's the suit he wore for his trial. Donna is wearing a white jacket and matching skirt, red court shoes, and two red roses in her jet black hair. She has nothing on under the jacket, and nearly two inches of cleavage is on display. She doesn't look saggy or tired, not like an old tart or anything, just busty.

They're standing against a wall, in front of a blue poster with a big white question mark. Gow is looking at the camera, his head tipped backward slightly because he's grinning so widely. His big banana hand is wrapped around her slim upper arm, pressing hard, gathering the white material. It looks as if he might have said something rude. Donna is looking down at her feet. She looks nervous and out of her depth, and it makes you worry for her, it really does.

The picture is very badly lit, which is typical of Susie's photography. White light spills in from the side, from another camera flash.

PHOTO THREE

This must be the official photograph, a copy of the one she had stuck to the skylight and Blu-Tacked over. He is holding her tiny hand in his big hand, and he is smiling but she isn't. She's looking at her hand and seems alarmed. She said in interviews at the time that she wasn't afraid he'd hurt her, that she knew he'd never hurt her. But she didn't think he'd ever get out.

Now that I have remembered last spring, I can hardly bring myself to leave it. Winter gave a death kick and we had a few random days of snow, but apart from that the weather was mild; the season was over before it had begun. I remember clouds of pink cherry blossoms blowing into the garden from next door, fleshy leaves carried on the water-clean smell of springtime. We had Margie, the renovations were done, and Susie had settled back into her job.

And then the murders started again.

chapter twenty-two

STEVIE RAY IS A BAD MAN, A SELFISH MAN WHO MAKES MONEY BY cashing in on the misery of others, but after meeting him it's hard to believe he actually means any harm to anyone. He is small and balding in a messy way, not a straightforward receding hairline. He has a brown hairy button on his forehead and thin wisps all over the top. He's short and fat as well and ties his raincoat belt in a knot at his swollen waist, which makes it look worse. He's simultaneously repellent and sympathetic. It's like he's got his charisma on backward.

I'd dropped Margie off at nursery, more of which later, and was sitting in Greggs waiting for him. I was about ten minutes early, so I ordered a fudge doughnut and a cup of tea (the coffee's terrible there). I was peeling the frosting off the cake when I heard a commotion at the door. Stevie Ray was a-coming. He'd got tangled up in a pram at the door and was trying to apologize, bow obsequiously, and extricate himself all at the same time. He almost tipped the child out, and the mother became so angry she started hitting him with a full Co-op bag. Things like that must happen everywhere he goes, because he didn't even mention it when he sat down opposite me. He just flattened a hand over his bald head as if he still had hair.

"*Foof,*" he said. "It's windy."

He ordered tea and a prawn and mayonnaise roll and chattered away about stuff, how bad everything was for him and how much he needed a break. If I hadn't told him beforehand that I would only buy him lunch and pay his bus fare, I'd have thought he was working up to asking to borrow money from me.

"I owe everyone," he said, shaking his head slowly. "I owe the car company, credit cards, the bank is after me, and I've got nothing coming in now, because of your missus." He looked up at me.

"I'm not going to pay you, Stevie," I said. "I know for a fact that my wife is innocent, and anyway, I haven't got any money."

He relaxed a bit. I think it was almost a relief to him not to have to try to chisel me. "You broke, too?" he asked.

"Lawyers don't come cheap," I said, thinking of our one and a half mil carefully tucked away. "So go easy on the tea."

After five minutes with Stevie I felt focused and go-getterish. It's as though he can't do status games and comes ready-capitulated. I bet that's why Gow wanted him to manage his affairs, so he could see him often and patronize him. But then, the thing to remember with Stevie Ray is that with no skills *whatever,* he made a nice living off the back of Gow. He's not a stupid man, and that's something to bear in mind. He filled in every conversational pause with a story about how much he'd lost to the car company, how much work he needed done on his house, how everyone thought he was rich. He was being so unchallenging it actually made me feel suspicious. The roll arrived and he took a massive bite and tried to talk about his troubles through milky lumps of bread.

I interrupted him and told him I wanted to talk about my wife. That shut him up.

I took out the notebook I'd written the questions in. I knew I'd crap out if I didn't have them written down, knew I'd end up asking how he was and finally if he needed any money. I asked the first question and wrote down notes of what he was saying to busy myself, so I didn't have to look at him while he answered.

Yes, he said, Gow did talk about Susie. He said she was a lovely lady and had been very helpful in getting Donna in to see him. She had okayed their first visit and was kind to Donna. He paused, finishing off his sandwich, and when I looked up, he was watching my face and all but asked me if he was doing it right. He was saying what he thought I wanted to hear.

"Look, Stevie," I said, "I want you to tell me the truth. I don't want you to dress it up."

Stevie smiled uncomfortably and chewed a hangnail, staring at the table.

"I know Gow didn't talk like that," I said.

"Can I have an éclair?"

"As long as you stop lying to me."

He ordered an éclair. The prawn and mayonnaise roll was the most expensive one on the menu, and the éclair was eighty pence. I think he'd checked it out beforehand to make sure he got good value.

Yeah, Gow did talk about Susie. Stevie glanced at my notebook, looked away, sipped his tea, and then smiled as if he was going to be sick. Gow wasn't nice about women generally. He said things, pretty bad things, actually. Stevie didn't agree with them, oh no, he doesn't think about women that way, but, well, ye know how men are together. His cake arrived and he took a bite.

I laughed and jollied him along. We don't mean it, I said. Stevie jumped on that, agreeing through a mouthful of pastry; no, nothing means anything, it's just guys talking, like, you know how guys are. This gave me reason to surmise that Gow had said sexual things about Susie, definitely, but Stevie wasn't about to tell me what they were. I wrote "JUST GUY STUFF" in the notebook so he could read it upside down.

He took another bite of his éclair and frowned at the page, taking about a minute to read the three complex words. Some of the cream had squished out of the side of the cake and got stuck to his chin. In the ensuing conversation it began to look more and more like a big lump of dried cum.

I saw him mouth the words "just guy stuff" and relax. "Gow said he fancied her, ye know, thought she was good-looking. A nice person and such."

"Look, Stevie, you can tell me what he said, I won't be offended." He looked unsure, so I added, "Susan and I have been living separate lives for a few years now." He still looked confused, so I spelled it out for him. I said I'd been seeing other people and Susie was free to do the same.

Stevie nodded nervously and took another bite. He kept his mouth open as his molars ground the pastry and cream and chocolate together, his tongue pushing the pale lumpy shit forward in his mouth in a rolling bovine rhythm. "Whose idea was that?" he asked.

"It was hers," I said, acting resentful, making it okay for him to start in on her.

"And whose is the kiddie, then?" I almost leaped across the table. I was prepared to lie to him and make myself a passive, cheated-on husband, but I'd die rather than denounce Margie.

"Mine," I said firmly, "she's mine."

Anyway, the fib worked. Gow talked about Susie a lot. He thought she had lovely tits. Stevie looked up at me and waited for me to punch him. When I didn't hit him or seem annoyed, he carried on, increasingly astonished by my passivity. Gow'd wanted to fuck her when he first came into the hospital. He thought she was an uppity cow who needed bringing down a peg or two. Gow liked quiet women. Susie wasn't his usual type, but he did like to tame women. He wanted to make them beg for it and then give it to them. He talked about them begging a lot. Stevie snickered when he reported this, as if he had experience of this scenario, as if any woman had ever begged Stevie to do anything but fuck off. He leaned across the table, lowering his voice. The cream/cum was still stuck to his chin and made him look like a porno gimp. Gow told him about this one time when he met a woman in a bar and she looked like a model but with great tits, right? She took him into the ladies' room. "I use the term loosely," he said smugly, obviously repeating a line of Gow's.

I couldn't stand him to be confident for a second longer, so I interrupted him to ask whether he was indicating a future intention to use the term "loosely" or whether he was using the term "ladies" in a reckless and all-inclusive manner?

He didn't understand and got flustered, so I repeated myself in a different way. The last one, he meant the last one. Anyway, this twat took him into the toilet in a pub and lifted her skirt and she had on stockings, garter belt, split crotch, *the lot*. Stevie went on about all the stuff she did and how she loved it and rubbed her tits on the dirty mirror, etc., etc. It was a jazz-mag story, obviously made up by Gow, either because he was an unimaginative fantasist or to take the piss out of Stevie Ray. Stevie believed it anyway. He went pink telling me about it; I'm sure he had a semi, it took him ages to sit back.

I said I'd heard that a lot of women wrote to Gow in prison.

Stevie nodded. "Yeah," he said, licking his fingertips lasciviously. "Lot of women sent in nude pics of themselves. A lot of them were done in, baggy tits and faces like buckets, but Andy used to say this about them: he'd say, 'It's just a hole, isn't it?'"

It's just a hole. I didn't know what to say. I nodded in shock and offered to get him another éclair. He said no but he'd take a strawberry tart instead. He ate it with gusto, getting jam on the corner of his lips. I couldn't stop looking at the wreckage of his mouth and chin and thinking menses/cum, cum/menses.

I asked about Susie again, and he paused.

"I'll tell you what *he* told *me*. Right?"

I nodded.

"This isn't me saying this, he told me this, right?"

I knew it had to be pretty bad, but when I heard what he had to say, I wanted to laugh. It got more and more difficult not to laugh as the conversation wore on. I knew then that she had never touched him, that she might have been in love with him, but my wife, my darling Susie, never ever had sex with Andrew Gow.

Gow told Stevie that Susie sucked him off in the office once. It was when she first came to Sunnyfields, back in '94. She walked right around the desk and did it. I managed to keep a straight face. Stevie was watching me carefully. I nodded and he carried on with the description. I wanted him to go on and say something else, more balm for my bitter heart. And he did as well.

It was rubbish, a series of schoolboy lies about a woman Gow'd never even touched, and I knew it. Gow saying that Susie had sucked him off once was probably intended to make it believable, but if she'd done it once, he'd have said she did it six times. And she'd *never* do it in the office. She might have sucked off a stranger, maybe even a dangerous stranger, but she wouldn't have done it in her office in '94. She was far too ambitious. Then Stevie handed me the big prize.

He said that Susie'd taken it up the arse for Gow because she didn't want to get pregnant. She knew about these things, being a doctor. I almost clapped my hands with glee. Susie wouldn't have worried about getting pregnant because she would have used a condom, she wasn't into anal, and she'd *never* have anal sex with a man who was arrested cruising a red-light district. The HIV risk factors in that scenario are worse than throwing yourself into the stick bin at a needle exchange. Stevie was in full flow now. It was as if he was so pleased I hadn't punched him that he couldn't stop himself. I sat back and let him pad the story out, where they did it and how often, once in this closet, once in that room. Susie asked Gow to take off her "panties," another jazz-mag term. I actually got bored listening to him. I got some money out and held up the bill for the waitress, and the reader's-letter recitation tailed off.

"Is that all you want to know, then?" he asked.

I said yeah, thanks for coming, hope you enjoyed the pastries. He did, he did, did I have my car with me? He wanted a lift. I said yeah, but I was in a hurry, sorry. Did he see a lot of Gow and Donna after he got out? Well, he said, they went up north a week after his release. Stevie brought Chinese food over to Donna's house in Kirki the night before they left. Whose idea was it to go up north? Donna's, he said. She really wanted to go. Gow couldn't stay in Glasgow really, too many guys wanting a piece of him. Couldn't even go out to a pub for a drink, but it was Donna's dream to live up there. She'd booked the hotel, and they were going to go and look for a house and jobs in Sutherland. I said it wasn't a very good plan. There was no work in Sutherland, and the seasonal waitressing jobs would all be gone in September, but Stevie just shrugged. Did Donna know anyone there? No. Had she been there before? No, but she'd seen pictures.

I said I wanted to ask him one more thing: Where was Lara Orr, and how could I get hold of her? He wiped his face as if he'd just realized he was covered in food.

"I've not seen her for ages," he said. "No one has. She's probably gone back to Liverpool."

Never mind, I said, and, once we were outside, thanks for coming to see me. Stevie flattened his hand over his bald head again, looked as if he was about to ask for money, but stopped. He nodded to himself and walked away, pulling his collar up, even though it wasn't windy anymore and it wasn't raining.

I felt great as I drove back to nursery. Susie hadn't slept with Gow. She might have been madly in love with him, the twisted little prick may even have been the love of her life, but they didn't have sex in prison, I was certain of it. And she'd been sacked before his appeal and was at home the whole time after he got out, so it didn't happen then.

I'm going to visit Susie in a few days and I'm actually quite excited. I'm going to ask about the hotel letter and about Gow. I hope she appreciates the trouble I'm going to. I've spent hours up here working on this.

But I was going to write about nursery. I had taken Margie there this morning with a light heart and slight tingle in my loins. I wondered if Harry's mum would be there, and, sure enough, she was wearing a gravitationally impossible low-cut top. I think it was actually a low back and she'd put it on the wrong way around by mistake. She must have gotten dressed in the dark. It is dark until about eight-thirty, give or take, and she has got three boys to get dressed and fed. The straps of her white bra were showing, and she kept having to yank the top down, showing the tops of the cups.

She didn't come over but gave me the eye, which I liked because she'd been so full on before, and not coming over suggested a little reticence. I went over and said something inoffensive like, "Hi, how are you today?" She laughed loudly, covering her mouth and pulling her top down at the hem.

What was she laughing at? Was she laughing at me? She seemed quite nervous, so I tried to diffuse the situation by saying, "Calm down," and she laughed again and said she didn't know what I meant. I just backed away and left, waving good-bye to Margie on the way out. She was rubbing the blackboard with a dolly's legs and ignored me.

I felt ridiculous when I got outside. What was the woman laughing about? Have I managed, in among all my other failures, to be bad at flirting, too? Maybe she was just nervous? She seems desperate. There's something of the bunny-boiler about her: a slight craziness around the eyes.

If Susie doesn't get out or for some other reason our marriage splits up, I'll be back on the dating scene. I don't know if I could stand all that guessing what people mean and getting knocked back and putting your emotional equilibrium in the hands of another person. In marriage at least there's an understanding that you can't just get dumped out of hand, that they definitely did like you once. It might have been long, long ago in a galaxy far away, but they definitely found you attractive and interesting at some point in the interaction.

I'm sure not all women are like Harry's mum; it must just be some of them. But what if all the ones who aren't like that are still married and only the ones like Harry's mum are back out on the range? What a depressing thought. I think I'd rather stay single than try to negotiate all that crap again. I don't want an intense face-to-face relationship. I want someone I can take for granted; someone I can not reply to when they call me from the other room. The older I get, the less often I meet new people that I can stand the sight of.

Anyway, after my encounter with Stevie Ray and his jazz-mag visage, I drove back to nursery to get Margie. One of the babies had been sick, and the heat was turned up high, so the whole room stank to high heaven of hot sour milk. Harry's mum was there again, hanging about near the toy cupboard, wearing a different T-shirt. She came toward me through the sour fog. As she approached, I could see her getting angry, and she said, "Don't look at me like that." I explained that I was wrinkling my nose at the milk smell, not at her, but she stayed annoyed and demanded to know how I was. I said I was fine, sorry, sorry. How was she? How were the boys getting along? Yes, nursery *was* super for them. She paused and whispered she'd like to call me, she had my number from the birthday party list. I said that would be nice, please do, and she tugged at the hem of her top, pulling it down and in.

She's gorgeous.

chapter twenty-three

YESTERDAY I FINISHED WRITING UP STEVIE RAY AT ELEVEN-THIRTY and went downstairs to watch telly. Feeling pretty smug, I remembered the video in Box 2. Yeni and Margie were in bed. I decided to watch it.

I sat on the settee, watching the TV with one eye, remote ready to hand in case I needed to turn it off quickly. The index showed that there were three items on it: a bit of home video followed by a one-hour documentary shown on Channel Four in February and then another portion of home video buried deep at the end of the tape, hidden beyond seventeen minutes of white noise and snow. If we didn't have the indexing facility on the tape player, you'd never watch to the end. The dates on the index show that the documentary was aired on television a good month before the last bit of home video. I wasn't sure which of them was relevant at first, but actually they're all relevant and tie into the research she'd started with Harvey Tucker.

Box 2 Document 9 ***Videotape***

PROGRAM 1: HOME MOVIE 1 3/1/98 3:18 P.M.

As it started, the image of a gray little office was tugged down the screen in jagged horizontal lines. Finally it resolved itself and, off-screen, Harvey Tucker says, "Brilliant."

I made extensive notes as I watched.

The room looks small and ugly. There is a shelf of books on the far wall above a metal desk. I can't actually read the titles, but I recognize the spines of some of the books and can see Susie's sports bag under the desk. This is her office, but I've never seen inside because she works in a secure institution. It is small and gray and low. Susie taped interviews with some of her patients, I remember. She brought the prison's camcorder home to film Margie's first Christmas. On one of the bookshelves, up high near the top of the wall, a tiny bright glint catches my eye. It is her wedding ring. The design we got was quite chunky, and she takes it off to work, just like I do when I'm typing things up here. That's how she lost it. She told security she went to put it back on again after typing a report and found it gone.

In the center of the static shot is a black plastic armchair with a low seat and wooden arms. Donna is sitting in it, looking nervously to the right of the camera, banging her knees together, a little I-want-to-please-you smile on her heavily made-up face. Her hair is thick, pulled loosely up in a ponytail at the crown.

In front of Donna's feet, on the floor, there is a long bright rectangle of sunlight. It is coming from a window behind the camera. The shadow from the window is so crisp that the four vertical bars can clearly be seen and I can make out the sharp shadow of someone's head and torso. (I assume it is Tucker but later realize it is Susie.)

It's painful to look at Donna, knowing she's lying dead somewhere, her voluptuous little body decomposing, waiting to be found. She seems so young and plump and ripe. She is dressed in a button-up black polka-dot dress with a scoop neck and a pair of clunky white court shoes. You don't really get a sense of her personality in static photos, but she is fidgety and shyer than she seemed in interviews. She covers her mouth when she smiles, which is often, and pulls her dark hair over her face. At one stage I can see her pull the edge of her hair toward her mouth as if she's going to start chewing it like a small girl. Then she remembers that she mustn't do that and tucks it away. Her skin is very pink.

"Hi, Donna," says Susie, and I can hear that she's smiling.

Donna grins back at her. "Hiya." She lifts her hand in a little wave, feels embarrassed about the gesture, and then covers her mouth and giggles as though she has done something wrong.

"Now," says Susie, "if at any point you feel uncomfortable with this, we want you to say so, okay?"

Donna nods.

Tucker emphasizes the point. "Yes. Any time you want us to stop filming, we will."

"'Kay."

She smiles at him, and I can hear in his voice that he is smiling back as he adds, "All you have to do is say so."

Tucker is not delineated in the shadow on the floor, and it makes his voice seem disembodied and God-like, coming from nowhere. Donna never really looks at him, either, so I have no real sense of where he is sitting in the room other than behind the camera somewhere. Donna looks at Susie all the time.

"Are you going to ask me personal things?" She has a lisp, and her accent is all over England. One minute she's from London, the next she's from Newcastle. I thought she was from Leicester.

"No," says Susie in a soothing voice, "nothing terribly private."

"Good. Good. I don't want to talk about my Andrew, either." She shivers with excitement. "I can't wait to meet him."

"I want to ask you about your attraction to Andrew and what made you write to him in the first place. Then I want to ask you about your feelings. Will that be all right?"

Donna shrugs and pulls her hair over her face. "S'pose." Her line of sight falls slightly, and I can tell from the moving shadow on the floor that Susie has just sat down. Only the shadow of her head is still visible.

"Okey-dokey," says Susie jovially, and Donna smiles again. "When did you first hear about Andrew Gow?"

"I saw him in the papers."

"You saw his photograph?"

"Yeah, the one where he's got the green jacket on. The one with the beard." (I realize suddenly that this is how Susie knew which photo Donna had seen of Gow; this is why she wrote "Donna's first view of G" on it and told the guy in *GLT* about it. I feel I'm really making sense of things, as if I'm finally breaking the back of the materials in this study.)

"And you liked that picture, did you?"

Donna rubs her leg and glances guiltily at the camera. "Yeah. I thought he looked kind."

Susie pauses. "You see, not everyone would take that out of that photograph. To a lot of people he might look a bit scary."

Donna smiles a little. "Not to me."

"Do you think he wanted to look kind in the photograph?"

Donna thinks about it. "Hmm. No, probably not, really."

"How do you think he wanted to look?"

She thinks about it, but I can tell she's a bit bored and doesn't really care. "Handsome?"

Susie makes a noncommittal noise and moves on. "What was happening in your own life at the time when you saw the photograph?"

"Oh." Donna flattens the skirt down over her knees and bows her head. "My divorce was just through, and then my dad died." She laughs unhappily.

"And how did that make you feel?"

"Dunno. Bit sad? Dad was a bastard and hit us from when I was a bairn . . . so . . . it wasn't all bad, and the divorce was good."

Tucker interjects. "But you looked after your father? You and your husband lived with him?"

Donna points her chin in Tucker's direction but keeps her eyes down. "Yeah. Then I put him out and stayed on myself."

"You must have felt some affection for your father, then?"

"Yeah, dunno." She turns back to Susie, clearly her preferred interviewer. "Where did you get those shoes?"

Susie is thrown. "Oh," she says. "Um . . . Shoe Nation, I think."

Donna grins and nods. "They're very nice." She sits forward, leaning out of frame. "I like that color of brown. Have you polished them up or . . . ?"

"No, they're patent leather. They're always that shiny."

Donna sat back, filling in the screen again. She looks at Susie and there is a pause.

Susie has spotted the fact that Donna shifted the subject from her father and moves on. "Where do you see your relationship with Andrew going?"

It would be a loaded question for a woman who was in love with Gow, but Susie's voice is steady and my heart leaps. I rewind and watch that bit over and over again until the nuances of her voice are completely lost to me. Truthful, not fucking him, and possibly not even loving him. This has been a great couple of days.

Donna shrugs, and Susie rephrases the question. "Have you thought how difficult it would be if you spent your lifetime visiting this prison? You might have to move up here."

"I've already moved here." I can see their surprised reactions reflected in her face: she smiles and nods. "Yeah," she says, almost surprised herself, "I'm renting a house in Lenzie."

(This is a real estate agent's lie. The house is in Kirkintilloch, not in Lenzie at all. Lenzie is nearby and twice as posh.)

Susie's voice is incredulous. "But you haven't even met him yet. Why did you do that?"

"Because I love him," Donna says. "I know in my heart that Andrew is an innocent man."

"Didn't you have friends or family back in Leicester?"

"Nope." She doesn't sound sad about it.

"Did you have a job?"

"Yeah."

"Where?"

Donna looks at her lap. "I worked in a health club, at the reception desk."

"Do you have a job up here now?" asks Tucker.

"Not yet, but I'll get one."

"Don't you think you'll miss your old job?" he says. "Don't you think you'll be lonely?"

"I don't feel alone when I'm near Andrew." She looks at Susie defiantly. "I may not be alone for very long, anyway."

"Hm," says Susie. "Do you think Andrew'll get out?"

"I don't care if he's in here for the rest of his life. I'll stand by him."

"Have you discussed the rapes and murders with him?"

Donna flinches. I think it's the use of the word "rapes" that offends her more than murders. "Not *those things* specifically, no. But he has told me that he was set up."

"And do you believe him?"

"Of course I do. I trust him."

"You trust him to tell you the truth?"

"Yes."

"Are you aware that other women write to him and he writes back?"

Donna flinches again but carries it off with aplomb. "Yes," she says. "Yes, I know that."

"Are you aware that other women visit him?"

"Yes, that's only to be expected. I hope that'll change after we meet."

"Will you be disappointed if it doesn't?"

"Aye, I will. Of course I will. I love him."

Susie pauses and I can hear the noise of paper turning. "Doesn't it seem very unfair," she says, "for him to be locked up in here for years? Doesn't it make you think he might be guilty?"

Donna is wide-eyed. "It is unfair," she says. "But life's unfair."

"Would you strive to make Andrew's life fair?"

She sits back and nods. "Oh, yeah."

"Do you participate in politics, then? Are you involved in any other campaigns?"

"No." Donna curls her lip. "You can only make life fair for you and yours, not for other people. There's no point, is there? Fighting for people you don't even know. People you don't know are bastards and deserve all they get."

There's a smirk in Susie's voice. "But Andrew isn't bad?"

"Not to me, no. I know him now, you see."

Susie shuffles some papers. It feels as if she's looking for the next question. "I think that's about it, Donna."

"Have I done all right?"

"You've done very well."

"Will I be allowed to meet him, then?"

"I'm pretty sure you will. Everything seems fine."

Susie had the final say in whether Donna gets in or not, but she doesn't let on. A lesser woman would have hinted at it and put Donna in her debt. "You seemed a bit nervous when you came in earlier, I wondered what you were afraid of." The shadow on the floor is shifting again and Susie is standing up. "I hope it wasn't us?"

Donna smiles flirtatiously. "Why, are you going to spank me?" For a millisecond an inadvertent smile bubbles up across her face. She catches herself, glances at the camera, looks at the ground, and by the time she looks back at Susie, the thought is suppressed.

I rewind a couple of times to check my impression, but I'm right. Donna said it, and realized she'd made a mistake as soon as it was out. Could it be some sort of S&M thing? Maybe she was into Gow's being a sadist and is pretending to be a naive idiot so she could meet him? She does seem genuine, I have to say, but there is something odd, definitely very, very odd about her.

PROGRAM 2: DOCUMENTARY

The documentary is about people writing letters to Peter Sutcliffe in prison. Having watched it, I can see why Susie kept it. The women, and they are all women, have written to him on a number of pretexts, each one more flimsy than the last.

One woman was going through a bad time herself, so she went to his trial to cheer herself up and fell in love with him. There are at least two grotesquely mismatched junctions in that sentence. Sutcliffe wrote back, and the letters got more frequent, with more and more exclamation marks and love declarations, just like Donna and Gow. Sutcliffe wrote poems for her as well. She did sketches of him sitting in a garden or at the seaside. I suppose it's the complement of wasting time on each other, really. Eventually she discovered she wasn't the only woman writing to him and got disillusioned. She felt that he deceived her. She'd given up access to her children for him. What is most startling is her complete unwillingness to take responsibility for her own behavior. She keeps saying he tricked her into trusting him. The man was in a state mental hospital for the criminally insane, a fact which might have served as something of a red flag to more self-protective women.

Next was a happily married woman, all wax jacket, Labradors, and warbling voice, who had seen him in court. She'd done a drawing of him from memory and wanted to visit him to see how accurate it was. She was, without a doubt, the most self-deluding. She couldn't even admit that her interest in him had a prurient element. Her husband drove her to the hospital once a month for visits and sat outside in the car.

The third woman was very worrying. She was a little old lady who was certain she had served Sutcliffe and another man in a café during the Yorkshire Ripper murders. The other man, Sutcliffe's friend, had a Sutherland accent that perfectly matched the voice on the bogus tapes sent to the police, the tapes that claimed responsibility and misdirected the investigation for months. Sutcliffe was released to kill again because he had the wrong accent. The old lady wanted Sutcliffe to confess and admit that he had an accomplice. A retired police officer was interviewed and said that it was plausible for two men to have been responsible for the murders. Her husband sat in the background, in a shadow against a wall, like Boo Radley. His face was blank, and he never spoke or moved until she looked at him. She showed off a lot of photographs of them with Sutcliffe. They were hugging him in one, then handing over Easter cards and Christmas presents. She showed off a collection of letters from Sutcliffe that they kept in plastic folders. The woman seemed to have forgotten all about truth and the mystery man by the time she got near to him. She said over and over that he was like a son to her but eventually got annoyed when Sutcliffe wouldn't admit to having an accomplice and stopped going to see him. She said he had made her trust him and then betrayed her. Exactly how was never made clear.

They had an expert on, and she said that women who form relationships with killers are all lying to themselves and are likely to be motivated by thrill-seeking and, often, a sense of loss. This ties in neatly with all the stuff in the prison-lovers book. I should start reading it again.

PROGRAM 3: HOME MOVIE 2 6/12/98 4:37 P.M.

The camera blanks and starts again. This is another interview, two weeks before Susie got sacked. Susie and Donna are alone this time. The light from the window is sharp on the floor, the shadow from the bars is crisp but shorter, more square-shaped, which means the sun is higher, so it's a few months nearer midsummer than the first interview. It's warm in the room too; lazy dust flecks are suspended in the treacly air. Donna is sitting in the chair, wearing a red dress with a scalloped frill around the hem and the V neck. She has the same white shoes on as before, has a matching white handbag leaning against her leg, and is smoking a cigarette. From Susie's shadow on the floor, I can see that she is smoking, too. The shadow-Susie lifts her hand to her face and exhales on oily gray cloud. I remember when I really smoked. I remember when I smoked as I walked home, smoked through colds, smoked in hot, airless rooms in the summer and made myself sick.

The tone between Donna and Susie has changed since the last interview. Donna is no longer acting like an insipid transsexual. She has her legs crossed and is sitting back, quite comfortable. Here's the strange thing about it: Donna seems to be completely in control. She is not disempowered and desperate to be looked after by a strong man as the book says she should be. She has an ashtray balanced on the arm of the chair and tap-tap-taps the ash, watching it and smirking, taking longer over the tapping than she needs to, as though she is avoiding looking up.

"Donna, where are you from?"

Susie sounds very annoyed with her. Donna stops tapping, glancing into the camera. "All over the place." She has lost her lisp. She covers her mouth with her left hand, looking knowingly at Susie over her fingers. Is she showing off that brand-new wedding ring? I look up and I can see Susie's wedding ring high up on the bookshelf. Behind the hand Donna smiles broadly.

"How do you feel about these murders, Donna?"

Donna shrugs. "Dunno. It's a shame."

"Did the police come and see you? Did they come and tell you about them?"

Donna nods and taps her fag. "Aye, they came to ask me where I was when they happened. Me. Can ye imagine?"

Susie takes a puff on her cigarette. The shadow of her exhalation creeps swiftly across the floor toward Donna's feet; the edge of an urgent white cloud enters the shot from the right and disperses in the oily air. "This last girl, Gina Wilson, she was a catering student."

"I know," says Donna, tapping quickly. "I heard about it."

"She was nineteen and liked line dancing. She lived with her parents."

"I already know that," says Donna, nodding and tapping, tapping and nodding. "I said I heard about it."

"You heard about 'her,' Donna. Not 'it,' 'her.' Did you know she was Catholic? She went to Lourdes every year—"

Donna leans forward in the chair, eyes open, voice raised. "I HEARD ABOUT IT." She seems to regret her outburst immediately. She throws herself back in the chair, tapping and grinding her jaw. "It's hard for me too, you know. I have feelings too."

"Two young girls are murdered and you have feelings too?"

"My husband has been wrongly imprisoned for five years, and it's only just coming out now. I'm bound to have some feelings about it."

Susie sighs and a long, thin stream of clear air punctures the swirling shadow of smoke on the floor. "Do you think he'll get out, Donna?"

Donna glances at her. "What do you mean?"

"Do you think that Andrew, your husband, will be released?"

Donna shakes her head slowly, still keeping her eyes down. "No."

"How would you feel if he did?"

Donna looks up and a deep, unspoken fear pinches at the corners of her mouth, taints her eyes. "That would be great," she says unconvincingly.

"Oh, for fucksake, Donna," snaps Susie, "stop pissing about."

It's so unprofessional, so out of character, that I freeze the tape and rewind to see the buildup. It seems to have come out of nothing. Susie is angry, and she isn't hiding it. "Do you think you'd be safe with him?"

"Who'd care?"

"Donna, you have to learn to take care of yourself. You're twenty-three. It's time to grow up."

Donna knows she has won a small victory. She looks at Susie and raises her eyebrows twice, like Groucho Marx, and then she glances at the camera, remembering it is there. She lowers her eyes.

"Where are you from, Donna?"

"We've been through this."

"Where did you start out?"

"Leicester."

"You don't sound as if you're from Leicester."

Donna looks up, coquettish and innocent. "Is that wrong of me?"

"What area of Leicester?"

"Highfields," she says. "The Highfields area."

"Is that near the middle or on the outskirts?"

It's obviously a test, to see if she even knows where it is. Donna meets it full on. "Near the middle. Why are you annoyed at me, Suse?"

Suse? Excuse me, *Suse? Suse*'s shadow can clearly be seen on the floor. She stands up and stubs her cigarette out in an ashtray. Messy tendrils of shadow spill across the floor like ink in water. She takes one step over to the camera tripod and switches it off.

Afterward I wished I hadn't watched the video. It's spoiled my optimistic feeling. Now I feel I have a lot of uncomfortable questions to ask Susie when I see her, only this time I really don't know what they are.

chapter twenty-four

LOOKING OVER ALL OF THE MATERIALS, I'M STRUCK BY HOW MUCH has happened since Donna first wrote to Gow in February. Donna wasn't bright, but some people are catalysts, and dramatic events follow them wherever they go. Like Morris, whose wife has put him out now—Nurse Julie wasn't bluffing. Donna was only twenty-three when she first wrote to Gow. She had been divorced and orphaned and was already starting a new life in a strange country. I hadn't even graduated when I was twenty-three. Donna and Gow married within two months of the first letter; the new Ripper murders started a month after Donna's first letter; and then Susie got sacked in June for stealing his files. The campaign for Gow's release had gathered momentum with a number of celebrity endorsements; he was out of prison by September, and he and Donna were both dead by the end of the month. Donna didn't even live to see her twenty-fourth birthday.

Box 2 Document 10 *News in Brief,* Glasgow Herald, *3/6/98*

In a disturbing replay of the Glaswegian Riverside Ripper murders of the early nineties, the body of a young woman was found next to the River Clyde yesterday. The woman, whom police have not yet named, was found dead under the city's Kingston bridge. A team working on the renovations to the bridge arrived for work yesterday morning to find the woman's body under a tarpaulin. The police had no comment to make as to a connection with the river murders but would say that the woman was not a prostitute and that there were significant differences between this and the 1993 cases.

Andrew Gow, the man convicted of the Riverside Ripper murders, recently hit the headlines when he remarried in Sunnyfields State Mental Hospital. He has maintained his innocence since shortly after his conviction. His new wife, Ms. Donna McGovern, was unavailable for comment yesterday.

I remember these new cases unfolding in the press and on television. I remember us watching the news reports about it. It seems strange, given how significant those events were to become in our lives, but I only really remember two specific conversations about it all.

One exchange was in the front room. It was spring and the room was bright, the window was wide open and outside the garden was very green and lush. I was ironing, and Margie was in the kitchen with Yeni. The television was on for the news, and Susie was slumped on the settee. We'd had an argument about her smoking in the house. Within a few short months Susie's position on domestic smoking had shifted from regarding it as a form of child abuse to arguing that it was justified if Margie was out of the room or looking away. We had fought about it, and afterward, when we reached a stalemate, the argument hung between us like a bad smell.

Have you noticed, I said, trying to be cheery, how they're using more attractive photographs of Gow on the telly as the campaign for his release gathers momentum?

She asked me straight out, "Do you think he's attractive?"

I laughed and asked her whether she was serious.

"Yeah, I'm serious." She pulled herself upright and looked at me with a face like an angry little fist. "Do you think he's attractive?"

I put the iron down. I didn't think he was attractive, but in the old mug shot they used to use on TV, he was scowling, looked very malnourished, and had black bags under his eyes. (He was working nights, she said. Driving the cab. That's why he looked so tired.) But in the new photos, taken more recently, he was smiling and seemed healthy.

Susie nodded into her lap and stood up, announced that she was going outside for a smoke, and left me alone to finish her blouses. At the time, I didn't think Gow's case was particularly relevant to us. Susie worked at Sunnyfields and knew him, of course, but everyone was talking about the campaign. It was big news.

I only remember one other specific conversation. We were out for dinner with Evelyn and Morris. I remember it because afterward Susie said she didn't want to go out with them again, that she didn't like getting that drunk anymore. It shocked me because I didn't think you could drop friends you'd made at university. I hadn't stopped to think what they were like—they were just Morris and Evelyn. But Susie was right: they are a bit seedy. They always remind me of how old we're getting and how undignified and ugly being pissed in a restaurant is. That night Evelyn needled Morris incessantly, making digs about money or something. They're not nice company, but the blessing is they both like a drink, so you can get pissed and not listen. I have to admit that they used to make me feel smug because at that time we were happier together than they were, and Susie hadn't let herself go and get massively fat like Evelyn did after the kids.

We were all extra pissed because we went to a new restaurant and there was something wrong with the food so they gave us a couple of bottles of free wine. Morris kept asking Susie about Gow and the murders, and Susie insisted that she couldn't talk about it because of her professional interest. Morris thought her unwillingness to gossip was ridiculous, and they had a heated argument about confidentiality. Morris said that it was just a principle, not a law, and wasn't meant to be applied absolutely. Susie said it actually was a law and she'd bloody hate to be one of Morris's patients. He was quite annoyed by that, which is unusual for him, and he insisted that his patients didn't deserve the level of care he gave them. They were assholes. Anyway, if she was half the psychiatrist she made out she was, she'd have spotted that the guy was innocent before the real murderer started up again.

Susie leaned across the table. "He is the real murderer."

"How d'you know?" said Evelyn. "Really—how d'you know?"

"For God's sake," said Susan quietly. "There was DNA evidence that he did it."

"Nah," said Morris, wagging a smug finger. "The bleach spoiled the sample."

"Morris, you're supposed to be a scientist," said Susie. "Bleach can kill cells stone dead, but it can't reconfigure the structure of DNA strands." (She said something like that. It was actually a neater summation of the scientific impossibility in six words or less.)

"Bullshit!" shouted Morris, who really was very drunk. "He's an innocent man. We should let the guy out so's he can bang his new missus."

But Susie was leaning over her plate. "He is a killer." A vein stood out on her temple, and I knew she was absolutely furious. None of us, myself included, knew whether she was really certain of his guilt or indignant about the slur on her professional reputation.

Morris, never a man to sit back from a fight with a woman, topped up her glass. "Oh, yeah? Why would someone kill this new lot then?"

"Well, obviously someone wants him out," said Susie.

Morris snorted. "That's ridiculous."

"So," said Evelyn, filling her wineglass. "Do you think it's—what's her name—Maria?"

"Donna. Her name's Donna, and no, it's not her."

"'Cause that would be quite romantic," slurred Evelyn. "In a sick way."

"He cuts their tongues out," Susie said flatly. "He rapes them and cuts their tongues out and douses their wounds in bleach and leaves them to bleed to death. Is that romantic?"

It would have been the start of a big scene if we'd been sober, but, too liberally lubricated, the conversation jolted onto another track.

Although those are the only two conversations I remember in detail, when I look back over the whole spread of things Susie said at the time, I know she was sure of two things: that Gow'd committed the original murders, and whoever was killing the new lot of women wanted him out of prison. She was probably right, because the murders stopped as soon as Gow was released.

I hunted about in the boxes and found this Fergus Donagh article from the same time. This article isn't as good as the previous series of articles. The *Guardian* prints photos of their featured writers, little disembodied heads next to their articles, and Donagh has ballooned since the '94 series. He has that bug-eyed look of a drunk whose liver is about to explode. Come to think of it, I never see his byline anymore.

Box 2 Document 11 ***Article by Fergus Donagh, "The Revival of the Riverside Ripper,"*** **Guardian 4/29/98**

It is cold as I stand by the river. A damp wind picks up and blows my hair around. My ears are numb. The gawkers are gathered beyond the police tape, breathing in the rank smell of bleach, hoping for a glimpse of the raised platform where the girl's mutilated body was found. We are standing under the Kingston bridge, a motorway overpass built in the seventies . . .

Well, that's wrong, for a start.

and already crumbling. The workmen were adding support to the two giant pillars on either side of the river. On the one hundredth day of the job, they came to work and found the murdered body of a teenage girl immolated on the raised platform.

The talk in the crowd is of the '93 murders, secondhand tales of women who narrowly escaped Gow's hand, of the people who knew him, were at school with him, danced with him, sold him his daily newspaper. They swear it couldn't have been him. Everyone has always known he was innocent. Even the people who brayed at his wife outside the court knew that he was innocent. We should let him go.

The police are certain it's a copycat killing. The official line is that Gow is guilty and this is a one-off by someone who has read a lot about it. But Glasgow is a tight-knit community, and gossip spreads quickly. Aspects of the original crimes have been reproduced perfectly. There are rumors of a DNA match with the original sample.

QC Alistair Swindon has strong feelings about the way the original investigation was conducted. Gow was a habitual confessor, although admittedly for very minor crimes. Swindon argues that apart from his confession, the sole piece of evidence to link him to the crimes was the presence of blood matching the victims in the back of his cab. He had no history of violence, and the DNA sample used was too degraded to give a reliable match.

Swindon has been arguing for an appeal for several years, and as one of Scotland's most prominent human rights advocates, his voice carries a lot of weight. "Convictions based on confessions alone are rarely watertight, and this holds particularly true for high-profile cases when the police are under pressure to get a conviction."

A blond man, Swindon has been a member of the Commission . . .

"A blond man"? This is rubbish. Donagh is jumping about all over the place. The germ of the article is that the conviction was a bit dubious and some people thought Gow should get an appeal. Donagh managed to drag it out for two pages with a supplementary column on page thirteen.

The article is accompanied by a moody twilight photograph of the underside of the Kingston bridge looking from the north to the south bank. The bridge's giant supporting strut is in the foreground, echoed on the far bank by the other leg, and a concrete ribbon is strung between the two. On the south bank the red and yellow neon lights of the entertainment complex cut through the gray evening. Susie and I used to go to the movies there. We liked it because it had a huge parking lot right outside the cinema doors and a Häagen-Dazs store. The last time we went there together was very subdued. Susie had just been sacked, and I bought her a big ice cream as a surprise while she was away at the toilet. She acted pleased, but she didn't want it. She nibbled at it until the lights went down and then sat the cup under her chair. I only know because she knocked it over on the way out, splashing gooey pink melt on her shoes. I don't even remember what film we saw, although I do remember coming home across the Kingston bridge, driving through the dark into the high glittering heart of the city and wondering if the area below the bridge was still cordoned off. They'd found the second body by then. Poor Gina Wilson. No one will ever forget her name.

I miss Susie now. Since seeing Stevie Ray I've been thinking about her fondly again and wishing she was here with me, in our bed, making tea, padding around upstairs and coming down to watch the news. The hotel letter probably means more to me than it would to an appeals court. Maybe she's already told Fitzgerald about it and he said it didn't matter, leave it, forget it.

I'm going to see her the day after next, and it feels like a date. I haven't been eating as much in the past couple of days and feel quite slim. I'm going to go and get my hair cut tomorrow, short at the sides. I might even buy something new to wear.

chapter twenty-five

IT'S FOUR-FORTY-FIVE AND IT'S ALREADY DARK OUTSIDE.

Last night I got a phone call from an unnamed newspaper, wanting to know about Dr. Susie and my swinging marriage. I hadn't a clue what they were talking about. They told me that Stevie Ray, true to bastard form, had sold the story of our sex-mad marriage to the paper and they wanted my comments. Could I tell them the name of the woman I've been having an affair with for several years? I told them to fuck off and hung up, which was probably the worst thing I could have done, but I wasn't thinking straight. I immediately realized that I should have been nicer and said Stevie Ray got the wrong end of the stick. I tried to call the journalist back but I didn't have his name or even the name of the paper. I dialed the last-caller ID code, but it said that the caller had withheld the number, a message that usually means they've come through a switchboard. I couldn't very well phone all the newspapers and ask which one was about to expose me.

I lay in bed wide awake, imagining Susie seeing the newspaper in prison and crying; imagining Margie as a grown-up coming across a copy of the paper and throwing it aside in disgust. First thing this morning I phoned Fitzgerald, livid, and asked about suing. He sighed, sounding uninterested, and said was there a grain of truth in it? I said no, there wasn't. It was a complete fabrication and they'd misunderstood something I said to someone. He sounded quite skeptical and hemmed and hawed and said, well, if you said it in any context they can publish it. To be honest, the smart thing to do is let it go. I should only sue if I wanted to (a) bankrupt myself and (b) have the allegations reprinted again and again in the papers for the next three years.

I mentioned the Durness phone-box thing and said I'd been thinking about getting a file together for the appeal about the press coverage and he said no, the papers have lawyers working for them and have to screen the articles before they're published. So forget it. I didn't want to mention the Donna letter in case Susie has already talked to him about it. I don't want him thinking she doesn't tell me things.

Changing the subject with hope-crushing swiftness, Fitzgerald told me that the reports are all in and Susie's sentencing hearing has been moved forward to five days' time.

Susie will see the newspaper article. I know she will. Some bastard will show it to her and she'll phone here, angry and wanting an explanation. It could cloud her appeal. It'll certainly cloud the coverage of her appeal. What the hell can I say to her? That I'm tramping around making us vulnerable to people like Stevie Ray because I didn't believe her? Although, subsequent to digging about in her private papers, I think she's probably not a complete and utter liar. If the article isn't in the papers tomorrow morning before I go to visit, I could try to explain preemptively. I could set the ground.

I shook all the way through my haircut. Afterward I went for a run. I ran for about six miles, until my knee hurt, long after my lungs began to smart. I was trying to tire myself out, aiming for ten consecutive minutes when I'm not absolutely furious. I bought some of those marzipan bars to bribe myself through the morning. I've eaten three of them already and I feel sick. I've had to hide the others from myself in the fridge.

This from an overlooked C-drive file titled *C:/misc/evington.doc.* I wouldn't have bothered with it because I thought you could only keep documents in the "My Documents" file, but I'd left the mouse pointer resting on it while I had a sip of tea and a blue box popped up on the screen that said

> Author: Dr. Susie Harriot
>
> Title: She called from Durness and I had to go. It's over. Sh

I opened the file and here it is, cut and pasted in its entirety:

She called from Durness and I had to go. It's over. She shouldn't have called me. There are loads of people she could have called who were nearer. She should have called the police, or I should have called them, because who the hell am I to think I can make anything all right for anyone? I thought it was my big chance and I could talk to Andrew. I know he respected me and would be surprised and pleased to see me. She said he was in a highly volatile state and had hit her several times. I knew he would need help, that it would be a shock being released just like that after five years without any training for freedom or help or support.

He was in the kitchen, reading the paper while fat Yeni dressed Margie upstairs. She irritates the pulsating living fucking shit out of me. She's so sweet and helpless and pointless and silent and stinks of dairy products and she's as fat as an elephant as well and eats all the time when she thinks I'm not looking. He looked up at me with his big stupid face and asked me where I was going, huneee. I got really angry and just said to the shops. He said well give us a kiss then, huneee. I couldn't explain how long I'd be away, I didn't know and there was too much to tell.

I was happy on the drive up. It was the last time I remember being happy, and in a way it was the first time as well because I felt free and didn't have anyone to be responsible to or fix or look after or make things all right for. I went across the bay in the boat on my own. That was the big mistake: going after them on my own, because at the time I thought I'd be able to talk to him, calm him, and get them off the hill.

He was on his side when I got there. He was facing away from me and I thought he was a stone or a rag. I saw a shoulder, then shook it, and he turned his face up to me and opened his mouth and gurgled.

I couldn't breathe and pushed him away and ran and ran and ran down the steep steep hill and over the wet in the sandy bay and into the hotel. The whiskey made me breathe in because I think I would have died if I hadn't taken a breath, and then I just stood there. I stood there drinking with two hands, shaking. I didn't know what to do because I couldn't phone the police or Lachlan or home and my mum and dad were dead and I kept seeing him in my mind. The whites of his eyes and all the black of his mouth.

They haven't found her yet. I can't believe she's dead. I'm having bad bad dreams, and I need to talk to someone about this, but Fitzgerald says not to until after the trial. If I have to give evidence, he wants me to cry when I talk about it.

I'm stuck in this fucking house until the trial comes up, and he's driving me nuts. I'd like to sack Yeni, but I'm afraid to leave him alone with Margie because he's feckless and won't be able to manage.

chapter twenty-six

IT'S LATER AND I'VE HAD A DRINK. SHE DIDN'T WANT ME TO FIND that document. That's the kindest thing I can say, that she tried to keep me from reading it. I'd like to talk to her tonight, point out that I'm so fucking feckless I've spent three and a half weeks searching a four-foot-by-four-foot room until I found it. Me and my big stupid face came up here day after day, night after night, until we found it. Susie didn't kill Gow, but it doesn't matter as much as it used to. She thought she could save her career by saving Donna.

I was in the kitchen, furious and agitated and drinking a scotch, when Yeni came in and grinned sweetly at Margie. She's not a secret eater. She does nothing but eat in front of me. I stormed across the kitchen and gave her one of the marzipan bars out of the fridge, secure in the knowledge that I had another two hidden in the frosted butter shelf. Yeni almost clapped her hands and her little button eyes lit up. Margie picked up on the excitement at the table, laughing and bouncing in her high chair. It was like Christmas or something. Yeni said the marzipan was good to her and thank you and she liked. Her English has definitely gotten better recently. Thinking about Margie's response has made me realize that I've been completely self-involved and maudlin for the past month. I must try to pretend I'm happy sometimes, if only for Margie's sake.

Anyway, Yeni said let's watch *Friends* and eat our marzipan, and we trotted through to the front room like a little family and put it on. I didn't know that they have reruns on at teatime now as well as Thursday nights and Sunday nights and Friday nights. Yeni shared her bar with me, and we three all sat on the sofa, watching and munching and smiling at the jokes. Every now and then Yeni broke off a little taste and fed it to an insistent Margie, who spat it out down her front. She's so good with her. I'll give her fantastic references when she goes. She might not want my name on her CV though, if she stays in Britain.

Yeni put Margie to bed and I went up to say good night. Margie didn't want a story, she wanted to hear her singing tape with the lullabies on it, so I put it on the chunky plastic tape recorder and I sat on the floor next to her crib, thinking about her future. She can't even talk properly yet and she's already got so much to overcome. It's a shame that she's an only child of two only children. Aunts or uncles or siblings could have shared the experience with her, protected her, diluted the shame. Maybe we should think about moving eventually, leave Britain and go abroad, change our names and cover our tracks. Margie struggled valiantly to stay awake, staggering around the crib like a punch-drunk boxer. She sighed as she fell asleep, and I was frightened for her because she's so small.

I don't want to go to the Vale of Leven ever again.

chapter twenty-seven

It'll be fine. I've written bitchy things about Susie before, and she did go to a lot of effort to try to keep me from seeing it. I was surprised by my nice hair when I spotted myself in the bathroom mirror this morning. I had my blue T-shirt on and realized that my belly has gone down a bit. Or maybe it hasn't. I look thinner in that T-shirt anyway, so I decided to wear it to the visit. I ran across the road to the newsagents, well, hobbled really, because I'm so stiff from my reckless, stretchless run yesterday. I'm not on the cover of any of the papers. The Evington file and everything, it doesn't change anything, although I feel far less worried about explaining the newspaper article to her now. Susie knows how slippery these newspaper people can be, she'll know I've been stitched up. She'll be glad to see Margie anyway.

I started off for the prison early with Susie's dry-cleaned court suit hanging off the jacket peg and Margie strapped into the car seat in the back. She nodded off within the first ten minutes of the drive and slept for most of it. The traffic was light, and I listened to a gratifying radio program about a dead writer whose genius wasn't recognized during his lifetime. The troll women weren't there when we arrived, just a man and a fat old woman with a child of about three. They were waiting outside the door, and sleepy Margie perked up when she saw the other girl.

We were all let in and gave our names, I handed over my phone, and the children played together while we waited to be let into the first waiting room. The other girl was dressed poorly and had her ears pierced, but she was an absolute gem. Her language was miles better than any other child of her age I've met. She actually said, "May I see your pretty socks?" to Margie at one point. Margie tried to bite her. She played beautifully with Margie and the rubber Tigger toy I'd brought with us. She was patient and understanding and smiled up at both of us when Margie screamed and tried to knock over a chair. The fat woman with her was too old to be her mum; I guessed she was her granny and they were there to visit her mum.

"What a beautifully behaved child she is," I said.

"She can be a right handful sometimes, but . . ." said the granny indulgently.

The prison guards are nearly all women. They're not as beefy as you'd expect, but they're nippy and unfriendly. It's like the Surly Lady Army. They're what I remember girls being like in early puberty: powerful and unwilling and terrifying.

They held us for too long in the first room. I could see them through the glass wall, talking to each other and looking through at us. The granny was getting agitated. She thought something had happened to the girl's mum; perhaps she'd killed herself or something. She got a bit tearful after we'd been kept waiting for ten minutes and tried to hide it from the child.

"Can't they tell us why we're waiting?" she said nervously.

Taking charge, I went to the door and rattled it, motioning to the guard at the reception desk to unlock it so I could come out and speak to her, but she shook her head and looked away from us, muttering to the other guard under her breath. I shook the door again, but she refused to look at me. The granny was weeping openly by this time, and I tried to comfort her by saying the delay might be nothing to do with her daughter.

"Ye dinna understand," she said. "She's tried it before." She snatched the child away from playing happily with Margie and hugged her tight.

Margie started to cry, and the three-year-old child tried to comfort both Margie and her gran at once, patting her Granny's back and making cheerful swoopy noises to Margie. She must have siblings at home, I thought. I told the granny to stop crying right now, and to my surprise she did. She put the child down to play, but the girl, who was unnaturally calm for a child of her age, kept hold of her granny's knee and used her free hand to play with Margie. I don't care if Margie does grow up to be a spoiled, selfish little princess. I never want her to have to do that for either of us. I want to attend to her every whim and keep her ignorant of that impotent need to save other people.

Eventually a different guard opened the door and asked me to wait for a moment while they took the granny through. She was sniveling in panic now, and the terrified child clung to her leg. The old lady disappeared out into the corridor, and they shut the door again. Margie, not knowing what it is to anticipate the next minute fearfully, ran the length of the room a couple of times and started making high-pitched noises. I was grinning at her, asking her what that meant exactly, hmm, Margie-Pargie? Whatever can you mean, you meaty little pudding?

A guard opened the door and invited me into the corridor, so I scooped Margie up and we followed her down to the second waiting room, which was already empty. I set Margie down. "I hope that lady's daughter is all right?" I said, imagining the granny sobbing her poor old broken heart out in a soundproof room next door.

The guard looked me up and down. "She's fine." And then she walked away behind the screen and through a small side door.

They left me waiting there for twenty-one minutes. I knocked on the side door several times, thinking bloody visiting would be over if they didn't let me in soon. When the guard finally came back, I was really annoyed and said that I shouldn't be penalized and miss my visiting time because another visit had gone wrong. The guard didn't know what I was talking about.

"The old lady who was in here," I explained, "she was very upset because we were held back." The guard shook her head and left again just as it dawned on me. The old woman was already in visiting her daughter. I was the one they'd held back.

It must have taken four minutes before two male guards came in, but I was doing deep breathing to slow my heart rate down and wondering how to get through the next ten minutes without punching someone.

"We'd like to search you please, sir," said the fat one.

I exhaled, bristling with relief because I realized that they wouldn't be worried about my passing contraband to Susie if she was dead. Impatiently, I dropped my coat to the chair and stood like a starfish, no-no-no-ing while he asked me if I had any drugs about my person, any sharp objects or needles. He patted me down while his friend looked on and got me to kick my shoes off so he could feel under my feet. Then he flicked a finger, giving me permission to put my stuff back on, and turned to the outside door. I followed him with my heel still working its way back into the shoe, holding Margie by the waist.

The grass strip was wet, and I felt eyes watching me from the little slit windows opposite. A woman shouted something I couldn't make out, and Margie shrieked a funny little piercing cry like a bird of prey. My coat was flapping open, one shoulder not pulled on properly, and I was walking unevenly, still stamping my right foot into the shoe. All I wanted was to get in there and see her, see she was all right and not dead.

When they opened the door from the inside, the first thing my eyes fell on was the old woman and the girl, sitting with a young woman, barely an adult herself, who was holding the child and beaming, pressing her cheek to the child's. The girl had her eyes shut, savoring the love. The old woman looked up at me pityingly as Margie clambered down and ran across the room to her mummy.

Susie was sitting in the corner, head back, propped between two walls. A very long cigarette was burning in her limp hand, and she had a red nose and swollen eyes. She didn't even put her cigarette down to pick up Margie, she just held her hands open and let Margie climb across her lap to the seat next to her.

In spite of what I read last night, I was pleased to see her too and scurried across the room in my half-on shoe, falling into the seat next to her. "Susie, Christ, are you okay?"

Her face crumpled and she sobbed against my chest, holding her cigarette up and away from me like an overwrought drunk at a party. I wrapped my arms around her and indulgently imagined that we were at home on the settee, she'd just been sacked and I was comforting her, and everything was fine, fine. We'd get the chance to spend time together now. We could take a new nanny and travel. Go to the Sahara and watch the sunrise over the High Atlas Mountains. I patted her shoulder and kissed her head.

It took Susie seven minutes to cry herself to a standstill, and during that time I was as happy as a man sitting in a prison visiting room can be without having a wank. I opened my eyes and saw her cigarette had burned all the way down and the ash had fallen into my lap in a perfect skeleton.

Finally, Susie patted my chest and sat herself up. "You are so good to me," she said, shaking her head and wiping her face. "It means so much, Lachie, I can't tell you. Especially just now, when things are so bad."

I took her hand and told her I loved her and would do anything—literally anything—to make things better for her. Carried away by my own rhetoric, I said it was the highlight of my life to come to this filthy room and see her. She looked beautiful, and, poor sweetheart, tell me why she was so sad.

"She's dead," she said, "Donna's dead."

I said, "Yeah, we knew that already."

No, Susie said. They found her body yesterday, on a hillside in Sutherland. A Ministry of Defense team on maneuvers had found her body at the bottom of a cliff. She'd been mutilated like the Riverside Ripper victims.

I didn't understand. "Was she killed recently?"

"It happened at the same time as Gow. They've only just found her." Susie sniffed. "The police have just left. I didn't really believe she was dead. I imagined her off somewhere, carrying on her life."

I didn't know what to say. Everyone knew Donna was dead. They'd found copious amounts of her blood in the boot of the Golf Polo after they found Gow. I asked if they were sure it was Donna. She nodded. "They've matched the dental records and a fractured clavicle she had when she was seven."

I nodded. We only had six minutes left. "Are they going to charge you with it?"

Susie said no as she lit another cigarette. "They've got me already. Waste of money."

We had four minutes left. "Susie," I said, "I have to ask you something stupid. Were you having an affair with Andrew Gow?" It sounded more sissy than I expected. Susie laughed loudly, like the laugh on the Dictaphone tape about Donna, but not bitter or scary.

Genuinely amused, she cupped my cheek in her hand. "Oh, Lachie," she said, exhaling my name like she used to during sex, "Lachie, how could you think such a thing?"

"When you said to Morris that someone had killed those girls to get Gow out, who was it you were talking about?"

She fell forward slightly from the waist. "Donna," she whispered.

"Donna killed those girls?"

She nodded.

"But you told Morris and Evelyn it wasn't."

"I only realized after. Anyway, I wouldn't confide my suspicions to that pair of arseholes."

(I didn't think about it until now, but she didn't share her suspicions with me, either.)

Shock hit her in a fresh wave and she started to cry again.

"But if Donna killed those girls, why did they find semen on them? How could they get a DNA match?"

She was crying so much that she couldn't talk. She tried but couldn't bring her lips together. She made a slight wanking motion with her hand, and I understood.

"Are you sure?"

She shrugged and carried on crying. It seemed to be compulsive. She covered her open mouth and tried to sit as though she were having a normal conversation, but her eyes dripped tears and her breath came in gulps. I told her about finding the hotel letter but hadn't the heart to give her a hard time about it. She carried on crying, listening and nodding but crying all the same.

"Shall I just hang on to the letter for now?" I said.

She nodded.

"For the appeal?"

She nodded.

Before I left she squeezed my arm tightly and apologized. "I am so, so sorry," she breathed, "sorry. I'm so sorry."

"Don't be silly."

She shook her head and said she was sorry again. It was only later that I wondered whether she was apologizing for crying or something else entirely.

I find what Susie said about Donna shocking, but it does make sense. Having seen her on the video, you know there's more going on in her head than she let on. I can't see her kneeling over a dead teenager, though, much less hacking at her mouth and throwing a sample of Gow's sperm on her.

It also occurred to me, during a moment when I was considering all the possible possibles, that if Susie believed Donna had killed those other girls to get Gow out, then it would be a perfect motive for killing Donna too. Susie might have thought that she was saving the world from a violent couple who would inevitably kill again.

Maybe Susie did kill them and genuinely doesn't remember. She often used to talk about patients who had blanked out committing their offenses because it was too painful. There's nothing in post-traumatic stress disorder that says they can't be responsible for the trauma; it just means that they were upset by it.

Still, possible possibles aside, I drove home happy. They announced on the radio that the remains of Donna McGovern, from Highfields in Leicester, had been found in Sutherland. I turned it off. I didn't want to hear about that. Susie may have said terrible things about me and Yeni, but she's not dead, she definitely wasn't fucking Gow, and she wasn't in love with him. I feel like I've been undivorced, uninsulted, uncuckolded. I've never felt more horny; it was like being a teenager again. Every time I passed an attractive woman on the drive home, I thought about Harry's little blond mum. I'd think of her being a little bit pissed and out of order, giggling and pulling down the hem of her top so that her round little tits pop out. I've struggled all evening not to open the kitchen drawer and find the birthday party list. It's eleven o'clock now, getting to the point where it's much too late to phone. It would be dangerous to start anything just because I'm relieved. She could so easily go straight to the papers. I'll leave it. I'll leave it for a bit.

chapter twenty-eight

I DON'T WANT SUSIE EVER TO READ THIS, BUT I NEED TO WRITE about it. I've changed the computer password to "Marzip." It wasn't meant as a big symbolic gesture or a shift of loyalties or anything. It doesn't mean anything, not at all. It's just that wrappers from marzipan bars are lying around the desk and I'm a bit nervous today, my mind's gone blank. I've slept with Yeni.

There, it's in the file now. I slept with her and liked it. We stayed up all night having fun and being nice to each other. I know she's young. I know she's lonely, and she probably did it because of that, and I'm older and it's wrong of me. But for the first time in weeks I was present in the moment, not speculating about the future or rewriting the past, and it felt like a month-long holiday.

I don't want Susie to stumble across this file the way I did hers. I suppose it would be just as bad if she found the stuff I've written before, about not trusting her and how I felt during the visits. I'll get rid of this computer. I'll say this one's broken and buy her a new one. I'll pretend it's a nice treat.

I said to Yeni this morning at five-thirty, "Yeni, we can't have an affair, I do have a wife."

And she said, "Hmm, Lachie, afster this day we're not talk about it again. This . . . hmm." She paused and dipped her chin to her bare knee as she tried to think of the words. "Friendly fuck, for friend." And she stroked my face.

It sounds sordid when I write it down, but it wasn't when she said it. It was tender and kind and sweet. Even her mustache looks kooky and sexy now. She is an amazing woman.

Before I left to drop Margie at nursery, I nipped back upstairs to her bedroom to tell her quickly that we were heading off. She was on her side, the duvet curled around her curves like a flattering strapless dress, her black hair fanned out over the white pillow. The moist air in the room was thick with pheromones and vigorous sweating. I crouched down and rolled my face into her soft hair, nuzzling her neck, and said I might come back from nursery and snuggle in beside her. She said no, she'd be asleep and now we were just friends. I love that. I keep wanting to wake her up and ask her if it's still all right, if she still likes me, if I'm a horrible predatory old bastard. But it wasn't me who started it.

I'd finished working up here at about eleven-thirty yesterday evening. I'd actually finished at eleven and went downstairs to get the phone. Bangor phoned to cancel our drinking session on Sunday: Evelyn's taken Morris back and he's not allowed out at night. She won't even let him work evenings. I came straight back up here because I didn't want to phone Harry's mum. I read a bit of the book about women who marry murderers. Maybe I should have chugged off, but it didn't occur to me. I thought Harry's mum was the danger, not me.

When I came down, Yeni was sitting watching television, some film with Kevin Bacon in it. I sat down in the opposite chair and said, "Oh God, how much longer does this crap go on for?"

She laughed and said, "Shut up, Lachie, it's very sad."

I pretended to cry, covering my face (a bit like Susie had during the day) and saying oh, poor Kevin Bacon, he so brave; Holy Mother protect him from the other actors, boo hoo. It got a laugh, but she was obviously engrossed, so I shut up and went to the kitchen. I got the two hidden marzipan bars out of the fridge. When I went back into the sitting room, I sort of went "ta-da" and held them up. She beamed at me. She reached out to take one with her right hand, and then her left hand came out of nowhere and snatched the other one as well. We were wrestling down by the side of the settee when she straddled me and sat up, panting and looking down at me with such an expression of approval and affection and, well, *enjoyment*. She wasn't tolerating me or being kind or keeping things going or hiding feelings from me. She genuinely enjoys me. I put my hand on her thigh and we looked at each other for an electric moment. Then Yeni toppled forward from the waist and kissed me hard on the lips.

Within minutes we were upstairs, in her room because it has a lock on the door, wrestling on the bed and giggling and eating marzipan and feeding it to each other. Before I had even touched her, she whipped off her top, yanked one of the cups of her bra down, and balanced a nugget of sweet golden paste on her tit, lying back and grinning. Her cherry nipple was the center of a swell of coffee skin, lighter than her caramel tummy, warmed in the sun for eighteen summers.

I climbed off the bed, unable to take my eyes off her breast (or indeed the marzipan—they both seemed enormously exciting to me at that moment). I stood there, bent over and panting. I asked if she was sure she wanted to do this. She seemed surprised at the question. I said that she was young and the house was mine and I didn't want her to feel she needed to do this or that it couldn't stop right now. She thought about it for a moment and looked at me, gasping like a man having a stroke. She laughed and made her delicious tits shudder. Looking up, looking me straight in the eye, she reached out and stroked my cock through my trousers.

Yeni is fat. She has big tits and love handles you could hang a bike on, but she doesn't care. Her stomach creases above her thighs, and a roll of flesh hangs down over her pubes, but she doesn't look like a second prize. She looks like a fertility goddess because she's so proud of herself. It makes her seem unbelievably dirty and sensual, like you could fuck her all night and then eat pizza off the cheeks of her ass, and she'd still laugh and like you.

I did ask her if it was all right, I did, but I feel I've done something unconscionable that I'll be held accountable for at some point in the future. The odd thing is, I feel as if I've done something bad to Yeni, not Susie. Susie barely comes into it. The only time I don't feel ambivalent about what happened is when I'm with Yeni. When I'm with her I know it's fine.

On the way to nursery all the newspapers had headlines about Donna's body being found. I bought one on the way. It said they'd found Donna's body, that she was from 18 North Street, Highfields, in Leicester (so she was telling the truth in the video). As a special-value bonus, there was a picture of Donna and Susie, and one of Gow, and the whole terrible tale again.

At the nursery everyone patted my elbow and said they were sorry to hear about, well, you know, as if Donna was a friend of mine.

Harry's mum was there and smiled over at me. I didn't want to encourage her attentions, so I sort of waved and yanked Margie out of her coat, trying to effect a quick getaway.

I was easing past a small boy when Harry's mum sidled over, calling, "Lachlan, hi." I turned back into the room so that we were talking publicly.

"How are you?" She smiled.

"Fine," I said. "How are you?"

She said, "Fine," and dipped her head down, dropping her voice. "I was wonder—"

"How's Harry? Is he okay?" I said it loudly, making it clear that I didn't want to have a private conversation, not today.

I was talking so loudly that Mrs. McLaughlin looked over. She had a sleeveless top on, one of those button-up ones with a collar. Her fat arms are red with angry stretch marks down the back like little lava flows.

"She should buy a shirt," said Harry's mum quietly, nodding over at her, "and hide her bingo wings." She smiled at me, raised her eyebrows a little, expecting me to laugh.

In hindsight I can see that she was trying to re-create the success she'd had with the "tanorexic" crack, but coming so soon afterward, it made her seem routinely unkind and wordplay obsessed.

I was tired and distracted and didn't get the joke this time. I nodded and pressed my lips together, and she had to explain—fat arms, bingo wings. "Oh, yeah, yeah," I said. "I see, yeah."

Harry's mum was wearing a tight red pencil skirt and little heels, which didn't seem all that appropriate. I know she's dressing like that for me, but looking at her today, I realized that she's not my type at all and would probably go to the papers if I as much as touched her bum.

I'm not sure why my interest in her has evaporated. I think it's because I'm not desperately horny anymore, because of Yeni. I don't want to feel that I could have shagged either one of them. I want my night with Yeni to mean something and be about more than me being selfish and betrayed and sexually frustrated, but maybe that's all it was. How depressing.

Yeni has kindly gone to pick Margie up because I was on the phone with Fitzgerald. He takes sooo long to say anything at all. I'm sure it's a lawyer's trick, because they charge by the hour. Yeni stood in front of me in the hall and touched her watch, motioning to the door. I raised a finger. She slumped her shoulders and dropped her head to the side. I shrugged helplessly as Fitzgerald droned on and on and on. Yeni pointed to herself, picked her jacket off the coat rack, and pointed at the door, tipping her head inquisitively. I nodded a thank you, I owe you one, and she kissed the tips of her fingers and wiggled them at me as she opened the front door and set off. I watched her through the window, walking away down the path. She has magnificently pear-shaped buttocks. When she wears those thin trousers, her bum looks like two jumbo plums quivering in a silk hankie.

Fitzgerald kept on talking about the sentencing hearing on Monday, telling me which court, what time. He reminded me not to expect any outcome other than the life sentence and said that there might be journalists there, I might like to think about whether I wanted to give them a statement this time. Every time I brought up the subject of the appeal, he swerved around it.

Finally I said it outright. "Well, Susie won't be in there very long, anyway. You know, because of the appeal."

Fitzgerald hummed gruffly. "Dr. Harriot, it was my understanding that you were going to visit your wife yesterday afternoon. Did you not go to see her after all?"

I said yes, I'd been out to see Susie in the Vale, although it wasn't a very satisfactory visit because the police had turned up at the same time and Susie had to see them first.

"So," he said (and he even took his time about that), "you are aware of the recent developments in the case, specifically those regarding the discovery of Donna McGovern's whereabouts?"

"Look," I said, "I know they found her body up in Cape Wrath."

He paused for a moment, as if waiting to see whether I would be adding to that statement. "Did your wife tell you, Dr. Harriot, that her wedding ring was discovered under Ms. McGovern's body?"

I was shocked and defensive. "What? That's rubbish. How could they possibly know it was Susie's wedding ring? They all look exactly the bloody same."

"No," said Fitzgerald, getting to the point. "When your wife was sacked from her job, she reported her wedding ring missing. She was quite concise about the inscription inside when she gave a description to the prison authorities. The ring found with Ms. McGovern has S&L'92 CORFU4EVER engraved inside it."

The inscription sounded puerile when he said it. It was a secret wedding vow, a commitment to keep on loving each other as we had that first holiday. I asked him whether Susie knew about this yesterday.

"Of course, Dr. Harriot. The police would certainly have mentioned it to her yesterday. It's a tremendously significant find. It certainly alters any possible course of action we might take over the case. In the event that we pursued an appeal against your wife's conviction for Mr. Gow's murder, she would inevitably be tried for Donna McGovern's death. We need to ask ourselves whether that is an efficacious use of your resources and funds, given that a success in one suit can only lead to another charge being levied and, in every potentiality, proved against your wife."

I put the phone down and came up here just to be alone for a while. Margie and Yeni are back. I can hear them playing in the back garden.

I'm trying not to take onboard what Fitzgerald said and what it all means. No wonder Susie was beside herself at the visit. No wonder. I can't even mentally berate her for not filling me in, because she would have had to explain the consequences, and I can't even think about them.

chapter twenty-nine

I CAN'T SLEEP, AND NOW I DON'T HAVE ANY OLD PEOPLE TO BLAME it on. The smoking isn't helping, that's for sure. Alarmingly, the crown broke off my tooth and fell out in my mouth at dinner this evening. It's a lower molar. I was eating some microwaved lasagna, bit down, and the porcelain on the cap just snapped off. I had a flush of adrenaline and thought for a moment that all my teeth were flooding out of my mouth. When I looked at the lump of porcelain on the tabletop, I found it was a dull yellow, yet it matches all my other teeth. The dentist's receptionist suggested that it could have been from grinding my teeth when I'm asleep. The only time they can take me is on Monday, after Susie's court appearance. I can't imagine that day getting any worse.

I still think we should give the Donna letter to Fitzgerald. I'll see what Susie says when I go to visit her, but I'm sure we could base an appeal on it. At least it shows that she was telling the truth.

I was watching telly with Yeni, sitting on the opposite settee so that she didn't think I was expecting anything. She winked at me a couple of times during the commercials, but I didn't respond. I was sort of waiting for her to take offense, but she didn't. She stood up at nine-thirty, said goodnight, and slipped out of the room. I watched the news and put the telly off, ready to come up here to work.

I stopped on the landing and knocked on Yeni's door. I wanted to say sorry for ignoring you there and thanks for a lovely time last night or something. I don't know what. I just wanted to see her, I suppose. She shouted, "Come in," and I put my head around the door. She was sitting in her bed, wearing a T-shirt nightie with pink bunnies on it and reading *Hello!* She dropped the magazine to her lap and wobbled her head back and forth in exasperation. I braced myself for trouble.

"Stephanie of Monaco is trash," she said, pronouncing it "trush," saying it as if they'd had a fight and Stephanie was refusing to give back Yeni's favorite jeans.

I went in and sat next to her on the bed. It felt very exciting, sitting right by her, not knowing whether we would ever touch again. We both had faint smiles on our faces and avoided looking straight at each other. She showed me a picture of the princess looking sulky at a party.

"Is that bad, what she's doing there?" I pointed to the picture unnecessarily and brushed the back of her finger where she was holding the page. A slight tremor ran through her, emanating from her hand. She blinked slowly and smiled at the page.

"Not so bad, but"—and she shook her head in disapproval, a curl of black hair falling over her face—"*trushy dress.*"

I smiled and pushed the hair back. "What would you know about trashy, Yeni?" I love the language barrier between us. She doesn't know my chat-up lines are crap, and we can't possibly have big conversations about ourselves or our relationship.

She put the magazine down and slid down in the bed, pulling the covers up over her face. "Good night, Lachlan." She giggled.

I leaned forward to kiss her. I only meant to kiss her on the forehead, but she pushed me off, giggling, and said, "Jyou *piss off,*" in a heavy accent.

I stood up and pretended to cry. "I'm as sad as Kevin Bacon."

She was laughing as I shut the door behind me, that big dirty laugh that makes her tits wobble. I won't try to kiss her again. I don't want to be pushy, but I hope that it isn't over between us. Her unavailability coupled with the complete sexual abandonment that lies beneath it is tremendously erotic. I can't remember if having to strive for sex was always this exciting. It feels as though there's a live possibility tingling between us in a way that never happens when you know for certain you're going to touch each other again.

I've been reading the prison-lovers book since I came up here and looking at the pictures of Donna, trying to feel sad about the fact that her body has been found. I can't remember what I came up here to say, but it was important enough to peel my carcass off the sofa and propel me up three flights of stairs. Possibly I had nothing to say, possibly I just had an urge to be up here, in this small space with a locked door between me and the rest of the world, restoring order through the cunning application of my rudimentary secretarial skills.

It seems bizarre that this article was published only three months ago:

Box 2 Document 12 *"Riverside Ripper Appeal to Go Ahead,"* Scotsman, *8/30/98*

This box is getting a bit full. I should get a new one.

A fresh appeal hearing was announced today for Andrew Gow, the Glasgow man convicted of the 1993 Riverside Ripper murders. The failure of the police to stem the murders of five Glasgow prostitutes in the early nineties led to the calls for the formation of a US-style EPCU policing database, capable of cross-referencing cases nationwide and identifying patterns. Gow, who was convicted on the basis of a confession, has become the subject of a local campaign for a retrial following the discovery of two new victims, apparently killed by the same offender. Gina Wilson and Nicola Hall both met their deaths while Gow was in prison. Samples found at the scene match the DNA profile found on the previous victims. It calls into question the use of DNA profiling when samples are degraded and the presentation of degrees of probability in DNA cases. Since his original confession, Gow has consistently denied committing the original series of murders.

The appeal will be heard on September 2 and is expected to attract international press attention. Mr. Gow was denied bail pending the hearing, but this is not thought to reflect his chance of a successful appeal, rather, the lack of reliable risk assessment reports at this time.

This was because Susie had been sacked. They had to get the reports redone by someone else because Susie's were challengeable.

A spokesman for Gow's new wife, Donna McGovern, 23, made a brief statement outside the court hearing in Glasgow: "Mrs. Gow is absolutely over the moon and delighted with the news." The couple plan to move away as soon as Mr. Gow is released.

See our DNA Special page 13: Racial Profiling, Probability, and How Hundreds Become Thousands on the Stand

I don't want to read about appeals just now really. It's twelve-ten and I should go downstairs and lie in bed with my eyes shut tight, straining to relax. I'll stop typing at one. I can't even get a cup of tea because my tooth's heat-sensitive. I'll put a hot-water bottle in my bed, come back up here, and definitely stop at one.

Box 2 Document 13 *Notes on Women Who Marry Murderers*

REASONS FOR MARRYING

1. Status, gives them social significance, attention-seeking.
2. Vicarious celebrity.
3. Vicarious murder.

4. Erotomania: killers ultimate macho men.

5. Inadequate intelligence.

6. Passion is fueled by deprivation of the physical presence of the other; suffering and anguish mistaken for passion.

All of which seem to apply to Donna.

Profile of Women:

1. Catholic; subjugation of women and sexual repression of Church ties in nicely to absent husband.

2. Often have had an unhappy first marriage at a young age, often to violent alkies.

3. Unstable upbringing, authoritarian father.

4. Recent death in family, often of abusing parent.

5. Low self-esteem and attachment to someone they think powerful.

6. When move to be closer to prison (usually six months to a year) lose all social support and become more vulnerable.

All of which absolutely *do* apply to Donna. Apart from the last one. She moved up before she had even met him.

Profile of Murderers:

1. Alcohol often present in commission of offense (*not Gow*).

2. Motive for marriage by prisoners: having stable relationship creates better basis for parole board (*not applicable; D&G were engaged even before there was any possibility of parole*).

3. These men are strivers in prison, often take degrees (*not Gow*).

4. Grandiose and narcissistic (*yes Gow*).

5. Killers exude self-confidence. Lack empathy and refuse to take responsibility for their behavior—blame others, often the victims. Claim victim status for themselves—killers victim of system. The whole relationship focus becomes saving poor man from victimization by the system (*yes to all of this re Gow*).

It is astonishing how many hits the woman who wrote this book made with Gow and Donna. It would be nice to write to her and let her know, but I can't be bothered. I was thinking about Donna moving up here before she was even sure she had permission to visit Gow, which kind of makes me wonder what she was moving from. If Donna did murder those women for Gow, then she must have killed the first one (Nicola Hall) before they were even married. Maybe she wanted to kill someone all along and getting Gow released was her excuse.

It's one-thirty and I've got to sleep. I'm glad I've had my hair cut. I hope I don't look awful in the photographs on Monday. I hope to God that Susie's all right. I hope they'll give her some sleeping pills and she isn't hassled by anyone on the Big Blue Bus.

Everything on earth feels precarious tonight. I've been down and looked in on Margie four times. On the way back up with a cup of tea, I was struck by the conviction that Yeni had buckled under the strain of having an affair with her employer and hanged herself. I couldn't resist the urge to look in on her to make sure she was okay. I just stood at the door to her room and peeked in with one eye. I hope she was asleep and doesn't know I did that.

chapter thirty

DRINKING STRAIGHT FROM A COGNAC BOTTLE IS NOT EASY WITH A half-frozen face. Let me correct that. Drinking straight from a cognac bottle is not economical with a half-frozen face. I had to take my new coat off in case I spilled any on it. I hung it behind the door. It is beautiful. I'm not going to drink any more tonight so that I can put it back on.

It is done. I went to court this morning and Susie was given life and taken away. Then I went straight to the dentist and had the tooth prepped for the cap. I sat for an hour with two people's hands in my mouth, let them grind my tooth, and then paid handsomely for the privilege. Can there by anything more counterintuitive than voluntarily subjecting yourself to dentistry? I slept so badly last night that I almost nodded off while my tooth was being drilled.

I came straight up here and have been reading reviews in the *State Literary Journal* for over an hour to try to bore my mind into a state of quiet.

Yeni has been wonderful. She looked after Margie all day and then let me come straight up here to be alone. She hasn't questioned me about my day, but she must have seen it all on TV. When I came home, I went into the kitchen and Yeni stroked my arm, but I think it was to feel the fabric on my new coat rather than to touch me. Maybe she just doesn't have the vocabulary to ask about the niceties of procedure in my murderous wife's sentencing. I'd smash this room up if I didn't like it so much and wasn't worried about messing up my lovely coat. I'm fucked right off.

I slept for about three hours last night and woke up at five-thirty, breathless with anxiety. It was the thought of facing the press again. I know that's self-obsessed and selfish, given the awful thing that was just about to happen to Susie, but it's the truth. I couldn't bear the thought of being seen by them, of them photographing me and making me ugly again. I feel all right when there's no one looking. When Yeni's looking at me, I feel handsome and funny and able, but when the press look at me, I feel ugly and pathetic and unlucky, like those grim photos they always print of a victim's family.

Anticipating being unable to drive when I came out of court again, I arrived early and left the car half a mile away in a long-term parking lot. I had thirty minutes to kill before I went to meet Fitzgerald, so I sat in the car and listened nervously to the radio. I definitely didn't want to have to hang around outside the court with the old women and the man who smelled of mustard. I was too jumpy to sit in the car—I kept thinking that the lot attendant was watching me from his little booth—so I got out and went for a circuit of the block, telling myself calmly, calmly, smooth blue ocean, smooth blue ocean, walk slowly and don't build up a sweat. Courts have the heating up high because they're sitting still for so long, whatever the weather outside. The day of Susie's bail hearing I had hurried in, arriving with a thin film of sweat on my face, and after five minutes I was peeling my shirt from my back. I was left distinctly rank.

I walked around the corner, shortening my stride, and came

across the Armani shop. Nerves made me misread the sign as the Armor shop and that attracted me to the door. I went inside and walked about in the soporific gray light, finding myself involuntarily slowing down. A shop assistant slithered over to me and inquired in a broad-voweled Italian accent whether he could help me. I thought of Yeni and smiled. I must have had a strange look on my face because he said, "Very well," and withdrew without prompting. Working out that it would take ten minutes to walk around the corner to the court and five to find Fitzgerald and get seated, I decided to leave at a quarter to, which gave me ten minutes to look around the shop. I found myself checking my watch every thirty seconds but managed to get it down to intervals of two minutes before I left.

Initially there didn't seem to be much to look at. Everything was gray and black and white, but when I looked more closely, I realized that these were incredibly expensive clothes, very well made. Even the T-shirts felt beautiful. I caught sight of myself in the mirror, and the overhead lights highlighted the rain creases between my lapels and shoulder pads. My hair didn't look bad, though. I was almost in front of the coats. I picked out a gray one and pulled at it, but there was a security chain along the arm. The assistant had to come over, unlock it, and stand there, staring at me as I tried it on. It's three-quarter-length with four buttons and a black velvet collar, like a frock coat. I looked great in it, slim and tall and cool. The lining is sky blue. The Italian guy was watching me, so I couldn't preen in the mirror or grin delightedly. Just before I threw my wallet in the air and shouted take what you need, you Italian fop, I slipped the coat off, the exquisite silky lining sliding gracefully down my shirtsleeves, and I looked at the price. Fuck me blind. It cost more than I used to live on in a year. But then I thought of the day ahead and of the comfort of wearing something that didn't make me feel like a two-bit loser creep, and I bought it anyway. I was glad I did, glad I had some armor on. The assistant had me pegged as a time-waster and was surprised when I said I'd take it. He tried to wrap it in tissue, but I said I'd wear it and put my old coat in the bag.

I walked around the corner, catching glimpses of myself in the windows of shops. Realizing that it would be grotesque to show up in court with a shopping bag, I dumped the Armani bag with the old coat in it at a charity shop.

There was no crowd at the court. No one thought of this as anything more than a formality. I found Fitzgerald around the back corridor, and he greeted me coldly. I don't know why he's so snooty to me. I've been perfectly nice to him and we pay him on time and everything. Maybe he's annoyed that he's lost the case, but that's hardly my fault. I saw him looking at my coat and was glad I'd dumped the bag. He said he liked it very much, that he hadn't seen me wearing this one before. Was it new? When I said yes, it was new, he looked away sharply. He asked me if I wanted to make a statement to the press afterward, because there were a couple of journalists kicking about. I said no, I didn't really want to. He told me to wait in the public galleries. I think he was jealous of my coat.

In the dark public gallery the mustard-smelling man was sitting next to two of the older women. I sat down in front of them, nodding hello. The dark gallery looks out onto the bright court, a proscenium arch framing the justice system for us viewers. I noticed as I sat down that the lady who brought the scones was missing from the gang. One of the other ladies leaned over to tell the mustard man that their friend had suffered a stroke since they were last here, and I turned without thinking and said, "Oh dear, how is she?" Not very well, apparently, but her friends looked shocked that I'd asked, so I turned away. My coat felt conspicuously wealthy and decadent in a world where wives were sentenced to life imprisonment and old ladies with scones had strokes. Still, my wondering whether I looked good or bad was a welcome break from thinking about whether or not the mother of my child was going down for life.

They brought Susie in from the side cells, and she looked awful, broken. The nice gray suit doesn't fit her anymore, she's lost so much weight around her hips. I thought of plump, sexy Yeni and felt a shooting pain of guilt. She caught my eye, and I suddenly realized that I must be looking dismayed. I smiled and waved. She ignored me and frowned at my overcoat. It was quite a light color for the court. Everyone else was wearing black or washed-out tones of green or pink or slate.

They sat Susie down, facing away from us. She straightened her back and, in a gesture of inarticulable grace, raised both hands to the nape of her neck and gathered her dull black hair, twisting it into a tidy rope and letting it drop. I felt suddenly unbelievably sad. I knew it was over, that Susie was gone, and by the time she got out of prison, I'd be gone, too. Margie would have done most of her growing up, would rebel against her pudgy old dad, and would always be wary of Susie. We were all three lost to each other, and there was nothing to be done but give witness to the unfolding disaster.

I'd left my handkerchief in the old overcoat pocket. I couldn't sniff because it would draw attention to me, and Susie would be pissed off. So I undid the cuff on my shirt and pulled the sleeve out, dabbing my nose with it.

God, I am fucking sick to death of being fucking miserable. Look at Morris: he thrashes about, fucking everything that moves. He fiddles his practice accounts and drinks too much, and he's happy. I'm sick of Susie looking at me as if I'm some sort of fucked-up weirdo freak. I wasn't the one who followed a serial killer and his ugly bride up north.

I stopped for a smoke there. I've cooled down.

Anyway, we were all sitting in the court, the journalists waiting and watching Susie, chatting to each other, smiling sometimes but never taking their eyes off her. She looked out-gunned sitting there between the two big male guards, suddenly small, like Margie. Eventually the judge came out, and after a bit of whispering among the lawyers and passing around of papers, he addressed Susie directly. Yak yak, he said, look at me up here in my big chair, yak bloody yak. He told her she had previously been of good character, was a successful psychiatrist, and had a small daughter. He was starting to sound like a miraculously insightful stage psychic when he said it was a shame she'd let herself down by committing this murder and ordered her to serve a life sentence with a recommended minimum of ten years.

I saw Susie slump in the chair; her hair slid forward over her shoulder, baring her neck to the ax. I was reminded of the photograph she took of Donna's neck, the white, white skin and tiny black freckle sitting between taut and slender ligaments.

The two big men on either side almost carried Susie out of the court. She didn't even look back at me. Everyone in the public gallery was staring at her and muttering about the state she was in. I watched and realized that I wasn't as involved with her as I had been. As for my indiscretion with Yeni, it wouldn't be so bad if only I had waited for six months. Susie would have been gone awhile, all her toiletries would be gone from our bathroom, her clothes would be washed and mothballed and packed away in the suitcases in the attic. I could justify it all much better to myself if I'd waited. What I've done is unforgivable, a peculiarly unkind and brutal kind of betrayal; I've staged a mental retreat from her just as she is broken. I'll keep looking for grounds for appeal. I owe her that much, but I have retreated from her. I feel nothing approaching the devastation I experienced at the trial. I knew I'd be fine to drive.

Outside the courts, a couple of journalists were gathered at the bottom of the steps. They were smoking, actually, and I wouldn't have known they were press if one of them hadn't shouted questions about my wife. He wasn't even asking questions, really, it was more like he was shouting abuse at me. I got flustered. The press have been intrusive and difficult, but there was always a sense that they knew I was having a hard time through no fault of my own. There was always an underlying sympathy. Now it seemed I was no longer privy to even this small courtesy.

"Hey, Harriot," he shouted as I walked past. "Where'd you get that fancy coat?"

No one even took a photo of me. Fuckers.

chapter thirty-one

I'VE BEEN TRYING TO PHONE SUSIE ALL MORNING BUT CAN'T GET through. So I sat down and wrote a long encouraging letter, telling her that I was thinking of her (true), that I missed her (not really true at the moment) and wished I was with her during this difficult time (outright lie). I'm going to try to write every day, give her news about Margie and send photos of her. If I were in Susie's position, I know I'd be thinking about killing myself, and she mustn't do that. She has to get through the next short while, for Margie's sake if nothing else. I want to remind Susie that she'd be increasing Margie's statistical chances of suicide by a factor of four if she kills herself, but I'm afraid that if I mention it I might be putting the idea in her head. I'm not against suicide per se, but I do think you lose the right to consider it once you've had kids.

The papers are full of Susie and Donna today. I bought five of them. Loads of people have sold their story. Our old nanny, Saskia, who went off to live with a hospital porter in Toryglen, has told her story exclusively to a local evening paper. It's funny to see her face again. She looks much older, scowling out from the front page, dark-eyed, with her wiry auburn hair cut short. Inside, she is sitting on a nasty armchair, in front of a horrible gas fire. I always thought she would live somewhere pretty, and I'm sadder about that than the fact that she sold her story. I showed the picture to Yeni, who nodded and smiled and carried on changing Margie. I wonder if she would ever sell her story. And what a story. She might have already sold it, I suppose. Journalists phone here all the time, so it wouldn't be hard for her to make contact. Alistair Garvie—the man from the *Mirror*—still leaves at least one message a day. She might even have seduced me just to have a unique spin on her story, but I don't think so. She's very detached from everything. She lives in a wee world of her own.

Another paper has a story from someone who worked at Sunnyfields with Susie, a disgraced social worker or something. Yet another interviewed the property agent who let Donna the Kirki house. He says she was nice but owed his firm back council tax (not such an interesting exclusive that one). The papers without interviews are rehashing all the old information. They've all managed to get in some of the details about the murders and what was done to those girls, which is hideously prurient. One has a huge teaser banner for Stevie Ray's story about me, which will be in tomorrow's edition. The very best I can hope for is that it gets lost in the rest of the coverage. One of the papers mentions the fact that no one has come forward to claim Donna's body. She had no one apart from Gow. Perhaps that is why she left Leicester without a backward glance and, according to Susie at least, was prepared to kill innocent girls not much younger than herself.

Mrs. Anthrobus came this morning. She hadn't even noticed the papers and seems to think that Susie is away on a business trip no matter how often I tell her she's in prison. She may be a daft old goat, but still I changed the sheets on Yeni's bed myself and washed them before she arrived.

Susie phoned this afternoon, sounding drugged and slow. She asked to speak to Margie, and I tried to warn her about the papers tomorrow, how they were going to say things about me that weren't true and not to mind them, but she said they were full of lies all the time. Who cares, she said, and I felt that she was speaking more broadly than just the particular.

Is Margie awake, she asked, what's she doing? I described what Margie was wearing and tried to get her to talk into the receiver, but she wouldn't. She didn't react at all when Susie called her. I don't know if she's stopped recognizing the voice or the drugs make Susie sound different, but Margie carried on picking up and dropping the snake draft-excluder to watch its eyes boggle about. I picked it and her up and took them out to the quiet hall to settle her down a little, but she was tired and just dribbled onto the receiver, staring through the door into the bright kitchen as she picked at the corduroy on her little trousers.

Susie called to her again, hopefully, desperately. She called to her through a medicated smog, across a thousand miles and a dozen centuries, but Margie didn't flinch. She was bored with me shaking the snake at her and tried to get down. I couldn't hold her anymore, and she wriggled off my knee and wandered off into the kitchen.

She was all the way across the kitchen, crouched and picking at something that had spilled and dried on the floor by the stove, but Susie was still calling her name. "Can she hear me, Lachie?"

"Oh yes, she's sitting up now. Yes, she is. Aren't you, Margie?" I spoke in that instinctive, weird falsetto that people only ever use with small kids. "Where's that coming from, hmm? Susie, I wish you could see her. She recognizes the voice but doesn't know where it's coming from."

Susie was pleased and called her again in the same high voice. "Hello, darling, it's Mummy. I'm your mummy, yes, I am. You remember me, don't you? I love you, Margie, I love you, my lovely girl."

"Where's that coming from, Margie-Pargie, eh?" I said. "That's right, it's Mummy, your mummy." I gave a hollow laugh. "Oh, she's looking round for you."

"I love you, Margie," said Susie, and I could tell she was crying,

"I love you, darling. You know me, don't you? I miss you. I do. I miss your little face."

"Yes," I said, clutching the knitted snake, "you know that voice, don't you? That's right. It's your mummy. Where's Mummy?"

"Where's Mummy, baby?"

"Where is Mummy?"

"I love you, baby." Susie sniffed hard and banged the receiver—or her head—on something: she banged something very hard off something else.

"She can't take it anymore, Susie. She's gone off to look for you."

Susie gave a wet gurgle of pleasure. They must have been giving her buckets of sedatives.

"That's right," I told the dark hall. "You go and find Mummy. Good girl." I don't know if she knew I was lying; if despite the medication Susie remembered that Margie is twenty months old and therefore intrinsically contrary. She sniffed and sighed. "Thanks, Lachie." And she hung up.

I immediately called the prison and said that I thought she was suicidal. After leaving me on hold for a while, the prison officer came back and told me that she was on suicide watch and not to worry. I'm only quite worried. More than worried, I'm bloody exhausted. I want a holiday from my head.

Box Two is very full now. I could file all these things in the other boxes, but it's best to keep the boxes thematic so that I can find things when I need to.

This article was interesting because the families of the later two women killed were much better off and had better representation. The press portrayal was more sympathetic, and the campaigning got under way immediately. This was a scant eight weeks after the second murder, and Susie had just been sacked.

Box 2 Document 14 *"Families of Ripper II Call for Investigation," 7/3/98*

> Gina Wilson and Nicola Hall never met when they were alive, but in death their families have come together to launch Families For Justice, an organization campaigning for the reopening of the original Riverside Ripper cases. Andrew Gow was convicted in 1994 of the spate of murders but has since always maintained his innocence, claiming more recently that his confession at the time was given under duress. Mr. Neil Wilson and his wife, Sheila, have pointed out that Gow had a history of confessing to crimes and this should have been noted at the time. "The police must answer for these deaths," said Mr. Wilson yesterday. "They knew how slim the evidence was and yet proceeded against Gow, abandoning the original investigation."

Neil Wilson went on to make something of a career of it. His organization Families For Justice (FFJ) developed into a body campaigning for more input from victims and victims' families in court cases. I don't think they ever got anywhere, but they were on all the debating shows. It was so different from the 1993 families and Karen Dempsey's mother, but the earlier families were poor and unable to use the media or afford lawyers. It just shows that justice is a commodity: if there were a battle between the victims' families from Lockerbie versus those from Zeebrugge, the Lockerbie families would win hands down every time because they had pricier tickets and are better resourced.

Neil Wilson was never off the telly at that time, I remember. We watched a lot of telly then. Susie was at home all day and gradually put the television on earlier and earlier. She got dressed later and later, as well. She was pretty depressed, I suppose, until the call came from up north.

I've been thinking about Donna and no one claiming her body for burial. How does a woman in her midtwenties with great tits and a chatty nature leave behind no one? Women can be friendless in their late forties, when they're past it, but any woman in her midtwenties with a tarty sense of dress will surely have someone. The ex-husband hasn't even surfaced to sell his story.

Mum and Dad have been on the phone telling me how awful everything is. Mum is embarrassed that it's all over the press. I hadn't the heart to tell her about tomorrow's papers.

Yeni came back from a walk, and I sat down at the table and lit a cigarette (in the kitchen!). I told her that some lies about me were going to appear in the papers tomorrow and I was nervous about it. She made a sad face and patted my head and called me "sorry Kevin Bacon." I made her sit down and asked her not to leave us, at least for the next couple of months, whatever happens. She said a very definite no and it took me five minutes of quizzing to work out whether she meant no, she wouldn't go or no, she couldn't give that sort of assurance. At the end of it she picked up my cigarette from the ashtray, took a puff and stubbed it out. Then she opened the French doors and made a sweeping motion to get the smoke out of the room on the grounds that "It's stinks."

Outside the French doors, across the green lawn, the Japanese maple and Boston ivy have turned a deep dark scarlet, making the back wall a frozen tidal wave of blood heading toward the house. Night falls very early now. My heavy heart feels as though I'm walking into a dark tunnel, and I wish today were over.

chapter thirty-two

YENI'S BEEN OUT FOR MILK AND BROUGHT THE PAPER BACK WITH her. We sat at the table and looked at it together. They used that horrible picture of me leaving the court on the day Susie was found guilty, the one where I look like Paul Weller's Fat Elvis years. Blinded by the low winter sun coming in through the French windows, I thought I caught Yeni looking at me strangely. I asked her if she believed all that stuff about me.

She said, "What is it?"

I couldn't be bothered elaborating. I said, well, you've been in this house for a year now, you know what goes on in here. She said yes, don't be angry, and, smiling, she stood up, leaned over, and kissed my eyelids. I pulled her onto my knee and thanked her. I said that I was so grateful for her support, I'd buy a truck made of marzipan for her. Happily such items are not readily available around here and she agreed to settle for a pizza later instead.

When the sun hits her brushed-cotton skin and she looks happy, I could wrap her up in my new Armani coat and run her to the airport and whip all three of us off to Greece or somewhere, to a place where fucking a dusky young beauty while your wife languishes in prison isn't regarded as an appalling thing to do. France maybe.

I asked her to take Margie to nursery tomorrow, and she actually said no to me.

"Jyou cannot hide, Lachie; you have done nothing. Jyou have to go with Margie."

She's right, of course, but I do want to hide. I said I'd get her a nice surprise if she did, and she agreed reluctantly, but said it would be better for me to go. She's very adult about everything.

I find the way she moves enchanting. It's like a dance. If she reaches for a thing, she sweeps her arm quickly and then catches herself, as though she needs to consciously conjure up memories of failure and caution. She raises her arm too high, halts it and slows, letting it alight on the object, then brings it back slowly. I love the confidence in that sweep, the lunge, the reaching for my cock because she wants to. I don't know if I envy her age and underlying belief that nothing can go wrong, or if I just like her. If it's her age and naïveté, then I'm a nasty old man. If it's her I like, then I have a crush on her, which isn't such a bad thing. Having a crush on someone could be my mind's way of tricking me into feeling something positive, a psychic trick to restart the endorphins after all the misery and insomnia.

I know that running off to France is only appealing because I want to hide my face. I don't want to be seen because I don't know what people will think of me. It's not true, none of it. Susie and I were never unfaithful to each other (because of Yeni I have to add "before"). We were never unfaithful to each other *before*. Stevie Ray's a spineless little shit.

Yeni and Margie were fast asleep in the house, and I was trying hard not to come up here and spend the tail hours of the evening speculating about everything, typing up five-odd pages that end on a self-pitying note, and then slink off to bed for a crappy sleep. I told myself I was going out for a smoking session in the car, but really I knew it was nothing of the kind. I'm smoking properly again, getting through about ten a day, and I can feel my heart rate rising every time I inhale, my bronchioles getting itchy and irritated, my lung capacity diminishing. It feels good.

Driving through the town at midnight, through the parallel universe that is pub closing time. All the newsagents had cloyingly alliterative posters, tattered and smudged from a day of windy rain: SEXY DR. SUSIE'S SWINGING SECRETS. I fret about smoking ten cigarettes a day and being slightly overweight at twenty-nine; the town was full of drunk, fat, laughing people smoking casually as they walked down the streets, stopping at late-night shops to buy fatsnax and yet more cigarettes. Half of them didn't even have enough clothes on for the weather. The young women especially, walking along with their tits hanging out and skirts up their arses. Susie said they are dressing to impress one another, but I don't think any heterosexual man would ever believe that. I'm not going to let Margie out until she's twenty-five. She can wear what she likes, but she's staying home with me.

The colors at night are yellow and blue and gray. Uplit faces are slow, drunk. People move gracelessly, laugh loudly, fall languorously. Hot chips spill onto litter-strewn streets, crying women hail cabs, and angry men go after them (Angela, you stupid bitch, Angela, fucking come back here). The red eyes of the car in front leave crusty, bloody trails in the yellow dark.

I cruised through the town, not going anywhere really, not consciously, until I found myself far out on the south side, on the council estate. It's built on the edge of a deep wood, with ugly concrete cottages from the fifties lining broad streets and a badly broken-up road surface. I had to snake along, veering back and forth across the road to miss axle-shattering chasms. I only saw two or three other cars there.

Beyond low brick walls were bare little gardens, overlooked by bright windows with curtains. They had ornaments arranged on the sill: a china cat, a nasty vase with dusty plastic flowers jagging out of it, a ceramic flower basket. None of the front gardens had anything growing in them. Stevie Ray's house had two small windows knocked into a much bigger one, but the surround wasn't finished on it and the white PVC frame sat inside chipped and crumbling brick. A pile of bricks and loose rubble sat in the middle of the front garden. The lights were off.

I drove past Stevie's house three, maybe four times before I pulled over just beyond it and stopped. I was so angry by this point I could have kicked his door in. I wanted to ask him how he could live with himself, did he think I was a wanker? Well, did he? I sat in the car, taking deep breaths so I wouldn't be too angry, smoking a cigarette, which made me angry again.

I glanced in the rearview mirror and saw Stevie Ray coming along the road toward me, back from a night in the pub. Next to him was a small blond woman, and I thought he'd got lucky. They were walking so close, smiling but chatting very little, it was a touching scene. I'd calmed down by this point and knew I'd have to work myself up into having a fight again, so I slid down in the seat, and as I watched, I realized that the woman looked familiar.

They turned into the garden. For a moment I worried that they'd notice my car. They could have, but at that moment the woman said something, flicking her finger toward the crap piled up in the front garden. The gesture was disapproving, but she dropped her shoulders in despair at the same time, as though she'd pointed it out a hundred times. Stevie didn't say anything, but his back tensed guiltily. From that one gesture and response, I knew immediately that they were living together and had been for a long, long time.

Then Lara Orr took out her keys and opened Stevie Ray's front door.

I was stubbing out my fifth cigarette, about to get out and knock on his door, when a rap at the window made me jump, the seatbelt yanking me back and hurting my shoulder. Stevie Ray was at my window, looking wary but curious. He was breathing frost, wearing stripy pajamas under a heavy woolen dressing gown and outdoor shoes on bare feet. I pressed the electronic button and Stevie reeled back as the window started and lowered. He'd been expecting me to punch him.

"Listen," he said, talking fast and hanging on to the wall behind him with both hands, "I'm sorry, but a guy's got to make a living. You've got everything—you wouldn't understand. You're clever and good-looking and you're a doctor. You've got a healthy daughter—"

"You prick," I said, brave inside my car. "My reputation's ruined because of you. What a cheap thing to do, even for you. It was cheap."

Stevie looked at the ground. "I needed the money," he said. "I'm sorry. I am a prick." He came closer, put a hand on the roof of the car, and drummed his fingers once, leaning down into the cab to speak. "Are you, um . . . d'you, um, want a cuppa?"

I looked up at him. He actually felt sorry for me. "Come away in and have a cup of tea with us," he said, sotto voce, eyes serene. "There's someone inside who wants to meet you."

"Lara Orr?"

Stevie nodded, glowing at the mention of her name. "She's been following you in the papers. She feels bad for you."

I was genuinely touched. How deeply kind, I thought. How good women can be sometimes.

All promise of a spiritual connection was shattered when I saw inside their house. All the paper had been ripped off the walls in the hall, and someone had painted over the scrappy mess in the cloying peachy color of artificial limbs. The real shock was the undulating dirt floor. It was actual dirt, muddy, sandy dirt for growing things in, but, being December, the frost was through it. Someone had laid bits of cardboard box down, but the freezing damp hung in the narrow hallway. There had been floorboards once, that much was clear from the struts sticking out of the side of the wall about an inch above the ground level.

Stevie saw me looking around at the mess. "I'm doing, ahem, some renovations."

The living-room floor was still intact. It was a steep step up from the hall and had a once-green carpet on the floor, now encrusted with dirt to the point where it was black and shiny at the doorway. Newspapers were spread over the floor to act as a protective cover. A midnight blue velvet settee with full ashtrays and plates and cups balanced on the arm stood just inside the doorway. A large television was precariously balanced on a red plastic child's chair next to a big gas fire. Standing there in the cold muddy hall, looking up into the floating platform of the warm living room, I felt like a soldier on the Somme dreaming of his modest home.

Lara Orr hove into view wearing a nightie, a dressing gown to match Stevie's, and a pair of low navy blue court shoes with fluffy yellow socks inside them. She's petite, nervously thin, and unattractive. Her eyes are so small they make her seem almost inbred.

"Wit's he doing here?" she snapped unpleasantly.

"I brought him in for a cup of tea."

"Look at the mess you've made of the place," she said, making it sound as if he'd done it all that evening. "I'm ashamed to have people in and you're bringing folk in here. . . ." She glanced at me, sphincter-mouthed. "It's twelve at night. And we don't even know him. Ye shouldnae invite folk in."

"Lara, shut it. Away and make some tea," said Stevie, affectionately.

"Naw," said Lara, looking me up and down and relaxing slightly. "You make some tea."

"It was me invited him in. You make the tea."

Lara was looking at my coat, and I could tell she liked it. I was expecting her to leave the room to make tea, but she clopped across to the sideboard and turned on a kettle that was sitting there. Stevie saw me staring open-mouthed at the arrangement.

"I'm doing up the kitchen as well," he explained, inviting me to sit on the sofa.

How extraordinary. I didn't want to sit on anything in my nice new coat, so I used the excuse of there being only two places on the settee and, lifting my coat at the back, balanced myself on the arm.

"I don't like living like this," snapped Lara at me.

"Neither of us likes it," retorted Stevie.

"Wasn't me that done it," said Lara.

Stevie shrugged. "It's just temporary," he said.

"It's been temporary for nearly two years."

He swiveled around. "Lara," he implored. "You're nipping my fucking head. Give us peace."

She raised her voice. "*You* give *me* peace," she shouted.

Stevie laughed softly and turned back to me, spreading his hands in an appeal for reason. "She could start a fight in an empty house," he said. If anyone had done that to my house, I'd have slapped them from sunup to sundown.

Lara busied herself at the sideboard, making us each a mug of tea. She asked me if I wanted sugar, and when I said yes, she shook some into the cup from a paper packet, stirring it with a suspiciously dun teaspoon. I think it was filthy but couldn't see it across the room. Lara saw me looking concerned and used her body to block my view. She gave us both disgusting, cloudy-looking tea in stained cups, and Stevie fell on his, sipping it with great relish as though it were a delicate soup. I wasn't about to drink mine. For an *amuse-gueule*, Lara opened a green bag of crisps and took out a handful for herself before handing them to me. She was still eating when she lit up a Rothmans from a packet in her dressing-gown pocket. I took out my Marlboros and offered them around. Stevie took one and put it behind his ear (for later, he explained). I sat the tea on the floor and pretended to be concerned with picking bits out of my handful of crisps and smoking. I found Lara a bit frightening. I didn't want her having a go at me.

"I hear they found Donna's body," she said, smoking through

a mouthful of cheese and onion. She opened her mouth to masticate, and smoke clung to the crisps, a wet landscape of smoldering rubble.

I nodded. "Yeah. Sad. Sorry, do you hate her?"

"No," said Lara genuinely. "We weren't friends. I never met her, but I was pleased that she took him off my hands."

"I knew her," smiled Stevie, sitting to attention. "I've got nice pictures of her."

I looked at Lara. "But I thought you were divorced from Gow long before she came on the scene?"

"Oh, aye. I divorced him, so he was going to kill me. He used to phone me and write letters. He was always talking to Stevie about what he'd do if he caught me." Stevie nodded helpfully. "I didn't get any peace until she came along."

"That's why we've never told anyone we were together," said Stevie. "He'd have killed her if he got out."

"Do you really believe he was capable of killing anyone?"

"Listen," said Lara with conviction. "Never you mind what the courts say. He killed those women."

"So you're not sad that he's dead?"

"No. I'm pleased," said Lara Orr. "When he was out, I had to go and stay in my sister's trailer in Prestwick to get a sleep. I didn't feel safe."

Stevie patted her knee. "That's why I saw him before he left for up north," he said. "I wanted to make sure he went away."

"I knew he'd kill Donna." She sat back smugly, shaking her head. "Didn't I, Stevie? I said, didn't I?"

Stevie nodded, first at her and then at me.

"But he didn't kill Donna," I said tentatively. "The court says that my wife killed her."

"Naw." Lara was certain. "Not Dr. Susie." She was talking about it as if it were a soap opera. "If you ask me, he killed Donna and someone else killed him. He was a killer through and through."

We sat on the settee and finished the bag of crisps, passing it among us. A freezing mist hung in the room, leeching the heat from the gas fire. I glanced at my watch. It was twelve-thirty-three. If I had been at home, I'd have been up here getting miserable.

"Do you want to see my pictures of her?"

Stevie got out a pile of photos from the sideboard and came and stood next to me, handing them to me one at a time, making sure I looked at them before he gave me the next one. They were big publicity shots he'd taken of Donna to sell to magazines. They weren't good photos, she didn't look relaxed or pretty, but there were a lot of them, and I realized that Stevie was looking to sell them to me. The way he went about it was clever too: he took out the pile of photos and started flicking through them saying I might like this one better, what about this one, isn't that nice? Of course this one's only two quid because it's a bit blurry. He stood too close to me, his soft womanly thigh tightly against mine so that I'd have agreed to almost anything to get away from the itchy heat gathering between our skins. There were a lot of photos.

"Where did you get these?" I said, showing I wasn't being shaken down.

"I took them," he said quite proudly. "Donna didn't agree to using these. She didn't like herself in these ones."

Stevie carried on flipping through: Donna smiling with red eyes; Dragon Donna (little trails of smoke trickling out of her nostrils); Donna outside, her back to a strong wind (the skirt of her coat blown up); Donna at a bus stop with one eye shut and the other rolled back. You could see her teeth in that one, which was unusual.

"Stevie, why do you think I would want to buy publicity shots of the woman my wife is accused of killing?"

"For your book," said Stevie simply.

I looked at Lara. She shook her head. Stevie nodded and carried on going through the photos.

"I'm not going to write a book, Stevie. And I'm not going to buy any photos from you, either. If I did you'd only go to the papers with the story."

He thought about it for a moment, then came around the other side, sat down on the settee, and looked up at me. "But," he said, "that's not much of a story, is it? Man buys photograph?"

I didn't want to fight with them, so we sat looking at the photos until we had all finished our cigarettes. Stevie turned to an indoors one of Donna leaning toward the camera across the top of a wooden surface. She was wearing a purple and white tie-dye top that swept down to her cleavage and a gold crucifix dangling between her boobs. She was smiling, pressing her lips tight together the way she always did in photos. It was quite a good picture.

"What's that scar there from?" I said, pointing to a pink mark that had caught the light.

"That's where she broke her collarbone when she was wee," said Stevie. "It was a bad break. She was in a cast for months."

I laughed but they didn't. Of course they didn't. They never went to medical school. They couldn't know that you can't use plaster to set a fractured clavicle. Old MacDonald used the same joke every year: it's like using an envelope to try to set jelly, he'd say, and the second-years would titter. Nor would Stevie know that a bone breaking through skin wouldn't leave a perfectly straight, small scar at ninety degrees to the bone. Donna's scar looked like a deep paper cut, it was so straight. And he wouldn't know that pink scar tissue is relatively recent.

He could see how intrigued I was by it. "You take that picture," said Stevie as I stood to leave.

"I don't want it," I said. He shoved it toward me.

"Take it, take it," he insisted, pushing it into my hands.

I'm sure it was meant kindly. Lara scrunched up her nose and crossed her arms, watching Stevie struggle hard to do the right thing.

"Okay," I said. "If you tell anyone I took it, I'll tell the papers about you two, right? And about the state of your hall."

Lara blushed at the thought. Stevie followed me outside. "You'll write a book about all of this," he said. "One day. You're clever."

"No," I said, "I won't write a book."

"Of all of us, you'll write the book."

"No, I won't."

He smiled imploringly. "Just make me nice in it."

I put the photo of Donna up here, stuck her to the edge of the shelf in front of me. Donna McGovern: curiouser and curiouser.

chapter thirty-three

I CAME UP HERE TO WRITE ABOUT NURSERY, BUT AS I WAS SETTLING down in the chair, putting the cup of tea down, etc., I was thinking about *evington.doc*, and I looked at the first letter Donna sent to Gow. It was sent from Evington Road, Evington, in Leicester, but Donna's address was not Evington. Her father's house was in Highfields, and her husband moved out a year before her father died. Two months after his death, she was still living there alone when she wrote to Gow. But why would she need a different correspondence address if she was living alone? She'd lived in North Street all her life and sold the place when she came up here. Susie must have called the file *"evington"* for some reason, perhaps to highlight the discrepancy?

I'm drawn to write about nursery. The women there are so nice and supportive, and the herd of wee wild kids reminds me that life goes on whether I want it to or not. I only went because Yeni refused to go back and collect Margie. I begged her and then acted stern but it had no effect whatever. I even tried bribery. I offered her a tenner (cheap, I know, but you don't want people to know you've got money; that's how you end up with none). She turned her nose up at the note and refused me on the pretext that she had "sjchores."

"Yeni, leave them," I said, slumping to my knees. "For the love of God, return my daughter to me, *please.*"

"Lachlan." She stood above me, her hands firmly on her hips, speaking as if to a naughty brother. "Jyou cannot hide in this house. These story papers: no one believe that for you."

I protested for a bit longer, but I felt she was probably right. I'm an unlikely swinger, having a morbid fear of both indignity and public nudity. It's not written on my T-shirt, but I think it's probably clear from the shamed way I carry myself. Anyway, I wore my new coat and walked slowly through the park.

Before Susie's arrest, the women at nursery were a bit suspicious of me and kept me out of their warm circle. Now when they see me approach the door, they make a point of waving and catching my eye and saying hello. They don't even really know anything about me other than I'm being made a monkey of in the papers. If I had walked in there this afternoon carrying a severed head, someone would have come up to me and said, "Poor you."

Some mums were gossiping at the top of the steps but stopped when they saw me coming. They said hi, calling me by name, and an unknown hand squeezed my elbow compassionately as I brushed past and went downstairs. Inside everyone smiled at me or waved. Harry's mum wasn't there, which was a relief and took the onus off me to make conversation or deal with any kind of situation. The small woman who once had vomit on her back came over and said, "Everyone knows that's crap," before scuttling off. I don't think she should swear in front of the kids so much, but I appreciated the gesture of solidarity.

Margie had bitten a boy on the tummy, and Mrs. McLaughlin needed to talk to me about it. She explained that Margie's gums hurt and she doesn't understand that biting doesn't feel good to everyone else as well as her. She needs the fact brought home whenever she bites anyone. As she talked, I could see her eyes trail across the shoulder and sleeve of my coat, taking in the quality of the material. I put my hand in my pocket so that the front flapped open and she got a glimpse of the lining. I saw her eyes widen at the shock of pale blue. I love this coat. I wonder what else they've got in that shop. Later, when we got home, Margie tried to bite me on the arm.

I've been thinking all afternoon about Stevie Ray and Lara Orr. It was eleven-thirty before I worked out that Donna's body's being found with Susie's wedding ring has been a terrible shock, and Lara and Stevie's romance, another shock, may well be completely unrelated. It feels as though one has something to do with the other because they both have a strong emotional resonance for me. It's the mental equivalent of mashing two mismatched jigsaw pieces together. I was hoping in some way that one might cancel the other out, like red and white wine on a carpet.

The ring is a giant, tectonic shock because it makes me think that Susie must be guilty after all. I look at my own ring now and feel sick. I took it off and put it on the shelf up here. The overhead light catches the gold, and the ring winks at me. We know, the ring and I, we know she may have done it. Everyone else in the world recognized it ages ago, dealt with it, accepted it, but not me. Only now, a full three months after she was charged, only now can I see her with a small knife in a dark bothy, the ragged, gaping neck of a family packet of wine gums sticking out of her pocket, leaning over Gow, reaching into his open mouth, his hands swelling up, big and purple enough to be mistaken for gloves.

Accepting it, just as a possibility, here, in the sanctuary of this secret room, feels strangely comfortable. It feels as though I have known all along that she might have done it and have sprained my brain trying not to admit it. Could all that pain and discomfort have come from my lack of acceptance? I wonder whether Susie could have given Gow her wedding ring as a sign of her loyalty. Then he could have killed Donna and left the ring there and Susie killed him in retaliation?

If she killed either of them, she's in the right place. If she did it, then Margie is better off growing up without her, and I'm better off by myself. I'm young enough to start again. I'm not in a bad position to be left alone. I live in a lovely house, I have a beautiful daughter who is healthy and adorable. I have access to a lot of money in my bank accounts—really, a lot of money. I'd never have to work again. I could get full-time child care in the house now and actually get down to some writing. I could buy a laptop, get rid of this machine, which is and always will be her machine, and make this my own study.

I can feel myself separating off from Susie, pulling away and slowly letting the skin between us split. It hurts. I feel the pull and ripping tug on the unripe scab. There will be a right time to pull away completely, but just now I cannot resist the urge, I pull and bleed, just to see what it will feel like to be Susie-free. It's a phantom pain, because the Susie I thought I was attached to was never there.

Box 3 (*overspill from 2*) **Document 15** ***"College Friends Mourn Gina's Death,"*** **Evening Times, 5/13/98**

A memorial service was held yesterday for Gina Wilson, victim number two in the second spate of Riverside Ripper murders. College and school friends joined Gina's family outside St. Michael's Chapel in Mount Vernon.

"She was a lovely girl," said a college friend, "we will all miss her."

Gina, 19, had been studying catering at the city's Central College of Catering and Hospitality Management. She was a popular girl who was active in her local church. She had given up her Easter holidays for the past four years to accompany groups of disabled children on pilgrimage to Lourdes.

I keep transcribing these things, and I don't know why I'm doing it. All they do is make me recall portions of our lives that I've forgotten.

Box 3 Document 16 *"Crimewatch Gina Offers No New Clues,"* Glasgow Herald, 5/15/98

Despite a reconstruction on the BBC's *Crimewatch* program, no new witnesses to Gina Wilson's movements have come forward. What is known is that Gina Wilson went missing on her way home from a nightclub in the city center after a night out with friends. Gina followed the Broomielaw down to the junction of Union Street looking for a taxi and then disappeared. Both her body and that of the previous victim, Nicola Hall, were found in locations bordering the river.

Ripperologists have warned that the murders could be following the original pattern of the Riverside Ripper slayings.

I'm trying to break the habit of coming up here in the middle of the night. There's no point in poring over the articles if there isn't going to be an appeal. I need to get back to sleeping properly. I come up here and spend hours smoking and hiding.

I was lying in the dark ten minutes ago, thinking about Susie. It is very dark tonight. It'll get worse before the winter's over. In the dank dark, right in front of my face, I saw Susie sitting in her cell, a miniature square of white, so small I had to squint hard to see, and my head began to hurt. She is sitting on her bed, looking at her hands. The light above her is bright, and her face is washed out with the whiteness of it. Susie is thinking about killing herself.

I see her being locked in her suicide-watch cell, the guard checking her through the eyepiece. Susie's sitting quite still on the edge of her bed, listening to the scuffling noises outside the door. She stares at her hands, exaggerating her medicated muddle, her jaw hanging open. From outside the door she hears the scratch of metal on metal as the guard slides the eye-shield down and moves on to check the next cell. They probably don't do that; it would be too obvious a signal that they had finished looking at the prisoner. They probably can't hear anything inside, but in the bright box Susie has some physical sign that she is no longer being watched. She suddenly becomes animated, moving too quickly as befits her fruit-fly size and mental excitement. She stands up and hurtles over to the wall, pulls a rope made from knotted bed linen out from her sleeve and loops it over the radiator. The light is bright in the room, and I have to squint once more to see. It's Susie but not Susie; it looks like her but it isn't her. She hooks the rope around her neck and grins, a smile so wide it almost splits her face. Her eyes are already dead as she sits down short of the floor, her hair jerks up and down, and she hangs, grinning, on the rope's end. My head is aching.

I sat up and did breathing exercises, trying to calm myself down. It's nonsense, like the monsters Margie thinks are in the toilet, or the ankle-grabbing hairy hand under the bed. And then I lay back down and saw her again.

The prison would have phoned me to tell me if anything had happened to Susie, but I keep thinking that she may have killed herself just one second ago. They are cutting her down, notifying the doctor, getting the death cert, before they contact me. It would take about thirty minutes to an hour for them to contact me, I think. And then I think, no, she's still alive, but I'm wishing her dead. I'm wishing her dead because it would make everything less complicated for me. Then I could be a sad rich widower and women would want to save me. I could step back from my sadness by writing about love and the empire, or loss and philosophy. Women would flock to me and men would seek my company. It would be so much less complicated than this peculiarly suburban mess of inching betrayal and small insults. Anything would be better than this.

In the deep dark night, I know Susie stopped loving me a long time ago. What I took to be familiarity was friendship and boredom. She loved Gow, not me, and she killed him and his wife. With a family pack of wine gums in her pocket, she followed them up north and killed them both.

She didn't even do me the honor of divorcing me. She just ignored me. No matter how hard I try not to care about her, I do.

But she doesn't reciprocate. You can't really fake that sort of disinterest.

She's the only person I'm close to, the only person I connect with. I don't remember being close to anyone before I knew her. Now I find that the island I've been rowing toward for seven years was a cloud on the horizon and I'm hopelessly adrift.

chapter thirty-four

I'VE JUST OPENED THE MAIL. TWO QUARTERLY STATEMENTS ARrived this morning, one from the high-interest savings account and one from the shares portfolio we have with Mercer. Both statements acknowledge the change of address to c/o Fitzgerald & Co. They also document substantial amounts of money being moved out of the accounts exactly one month ago, just after her conviction. Susie's moving money out of my reach, but she can't get to the bank. That's why she's using all her phonecards to call Fitzgerald. It also explains why Fitzgerald keeps acting as if I'm a filthy upstart. He's been organizing moves of raw cash and putting it where I can't touch it.

It's the lack of trust that I can't get over. Susie may have had an affair, could have killed two people, has certainly been convicted, and she's moving the money away *from me.* She might be able to move the three Mercer portfolios unilaterally, but she can't move the money from the Imcras account or the Donaldson ISA funds without my consent. If I divorced her, I could get all of it; I'm looking after Margie, after all. There's a bit of her old man in her; he was a sneaky, secretive old bugger too. She must have glue for blood.

* * *

Among all the papers and articles Susie has amassed up here, she has only two things about Gow's release: this short article and the picture from the newspaper, the one where Gow and Stevie Ray are holding hands and Donna is lurking in the background. I think Susie was losing the urge to collect things about it by this time. She was at home full-time and she didn't get as many opportunities to buy the papers.

Box 3 Document 17 ***"Ripper Appeal Hearing Set for Wednesday,"*** **Daily Telegraph,** ***8/31/98***

The Riverside Ripper's appeal against his conviction for a spate of killings of 1993 is to begin on Wednesday.

At a preliminary hearing in Glasgow, Andrew Gow's counsel lodged the outline of its arguments. The Crown Office has had four weeks to respond, and the court will begin to hear the case on September 2.

What's the point in my doing this? No one cares. No one doubts the verdict but me.

chapter thirty-five

YESTERDAY MORNING, I GOT BORED OF TYPING OUT IRRELEVANT news reports and decided to go and visit 48 Evington Road, Leicester. I told Yeni that I might be away overnight. She agreed to look after Margie, saying she'd take her to the park after nursery and they would have a lovely little day together. Then she poked Margie in the tummy, and Margie threw her big bald square head back and laughed like a sailor.

I went into the hall and called Glasgow Airport, got put through to British Airways, and booked a ticket on my credit card. The plane was due to take off in three hours. It only takes fifteen minutes to get to the airport, so I took my time getting ready, filling a bag with shaving things and deodorant and a change of shirt.

I left the car in the long-term lot and went off to kill an hour and ten minutes in the terminal. It was quieter than I expected; there were no long, snaking lines inside; I'm used to long lines for planes to Spain in midsummer. It only took me four minutes to check in because I didn't have any luggage. Upstairs I decided to take a wander around the shops and found an electronics store. I made straight for the counter at the back. The prices were not good, I know that, but I saw myself tapping out notes for essays and short stories in the side-walk cafés of Paris and Rome, on Gauguinesque beaches, and I bought myself a laptop. It fits neatly into a small black nylon brief-case and weighs eight and a half pounds.

Breathless with excitement, I checked through security. I asked the official if the X-ray machine could damage my laptop, and he had to ask his superior. It wouldn't, they assured me. I walked to the end terminal, taking my time, feeling purposeful and professional. I sat next to the other businessmen and looked worried. I kept check-ing my watch for no real reason.

It was a small plane with single seats on the right and a few rows of three on the left. In a fit of bravura I had accepted a window seat and now doubted the wisdom of it. Luckily there were only eight of us onboard, and no one sat next to me. I'm not a very comfortable traveler at the best of times and felt pretty sick as the plane took off. I drank a whiskey, less as a calmer than to treat myself for being so brave. It was a clear day outside, and I could see perfectly how far we had to drop and exactly which rocky outcrop my soft head would squelch on. I spent the next hour doing battle with the laptop in-structions manual, just to keep my eyes off the window.

I only bought the laptop to spite Susie over the quarterly statements. The idea was that I'd be able to get all of my impressions down at the time and wouldn't need to write it all up afterward. What I hadn't realized is that there would be so much about the machine that was different and that I would need to get the hang of. In the end I wrote diary notes in longhand on bits of paper.

I realized while I was on the plane that even if I could get the lap-top going, I'd feel self-conscious writing in front of other people. I talk to myself, I realize; I say out loud the next line I'm going to write whenever I stop to scratch or pick or take a drink of tea, all of which I do often.

Anyway, once I get the hang of the laptop, I'll give this clumsy machine away. Morris is trapped in the house with fat Evelyn and could use it to work on in the evenings. I'll delete all these files. I can start again with my writing, now that I'm in the habit and have no duty to anyone else. I've been thinking about starting with the Foucault idea, the one about the history lecturer and his mistress.

I'm going on about the laptop, but I'm sure it will be a good buy in the long run. I'll be glad to get rid of this one anyway. It reminds me of her. I look down through the buttons on the keyboard and see what I assume are her hairs, flakes from her skin, Susie crumbs.

We had to walk across the tarmac to get into the terminal. East Midlands Airport is really just a giant room with a high ceiling and a drugstore inside. No one checked our bags or anything, which I found surprising. I swept through the arrival gate with my shoulder going into spasm from carrying the laptop a hundred yards and found the taxi stand outside.

Forty minutes on the M1 later I was checking into the Travel Fast in Leicester town center, principally so that I would have somewhere to leave the bloody laptop while I went about my business. I slid it under the bed, checking that I had the receipt on me. I was half hoping someone would steal it, actually, so I could get the money back on my card, but it was still there when I got back from Evington.

I've never known anything about Leicester. I couldn't have pointed to it on a map. The only thing I knew about it was that they made crisps there, and I once heard that when Idi Amin expelled all the Asians from Uganda, a large number of refugees settled in Leicester. Apparently Leicester City Council was alarmed at the number of immigrants and took out an ad in a prominent Ugandan newspaper telling people not to come to Leicester, that Asians weren't welcome in Leicester and would not be given work in Leicester. The Ugandans were running for their lives and weren't bothered about a warm welcome. They only knew the name of one place in England, and all fled to Leicester as fast as they could and stayed there.

It's very flat country. Everything looks new and seems to be built from small red bricks. There were some nice buildings: next to the hotel there was a building with a semicircular portico, but it was overrestored and looked like a mock-up of something old, Disneyland Georgian.

The Evington area is just outside the town center. It's beyond an old steel bridge over the railway, up and over a sharp little hill that turns out to be Highfields. Evington is full of teeny-tiny redbrick terrace houses with front doors and two windows, one above the other. The sidewalks run right outside the bottom windows, which means having your eyes drawn into someone else's front room as you walk down the street. A lot of the front rooms are empty or have the curtains pulled. The inset brickwork is nice: sunny yellow brick fans above the front doors.

Unfortunately Evington is a slightly run-down student area with a high turnover of residents. Number 48 was on the main road and was taller than the redbrick two-up-two-downs. It was a narrow four-story terrace that, judging from the jungle of buzzers on the door, had been converted into many flats. The front door was set back from the road, behind a bus stop, tucked in the shadow of a small shop selling model-airplane kits and supplies. The building seemed fatally compromised by subsidence, with a lintel above the door angled sharply to the left. The ground-floor window was filthy and blacked out with a poster of the girl from *Trainspotting*.

I knocked at the front door and waited but got no answer. Eventually I tried the door and found it open. The hallway was narrow, with a flight of rickety wooden stairs at the far end, lit by a window on the landing. A narrow shelf by the door was spilling over with letters, junk mail, books of coupons from supermarkets, and free newspapers. I knocked at a door on the ground floor and spoke to a bloke wearing a red and green striped rugby shirt. He was eating a bowl of cereal and didn't seem surprised to find a stranger at his door asking after a missing girl. His name was Mark, and he and his chums had moved in two months ago at the start of the new academic year. They didn't know any of the last tenants, but they left the place pretty clean. The mail just got chucked into the hall by the postman. He said they delivered letters to this address when they didn't know where else to send it, or if it was a funny shape, because the door was always open. He said he liked my coat.

I stood outside the house and pretended to wait for the bus. I showed every person who came past Stevie Ray's photo of Donna and asked whether they had seen this woman. No one had. A businessman in a pinstripe suit came down from the top-floor flat (I heard him walk down the full length of the wooden staircase). Two students were waiting at the bus stop, and neither of them had ever seen Donna.

Thinking deductively, I worked out that since Donna smoked, if she had lived here, there would certainly have come a time when she'd need late-night cigarettes. I asked in the local newsagent's, but they didn't recognize her. The liquor store didn't, either. I asked in the local Spar supermarket, and they didn't know her.

It is quite possible that Donna never lived there and used the address as a letter drop. She might have counted on walking in and taking a letter addressed to her from Gow. But the question remains: Why couldn't she get letters at home?

The hotel room was small. There was a two-foot path around the bed and a chair in the corner. Everything was slightly old and a little bit broken. The curtain had come off its track in the middle, just enough to look saggy. The television was hidden inside a cabinet with peeling veneer. In the cupboard below sat a mini-bar (with rust spots around the seal) containing an enticing, sensuous selection of a small beer, a yellow wine, a purple wine, a mini gin, a Coke, nuts, a chocolate bar, crisps. I ordered up a sandwich from room service and while I was waiting for it to arrive, I ate all the food in the mini-bar.

I put the telly on at the end of the bed and flicked through twenty or so channels. I arrived at a blurry screen with a blue sign in the corner that said the signal was blocked. Behind the blur two women were either fucking or jogging through a very pleasing cake sale; breathless delight met ecstatic groan, to a backing track of a wailing saxophone. I'd have requested it and happily paid, but I was worried a newspaper would find out and tell everyone in Britain I'd had a wank in Leicester, so I sat on the end of the bed in my underpants, listening and eating a dry sandwich. The glamour of travel.

The next morning I awoke early, sweating wildly into the sheets, feeling completely exhausted. The room was overheated, and I fell out of bed, throwing myself at the double glazing, trying to work out the puzzle of the windows and get one open before I suffocated. My breakfast was outside the door with the paper I had requested. I could hear showers and televisions down the hall and the noise of elevators at the far end whirring up and down, giving out a warning "tink" as they landed.

As I stood under the shower like a limp washrag, I thought about the distance I saw in Susie's eyes during my visits. She loved someone else. The hours in the office with Donna suddenly made sense, the pictures of her up all over the study, the mole nestling on the back of her neck, the tension between them on the video, it all made perfect sense. I felt like a fucking idiot. I knew two things absolutely and fundamentally:

1. That the night we went to see *Duke Bluebeard's Castle,* Susan had been telling the truth about her buxom friend from the sixth form.

2. That my wife and Donna McGovern had been having a love affair in which I featured not one jot. I was not a special guest star. I was not invited in as a spectator. I would not come in at the end of the film and satisfy them with my huge cock. Susan loved Donna, not me. She loved her. When she looked at Donna, her mouth watered, her pupils dilated, her heart sang.

I spewed my guts up into the sink. I spewed the last speck of compassion and sympathy out of my rotten gut and flushed it away. I spewed and washed the taste away with chewy toast and bitter coffee. I sat on the side of the bed and felt my penis shrivel back into my body.

I went downstairs, left the laptop behind the desk for safekeeping, and set off for Highfields on foot.

It was cold and raining, a thin misty rain, and I worried about my coat. Then I thought, fuck her, I'll buy another one. I walked through an industrial district as nondescript and unremarkable as the town itself, then followed a snaking road past the railway station and over the hill. I asked a woman at a bus stop to direct me to the Highfields address. The woman said that I should be careful up there if I was a stranger, it was quite a rough area.

Highfields actually has nicer houses than Evington. They are still tiny and crammed up close to each other, but the facades are iridescent because of a glassy-flint pebble dash. It's odd to go somewhere like that and have someone tell you it's a rough area. In Glasgow roughness is obvious from the hideous housing and the burned-out cars and rubbish everywhere. I saw a drunk couple sitting in a bare ornamental garden in the middle of a busy roundabout. They were very thin and hanging on to each other, passing a cigarette back and forth. Other than that it seemed a nice place. Donna's street was littered with children. I heard a bell ring, and they all disappeared around the back of one of the houses.

I found the door of Donna's house and knocked. After a while a gray-haired Asian woman came to the door. She wore a nice green sari and did me the favor of looking at the photo, but her vocabulary seemed to consist entirely of the word "no." She kept trying to push the door shut while I was talking. Eventually I gave up trying and let her shut her door, rude cow. The woman next door had been listening through the wall, I think. I knocked, and my hand was barely back at my side when she opened the door and looked at the photo of Donna. The lady nodded. She was tiny, very dark-skinned, and had a thick accent.

She kept me on the doorstep, but I could see that the house behind her was immaculately clean. There was something lovely cooking; it smelled like seed cake. I didn't know if she'd feel comfortable talking to a man, but I tried to make myself less threatening by saying I was looking for a friend of my daughter's. Without getting the photo out, I asked about the McGoverns from next door.

"Yeees, that's right. Yeees." She drew the word out, opening her mouth wider as she got to the end. "Yeees. They did live here for many years, left not so long ago. Last year. I live here for thirty years. Yees, all married life. He died. The man, father? Yeees. Died. Very, very sad. Not nice man. Not happy family. Husband left. Shouting."

She put a hand behind her ear to show she had been listening through the wall. "Donna nice girl, yees, good girl, work hard for family. Modest girl. Good for family." It didn't sound like blousy, over-made-up Donna at all.

I told her that the current owner hadn't been all that keen to talk to me, and she sucked her teeth in a way that suggested she didn't altogether approve. "Cheeky old dog," she whispered, and we had a little laugh together.

"I heard," the woman said, hand on her heart, "that Donna is dead." She opened her hand heavenward, flicking the fingers out to show that Donna was gone like a seed from a pod.

I nodded. "It's very sad. She was very young."

"Good girl. She sold house when father died, took money, and they went away. Traveling, you know."

"*They* went away?"

"Donna and friend. Girl who stay there for while. I didn't see. Donna I know all her life."

"Were you here when she broke her collarbone?"

I could see the memory coming back to her. She smiled warmly and nodded. "Yees, fell off bike. Very sore." She pointed to a pavement curb farther up and opened her eyes wide. "OUCH!" she said, and we had another little laugh together.

"What did the doctors do for her when she broke it?"

"Bandage." She gestured to both shoulders, making the shape of a figure-eight belt. No plaster. Donna had broken her collarbone after all, but by falling off her bike and not at the hand of her father, as she'd told Susie.

Suddenly the woman started saying something that I had trouble making sense of. When I looked up, I saw that she was talking Urdu or something to a young woman behind me in the street. They nodded solemnly to each other, and the passer-by glanced at my legs as she moved off along the pavement. They were obviously talking about me, but the woman didn't feel the need to explain herself.

She leaned out the door and looked down the street, then stood straight again. I took the photo out of my pocket and showed it to her.

"Who that in photo? Who girl? Your daughter?"

chapter thirty six

I MADE THESE NOTES ON THE PLANE ON THE WAY HOME.

FACTS

1. Donna McGovern lived in Leicester and grew up there. She lived with her father, who died, and she broke her collarbone when she was small.

2. A body was discovered recently that matched the dental records and medical history of the real Donna McGovern, whose blood was found in the Golf Polo.

Conclusion: Donna McGovern is dead.

The woman Susan has been dealing with was not Donna McGovern. I will now refer to her as Donna II.

FACTS ABOUT DONNA II

1. She knew Donna McGovern, well enough to know that she had broken her collarbone when she was little.

2. Someone set off from Leicester with Donna I in the white Golf Polo, but only Donna II ever made it to that house in Kirkintilloch.

3. Donna I's body was apparently only recently dead, but she can't have been kept as a prisoner in Kirki. Journalists were hanging around the house. Anyone could have found her. Could she have been killed in the Golf on the way up and stored in the humming deep freezer in the garage? As long as she was eventually deposited somewhere obscure enough and allowed to defrost properly, there would be no evidence of freezing at the cellular level unless she was defrosted and refrozen several times. It would explain Donna's renting such an isolated cottage: she'd need somewhere private with a big deep freeze.

Conclusion: Donna II is probably not dead.

Having considered this list for most of the journey, I can now draw up the following list of important questions:

1. This woman passed herself off as Donna to meet Gow. Why would it be necessary to complicate it and pass herself off as someone living to get in? Why not go as a nonexistent person?
2. Who the fuck is she?

Did Susie know Donna II wasn't Donna? I think she had an idea that something didn't add up, judging from the video interview of Donna, the Evington title for her account of Cape Wrath, and the fact that she suspected Donna of the murders. But she didn't tell anyone or hand over the hotel letter.

And why did Donna II need to pass herself off as someone else? She must have known that she, as herself, wouldn't get through the security checks to see Gow. She needed a plausible, real identity that would stand up to scrutiny: when she met Donna I in Leicester, she must have known she would fit the profile. I imagine Donna I with downcast eyes and work-sore hands. For an Asian woman with a house that clean to say she was a good, modest girl, she must have been madly passive. And along comes Donna II and takes her firmly by the hand, introducing her to a whole new world of sensuality and control, until she pulls over in the car on the way to Scotland and kills her, the downcast eyes wild with fright and confusion, the work-sore hands scrabbling at a handle, at a seat, fighting back for once, and losing. During their time together, did Susie give Donna her wedding ring as a sign of loyalty and cover up by claiming it had been stolen? Susie said it was over in *evington.doc.* Perhaps Donna and Gow got it together and went up north. Donna called and Susie went for her, and maybe one more rejection drove Susie to kill.

It's the audacity of Donna II that astonishes me. She gave interview after interview to the papers and charged a fortune, had her photo taken a hundred times. Donna II always covered her teeth. She covered her teeth when she smiled in the video, and she didn't let Stevie Ray use photos where her teeth showed. She did that because she knew there must be no photographic record to compare with the body when it was eventually found. How much foresight and presence of mind must it take to always remember to cover your teeth? She had planned this months ahead, at least from the first videotaped interview, perhaps from the first untraceable letter to the discovery of Donna's body.

She must have had a lot of nerve. She stood in front of the press, asking them to look at her, demanding their attention, charging money. There couldn't be a better way to avoid examination.

There is a lesson there for me, and it's a startling one. If I gave one interview to a paper and said nothing interesting, no one would bother me again. More important, they'd stop watching me.

I could go abroad. I could do what I like.

chapter thirty-seven

IT WAS MIDAFTERNOON WHEN I GOT BACK FROM LEICESTER. I sent Yeni over to the deli to buy us a late lunch, and she spent the entire twenty-quid note I had given her. She came back with twenty-three pence change and a bag of perishable groceries that needed to be eaten more or less right this very minute: dolmas and taramosalata, which she claimed came from Spain.

"No, Yeni," I said. "That's from Greece."

"*Sí,*" she said nodding. "In Spain. Is very good."

She had also bought a half-bottle of wine, a packet of Nabisco Grahams for four pounds fifty (!), some fresh smoked haddock soup, a very heavy loaf of brown bread, and two slices of chocolate tart.

We heated up the soup in the microwave, and she broke crackers into it and served it with bread and taramosalata. It's the most expensive bowl of soup I've ever had, but it was nice. Not a tenner nice, but still nice. She poured us both a glass of wine, and we sat down opposite each other at the kitchen table and ate. It all felt very civilized. We didn't talk. Her English is so bad that we've kind of given up. I think she must have a tin ear for language. She should be fluent by now, given the amount of television she watches.

The tarts had broken in the bag, so she put the bits on a communal plate in the center of the table. It was lovely bitter chocolate, smooth and rich and yet not filling. As we each broke off sweet nibbles, our fingertips touched, and then our hands. Yeni held on to my fingers and tugged at me, smirking languidly, trying to pull me across the table to her. I was angry and sickened by Susie. I like Yeni, I don't want to use her to spite Susie; I really do like her, so I resisted, but then she stood up and came around the table, sitting next to me in a chair and bringing her soft big mouth to my tingling ear.

"Lachlan," she said, brushing the lobe with her lips. I heard the warm saliva slack under her tongue as she whispered to me, "Baby asleep. You come with me?"

She didn't give me a chance to answer. She slid a hand between my legs, easing her fingers down my inner thigh and pulling me toward her. I was still a bit reticent, but when I looked at her, her lips stained with the wine and smelling of haddock, I knew it wasn't about Susie.

I grinned at her. "Yeni," I said, "you're very bad."

She smiled back. "Lachlan, I'm want you to fuck with me."

It's the closest thing to a grammatically correct sentence I've ever heard from her, so I had to.

We were lying in bed afterward, watching the circus clock on her sideboard creep toward five, knowing that Margie would wake up soon. Yeni was snuggled into the pit of my arm when I asked her what she wants from this. She shook her head and shrugged, but I made her sit up.

"Come on, Yeni," I said, trying to be kind. "You're a bright girl. This has happened twice now. Are you hoping for a relationship?"

She looked a bit insulted. I had expected her to say yes and then I'd have mollycoddled her a little, softened the blow, but let her know that it wasn't really on, because I was married. She pulled the duvet around herself, suddenly ashamed of her fantastic tits. As she flattened the bedspread over her chest, the generous fat on her upper arms splayed unattractively. She lost her beauty in the act of hiding, like Eve discovering shame.

"I know you understand English better than you speak it," I said.

She sighed and chewed her lip. "I like," she said, after a few faltering starts at the statement, "that we cannot speak."

"You like that?"

"*Sí.*"

When she saw how much I brightened, she grinned back at me and put up a hand, covering my face, and pushed me back on the pillow. She let go of the duvet and slid down the bed. She had never had any intention of learning English. She's the eldest in the family of five. She came to Glasgow for a rest.

As we lay next to each other, our heads dovetailed on the pillow, I think I fell a little bit in love with her. I felt I had descended to somewhere warm, like a presleep drop in blood pressure that shocks you awake. I might be wrong, but I felt that I could write if I stayed with her. I would not spill my seed in conversation and existence; I'd save it all for the page.

Through the open door at the end of the bed, we heard the *ching-ching* of Margie's crib clown, and we grinned in unison up at the ceiling. Any second now she'd start screaming.

"Yeni, if I went to France, would you come with me?"

She looked wary. "No south?"

"No, not anywhere near Spain. Perhaps not even France, perhaps Greece?"

"*Sí,*" she said simply, "I like. We can hchave satellite?"

"Satellite TV?"

"*Sí.*"

"In Greece?"

"*Sí.* For *Friends.*"

"Yeah." I took her small, cool hand, touching the sensitive tip of each of her tapered fingers. "We could just about afford that."

* * *

Yeni was in her dressing gown, chasing Margie back and forth in front of the telly, when I left them and came up here. I've been taking shots of Margie with the instant camera so that I can enclose them with the daily letters to Susie. When I think about Donna and the money and how sneaky and rude it is for her to move it, I wonder why the fuck I'm bothering.

This evening Yeni said to me, "Jyou very serious."

I shrugged, and she waited for me to explain. Eventually she walked out of the room and came back with her coat on. She said she was going to see her friends from the English class. I nodded and gave her a hundred quid and said have a nice time. She tried to give me the money back, but I insisted.

"For baby-sitting." I pressed the money into her hand. "For baby-sitting for a whole night. Take it. You have a good time, honey."

She brushed my cheek with the back of her hand and made a precious little "o" with her mouth when I called her that. She didn't cringe or grimace or get pissed off. I heard the front door slam behind her. I hope she genuinely doesn't want to talk and didn't just say that so that I would like her more. I hope she never wants to talk.

Susie is a cunt. She's a duplicitous, faithless, disloyal cunt, and she'll leave me broken if I don't do something soon. If this ever gets out, I will be the world's biggest, most widely recognized, dickless idiot. She's been laughing at me from the very beginning, from before Otago Street.

The gloves are off, as far as I'm concerned.

chapter thirty-eight

IT'S THREE-TEN A.M. I WAS LYING IN BED JUST NOW, LISTENING TO the cold wind shake the dry leaves from the trees, and a thought occurred to me out of the blue. I carefully worked my arm out from under Yeni, slid out of the bed, and pulled on some pajama bottoms and a sweater. I left her in the warm dark, snoring softly in Spanish through the ripe segments of her lips, and went into the bathroom, staring at myself in the mirror, at my red eyes, round shoulders, and sagging belly.

Donna II knew that there would be background checks. That is why she knew she couldn't just assume a made-up name but would need a plausible identity in order to get in to see Gow. But how could she possibly know that? Tucker and Susie's security checks weren't a matter of public knowledge. No one else knew they were doing the research. I think she had tried to get in to see Gow before and been knocked back. I think this occurred to Susie, and that was why she took the file and destroyed all the other copies of it. She was protecting Donna II, still protecting her, even after being charged with a murder she thought Donna had committed. When I think of how much she loved me in Otago Street, I don't doubt that she would have done the same for me.

I opened the Gow correspondents research file. Three-quarters of them are men and can be discounted immediately. Then there are fifty-six women, thirty-one of whom first contacted Gow around the time of his wedding, when he was in the papers a lot. From the twenty-five women who contacted him before, only twelve of them were before the Donna McGovern letters started in February 1998.

1. The first is a psychic who wrote only once and said she had seen what he did to those women through a spirit guide. She was going to kill him through sending out bad thoughts (no request to visit). Her brain must have fried when he died a gruesome death.

2. There were a series of sexy letters from a Linda Slaintan. The file notes "photo encl., sexually explicit." She wrote nine times and asked him to call her back. She then wrote several angry letters after Gow's engagement to Donna was announced in the press, accusing him of misleading her.

3. Patricia Gallon was a member of the Plymouth Brethren in Lewisham. She wrote only once, saying that she would pray for his salvation.

4. A woman from the Isle of Harris believed her husband was Gow's accomplice on the first murder. The couple were separated, and she promised not to tell the police but wanted to know. Her husband was called Hugh Kean and he drank in the Park Bar.

5. A web designer with a vowel-free surname (Anna Trsykt) asked permission to use Gow's picture for a competition.

6. Mrs. Tate, a teacher from Bridgeton, knew him when he was a boy. She wrote once to ask him where he went wrong.

7. Brenda Rumney from Newcastle thinks he met her mum once.

8. Nine plaintive letters from his little sister, Alison, asked him to contact her and told him family news. She's had a miscarriage and was quite ill but recovered before the file ended.

9. Three letters from a woman in London who offered to be his manager. She said she'd give him a ninety-ten cut of all profits and get him more coverage than Stevie Ray.

10. Doreen Armitage wrote sexy letters with "photo encl., featuring bondage." Some cheeky scamp has noted in the file "correspondent breathtakingly unattractive." Doesn't sound like Tucker, somehow. Doreen wrote four times.

11. Marti Gibbon, a priest from America, may or may not have been a woman. Marti wrote a few times, proposing to write a screenplay of Gow's life. The return address is Santa Monica. I guess that deal fell apart when Gow was acquitted.

12. A woman from Lanarkshire asked whether her dad was involved in the first few murders. She gives a detailed account of her father's movements around that time, where he was and what he did for a living. "Photos encl." The file doesn't say whether the photos were of her or her father.

I don't know how to discriminate among these. It's four-thirty in the morning and I'm on my third cup of coffee. I shouldn't be drinking coffee, it'll just keep me awake, but I need something to keep me warm, and decaf doesn't seem determined enough for sorting through this file.

NOT EXCLUDED BY SECURITY CHECKS:

1. His wee sister.
2. The American priest.
3. Manager woman; I think he would have seen her.
4. Sexy lady 1.
5. The brethren woman didn't ask for a visit.
6. Neither did the web designer.
7. Nor the psychic.

EXCLUDED BY SECURITY CHECKS:

1, 2. Both women who thought they knew his accomplice. Gow refused to see them because he was maintaining his innocence.

3. Sexy lady 2: Doreen would have thought that the promise of sex would get her an invite to visit. She would have been rejected by Susie and Tucker because of their antihubristophiliac stance.

4. Mrs. Tate rejected by Gow. No one would want to see an accusing old teacher.

5. Brenda was rejected, presumably by Gow, for having a boring connection.

That's it, down to five, but not one of them had a return address in Leicester.

The perfect fit of Donna McGovern and the profile of a prison romancer seems very sinister now. It feels as if Donna II went hunting for a front. She knew that by using Donna's background and history she could easily pass the interview with Susie and Tucker. But what's behind it all? Why bother to come up here at all?

I feel completely detached from Susie now. I can't even conjure up good feelings toward her when I think of her as Margie's mother. Even that. It leaves me cold.

chapter thirty-nine

I SPENT AN HOUR ALONE THIS MORNING SITTING IN THE KITCHEN, looking out the window. Yeni took Margie to nursery. I sat still, staring out the window and thinking vaguely about everything. I came up here to get a note of the phone numbers of the women who might have been refused access.

Before I started calling the numbers, I phoned the bank and the investment firms and asked them to send detailed statements for all of our accounts going back over the full five years of our marriage. Then I made some phone calls. My interview with Alistair Garvie is tomorrow. I'm flying down to London in the morning and coming back the same night. I'm not going to say anything interesting; I'll keep it all as bland as possible.

I phoned each of the women's numbers in turn. I had worked my story out: I would claim to be a friend from Leicester, say that I had a silver necklace belonging to Doreen/Mrs. Tate/Brenda/etc. that I dearly wanted to return. It was early afternoon.

Doreen had a baby crying in the background and two small children shouting at each other in the foreground. She sounded exhausted. Mrs. Tate was about 110 years old. Neither of the women who suspected members of their family was in. And then I came to Brenda Rumney.

Brenda's phone was answered by an old woman. She warbled like a deaf canary, and occasionally, during the course of the conversation, I could hear her dentures clack together.

"Hello?" she said.

"Hello, Brenda?"

"Brenda? No, dear, I'm not Brenda. She's not here. I'm Mrs. Rumney."

We paused momentarily while I took this in. "Will she be coming back soon?"

"No. She doesn't live here anymore. She lives in London now. She's gone back to live in London."

I was well practiced now, having given the story to a few people, and I started in on my spiel. "Ah, I see, well, the thing is, I'm trying to get hold of her because I have a necklace. It's silver and she—"

"Oh God. . . ." The woman stifled a sob.

"I'm sorry?" I said, mentally racing back through everything I had just said. Was it the necklace that upset her? Had she been necklaced? "Are you all right?"

"It's a shock, I'm sorry. You . . ." Her voice dropped, and she whispered as if broaching a terrible truth. "You're from Glasgow, aren't you? I can hear it in your voice. You are, aren't you?"

I hesitated. "Yes?"

"Oh. Are you a relative of Brenda's? Does she have a family there?"

I thought the woman was Brenda's mother, and the question made no sense. I didn't know what to say, so I stumbled on with the story I'd rehearsed. "I, um, I have a necklace for her. It belongs to her. She lost it when she was in Leicester and I want to give it back. We are talking about Brenda who was in Leicester, aren't we?"

"She was there for a short while last year. She was transferred with her job, but then left. How did you get this number?"

"Well, Brenda gave it to me."

The old lady's voice lightened. "She gave you this number?"

"Yes, she gave this number." It wasn't a lie really, it was the number on the letter.

"Oh!" The woman was crying. "I can't tell you what that means to me. . . . We haven't seen her for over a year."

She wept openly now. I apologized, but she sobbed that there was no need to be sorry. It wasn't my fault. It was no one's fault. She should have told Brenda sooner. I didn't want to pry, so I asked if she was Brenda's mother. She gave a little squeaky yes and shuddered as she inhaled.

"We got Brenda when she was just five weeks old. We hoped she would settle. We put off telling her she was adopted, but she was always a strange little girl, always cold and withdrawn. It sent her off the rails when we eventually did tell her. She was twenty. She left university and just disappeared."

I thought about Margie and what I'd probably want to hear if she turned against me and couldn't be found. "She loves you very much—" I said off the top of my head.

"I know." I heard a hankie being dragged across the receiver and a slight nose-blowing episode.

"She loves you very much indeed."

"I know. She's just got a funny way of showing it. We should have told her."

"But she does love you. . . ."

"You're kind. What's your name?"

I didn't want to give my own name. "Um . . . ," I said. "Morris."

"Morris Roberts, then, is it?"

I hmmed again noncommittally. "Mrs. Rumney, did you receive a call about a year and a half ago from either Susie Harriot or Harvey Tucker at Sunnyfields State Mental Hospital?"

Confused by the change of topic, she hesitated. "Yes. I didn't know where she was calling from, but a Dr. Harriot did call."

"And what did she ask you?"

"About Brenda contacting her mother. I thought she was from

the adoption people. Brenda was upset about the whole thing. We should have told her earlier. She just disappeared."

"Mrs. Rumney, you don't have an address for her in London, do you?"

"No, she wouldn't give me one." She blew her nose. "She doesn't want me going after her, you see. She'll only"—she paused to blow again—"only have contact on her own terms. She does phone here sometimes, but there's a lot she won't talk about. I'm surprised she's not in touch with you. I didn't know she had a relative up there."

"Well, you know. I'd love to see her again."

She tutted. "Our Sean met her old boss at the football, and he said he'd been asked for a reference for her. She's working in the sweets department of Selfridges in Oxford Street. Is Mary-Ann still alive, then? Brenda won't tell us a thing about how it went."

It took me about ten minutes to put the two names together, and when I did, I felt sure I knew more about all of this than anyone else, more than Susie, more than Gow, more than Stevie Ray.

Mary-Ann Roberts. Mary-Ann Roberts, died aged forty-one. No surviving relatives; no one cared. The victim's photograph is a blur, taken in a photo booth, overexposed. Heavy eyes looking upward, staring at the top of the frame. Thin lips drawn on with pencil, slightly parted, the pointed tip of her tongue just visible, glistening. Mary-Ann Roberts, twenty-two years scraping a living on the game, a face hardened by cigarettes and cheap gin. I cut the picture out of the yellowed newspaper clipping and put it next to Stevie Ray's photograph. Two dimpled chins. Two sets of brown eyes. Two long noses, flared at the bottom. Brenda was fatter than her mother. She would have been eighteen when her mother was murdered. Two years later she went looking for her and found an overexposed booth photo, features washed out. Her mother's eyes, bitter eyes, gone after she met Andrew Gow. Gone after Gow.

chapter forty

YENI WASN'T PLEASED AT ALL, EVEN THOUGH IT WASN'T OVERnight this time, just a day. Down at nine, back at six, home by eight with no delays. I gave her two hundred quid this time and promised to make her dinner. I have money. It's the one thing I do have.

I came through the gates at Heathrow and was met by a driver dressed in a perfect, crisp gray suit and hat. Carrying my briefcase, he escorted me across the road to an enclosed parking garage and showed me into the comfy backseat of a large silver Benz. I sat there, anxious about the interview to come, watching the outskirts of London pass by the window. People must live like this all the time, I thought, be driven everywhere, be provided for, have teams of people to attend them. If I had all of Susie's money, I could have someone to drive me all the time. I could pay for a nanny to do stimulating play with Margie all day. I could feel as good about all of my clothes as I do about my Armani coat.

I asked the driver how long it would take to get into town, and after telling me about twenty minutes, he said it depended on the traffic, you know. Sometimes it's good, sometimes it's bad, you know, more often bad nowadays. He said he'd been in Glasgow for a wedding once and we sure knew how to drink up there, eh? I said yeah and looked out of the window.

It wasn't long before we were passing the Ritz hotel, crawling along toward Piccadilly Circus. The driver pulled the graceful car across the traffic, down a side street, and into a bay in front of the hotel. A doorman in a top hat and gray tailcoat opened my door, and I stepped out onto the marble concourse. My driver stood up and told me he'd park and wait to take me back to the airport, just ask the doorman, he'll find me. The doorman tipped his hat.

The hotel lobby was clean and smart but nothing special. A gaggle of fat tourists gathered at reception, either checking in or checking out. They were surrounded by suitcases and suit bags. They seemed to be having a dispute among themselves. A young woman behind the desk called me aside and asked if she could help. Alistair Garvie had taken a room on the eighth floor and was expecting me. Go right on up.

The mirrored elevator had posters for *Cats* and *Starlight Express* and *Les Miserables* on the walls. I smoked a cigarette on the way up, trying to get my heart rate up a bit, get ready for a fight, but I needn't have. Margie could have beaten Alistair Garvie in an arm wrestle.

He is tall and skinny, with a shock of gray hair and a smoker's pasty pallor. I was expecting a young man, and it was only as I sat and smoked and drank the beer and vodka provided that I realized: Alistair Garvie *is* a young man. He's a young man who has taken extremely bad care of himself and smokes more often than he breathes. He asked me to sit down. They were going to do the pictures first because the photographer had to be somewhere else at one o'clock.

The photographer asked me to take my coat off. I didn't want to, but it would have sounded vain and stupid to insist, so I left it on the bed and sat on a low chair in my shirtsleeves and tie, looking out of the window over the London rooftops, resting my chin in my hand.

Big silver umbrellas reflected the lights onto me, and I became very hot. Garvie sat on the end of the bed all the while, watching a chat show on telly as he sipped vodka and chain-smoked.

I stared out of the window for half an hour while the photographer took my picture. It was amazingly boring. I asked if I could have a cigarette and, while I lit up, suggested to the photographer that we could take some of me wearing my coat, standing in front of the smart dresser over in the corner. He looked at the dresser for a moment and then said, "Yeah, okay, why not? Let's just get these ones first."

Garvie picked up the phone and ordered another bottle of vodka from room service and two packs of cigarettes. We hadn't drunk half of the first bottle yet. I think he wanted them to take home.

The photographer took a long time to finish. He took four rolls of me looking out of the window, sitting in front of the white background, drinking vodka out of a mug that was supposed to be tea. By the time he had packed up and left, my face hurt from maintaining a sad frown for him. It was only when I was sitting on the plane coming home later that I realized he never did take the pictures of me with my coat on.

As the photographer packed up, Garvie turned the telly off and talked, topping up my vodka and orange. His marriage had split up, too, so he understood what I was going through. His missus had an affair, with a window cleaner of all people. The guy was old, that was what really got to him, and he was a window cleaner. How much could he have been making a year? Fifteen thou tops. He couldn't believe she'd done that to him. They'd been childhood sweethearts and had three kids. I asked what ages they were, and he said three, six, and nine. As a joke I said that was pretty precise spacing, wasn't it? He hesitated and laughed. Yeah, he said, it was. I was starting to doubt the story about his wife. I think he was trying to get me to have an outburst and give a whole load of stuff away. I trusted myself to say nothing interesting (*never* a problem for me) but didn't know if that was what they'd print. I fumbled in my briefcase and took out Susie's Dictaphone.

"I hope you don't mind my using this?" I said sheepishly. "But my lawyer insisted. He won't speak to me if I go home without it." I whinnied a stupid laugh, and Garvie stared at the machine. He seemed hurt.

"Don't you trust me, Lachlan?"

"Of course I do," I said. "It's for my lawyer. He wants to know what I say in case it has a negative impact on the appeal. I'll do anything I can to help the appeal."

Garvie nodded and lit another cigarette. "There's going to be an appeal, then?"

"Oh, yes, definitely. We've got to keep hoping."

"Right? See, I've heard that there won't be an appeal."

"No, there definitely will be. We're just looking for the grounds at the minute. Susie'll be coming home soon."

"And how will your mistress of several years take that?" He laughed unkindly, and I wanted to say fuck you, you'll be dead at forty-five, but I knew I couldn't be rude. He'd gut me if I was a smartarse.

"That was a misunderstanding. Stevie Ray asked me about the allegations in court about Susie and Gow having a love affair, and I didn't want to talk about it. He took it the wrong way."

"So the other papers are lying?"

"Well, no, I —"

"Do you think your missus was having an affair with Gow?"

"I know they weren't. Susie is innocent of this terrible crime and I don't doubt that she has been faithful to me. We love each other very much, and we're looking forward to our future together."

Listening to the tape again this evening, I sound as if I'm writing the headlines for him, I realize, but what I was doing was saying things I wouldn't mind Margie hearing from my mouth when she is a little older, in say ten or fifteen years' time. These are the things I'd like her to hear me say about her mother. These are the things I'd like to be true.

The tape goes on for quite a long time afterward. Garvie tries different ploys to get me to say something nasty about Susie, but my guard is up. He never mentions his faithless wife or equidistant children again. I'm sure it was a lie. We smoked and drank, and I said nothing. Eventually I saw the fight go out of Garvie's eyes, and he dismissed me. He gave me a check for four thousand pounds, which doesn't seem like much to me.

As he handed it over, he smiled. "You should have given us an interview a month ago," he said. "You could have got three times that."

I told him the check was going to charity, and he suddenly looked very angry. It will be in the paper in a couple of days, apparently; they're going to serialize it over three days. He'll let me know. I don't think he will.

Dizzy with smoking and midday alcohol, I stood in the elevator and gathered myself together. I should have eaten, but there wasn't any time. I noted a spark of alarm in the doorman's eyes as he looked at me. I straightened myself as best I could. The afternoon light seemed impertinently bright, and I felt stale and soiled, as if I had spent the last two hours having sex with a reluctant partner. Or maybe I was the reluctant partner. It didn't feel very nice, anyway. The driver pulled the Benz under the carport and jumped out to open the door. I opened the door myself before he had a chance to get around the hood, and he had to jump back in.

"Thanks, anyway." I smiled into the rearview mirror, pleased to be with anyone who wasn't Garvie.

"Straight to the airport, is it, sir?"

"No, I want to . . ." It was an exaggeration. I didn't want to. I specifically didn't want to with a belly full of cold vodka and no lunch, but I would never forgive myself if I didn't take the chance. I would always wonder about it. "I want to stop at Selfridges. Could you wait outside for ten minutes while I pop in?"

"Certainly, sir."

"Thank you." I nodded. I saw him cast a concerned look at me in the rearview and I hoped I wasn't much, much drunker than I thought I was.

Selfridges' candy department is tucked away behind the cosmetics. The ceiling is lower than the rest of the shop, and it's a dizzying array of bright colors and deliciously enticing smells. It is a subfranchise arrangement: different chocolatiers have stalls there, and they're all very expensive. The servers are handsome young women, well groomed and nicely presented in clean white shirts and black skirts, using plastic gloves and mock silver tongs to pick up the merchandise. Freestanding tables on the shop floor hold displays of different brands of sweets: there is a pile of organic licorice, a wall of jelly beans in clear plastic dispensers, a papier-mâché mountain forested by pink and green lollipops with a small tin train running endlessly around the base.

I stood behind the jelly-bean wall, trying to sober up through force of will, and watched the faces behind the counters. Above a multicolored dune, the beautiful young women's faces distorted and spread through the thick plastic. I moved left a little to see the woman on a distant register and found myself weak with the need for Yeni and home and the sight of little Margie. I leaned against a pillar. I could smell marzipan. I turned and found that I was leaning against shelf after shelf of marzipan. I picked up a big round box and sniffed. It smelled of my dear, soft Yeni. I raised my eyes to the back of the shop and my heart stopped.

I blinked, looked again, and then I was floating slowly in the direction of a gourmet chocolate stall, tucked into a little cul-de-sac under the stairs leading up to the food hall.

An intoxicating stench of real vanilla made my saliva glands ache and flood in an oral orgasm. Resting on the glass shelves were chocolates the size of small cakes. The light was too harsh, the glass counter a sheet of brilliant white so clinically bright it sent a pain through my eyes that ricocheted to the back of my brain.

"May I help you, sir? Sir? Which box would you like?"

Behind the counter, next to the register, sat different-sized scarlet boxes. I raised a finger.

"This one?" She sounded Spanish. Like Yeni. And she had black hair and sallow skin and a dimple on her chin. She was very thin. "Sir, is it this one?"

I nodded.

From below the counter she took out a large red box the size of a box of tissues. She took off the lid, laid it on the counter, unfolded the tissue flats, and lifted her silver tongs. She looked at me blankly, hardly a sign on her face that she recognized me. Why would there be? She had never met me before. I had never met her before. But even through a gossamer haze of drink, her gaze locked on mine too hard and firm to be accidental. We were strangers, but each knew the other's darkest secrets, my hollow marriage, her many lives, my wife's loathing and disgust, her mother's lonely death.

We said nothing. Together these two strangers chose a box of chocolates. White chocolate strawberry crème. Nougat enrobed in white and dark chocolate. The famous coca truffle. Maple caramel with almond. Crisp-shelled praline. Ganache—that one has marzipan in it, sir. Do you wish marzipan? I see you have already chosen a box. I looked down and found I was clutching a gold treasure chest of marzipan. Yes, I said, running my hand fondly over the yellow lid, yes, I have already chosen. A superior brand of marzipan, sir. Have you tried their coffee chocolate? Quite exceptional. Still the Spanish accent. Still the blankness in the eyes. Yes, that's all, thanks. Forty-three pounds, then, sir, for the chocolates and the marzipan together. I gave her a fifty-quid note.

She turned away to the register, bent her little head forward, and there, between the elegant long ligaments on her neck, was a tiny black mole, nestling among the fine hairs.

My stomach lurched, and I shut my eyes. What could I do? Tell her employers? Tell the police? Confront her? She has killed four times; she let a woman who adored her be convicted in her place; she killed four times to avenge a mother she had never even met.

"Your change, sir. Sir? Your change. Thank you."

Picking up my chocolates, I turned and walked away.

chapter forty-one

THE DRIVE TO THE VALE OF LEVEN SEEMED TO TAKE HOURS AND hours. They are doing roadwork on the narrowest stretch of road outside Coatbridge, and half a mile of the motorway is reduced to a single-lane obstacle course. Margie started whimpering softly in the back. For three miles I didn't get above twenty, and each time we came to a break in the divider, I imagined myself pulling a U-ey, turning us around, and heading home. I saw myself at home in the bedroom, throwing clothes into bags, packing Yeni and Margie into the car, and driving us all to Dover. We were having lunch in France, sitting outside on a pavement café somewhere charming and tranquil, when Margie's shouting from the backseat turned into a full-blast screaming panic attack. I found it hard to care. I turned the radio up for a while, but she was losing her breath. I pulled over and found her diaper was full; she was sitting in cold shit. She had been crying for ten minutes. I almost drove all the way there with her in that state.

Worse than that, I smoked in the car with Margie in the back. That's probably the real reason she was crying. I opened the window to make myself feel better, but that just streamed the smoke right into her precious little face.

When Yeni was bathing her later she said, "Baby hair smell of smoke," and I shrugged.

"Susie," I explained.

Yeni frowned. "Ver' bad."

"I know, Yeni, I know."

I stopped at the village and left Margie in her seat for a minute while I nipped into the shop and bought a bag of toffees like the first time I went there. They didn't taste as nice, and they didn't have the same pacifying effect, either. They tasted dull after all the rich sickly gourmet chocolates I'd eaten.

I see Cape Wrath quite differently today. I see Susie getting the call and her heart leaping at Donna's voice. I see her turning away from me, looking down the hall, and her cheeks turning quite pink, her clit stiffening. Of course I'll come. I see myself sitting in the kitchen, asking where she's going, and Susie smirking at me, huneee, won't be long, huneee. I see her driving, happy at last because she has made her choice, arriving at dusk and sitting in the little wobbling boat across the beautiful kyle, worried by the letter but determined, going to save Donna for herself. I see Brenda Rumney standing in the filthy bothy, immaculate in her white shirt and black skirt, holding the supine Gow's tongue between little silver tongs, pulling it out as far as it will go and slicing it off slowly. Will that be all, sir? I see Brenda, panting as she walks across the wet sands with the heavy weighted sling, climbing to the foot of a cliff and letting out Donna McGovern, her solid eyes still open, frozen blood all around her mouth. I see her placing the golden ring under her playmate's body. Later she stands in the dark and sees Susie run back across the wet sands. She sees Susie run into the hotel. Through a small window she watches her order a drink of whiskey, and Brenda smirks at her, huneee. See Susie run. Run, Susie, run.

Susie was a gift for Brenda. She must have thought that modest, lonely Donna was a good cover for her, but what luck to stumble upon Susie, another love-hungry lady, willing to be duped and used, driving for eight hours on the promise of a kiss after being passed over for a prick like Gow.

The sky before me was dull as I approached the flat plain of the prison. The guard on reception asked for my mobile phone, to see my bag, and for me to lift the raincoat Margie was wearing so she could see her legs and tummy. It makes me despair of the world when there are people in it who'd smuggle contraband into prison strapped to their children's legs.

There were other visitors waiting in the glass-walled room, but I didn't really notice them. Margie had worn herself out crying in the car and sat quietly on my knee, sucking her fingers, burying her face in my chest when anyone tried to talk to her and no doubt thanking her lucky stars that she was no longer sitting in cold shit while being suffocated by her selfish father.

For the past two days I feel as if I've been walking through thick custard, trying to think through cotton wool. All I can see clearly is Susie's betrayal, Susie tossing aside the empty husk of my dignity. She must despise me.

I saw a laminated photocopy of the official rules on the wall of the waiting room: They can't ask you to take your clothes off. It turns out they can only ask you to take your coat off, pat you down, and check your mouth and feet. They weren't being nice when they let me keep my clothes on. They're not allowed to ask me to do more. I didn't care, I didn't care. I don't care. None of it matters now.

We tripped through the door, across the cold, wet, grassy verge, and through the far door to the visiting room. Margie, perched on my hip, saw Susie sitting nearby and pointed her wet little finger at her. I held her out to her mother, and Susie stood up to take her. She offered me her cheek again, but I pretended not to notice and sat down.

"Well," said Susie to Margie, with a lightness in her voice I hadn't expected. "Daddy's annoyed with me for some reason."

Margie wriggled and squealed until Susie put her down. We both watched her stagger over to the table and grab the plastic ashtray, banging it off the tabletop. "Which is odd, because he's been having affairs with half of Glasgow, apparently."

"You saw the paper, then?"

Susie didn't answer.

A slim prisoner with bleached white hair and a pierced nose walked past and smiled at Margie. "She's beautiful, Susie," she muttered and walked on.

Susie waited until she had gone. "Yeah, a helpful screw saved it for me. What have you been doing?"

I looked up at her. "What?"

"I said, Lachlan, 'What have you been doing?'"

Distracted, she turned away from me and waved over at a prisoner with a five-year-old boy standing sulkily next to her. "Hello, Patrick," she called to the boy. She looked at me again and saw that I was perplexed. "What have you been doing since I last saw you? Have you been swimming, or for tea with the queen?" I shook my head a little. "Tell me all your news, Lachlan. We have to talk about something during these visits. It can't all be high emotion, you know."

And there she was. Back in control. Mr. and Mrs. Wilkens's little Princess Susie. In ten years' time she would get out and come home and take my life over again. She would make all the decisions and oust me from whatever small encroachments I had made. She'd come home and get her own way every day and in every way, jollying me along into my grave.

I lit a cigarette. "I need to talk to you," I said quietly.

She gave me a sharp smile and opened her mouth, ready to ridicule me, but her expression dissolved when she saw how serious I was. "What about?"

"I know, Susie," I said, "I know what you've been doing."

She narrowed her eyes, impatient because I was calling the shots. "And what have I been doing?"

I took a deep breath. "Moving money." I took a deep draw on my cigarette. "Away from me."

She was surprised I knew, I could tell that. She picked up Margie as a distraction. She smiled again, trying to act calm, but I could tell she wasn't. "You should get a job, Lachlan. You're a fit young man. You can't sit about at home living off my dad's money forever. There won't be anything left for Margie if you do."

This made me really angry. "I gave up my job to . . . Someone has to bring up Margie, and you obviously weren't going to do it."

"We had to let Saskia go because you gave up your job without even asking me—"

"No, Susan, *we* didn't do anything. *You* let Saskia go. I didn't want her to go. I gave up my career so that Margie could be cared for by her own family."

She gave me a sidelong smirk. "Career?" she said. "Exactly which dazzling career is that, Lachlan? Your medical career? Your brilliant career as an insurance salesman? Or is it your literary career? Are you still waiting for your big idea? How long has it been? A year and a half full-time and twenty-seven part-time?"

She had raised her voice. Other people in the visiting room were aware of us and spoke quietly, looking everywhere but in our direction. The guard who makes the women stand in tidy lines by the door was watching us from the other side of the room, waiting for trouble to erupt.

I took out a packet of cigarettes from my pocket and looked up at her. "A gift," I said, putting them on the table, standing them on end.

She didn't want to take them, but she wasn't in a position to knock the kindness. She snatched them away, afraid I'd change my mind. She took one out and lit it cautiously.

I could have said to her: You know, Susie, I might have fucked up my career, but at least I'm going home tonight. I'm a good dad. No lesbiotic con artist got me to hand over my life. I could have told her that I do have things to say, I will write something one day, you'll see.

I could have said at least I stayed faithful to you, and you were off fucking a woman whose name you didn't even know. She made you love her, and let you watch as she chose Gow over you. I could have said she tricked you, you stupid cow. You ridiculous, bourgeois faux-sophisticate. You daft faithless fucking whoring bitch. You've laughed at me for the last fucking time, you witless, cheap cunt.

Instead I cleared my throat. "I've saved all the documentation about the money, so don't even try to lie about it. I want a divorce, Susie. Trisha can bring Margie to visit you in the future, because I'm not coming back here."

I stood up and looked down at her, shrinking into her chair, shriveling smaller and smaller until she was a sobbing, wet-faced speck in her ripped yellow nylon chair. I picked Margie up by the waist and left her mother crying in the stinking visiting room.

I'm not going back there. I'm never going back there.

epilogue

In the four years since the diaries were uncovered by Dr. Welsh, the veracity of the contents have generated a tremendous volume of materials: immeasurable column inches worldwide, several television documentaries (one British, one American, and two Japanese), five books, and a TV film. Despite valiant efforts, these investigations have turned up little or no hard evidence. Lachlan Harriot himself claims that the diaries were nothing more than a fiction-writing exercise and now refuses to discuss them.

A woman named Brenda Rumney had worked at Selfridges, but her temporary contract came to a natural conclusion three days after Lachlan Harriot claimed he was in the shop. Brenda was adopted and had been estranged from her adoptive family, a fact that may help explain why she disappeared after leaving work in Selfridges. She has not been found but has been sighted in Australia, New York, Bali, and Cardiff. Her adoption papers cannot be accessed by anyone other than Brenda herself, so there is no conclusive evidence to link her to Mary-Ann Roberts.

An unnamed and unidentified woman did move in with Donna McGovern after the death of her father but may have left the house before Donna moved to Glasgow. Brenda Rumney's photograph was consistently overlooked by the Leicester witnesses who tried to pick her out.[1]

Donna McGovern's husband disputes that their marriage was violent and has written a book about their relationship, which is as yet unpublished.

The freezer in Kirkintilloch was an upright, and in laboratory tests, it has been established that similar models could barely accommodate a small woman's body without necessitating the breaking of bones.[2] The body of Donna McGovern had no broken bones.

Expert forensic odontologists have drawn comparisons and discrepancies between the skull of Donna McGovern and photographs of the woman who married Andrew Gow in Sunnyfields.[3] There are few photographs and, unfortunately, none from which scientifically meaningful conclusions can be drawn.

Upon the advice of his lawyer, Eamon Fitzgerald, Lachlan Harriot invited Strathclyde Police to conduct a search of his home. Neither the video, the hotel letter, the list of correspondents to Andrew Gow, nor his prison files was ever found. In contrast to this, Dr. Harvey Tucker has given an affidavit claiming that the videotaped interview with Donna McGovern was word for word as Lachlan Harriot claimed, as was the list of correspondents.

And so debate about the case continues. Meanwhile Dr. Susie Wilkens (now divorced) has become the subject of a campaign for an appeal, largely funded by the FFJ. She is due to be paroled in 2008. Lachlan Harriot and Yeni Tarrossannani married on New Year's Eve 2000 in Acapulco. They have two children of their own and custody of Margie Harriot. They live year-round in their villa in Malta.

Denise Mina
Glasgow, 2002

[1] *Brenda's Missing Years,* ATV, first broadcast March 1999.

[2] "The Missing Link in the Donna McGovern Myth," Bernard Livivin, *St. Louis Times,* 9/12/01.

[3] *True to Death: The Donna McGovern Story,* SNM, first broadcast January 2002.

About the Author

DENISE MINA is also the author of four other widely praised crime novels: the Garnethill trilogy — comprising *Garnethill,* which won the John Creasey Memorial Dagger for best first crime novel; *Exile;* and *Resolution* — and, most recently, *Field of Blood.* She lives in Glasgow.

deception

A novel by

Denise Mina

A Reading Group Guide

Violent Femme

The author of *Deception* talks with Margy Rochlin for the *LA Weekly*

When the critic Terrence Rafferty called the Glasgow-based crime-fiction writer Denise Mina "another plate of haggis altogether," he wasn't just riffing on her country's affection for the boiled pudding of suet, oatmeal, and minced organ meats. Mina's work feels internal and — to an American reader — exotically Scottish. Maureen O'Donnell, the messy heroine of Mina's award-winning trilogy — *Garnethill, Exile,* and *Resolution* — is boozy, expletive-happy, fresh from a stint at a mental hospital, and unwittingly thrust into grisly murder scenarios involving Glasgow's dispossessed that have her playing detective.

The protagonist of Mina's latest critically acclaimed book, *Deception,* isn't what you'd call a professional gumshoe, either. The book unfolds, diary-style, with downtrodden househusband Lachlan Harriot trying to prove the innocence of his prison-psychiatrist wife, Susie, convicted of murdering her serial-killer patient.

Recently, Mina spoke to the *LA Weekly* about her special brand of gritty, emotional-tailspin crime writing; why the U.S. version of *Deception* was slightly altered; and why her lively Scottish brogue wasn't the only reason she was hard to understand long-distance. "You're phoning me on the tiniest mobile phone in the world," she said. "I mean, I'm holding a matchbox to my head. It's probably very bad reception."

You started writing crime fiction because you were, and I quote, "fed up with big men solving crimes with women in the background."

Yeah, absolutely! I don't know how it is in L.A., but everywhere I go in Glasgow, there are wee guys shouting abuse at you. "Show us yer tits!" That just doesn't happen to male protagonists at all. I think it's a very different landscape if you're a woman.

Do you see crime differently in Glasgow, where you've set all your books?

Glasgow has the highest per capita imprisonment rate anywhere in Western Europe. If you're working class or lower middle class, you'll know somebody who's been in prison. There's a kind of socialist assumption in Glasgow. Everybody assumes that sticking it to the man is a good thing. They have a real respect for criminals. Criminality is not someone else, someplace else in Glasgow. It's part of the culture.

Because of your father's engineering job, you were raised all over the world — Paris, Amsterdam, London. What made you decide to call Glasgow home?

I have a huge extended family here. But, also, Glasgow is a nice place to be poor, because everybody is. In Glasgow, instead of saying to people, "What do you do for a living?" and judging them on their job, everyone says, "Do you have a job? Have you ever worked?" In 1986, the recession was at the tail end. I'd come from London, which at the time was very Tory and very money-oriented, to stay with my mum to get enough money to go back, and I just fell in love. It was a different world: everyone at bus stops would introduce themselves to you. It was like the war had just finished.

What do you and Lachlan Harriot, the narrator of Deception, *have in common?*

He's really self-obsessed, always taking his emotional temperature and arriving at big conclusions. He's not dishonest about much, though. I think he's quite brutal with himself about how foolish he is. Some men find it hard to stomach how emasculated he is, how much he loves his wife. Women are more sympathetic — they get emasculated all the time. To be a woman is to feel very foolish.

How did you come up with using murder mystery as a device to explore complex social issues like alcoholism, sexual abuse, mental illness, and battering?

I was doing a PhD on mental illness and female offenders, and I realized that six people would read it. I thought if I could write a crime novel with the same stuff in it, hundreds of people would read it. I never realized that it would be, like, thousands.

What was your thesis about?

The judicial system ascribes mental illness in a different way for men and women. If a man asserts himself in an antisocial way, he's regarded as very bad and is sent to prison. If a woman behaves in an antisocial way, she's regarded as irrational and is sent to a mental hospital. But what could be more rational than a woman who is failed by the judicial system and her family, who decides to take her life into her own hands and impress her will on the world?

You used your PhD grant to support yourself while writing Garnethill. *Did you have to pay it back?*

No! I'd gotten stuck in a theoretical cul-de-sac. It was a nightmare. I'm sweating just talking to you about it. I did say to my academic supervisor, "I don't think I'm going to finish my piece. Do you think I'm going to run off and be a crime writer?" And he said, "If I were you, I would."

Little, Brown chose to reword some of the Scottish slang in Deception. *Why?*

Personally, I love reading something where you read a sentence over and over to get a sense of what a word means. But I think a lot of people find it very frustrating. I get letters from American people saying, "What is a skank?"

You're working on a new series, right?

Yes, about a journalist working in Glasgow in 1981. She's a crime reporter, Paddy Meehan, named after a criminal who was the subject of quite a miscarriage of justice in Glasgow. [Wrongfully convicted of the murder of Rachel Ross in 1969, Meehan received a royal pardon in 1976, seven years into his life sentence.] There's a stream of true crimes through the book — it's fiction and true crime together.

You have a ten-month-old son. Has motherhood changed how you think about violence?

People said to me, "Once you've had a baby, you'll never write about violence again." What shite! I'm very happy — and I write much quicker. Your time is very precious, and the best toy in the world is right next door.

The complete text of Margy Rochlin's interview with Denise Mina originally appeared in the issue of the *LA Weekly* dated September 17–23, 2004. Reprinted with permission.

Questions and Topics for Discussion

1. Do you have to tell a long-term serious partner everything about yourself? What if the information you're holding back could only make your partner feel inadequate or insecure or, worse, end the relationship?

2. Susie's office is so off-limits that Lachlan hesitates to enter it even after she's convicted of murder. Is it wrong to ask for a private room in a family home? Can anyone truly expect that privacy be respected? Is it different for a man than for a woman?

3. The consequences of Susie's choices cannot be concealed and affect not only her relationship with Andrew Gow and "Donna," but ultimately her entire family. Do you agree with Susie's actions? Do we choose to fall in love — is there an element of volition — or is it an accident, like falling over? Can we really be responsible for the actions that love inspires us to commit?

4. Lachlan takes particular delight in sporting his new Armani coat during Susie's trial. Is it wrong to want to look good at tragic events like funerals? Is Lachlan's vanity an indication of his indifference, or just a by-product of his privileged existence? How do the luxuries Lachlan enjoys prevent him from understanding Susie's affiliation with Andrew Gow?

5. Marzipan fuels madness in *Deception*. Do you think eating a lot of sugar can enhance an erotic experience? or does it just make you feel suddenly tired? What other unlikely catalysts for romance appear in the novel?

6. Lachlan's diary entries are written as he would speak. If you kept a diary, would you alter your voice in any way? Would it be for others

to read? Do you think people ever tell the truth about themselves, even in something as private as a journal?

7. Yeni and Lachlan make an unlikely but quite suitable pair. How can a woman so different from Susie take Susie's place? Does Lachlan's attraction to Yeni despite their obvious differences say anything about Susie's unusual and secret love? Is one right and the other wrong?

8. At the most difficult time in his life, Lachlan refuses the help of his extended family. If you were in his shoes, would you do the same, or do you think family is the only source of comfort and strength in trying times?

9. Think of your deepest, darkest secret. Is it hidden well? If circumstances were beyond your control, would someone be able to unearth a trail to the truth?

Denise Mina's Suggestions for Further Reading

Some of my favorite reads:

The Master and Margarita by Mikhail Bulgakov

This book is about the Devil coming to Moscow. It cuts back and forth between two narratives and the structure shouldn't work because nothing you think is going to happen does happen: no good guys are saved or anything like that. Bulgakov wrote it when he was old and blind and had asked permission to leave the USSR. Stalin phoned him directly to say no, and Bulgakov had given up on any of his work ever being published again. He spent the rest of his life rewriting this book. It's as close to an unedited manuscript as can be and rambles, is hateful and structurally unsound but utterly compelling because of that.

Heart of a Dog by Mikhail Bulgakov

A political fable about a dog who gets a human pituitary and starts demanding housing rights and equal treatment. It's very funny and visceral. The dog gets a job as a cat strangler. It's like Orwell's political fables but leaves enough of a gap between the political point and the story for it to be enjoyable on both levels. I love that space between a book and a writer's point where it resolves itself in a reader's mind. It's much more pleasing than telling someone what to think.

Lolita by Vladimir Nabokov

Just the greatest book for the quality of the writing and the awful tension between loving Humbert Humbert for that and hating him for harming the child so much. Absolutely brilliant jokes as well and a beautiful reflection of the grandiose aspirations of a failed academic.

I remember lines from it all the time: "jumbo crumbs" and "the whince of a child" never leave me.

Keep the Aspidistra Flying by George Orwell

I really don't know why I loved this book so much. It's by no means his best but I think the portrayal of someone really trying to live a good life by their own measure is very touching and very real to a lot of people. The hero's inability to compromise his principles means that he has to forfeit so much, and the idea of rejecting money seemed wildly radical to me as a youngster in Thatcher's Britain.

To Kill a Mockingbird by Harper Lee

I read and reread this book many times when I was a child and always skipped the first chapter because it's a bit boring. I loved the children's games and the idea of a fascinating friend who periodically comes and makes things more interesting. I didn't understand the rape in it or even the racism, but I recognized an opportunity to identify with a downtrodden person — and a withered hand! This guy had no luck at all! My niece had a book fair at her school and all the little girls bought *A Child Called It*. There's something delightfully morbid and morose about children.

The Curious Incident of the Dog in the Night-Time by Mark Haddon

A truly beautiful book in which a character with autism tries to unravel the mystery of other people's feelings using rational deduction. Haddon manages to maintain the voice of a child with autism so consistently and lovingly that everyone else in the story seems wrong-headed by the end-up.

Nice Cup of Tea and a Sit Down by Nicey and Wifey

This sounds like a load of smug crap but it is a lovely read about nothing at all. The various consistencies of biscuits are examined, there are whole chapters on the milk-in-first controversy. He suggests that putting things on top of certain biscuits is like dressing up an old dog in a hat and sunglasses because it's too old to run away. It also includes a Venn diagram of crackers / biscuits / chocolate bars.

I love true crime and had an excuse to read these books when I was teaching criminology. Now I just read them for pleasure.

Happy Like Murderers by Gordon Burn

A true-crime book about the Wests, a couple who killed young women who came to stay in their house as well as their own children. It's a beautifully written book, which makes the story even creepier. Up there with Capote's *In Cold Blood* and *The Executioner's Song* by Norman Mailer for quality.

Dream Lovers: Women Who Marry Men Behind Bars by Jacquelynne Willcox-Bailey

This is a series of interviews with women who have married — you guessed it — men who are behind bars. It's a sad book and manages to trace the relationships in a truly sympathetic way. It's tense because you suddenly realize someone's story is being told for her by her sister and read on to find out what happened. It stops reading as a freak show and becomes just about all relationships and the problems everyone faces in trying to tolerate other people.

The Godson: A True-Life Account of 20 Years Inside the Mob by Willie Fopiano with John Harney

This was one of the funniest books I have ever read. Fopiano was a deluded hanger-on thug who kept trying to implicate himself in the lives of far nastier mobsters. In the end you think he might be a rather nice man who could come over to your house and boast about his crimes. Fiercely anti-drugs, he keeps breaking off from being a major mobster to beat up drug addicts ("a cancer on our society as we know it"). His imminent career as Meyer Lansky's right-hand man never happened because of a spot of bad timing: he got done for robbing a post office.

Look for Denise Mina's new novel

Field of Blood

"Denise Mina's work is really quite wonderful. She has an original voice, rough-and-tumble one moment, heart-touching the next. She paints a big picture with the subtleties of true life. It took only one book for me to become a true fan." — Michael Connelly

"Denise Mina is quite simply a must-read writer for anybody looking for crime fiction as important as it is entertaining. This is powerful, passionate, and compelling stuff. Mina can chill your blood and break your heart in the same sentence, and *Field of Blood* is the start of what will surely be a remarkable new series."
— Mark Billingham, author of *Scaredy Cat* and *Sleepyhead*

Published by Little, Brown and Company

Available in hardcover in July 2005

Also available in paperback

Absolute Friends

A novel by John le Carré

"Unfailingly entertaining. . . . A terrific achievement by the best spy novelist out there—as engrossing, well crafted, and satisfying as anything this observer of the unobserved has produced."

—Matt Konrad, *Minneapolis Star Tribune*

Heart of the Hunter

A novel by Deon Meyer

"Compelling . . . exciting. . . . *Heart of the Hunter* is the dark, explosive side of Alexander McCall Smith's *No. 1 Ladies' Detective Agency* books." —Dick Adler, *Chicago Tribune*

A Question of Blood

A novel by Ian Rankin

"The baddest of the bad boys of modern crime fiction. . . . *A Question of Blood* can certainly bear comparison with the best of today's American crime writing."

—Patrick Anderson, *Washington Post Book World*

Also available in paperback

The Hamilton Case

A novel by Michelle de Kretser

"A miniature masterpiece of a mystery. . . . De Kretser's prose is stunning . . . evoking the glittering excesses of colonial life and the tropical fecundity of Ceylon with equally irresistible power."
— Lev Grossman, *Time*

The Dogs of Babel

A novel by Carolyn Parkhurst

"A searing portrait of grief that's also a love story and an engrossing mystery." — Joanna Smith Rakoff, *Time Out New York*

"A book with a staggering emotional wallop."
— Holly J. Morris, *U.S. News & World Report*

The Lovely Bones

A novel by Alice Sebold

"Mesmerizing. . . . *The Lovely Bones* takes the stuff of neighborhood tragedy — the unexplained disappearance of a child, the shattered family alone with its grief — and turns it into literature."
— Katherine Bouton, *New York Times Book Review*

Back Bay Books • Available wherever books are sold